PRA

COLIN M

Winner of the Edinburgh Inte

Award, for *The Letters of Ivor Punch*

'Warm, funny and beguiling, authentically infused with salt spray and whisky fumes'

CHRIS BROOKMYRE

'This is a vivid and exciting piece of writing in which there is not a dull page. A gripping read'

ALEXANDER McCALL SMITH

'One of my favourite songwriters of all time'

IRVINE WELSH

'A storyteller with a unique imagination and clarity of style'

THE SCOTSMAN

'A twisty mystery set on Mull, the island being a character in itself. Ivor Punch is a detective well worth spending time (and a dram) with'

IAN RANKIN

'A truly original and enthralling novel. Ivor Punch is a magnificent creation and his story is mischievous, sad, funny and truthful'

STEPHEN KELMAN, BOOKER-SHORTLISTED AUTHOR OF *PIGEON ENGLISH*

'I raced through this clever, poignant, beautiful book in one sitting. It's peopled by a cast of brilliantly off-the-wall characters, and full of keen-eyed observations about life on a remote Scottish island – and, by extension, everywhere. A must-read'

LAURA BARNETT, BESTSELLING AUTHOR OF *THE VERSIONS OF US*

'Tragedy and superstition hang over the characters like a mist, and the sea laps against every page. These are beguiling tales built on secrets and sadness, each of them with a keen sense of place'

THE INDEPENDENT

AN ISLAND BURNING

COLIN MACINTYRE

AN ISLAND BURNING

Black&White

First published in the UK in 2026 by Black & White Publishing
An imprint of Bonnier Books UK
5th Floor, HYLO, 105 Bunhill Row,
London, EC1Y 8LZ

A CIP catalogue record for this book is available from the British Library.

Paperback ISBN: 978-1-78530-527-6

Also available as an ebook and an audiobook

1 3 5 7 9 10 8 6 4 2

Typeset by Data Connection
Printed and bound in Great Britain by CPI (UK) Ltd, Croydon CR0 4YY

FSC www.fsc.org MIX Paper | Supporting responsible forestry FSC® C013604

The authorised representative in the EEA is
Bonnier Books UK (Ireland) Limited.
Registered office address:
Block B, The Crescent Building
Northwood, Santry
Dublin 9, D09 C6X8
Ireland
compliance@bonnierbooks.ie
www.bonnierbooks.co.uk

For my daughters, Sian and Reegan, great lovers of Mull; with all my love, forever and beyond, to all eternity.
(And to read when you turn eighteen!)

Author's Note

This is a work of fiction; I would like to emphasise that the characters are entirely made up. Any resemblance to real people, events or places they might be connected to, I would only wish to be taken as a tribute to a time, a place, a people and an island.

'The war of life was still conducted in the open and on free barbaric terms.'

Robert Louis Stevenson, *The Amateur Emigrant*

'Less is known than people think.'

David Hockney

'Some people feel the rain, others just get wet.'

Bob Dylan

'And fuck.'

Ivor Punch

PLEASE TAKE YOUR SEATS

THURSDAY

TEETH. STILLED. REMOVED. TWO SETS. Taken from two charred cadavers. That's the correct term. 'Corpse' implies a more traditional afterlife. The actual bodies I transported last night and are safely hidden elsewhere. I'm sitting within one of two burnt-out cars on Glen Bellart, a fourteen-mile stretch of single-track road through barren moorlands known on Mull simply as 'the Glen'. The teeth I've returned to the scene, to keep folk – more precisely, *Punch* – guessing. Two sets of bones also, for good measure. It's like I'm competing in the Mull Rally, *arsonists* category.

I couldn't resist coming back before dawn to check my job was done properly. The burning, that is. Both cars' interiors have perished. As intended. Like the work of a *Texas Chainsaw Massacre*-themed drive-through. Though we don't have a drive-through, of any category, on the island. In case you don't know the geography, the Glen starts at Aros Bridge and runs across the heart of the map of Mull, linking the Tobermory to Salen road to the village of Dervaig. We were always told in school that the island's shape resembles a snoozing bear. Quite appropriate really, given the company I keep.

Only the fixings of the seats remain. The seats I made sure to recover. I've a plan for them. Finton will be happy with those.

We all have teeth, even in the Hebrides. Or we start out with them. The ill-equipped dentist's van that comes off the ferry once a month doesn't exactly help. We're supposed to take care of them, so we can flash a smile. Though that's not a likely scenario in front of me now – I'm good, but I'm not a bloody magician. Even when just doing their everyday job as part of a living, human face, teeth, to me, are a glimpse not of life, but of death. A white hardness that persists when all other soft matter has gone. Admirable, in a way. The real terror is the thought that, sometime in the hours ahead, my own flesh also won't exist. Or should that be a comfort? Beauty, even?

I've studied the order of decline: first, flesh turns spectral, then comes the stages of epidermis, dermis and fat dying off. Until all biological tissue is gone. Next to teeth, flesh is a flash in the pan. Like mainland to island. In this, teeth are the close cousins of bones. Aye, long after the soul – which, along with the spirit, is lost to the mysteries of earth, wind and other band names – gnashers hang around. They prevail as the most steadfast, indestructible testament of you. Me. Punch, even. The sadness is, we don't all get to witness a human's end. Only a select few have that pleasure, that privilege. And for these teeth, these bones, before me now, as dawn breaks on a crisp January morning – that honour is mine. All mine.

Maybe yours will be next?

I'll bask in the indescribable stench. The smell of an island. Burning.

Oh – my name?

Call me Bearfoot.

ACT I

SCENE I

WEDNESDAY

HE FELT THE MIDDAY FERRY leaving Oban; *un-kissing* the mainland, as he always saw it. Now Davud experienced it more as relief, like he was escaping from its clutches.

It was late January 2000, the early days of a new millennium. Davud looked at the cafeteria clock. *12.02*. He logged the departure time in his sketchbook, next to his prediction of *12.03*. The three additional minutes had felt like a form of torture. As though the big hand of Oban or, more specifically, one of its gangsters – a man called Gerard McNair – might still reach out and claim him. Just trying to right a few wrongs, Bearfoot had said. It was he who had got Davud caught up in these clutches. Just the description of McNair had sent shivers up Davud's spine.

The dark island loomed ahead, out through the mist. He had never been so keen to get to Mull, away from his first-year studies. It was a strange feeling, because even after seven years, the island didn't feel like home to him, not in the way Bosnia did in his mind. But you couldn't take a ferry to your mind, to friends who were not now there. To war. To the dead. The country of his birth was no longer even a separate entity, instead it was part of a collective idea called 'the mainland'. He knew now that living on an island could do that to you. Mull, to give it its due, did feel less likely to be set alight, or bombed. But more likely to float away? That aspect never seemed to bother him. Especially today. Just as long as he was floating with it, from the things he had done. But, given the alien contents of his rucksack, the mainland was, in a way – in a frightening, unknown way – floating with him.

Even on Mull, war was never far away. The sounds of the clay pigeon shoots outside Dervaig – the village on the north-west Atlantic coast of the island, where he and his mother had been relocated as refugees – still had him flinching, anticipating the front door of their long caravan on the edge of the village was about to be booted in. The fact it was propped on bricks was too permanent. Those raids were his abiding memory of the place he used to call home. In Sarajevo, he had lived in an apartment *made* of bricks, not propped on them. Until his home became a pile of them. There, he had a family. Friends. A dad. Nobody seemed to understand how war relocated with you.

Rarely had he left the island since settling there, and then it was only to Oban with his mum. But now he was studying in Glasgow, three months into his first year, and cities were a part of him again. It was five full years since the war had ended, or ended in Bosnia. But it was still raging on Mull, in his head, and in his mum's too, he suspected. He didn't completely trust the door of his classroom in the art school, often keeping an eye on it in case soldiers arrived to drag him back to his country of birth now that, at nineteen, he was of conscription age. War was like dawn to him; it seemed to rise up every day. He felt the weight of it on his shoulders. But not on his pencil. Not on his drawing board. On there he could fly, briefly silence war.

The sea lay ahead like a fresh page. Hearing the ferry's engines firing up and seeing the waters frothing down below always indicated that the threat of the mainland's influence was retreating. War, retreating. Though a new thought came to him now, which was that by leaving the pier he was in a way also *un-kissing* his father. Leaving him for dead, again. For definitely dead. The last time he saw his father he was aflame. The scene was frozen in his mind. If only all this water around him could dowse the flames, the war, the image. And now he had got caught up in a new war. But he was doing it for Bearfoot. His only friend on Mull. To rubber-stamp them as blood brothers.

He would never forget the feeling of first arriving in this new country, just him and his mum remaining. But for him, accepting help, accepting Scotland, accepting refugee status – all these were in themselves acts of turning their backs on his dad, on her husband. Though Petar had pleaded with them to go. Davud still took that as his father's acknowledgement it had won – the war had won. The university Petar had worked in had been flattened.

Davud had been eleven. He had just completed primary school in Sarajevo and was due to start Tobermory High. But due to what the adults around him called 'trauma', which to Davud meant a hole inside him the size of Sarajevo, his mother and the headteachers of both Dervaig primary and

Tobermory High had agreed he should repeat his final year of primary. He had therefore always been one year older than his peers. That was just another factor, along with his accent – which, mostly, by now had retreated too, allowing the inflections of his new country to invade – together with the fact everyone knew of his close proximity to death, conspiring to further isolate him as 'other', as something even beyond 'mainlander'.

His name had stood him out too. Davud had hung onto the 'u', instead of giving in to the English 'i'; he wondered whether, had he been able to stop the flames and flee with them, his father would by now have done away with the 'a' in his name, succumbing to a second 'e'. Bosnia, his father, both were mostly a blur now, accompanied by snipers, fires, bombs and stacked rubble. To everyone else, including his mother it appeared, the village of Dervaig apparently had none of these. A new language, new country, new home, school, weather, football teams had erased what he had known. He had tried to sketch his old life but gradually the lines had faded in his memory.

His mum didn't even display old photos anymore. And he hadn't expected a new dad, or somebody trying to act like one, to arrive in their place.

As he gazed back at Oban growing smaller, he felt at least a little safer. He had been expecting the Gerard McNair man to meet him, the one Bearfoot said would give him the packages. But it had been a girl. Or a young woman, maybe just a bit older than he was. She had spoken like somebody from Oban, deep-voiced with rounded vowels, but seemed more built for war than he was. The spits of rain running down the cafeteria windows gave the impression the promenade buildings were dropping to the sea, and maybe the girl with them? He had seen buildings fall like that before, the whole earth crumbling. Oban was falling to its knees, like Sarajevo. Maybe because of what he had done? Of what he was carrying?

Davud knew this fear of collapsing villages, towns and cities was the real reason why he was studying architecture. It was to make buildings, houses, villages, towns, islands – and then, with *them* secured – language, stadia, grandparents, fathers, friends and families too; all strong enough to withstand war. Every other subject he had experienced in Tob High – to which he had travelled every school day by bus on winding roads full of what the locals called *hairpin bends* – had mostly passed him by. But drawing and connecting lines seemed to 'speak' to him. It was a universal language he could understand.

He had the packages from the Oban girl in his rucksack. When he had walked away from her in the unit located in the alleyway near the train platform on Oban pier, he hadn't expected them to feel like bombs. Like he was carrying somebody else's war. Might the ferry blow up at any moment?

He looked out of the windows on the other side of the cafeteria, across to the horizon interrupted by Lismore lighthouse. Unlike him, its very purpose was to be noticed. He placed his forefinger on the tower, appreciating how readily he could summon perspective, confuse scale and dimension, with just his fingertip. Like being a messenger – it was an act of power, as was all design.

The crackle of the ferry's public address system kicked in with the familiar musical chimes. Davud waited for the man's voice that always followed. There was a strange comfort in mistaking the address for the Tannoy voices ordering the residents of Sarajevo to flee. He was always the first one out of the cafeteria, ready to gather at the alighting point when it was time to exit.

He watched from the window as Oban gradually, thankfully, disappeared, giving way to sea, and only sea. His breath was still bigger than his chest. He really wished he wasn't involved in transferring the packages. None of it felt safe. Bearfoot had said the caves were about them being safe, about having their own world to live in. That Dervaig had once had bears roaming the village and caves where they lived. He'd said when Davud had fastened the packages where they were to go, that he should head for their particular cave. Where Bearfoot would be waiting. Bearfoot had even got him to roar.

But was their plan still working?

He looked to a seagull holding on outside the cafeteria window, gliding alongside the vessel. *Petar*, he imagined. Hoped.

There was something else out there he was looking for, that he had seen off Mull's Atlantic coast back in September, technically in the last century. He had seen it from the vantage point of the bear caves. It was just before leaving Bearfoot, to start art school. Only he had seen it. And he hadn't told anyone. Not even his friend.

An island. Where, before, there hadn't been one.

SCENE II

'NECKRINGABLE.'

Punch could see a skipper's cap hovering outside his window, hands cupped around the face, trying to peer into the Tobermory police station house, which, together with the station next door, he had coined 'Pebbledash HQ'.

'An upgrade on an irritation. And fuck.' It was even more annoying as he was just at the point when Rod Stewart was about to grab the mic stand and really give it laldy. Always the broom-handle stand, with the sturdy circular base to stop it falling over, or maybe the singer. The jury was still out on the sergeant.

'How can any bugger be expected to keep the beat . . .' He put down the imaginary drumsticks, pulled off his headphones, silencing Rod and the rest of The Faces. He rolled off the couch in the station house. Checked the clock.

8 a.m. Thursday. Unfortunately, it was the year 2000 and not 1973,

Rod's golden period.

'Middle of the night. Bastard'n island.'

He was halfway to the door when he realised he had not the microphone but a bottle of Tobermory Malt still in hand. *Christ, Ivor.* He turned and walked to the kitchenette, to place the offending bottle under the sink where he kept the security bottle of Bell's. He moved to lift the needle off the vinyl. Checked his trousers were definitely part of the equation.

He turned the key and pulled the door. It didn't budge. *High security*. He turned the key again and released the door.

'Have you seen it, sergeant?' came the voice, high-pitched and alarmed, as though a boot was on its throat. *It could be arranged*. 'I was knocking half of three minutes!'

'Eh?' Punch narrowed his eyes to the onrush of light, sky, sea, island; *'Humanity' would be an overstatement*. He looked to his visitor and then turned back to the room, to the expectation of Rod, the band and the stage, not to mention the screaming fans – none of it present; at this rate he'd be missing the after-show too. *How could all of that be constrained within headphones?* 'Right. Eh, aye, I was deep in paperwork, Skerry. Never heard you. You know it's an offence to go looking in the police house.'

It was Skerryvore. Tall, thin, with a face Punch considered more suited to bird analysis, to Darwinian inspection, than criminal. The old man could barely get his words out, rope around his waist. The glassy slits-for-eyes were reflecting the sky, staring upwards as though Punch was there. *Another bottle and it was likely.*

'What's the bother anyway, Skerry?' Punch watched his whisky breath – eighty years matured – surround Skerryvore. Still, there was no threat of it penetrating the cloud of distillery around the old man. 'I'm busy I said.'

Skerryvore glanced at Punch and then back to the sky.

Sometimes Punch expected that a stare from the man's eyes could cut his flesh. Originally from the Isle of Tiree, the man was named after the lighthouse situated some twelve miles off that island's southern tip. Still the oldest, and tallest, in Scotland. But to Punch, Skerryvore, the *man*, though harmless enough, was minus the light bulb.

'Mull!' Skerryvore said, pointing upwards. 'In the sky?'

'Eh?' Punch narrowed his eyes.

The old man was a mainstay on Tobermory Main Street, but lived in not much more than a hut up behind Rockfield at the top of the town. '*Hayfield Hotel, no door no bell!*' Skerryvore would say of it. Everyone knew he had rowed to the town from his native island some fifty years earlier. 'No passport required,' he always said. Even passing tourists were not spared Skerryvore's claim he was a descendant of the man who had placed the final brick in the lighthouse in 1844.

'The shape of Mull, Ivor!' Skerryvore persisted. 'I tell you! Up in the sky!'

Punch was well aware of Skerryvore's tales, which the man often recounted – usually with a prayer attached for maximum impact – while mooching drinks in the bars of the Mishnish, the MacDonald Arms and Macgochans. The more upmarket Western Isles Hotel having long since spat him out of their revolving door. The man would speak of those Victorian men who built the tower, of how they were sourced from many of the neighbouring islands, of how they had erected the lighthouse on a lump of rock not much bigger than the size of a postage stamp in the warring Skerry waters. Stand still long enough outside the Co-op down on the Main Street, and Skerryvore would even tell you of his family's connection to not only the workmen, but also the lighthouse's architect, Alan Stevenson, uncle of the famous writer; to the extent Punch anticipated Skerryvore might soon claim he had penned not just the Bible, but *Treasure* bloody *Island* and *The Strange Case of Dr Jekyll and Mr Hyde* too.

'In the clouds?' Punch pretended to look up, hoping to be rid of the man smartish. The final note of Ronnie Wood's guitar would by now have rung out, roadies busy flight-casing amps and bottles of Bacardi, ensuring Rod and the boys get to another town, hotel, to another set of groupies and TV sets ready for the swimming pool treatment. He gazed to where Skerryvore was pointing; there *was* something there, in the clouds, clearly visible, but he wasn't about to toast it. 'Aye, well; look, it's not a bad likeness. Though God could do with a night class or two. Look, Skerry, I must get back to . . .'

'Think it's something to do with thon wind farm they're talking about building around Dervaig way? You know, that we're getting their wind? A special kind of wind capable of this? Could be a sign?'

'From who?'

'Our *maker*!'

'Kenneth MacAlpin?'

'Revelation 16:16. I'm telling you, Ivor! Armageddon!'

'More like Arms-*MacDonald*.' Punch stared Skerryvore in the eye. 'And call me sergeant when I'm in uniform, man.' He looked down at his ruffled shirt and stockinged soles. 'Out of it too.' Punch went patting for his tobacco, but realised it was inside, packed up and flying halfway to Madison Square Garden by now for all he knew.

'Well, they're saying it's getting heated around there, Sarge, between the campaigners and the folk who make those Godawful structures.'

'That's a hellish thing to say about Dervaig Main Street . . .'

'Wind farms! That's what they're calling them! On Hi-Pockets Lennox's land.' Skerryvore looked to the sky and touched the rim of his cap by way of an apology. 'For the profanity, my Lord.'

Punch saw Skerryvore's gesture as apologising to weather, bad art, Darwin even. There was still talk locally that the famed naturalist had once visited Mull, though Punch was certain the man's journey, unlike Skerryvore's, was unlikely to have been powered by exclusive means of whisky and the almighty. Punch's own proximity to God extended only as far as his weekly transportations of his mother to Tobermory's Church of Scotland, which she called MacLean's, after the minister.

'Want me to arrest the Atlantic, Skerry, for the wind? Caliach Point? Or be done with it and pull the entire continent of North bloody America in for questioning? God?'

'Look, sergeant!' Skerryvore pointed forcibly again in the direction of the cloud formation. 'The sleeping bear, Mull. A sign! I'm telling you!'

'Whatever you're seeing, man, it's a long way from a crime. Even if it were, I'm not sure God could stand a night on the porcelain in my cell without bog roll, or minus the fan heater.'

'The cell?' Skerryvore forgot the sky and eyeballed Punch, becoming even more serious. 'I've never seen the cell, sergeant.'

Punch knew of the town's fascination with the cell; there were for ever kids at the police station door firing questions at him, asking if they could see beyond the thick blue door, only to have it momentarily closed on them, the key turned.

Do you get a pillow? Would we need a lawyer? Is there really a toilet inside? With no seat? 'Aye,' Punch would hiss, 'and imprisoned pirates too, from the Spanish Armada sunk in the bay! If you listen hard enough you'll hear them speaking Spanish . . . counting their gold bullion!'

'Can you believe it, sergeant?' Skerryvore marvelled. 'They're now farming air?'

'But not technically a crime, Skerry. Wasn't mentioned at Police College in Tulliallen in any case. Look, if you've never seen the cell then best keep it that way.' Punch stepped back inside. 'I've got important work here. Wasting police time is an offence you know.'

'Aye. Okay, sorry, Ivor.'

'Or, as Mick and Keith would have it – get *off of my cloud*.'

'Eh?'

'Nothing.' Punch felt his face heat up. He knew, ironically, he could never delivery a punchline; his cleaner, who was more than a cleaner, Mary MacBeth, had told him often enough, dating back to their time at Tob primary school.

'Right you are, sorry, sergeant.' Skerryvore turned. 'But now I remember why I was coming to you in the first place!'

'So it wasn't the weather report? And I don't mean the band.'

'It was the burning. Do you smell burning, sergeant? I'm sure I smell burning.'

All Punch could detect in the air was pine. And maybe – even from this remove from the Forestry office at Aros Mains eight miles away – a hint of Randy's aftershave, his friend from a misspent Tobermory childhood who was not really his friend. Despite having been born on Mull, Punch knew a police sergeant on an island has *no* friends. Only potential suspects:

neckringables. That suited him fine.

'No. No, I don't, Skerry. Look – was the burning at the Hayfield Hotel? I've warned you before about fires.'

'No! I smelled it in the wind. Like it was coming from the west?'

'Where?'

'But I might've dreamed it.'

'Christ! Enough, man!'

'An island in the sky! Burning!'

'Total shite, Skerry.' Punch grabbed the door.

'But maybe not Mull, sergeant!' Skerryvore placed a dilapidated boot to stop the door closing. 'It's the island nobody knows about . . . *the Looming*!'

SCENE III

'HULLO.' DAVUD HEARD.

He startled. Became still as a watched squirrel. Had the *seagull* spoken? He *did* speak to horses when he was alone with them, belonging to a bear-like, unsmiling Dervaig farmer named Hi-Pockets Lennox, but they had never actually spoken back. Not even Bearfoot knew about that.

Davud stole a glance.

It was Duck, standing at his table, dressed in what the locals called Highland dress.

'Aye, aye,' Duck said.

Davud calculated Duck must be in his late twenties now, though he seemed much older, almost already in decline, like a statue left hundreds of years in the elements. Given Davud had Dervaig's current population logged as 198, he knew – even discounting their nocturnal cohabitation of the same caravan – that it was statistically, geographically, impossible for him and Duck not to have been aware of each other.

He looked to the new TV mounted on the cafeteria wall. On it was an image of a small boy. His dead body washed ashore on a beach in France, the text said. Could that have been his fate? He had never before thought of the sea as a liquid bridge. He started rocking, looked intently to the sea. There was another reason he was keen to get to the island: the night before he had set a line of Glasgow rubbish bins on fire – he had briefly felt in control, in command, of war, of his father's flame.

'Well, I'll take the load off . . . these bacon rolls won't eat themselves.' Duck gestured with his plate to the seat opposite Davud. 'Feels like there's a piano tuner at work in ma skull.' Duck collapsed onto the yellow seat. 'Shite!' He had spilled coffee from his mug on his kilt. Used his hand to wipe it off.

Davud felt a minor earthquake. The rolls – all three of them – somehow stayed on the plate. He remembered how children in the village had used to flock around Duck. He had been one of them. Not long after he had arrived on Mull, he had been among many children lying at the bottom of Dervaig football pitch, looking up to see Duck flying high above them on a motorbike. Duck had seemed *beyond* adulthood to Davud, almost superhuman.

Duck nodded to the wall. 'Just out the wrapper, eh?'

Davud looked to his sketchpad. He had sketched the mystery island from memory. He thought of it as Trauma Island. But now the image had disappeared from the page. He caught a glance at how aggressively Duck attacked his first roll, his cheeks flushed, each one a Japanese flag.

'The new TV?' Duck said. He looked to the cashier's position and whispered to Davud, 'But all too serious. Change the bloody channel, love.'

Duck dropped his keys on the table. Davud flinched. He preferred to be warned if sudden explosions were going to happen. That was why he liked the musical chimes of the ferry address system, that they came *before* the ferry announcer's voice. He opened a new page and wrote, *In war everyone should carry a glockenspiel.*

'Always at the scribbling, eh?' Duck croaked.

Davud smelled the concoction of hair gel, bacon fat and alcohol wafting from across the table. Duck was almost an Oasis song. He was nothing like a motorbike-riding rock star anymore. He looked more like someone who had been experimented on in a horror film.

Davud looked to the TV and very briefly saw close-up images of smouldering embers, emergency vehicles in Glasgow, before new images showed a footballer running and scoring a goal with hair that didn't move. Lots of people seemed to be applauding this feat of the man's hair.

Duck gestured his Coke bottle towards the ceiling. Raised his eyebrows wearily to the public address coming from the speaker.

'What a fucking racket. We *know* by now you have trinkets in the fucking ferry shop! Christ, the boys at Costco must be quaking in their moccasins . . .'

Davud remembered how Duck had ensured that he, as one of the youngest in the line of bodies lain alongside each other like sardines on the ground, was safely positioned nearest the ramp for one particular jump. A feat that was recognised as a Mull record with some distance to spare. Davud had quickly realised no one else locally would have attempted such a jump. No one else could have commanded so many willing participants. Now he wasn't sure if his positioning in the lineup was only to do with his age.

He caught a glimpse of Duck's rugged, sad features. He could barely discern the heroic face from that record-breaking day. It was a bloated, unshaven face now; the man had turned even paler since sitting down. With the black rings around his eyes, Davud saw the complexion of one of Hi-Pocket Lennox's dairy cows. The red biker's jacket that Davud remembered Duck wearing – which he had included in a drawing of the scene in one of his first sketchbooks at the time – had been replaced with an ill-fitting, off-white shirt and black tie. It looked like a football had been stuffed under it. The knot of the tie was hanging limply, the top button not done up.

'I'd several too many last night.' Duck looked at Davud and then away. 'I was up half the night on the hotel porn. Dildos, the lot.'

Davud had no idea what 'dildos' meant. He was struck, even now, with how strangely proud he felt to have been included in the lineup. It seemed almost unbelievable that he was among the chosen that day. He had felt like the embodiment of one of Evel Knievel's red buses, a line of which he had seen the white-suited man jump at Wembley Stadium when it was replayed on TV. And here was the man-boy sitting next to him. News of the record jump had quickly travelled around the island on the teenage grapevine, aided by Duck's bin lorry route. In the days after, those involved had felt not only an afterglow, but a sense of notoriety in almost being maimed.

'The man was no virgin himself, of course,' Duck said.

'Evel?'

'Sorry? No, no. Burns. I saw they'd haggis on the menu.' Duck shifted uncomfortably. 'You always look hellish serious, lad. Like you're hiding something?'

Davud gulped heavily. Did Duck know about the packages in his rucksack? He had heard Duck in their caravan. Late at night. Adding to the weight on the bricks. Felt him leaving before morning, quietly sealing the door. Only his scent remained. The smell of the Bellachroy Hotel from along the road in Dervaig. Davud wasn't used to people sitting beside him. Not even in lectures, unless it couldn't be avoided, in which case he would be asked by a gleeful classmate to again recount the Oban to Glasgow ScotRail timetables that had been his only words uttered in Freshers Week. He had spouted his predicted arrival times at each station and told how he would crosscheck them with the ScotRail planner. Nobody had sat near him since. Sometimes he wondered if it was the war. If it had followed him. If people could smell the flames? Only Bearfoot seemed able to take the heat. His friend had said the packages were a way they could be closer. Closer than brothers.

'Painted any nudies yet?' Duck nodded to Davud's sketchbook.

'Erm ... no. I'm, eh, studying buildings not people. Not naked people.'

Davud remembered a secret thought at the time of the record jump, which was a desire to have been last in the line, so that a wheel might have come down on him. Then he would have been noticed. And the war, and his father, too. He had felt guilty about that ever since, given the horror of what happened the following week. As though he'd had a premonition and could have stopped it.

He closed the sketchbook and put it into his rucksack. Careful to keep the rucksack shielded as he did so. Not to bump it. Had Bearfoot implied they were bombs? He felt sweat running down his back. He looked to the window and wondered if the ferry had made up the lost two minutes yet. He had read that scientists were planning to add two seconds to the end of the year 2000. To make Earth run bang on time, they said. He decided not to mention it.

'Easy access at least.' Duck munched.

'Sorry?'

'The kilt.'

'Oh?' Davud had seen enough of Duck's piss on the caravan's toilet floor. Bearfoot had said he had seen that, too. That there were ways of making that stop. Davud wondered: were the bombs part of that plan?

'Wharra skull right enough.' Duck held his head in both hands. 'D'you see Dave the Grave handy? Our undertaker?'

'Erm . . .?' Davud quickly looked for the bald man dressed in all black he had seen driving the long, black car on the island. He didn't want to think about the dead. 'Here in the cafeteria? No. I don't.'

'I think I'm ready for his preparation table.'

Usually by now Davud would have sketched what was around him. He had entire books designated to ferry drawings, with internal workings revealing all the details he imagined inside. In the way he had learned Leonardo da Vinci had done with not only machines, but bodies. *Leonardo* – that had been the secret 'Brother' name Bearfoot had given him. Everyone on Mull seemed to have a nickname. Like it was their true identity, the one the mainland couldn't see.

'Not busy . . .' Duck chewed, summoning the cafeteria with his half-eaten roll. 'Midweek, of course.'

'It's twelve weeks into CalMac's winter timetable,' Davud said.

'I'd bet my pig rolls on it. Aye, aye.'

Davud counted the forty-four tables on the cafeteria floor. He noted eleven were occupied, which meant the cafeteria was operating at 25 per cent capacity. Everything could be determined by calculation. Even casualties.

He was never sure if his drawings were depictions of what he *actually* last saw of his father – his desperate face surrounded by burnt-out cars, gunshot and crumbling buildings on fire – or if they were, in fact, more like reinterpretations of events, possibly misrepresentations. He wished now to see back into that blur; he still felt the burning. A comfort in it. That was why the previous night he had set fire to the bins at the back of the Glasgow School of Art. He had run back to his room in the halls of residence afterwards, listening to the sirens from the fire engines, and something about the distance, the remove – only hearing the alarm he had caused rather than seeing it – made him feel connected to his father. But only momentarily. His mother didn't keep his father's photograph out anymore. She had become too distracted recently with the man opposite, and fighting something called a wind farm that the locals believed was being planned by Mr Lennox. There were posters everywhere about it. His mother and other campaigners had marched through the village, chanting all the way to Tobermory. She seemed too eager to forget their past, too keen to take Petar's order to run. Davud wondered, was his mum trying to turn the Mull wind into a war?

There were lots of people now on the TV screen walking alongside a motorway. Being shepherded like Hi-Pockets' sheep. *BREAKING NEWS*, it read. Some people were carrying others on their backs. Many had no shoes. Everything seemed to qualify as *breaking news*. There seemed to him more space available than there was genuine news to fit it. Poor design, he thought. He read the subtitles: *NATO have started a military air strike in Kosovo, in the name of a humanitarian war. Albanians are fleeing from Kosovo to neighbouring countries.*

The prime minister's face appeared.

'Blair,' Duck said. 'Talking of dildos.'

Davud looked away. So now he knew what one was.

'Politicians are always happy to send folk into their wars . . .' Duck looked sheepishly at Davud. 'Er, sorry, lad. Aye, aye.'

'We weren't taken by road. We were on plane,' Davud said, looking to the screen. 'Special flight to Edinburgh.'

'Right. Right.'

Davud remembered one boy who was a bit older than him in school, and his family were on that flight. But he had never seen the boy again. His mother had said maybe a Scottish castle was waiting for them. But Dervaig had no castles, only a church tower and a graveyard of people who had been properly buried, with gravestones.

He was sitting where he sat on all crossings, directly below one of the speakers against the back wall. He could hide while still being able to sketch everyone present. He was used to trying not to be noticed. Though villages, islands, weren't good for that. It was only to Mr Lennox's fields that he could really escape. The man, he'd learned, was known as Hi-Pockets because he always gripped his hands where his overalls met his neck; though his mum had said it was because when it came to his round in the Bellachroy Hotel the men claimed his money was always out of reach. Mr Lennox had told Davud he could go to the horses anytime. But more recently Davud's mother hadn't wanted him to go. And then the horses were removed from the fields altogether. There had been talk of Mr Lennox firing a shot where the protestors were gathering at the entrance to his farm. Bearfoot had said he could play that game too.

'So you're a scholar now, eh?' Duck said, gesturing his roll towards Davud. 'In the big city?'

'Not really,' Davud said.

Hi-Pockets Lennox's land also took in the caves on the coastline. It was there that Davud and Bearfoot would go. Bearfoot had told him he needed to meet the woman in Oban, but nobody could know about it. That the goods were for the MacMaster man at the Wee Theatre, situated near Davud's caravan. Davud was starting to wonder if Bearfoot liked the theatre man more than him. His friend also seemed jealous of the attention Davud received from the horses. Had it been Bearfoot who had cleared them?

Davud watched the sea arguing with itself. It occurred to him what had been so strange about the sensation of having caused those sirens in Glasgow – he wasn't invisible.

'The power of education, eh, lad?' Duck beamed. 'I'd a bit of it myself piping at the hotel do last night. Hence the rigout. Burns Supper. Posh one!'

'Education?'

'Power. Christ, the doors of the hotel even opened without me touching them!'

Davud could tell Duck was trying to find a connection with him. The record jump wasn't enough. Especially after the death that occurred the following week. When a skull *was* crushed.

'Even if my mum doesn't think I do, I know it's you,' Davud said. 'Leaving in the night.'

SCENE IV

THURSDAY

THE SOUND OF AN ENGINE APPROACHED.

Punch had almost closed the door on Skerryvore when he saw the sheer white Ford Ranger pull into the front of the station alongside his perpetually-in-need-of-a-wash own. He almost baulked at the ten-to-two leather-gloved hand-action on the steering wheel; it was only a matter of time, thought Punch, until the vehicle was connected to the two new station computers. His own was a glorified hatstand. The front wheels were straightened before the engine was turned off. All that was missing was an extravagant bow and the judges' scores.

Punch's deputy, PC Cluny – Bearsden U-16 badminton champion, Milngavie U-18 chess master, teetotaller and recent arrival from Tulliallen Police College – turned off the engine and made a theatre of applying the handbrake. Punch would just as soon have an interface wedged between his deputy's bum cheeks. He had already had more than enough of the posh accent, the tiepins, Harry Potter glasses, crisp moth-ball-scented shirts and cufflinks.

'I said I sense burning! Sergeant?' Skerry tried again, apparently oblivious to the arrival of more officialdom.

'Did I not tell you to be off, man? There's no burning. Not unless it's PC Cluny's wallet.'

'Sarge!' PC Cluny jumped from his Ranger.

Too keen, thought Punch; the man was for ever appearing like he'd just been stung by a wasp.

'PC Jonathan Ambrose Cluny,' Cluny said, outstretching his hand to Skerryvore. 'We haven't met but I've seen you about. Indeed.'

Punch watched how Cluny's shock of blond hair – which, atop the black uniform, had given rise to Punch nicknaming his deputy *Guinness* – arrived like a lighthouse itself in the grey afternoon.

'Aye, lad,' Skerryvore said, keeping his hands to himself, clearly uncomfortable with such formal address. A rope no match for a tiepin. 'I was telling Ivor here about a smell of burning.'

'Well, it can't be the art school.' Cluny licked the end of his forefinger and held it in the air. 'Not unless we're *seriously* upwind.'

'Eh?' Skerryvore said, screwing up the tip of his nose until it was almost in between his eyes.

'Heard it on the news in the car, Sarge. Big fire. Huge loss to Glasgow. And this is a Glaswegian speaking.'

'Jesus.' Punch puffed the word out. 'Good of you to take some time away from the shipyards. Hate to break up this love-in, but I've paperwork falling out the door.' Punch motioned to the station house. He could smell Cluny's mother's talc. 'On your way, Skerry.'

'You know,' Skerryvore blurted, not looking at either of the men and gazing blankly to the sea, 'when I rowed into Tobermory Bay it was the first time I had ever seen them? I had never left Tiree . . .' He looked absently to Cluny. 'I just hadn't seen them before.'

'What, Mr Skerryvore?' Cluny said, pushing his round-rimmed glasses up his nose. An action that was currently standing at no. 8 in Punch's top ten irritations. Next the man would be inventing new games using broomsticks, tattooing a scar on his forehead and sending owls to collect the locals' car keys from outside the pubs come closing time.

'Trees,' Punch completed.

'We have none on Tiree!' Skerryvore added. 'Flat it is, too. The old man called it "the Pancake". Last I saw of it was when I set off in the boat. I looked back at Tiree and Coll and each was hovering like two gulls on the horizon. That was the sum of it. My life there.' Skerryvore took a roll-up from behind his ear and sparked a match behind a shielded hand. 'Aye, something brought me here, but now I don't know what.'

'To Mull, or to the station?' Cluny asked, his notepad and pencil already in hand.

'Both,' Skerryvore said. 'My dog came in a suitcase, but that's another story. Your fly's down.' Skerryvore drifted away, still surveying the sky, not unlike a travelling cloud himself with the puffs of smoke.

Punch observed Cluny's inspection of his own trousers, and then his superior's.

'You want a night behind the thick blue door?' Punch zipped up and turned to board the private jet.

'Erm, can I help you with that paperwork, Sarge? Maybe open a new folder on the computer. Head Office are sending directives to digitise more.'

'I'm a Mull native, PC,' Punch said, 'not a digital one. Digitise the cloud,' he offered, pointing to the sky as he turned. 'We have an escaping island to investigate.'

'Eh, Sarge?'

'Nothing. I'll be through later, PC. Do a round of the town at five to show folk we're alive. Macgochans and the Mish will need an owl later.'

'Eh?'

'Nothing. Leave the car keys to me.'

'Right, Sarge.'

Punch watched his deputy turn on a penny and make eagerly for the station. *Like a bloody dog hunting truffle*. He closed the door and went immediately for the cupboard under the sink and the bottle of Tobermory. *Maybe catch Rod and the boys before they leave for LAX*. He turned for the headphones. The sticks.

'What the fuck?' Punch stumbled backwards to the sink. Taking his weight on his right arm, feeling unbalanced.

A man was sitting in the station house. Propped on the edge of the couch.

'I said what the . . .?' Punch straightened up.

The man was wearing long boots, breeches and a frilly shirt. None of it clothing of the time, even by Mull standards.

'How'd you get in here?' Punch reached instinctively to his chest for his radio and the red alert button. But found he had left it in the car, safe from Cluny. Somehow he didn't feel under immediate threat.

The man's hair was parted in an old-fashioned style, longer at the front. But there was something futuristic about him too. There was a stain of possibly ink by his shirt pocket. He sported a musketeer's moustache and had brought a musty smell into the room. But with it, a kind of serenity.

The visitor slowly stood and offered a confident smile.

Punch stepped forwards.

The man was about Punch's build, just a bit taller. He had a similar badger-like effect of greying at his temples. Though it looked more fabricated. He presented an outstretched, gloved hand.

'I'm Robert Louis Stevenson.'

SCENE V

'DID THAT CLOWN RANDY PUT you up to this pish?' Punch said, keeping an eye on his strange, apparently out-of-time visitor. 'Have to say you've aged bloody well. Eh? And fuck!'

'*Randy?*' Punch's visitor stood from the couch, smiled elegantly. 'I do love the Hebridean single-word character assessments. The fellow sounds mightily, erm, *busy* . . .'

'You took a wrong turn if you're looking for Mull's Wee Theatre – it's in Dervaig?'

The man sat down again, realising Punch wasn't going to take up his offer of a handshake. Punch heard the accent as confused. Scottish, refined, guttural, but a bit put on.

'No. Good fellow. I am who I say I am.'

'Look,' Punch said, ruffling his keys. 'I've a thick blue door with your name on it across the way if you're not careful, whoever you are – so enough of this bullshit. Entering a police building without permission is an offence. In *any* century. Joke's over!'

'Surely, entering *any* building, that is not one's own, sergeant? Or have the laws changed now?'

'Smart arse, eh? That's you lost your bog roll.'

The man looked at the whisky bottle.

'Ah, Tobermory, I see. A fine drop. Would you consider relinquishing a measure of the good stuff to a thirsty visitor?'

'Neckringable! Look, pal, I've had enough of this bullsh—'

'The old fellow is looking in the wrong place, sergeant.'

'What? Who?'

'The lighthouse keeper.'

'Skerryvore? The man lives in a glorified rabbit's burrow and can hardly keep a roll-up lit, let alone man a bloody lighthouse. Boats would be crashing into each other all over the bloody place. Look—'

'The island he talks of is not in the sky, sergeant.'

'I'd bloody guessed that much.' Punch noted how precisely the man spoke, so sure of his words, like it was a script he was reciting. He had him down as being in his late forties or early fifties, but it was hard to tell, given the rig-out.

Punch took hold of his tumbler and downed the contents. A warm flame danced in his chest. He troubled the bottle again.

'I sent him to you,' the man said.

'Who?'

'Skerryvore.'

'Today, or to the island?'

'Did you not notice how his words arrived themselves like beacons of light, even if received incorrectly. You see, my uncle, Alan Stevenson, the Skerryvore lighthouse architect, once told me we must all aim to use sentences like they are small acts of design, of foundation, structure and careful planning. Word as brick.'

'Well, try these ones out for size—' Punch reached for his handcuffs. 'You're nicked!'

The man stood, moved away from Punch's advances.

'Please, sergeant. Please! Allow me!' He tentatively sat again. 'You see, the point being it wasn't a writer who taught me to construct sentences, stories – it was an architect. As a result, I have always viewed my books as brick upon brick, as reaching for light. Might that be how you see your work? Clue cemented upon clue?'

'Okay, Doctor bloody Jekyll, enough . . .' Punch reached for the man with his left arm, but something stopped him making contact. Possibly because the man didn't move.

'The island is not in the sky, no!' The man crossed his booted legs. '"Simply say the things the sentence already knows," my uncle would say. And I am here because I know something, sergeant. Something I feel you should know too.'

Punch was beyond feeling like an idiot for entertaining the man this long. There was a duality about his visitor right enough, gruff but refined.

'But it is a danger, sergeant. If a person ever sees it, the island, then they are cursed. They will see the dead. Be surrounded by them. Alas.'

'Alas.' Punch reached for the bottle. The Faces would be three margaritas in and cavorting behind a cordon in the Whisky a Go Go by now, gate-crashing John Lennon's Lost Weekend. And all the while he was left here on the runway, with this comedian, facing the penance of a lifetime of badminton and spreadsheets with Guinness.

'The Looming.' The man spoke with an even more precise delivery.

'The what now?' Punch poured another finger-measure – late-period Marlon Brando proportions. It was the same name Skerryvore had spouted.

'The island. *The Looming*.' The man reached for a second glass on the table, a remnant of Punch's intake from the night before. Though only Mary MacBeth was counting.

Punch prepared himself to jump the bastard. Cluny was next door masquerading as some form of backup if needed, busy typing love letters about his new interface no doubt to the island's undertaker and Mull Millennium Bug Task Force Chairperson, Dave the Grave. Somehow, with this man's presence, Punch's deputy seemed even more an inhabitant of the future.

'Indeed,' the man said, pouring himself a measure and holding it by his mouth. 'Let me run a specimen over to the lab.'

The man drank from the glass with no little elegance, but failed, Punch noted, to hide a deep-set taste for the stuff. He recognised the trait.

'So you'd be mightily unfortunate to see it, sergeant, the Looming. Wretched happenstance, in fact. For any person.'

Punch couldn't believe he was tolerating this crap. He was half expecting some bugger off the TV with a microphone and camera pointing at him to spring through the door confirming the whole thing to be an elaborate gotcha; there was plenty of this shite on the box these days. It was hard to tell if his mother – upon whom the tightening stranglehold of dementia was increasingly playing out as a form of reality TV itself – would be even more lost to the rivers of confusion with or without this fare on her TV.

'And why would someone be unfortunate to see the thing?' Punch managed, shaking his head. 'For Christ's sake . . .' He was about to walk into the cell himself.

'Well, that is a full bottle of Tobermory question . . .' the man said, pouring again. 'But, in summary, it is believed to be a curse if a person witnesses it. I saw it, sergeant.'

'The island?'

'The Looming, yes. I died within weeks.'

'But you're here now?'

'Only as a messenger.'

Punch noted the accent had dropped. Still couldn't place it. He held his glass up to his eyes for inspection. 'Were it that Bell's shite I was on then this would be more explainable . . .'

'Mendelssohn had warned me, sergeant. The fellow thought it did for him too on his noteworthy sailing by Staffa. A different overture altogether. Folk even used to camp out for weeks in the hopes of seeing the Looming – like they do now with this creature at Loch Ness – before realising it was cursed. I thought I was blessed to see it on my first and only jaunt around Mull's west coast. But that was not the case. I suppose one island made me, and another broke me.'

'Aye . . . well, they say we have treasure on this island too. Mull, I mean.'

'I know this. It informed my own fictional island, in fact. Nobody else knows that.'

'Right.' Punch took a deep breath of what he hoped was reality, of sense, returning. 'Enough, pal.'

He necked his measure, aware he was only one more request for office plant space away from Guinness bursting through his door to find him talking to his couch; he would have to lay off the sauce for a day or two. He feared handcuffing the man would be like arresting the wind. Which would at least get him Dervaig's vote, going by the local posters and articles he had seen. 'Panto season is over! I need all your details; this is not okay. Here on *real* islands, breaking and entering is still an offence. Whoever the hell you are!'

'Yes! I was sailing, *sailing*, sergeant!' the man almost sang.

'Like fucking Rod? Okay, I get it now. Joke's over. Your accent's slipping too. Randy or Appy bunged you a few bob? I get it . . .'

'Sergeant!' The man reached for Punch's right arm. The shorter one. Deliberately, Punch could tell. He felt the flesh and bone of the man. He pulled away. 'Hear me, the waves were rising incongruously on the almost endless wild stretch of the Skerry! As though someone had shaken a blanket!' The man used his gloved hands to demonstrate waves. 'I was with my, eh, uncle, aye, let's call him that, and he proudly showed off the completed tower rising out of the sea like a light beam reaching to the gods. It was then that my uncle told me about the mythology of the Looming. And how the men who built the tower were firm believers in the island's existence; how it would only appear twice a century; and if you were afforded the opportunity to see it, situated between Mull and Tiree, then any child born on one of those two days was noteworthy, but cursed.'

'Enough I said! And fuck.' Punch moved towards the man again but found himself holding back. 'Time to sling your hook, Long John!'

'Sergeant! You see, those hardy men who were away for long stretches building the tower would look for trousers or a dress hung at the watchtower on Tiree . . .'

'What pish is this now?'

'It was to inform the men of the sex of their newborn child. More *marital*, than maritime, but that was how it worked . . .'

'Why the hell do I need to know about any of this crazy shite, man?' Punch was unable to move. He was thinking of the pram that was never required, still hidden under a now off-white bedsheet out in the station lockup. His *almost* child, gathering dust, fading, diminishing of light. Mary MacBeth, an *almost* mother, had never seen it. Too painful for her. He knew that.

His visitor sat and put a finger onto his moustache.

'And on one of those days, if tradition were being observed, a child's clothing would be replaced with a white bedsheet. And the expectant father would see the island appear. West of Mull, in the Atlantic. The Looming, the men called it. Signifying the child's death at birth.'

'Eh?' Punch rubbed his badger temples. 'Enough I said!'

'And *you* lost a child, sergeant, did you not? And you never knew the child's sex, did you not? Never had that courtesy?'

'How the fuck do you know about that?'

SCENE VI

WEDNESDAY

'SHOOTIN' DIARRHOEA,' DUCK SAID. He nodded to the steps leading to the toilet in the middle of the cafeteria. 'Almost needed the Council boys ... Takeaway curry on Sauchiehall Street last night. Criminal.'

Davud froze at the word. He was also glad he hadn't shaken Duck's hand. He pressed against the back of the hard seat. Given Duck drove the Mull bin lorry, he had a growing fear Duck knew about the Glasgow bins. Or did Duck *really* want to replace the burning man? Bearfoot had talked about burning Duck.

'A kilt among the clubbers!' Duck smiled. 'Aye, aye, that was me.'

Davud thought about something a tutor at the art school had said on day one of his studies; it was about Michelangelo, who, when asked about the difficulties he encountered in sculpting his man-mountain, and namesake of Davud, had replied: 'It's easy. You just chip away the stone that *doesn't* look like David.' Davud wondered if that was what war had done to him. Or was it the island? Was the Philistine giant represented by Duck? He couldn't detect if Duck knew he had in fact followed him on Sauchiehall Street, before the bins, before Duck's piping gig? Bearfoot had tipped him off.

'Home for some grub?' Duck said, waving his bacon roll. 'That it?'

Davud could tell Duck preferred his mention of the caravan to just hang in the air; to be swallowed up in this unseen faultline between the mainland and the island. He wondered if his mum ever talked to Duck about him. Maybe that wasn't the arrangement. He had never seen them together. He hoped Duck's joining him wasn't about becoming his father. That thought was worthy of a match alone.

'Fair swirl out there coming off the Skerry . . .' Duck said, nodding to the sea. 'Lucky we got away on time. I'll prepare a puff. Aye, aye.'

Davud didn't bother correcting. He watched Duck preparing a roll-up and it made him think of his dad; how as a child he was never sure if the tobacco tin that was a permanent rectangular outline in the breast pocket of his university lecturer's jacket was part of the clothing or of his father. Like he had a rectangular heart. The tin seemed to be there even when he knew it wasn't. That was how he thought of his father now.

'All the parts of my dad have been chipped away,' Davud spouted. He recoiled, unsure why he kept saying his thoughts aloud.

'Eh, so I see he's almost done with the presidency!' Duck said quickly.

'But he was a lecturer?'

'Clinton.' Duck nodded to the images of the president on the TV screen. 'It'll take them long enough to clear out his condoms.'

Davud hadn't told his mum he was returning so soon. He would need an excuse. He had an idea about that; his birthday had been the night before. He was supposed to have called his mum. He wondered if Duck was in the caravan more often now that he was away.

'Oh, hello, Donald.'

Davud turned to the voice. A woman he didn't recognise was nodding to Duck and collecting her cutlery from the stand. He tried to smile.

'Greetings, lad,' she added. He knew another word for it was *salutation*. The word had stuck with him from reading *Charlotte's Web* in Dervaig primary. His first completed book in English. Even when the others were on Shakespeare, and new, confusing people, called Stevenson and Burns.

'In the kilt I see?' she said. 'Hardly recognised you out of the hi-vis! You been visiting the queen?'

'Just collecting her rubbish, Jeanie. Knighthood's in the post!'

The woman moved away, a sachet of sweetener between her lips.

'Sweet enough, Jeanie,' Duck enthused, 'you're sweet enough!'

Davud eyed Duck, who was watching the woman settle at a faraway table. He could detect the man-boy was, even now, seven years after his bike landed on a body, still in need of the warm arms of the village, of the island, around him. Was that what his mother was doing?

'Do people really like me do you think?' Duck said.

Davud looked to the waves. The sea made everything of the now.

'Or is it just the idea of redemption?' Duck said. 'Do they *take* to me? Or do they see . . . a killer?'

Davud's eyes widened; he wanted to flee. He remembered it being called 'the *incident*'. Even now it was a word he confused with *accident*. Duck was referring to the week after the record jump. When he'd tried to break it again.

'The whole village became overrun with gawkers in the aftermath . . .' Duck said, still not looking at Davud. 'They even took me off the bin lorry for a spell.'

Davud remembered the police and ambulance sirens on Dervaig's otherwise sleepy main street. Like a kind of theatre of war. Duck's motorbike, in the seconds after, spinning on its own on the football pitch. Later his mother called it a 'catastrophe'. The word at the time had seemed to him not at all like the other English words he had been soaking up at full speed.

'Well, I know they *take* to me,' Duck said. 'I know they put their bins out for me, but do they actually *like* me? Or feel sorry for me? Hate me? I thought you'd know . . .'

'Why would I?' Davud wondered if by 'like' Duck really meant 'forgive'? His mum had said forgiveness was the way to douse flame.

'I was never supposed to be here . . .' Davud heard himself saying.

'I know, lad.' Duck slowly nodded.

'I mean in this seat, too.'

'I know.'

Davud looked at Duck. To the man who had been not much more than a boy when he killed somebody. Davud remembered he had gotten off the ground and sought his own escape, to the horses. It was the day before he found the caves and became aware of Bearfoot. Was Duck now living on Trauma Island too?

'I thought I made it happen,' Davud said.

'Me sitting here?'

'No. The death.'

'Your dad?'

'No. On the pitch.'

SCENE VII

THURSDAY

THE SUN IS NOW FULLY UP ON THE GLEN.

I'm still with the teeth, the bones. A little firepit on the go.

But I must leave soon. To the caves. Where I said I'd meet Leonardo. The charred remains of the bodies are there, lying alongside each other, like the two burnt-out cars nearby – each stripped of their colour, and their seats.

Despite the devastation, and the obvious signs of ruin, the cars are more about sanctuary, stillness, peace; no doubt even somebody's idea of beauty. I know how death, dead things, can do that.

I'm feeling a pang of pride, an adrenalin rush of electricity running through me. Maybe like one of those art restorers with magnifying equipment I watch on the TV with Fintan, my mentor. With only the ghostly traces of sketched lines on canvas to go on, invisible to the human eye; indicators of how the long-dead artist had, when alive, intended to complete the unfinished work with paint. But the question hangs in the putrid air – who is the artist, or architect, curator even, of this scene? Me or Leonardo? And is Fintan the prize?

Life, thankfully – unlike lost masterpieces – cannot be so easily restored. Crouched here over flame, it seems the purpose of the dead is to make the living feel more alive. And I feel it. It's like I'd imagine a war. Golden eagles circling above me as sirens.

The gawking fir trees form an amphitheatre. It all gives the impression of being part of something; it makes you think you are of some real value to an island that otherwise seems to ignore you unless their dead needs some rouge. This is going to be *my* stage now. It could pass as the opening shot of a film, or even the first line to a riddle: *Two cars enter a glen, but only two bodies get out . . .*

Under a mackerel sky, for a few minutes more, I'll enjoy the sense of desolation, of peace, scale; of being a living entity amid death in a winter death scene on a Hebridean island. That is the privilege – alongside the sense of all clocks, all sounds, wildlife, crime, life, tides and ferries having been momentarily stopped – of being alone with teeth and bones.

But I need to think about Punch. The sergeant will surely find out soon. I'll dowse the fire and remove myself from the scene. To the caves! To be fully immersed in the gases of death and to study the bodies further; to try to piece back together the once-intact, not paintings, but bones and teeth. The way Darwin did with the bone-maps of mockingbirds and tortoises.

I feel outsized, bigger than the original plan, more expansive than a forest, more singular than any island. It makes me feel like not the investigator, nor the discoverer, of human demise, not creator nor restorer – but architect! That's what I said to

Leonardo we could be. We made a pact to find reason in everything. We call ourselves *Architects of the Post-Truth World*. Our own secret society. Of two. Like it's our band name. A duo. Of truth. He's invested in that. I knew that would hook him in.

SCENE VIII

THURSDAY

PUNCH LOOKED HELPLESSLY BEYOND THE man purporting to be Stevenson to address the station house door, from where Skerryvore had vacated not twenty minutes before. 'What in God's name did you bring with you, Skerry? An offending cloud would've been easier to do the paperwork on.'

'Oh,' said Stevenson. 'I was here already, sergeant.' He poured himself another measure. 'Listen, I mean no harm. Just a thirsty fellow looking to tell a story or two. Stories are how we connect, even between centuries. It's what makes time *time*, place *place*, and a people *a people*. You are my people.'

'I am?' Punch took a step back. Checked the door was properly closed. 'Right, so I'll play silly buggers . . . even if you *are* who you say you are, how the hell could you be *here*? *Now?*' He studied the man more closely, saw how the skin did not seem alive, more porcelain than epidermis; not a well-looking man at all, more befitting of Dave's embalming table. If he looked closer he half expected evidence of barnacles and sun bleach. And yet, how could the man know his secrets?

The man angled his head away from Punch, becoming more forlorn. He clasped his glass in both gloves. Punch could see the glass was not hanging freely in mid-air; it definitely had a man attached to it. Boots were on his carpet. Indentation on the couch.

'One of those people born on the day the Looming presented itself, sergeant ... was ...'

'My child,' Punch said. He stole a deep intake of breath through his nose. Reached for the bottle and took a swig. 'Well, my *almost* child.'

The man nodded. Brought the glass to his lips and pulled it away.

'Sergeant. My being here is not with the intent of harm; nor is it as a pedlar of fiction. I am done with fiction. The world out there has had enough of fiction. My role here is simply reportage. Even if it means my news, frankly, is more worthy of the sewer.'

'That's one word for Oban.'

'Why, erm ... Oban?'

'The start of the world out there ...'

'Ah? Well, better the truth than the quill, as my father used to say. He was also an engineer and lighthouse designer. Though, as meteorologist too, he might have given airtime to your friend's version of events ...'

'Eh?'

'Skerryvore, the man.' Stevenson pointed a finger to the sky.

'Not my friend. Your father had enough professions?'

'Aye. As a result he was, how can I put it, over*seas* a lot. Aye.'

The man sat back on the couch, accepted the glass at his lips.

'You've learned your lines well, pal, I'll give you that.' Punch spoke more matter-of-factly. He turned away from the couch and fetched behind his ear for a roll-up, but there wasn't one prepared. 'Whoever put you up to this bullshit has earned their notes, or shillings, farthings ...'

'No recompense has crossed a palm, sergeant.' The man sat forwards. 'There are two sides to every man, Mr Punch. I myself know a thing or two about constructing such duality. But the lighthouse in all its glory was all *singularity*. And I see in you that same quality. But your role here on Mull speaks inherently of inner conflict, of dichotomy: you are one of them, but at the same time you cannot be. You cannot allow a hint of vulnerability for the destitutes in your community to exploit. A lot of pressure on you. I know about that. Somebody once took something from me too.'

'Tulloch, my sergeant in Inverness, did advise as much ...'

'And when you question my purpose here ... can I request of you to ask yourself how else I would have known about your unborn child?'

'You *want* the cell?' Punch gripped his ring of keys. 'I'm God in this room, town, island! And fuck!'

He looked to the clock with the Tobermory Highland Games engraving positioned above the sink stacked with dirty dishes. Mary MacBeth would be calling soon. Her weekly shift to tidy his life, if not his mind. Whether his Yoko Ono or May Pang, he couldn't decide.

'Well, is that not just the very concern of the moment here, sergeant?'

'The cell?'

The man leaned closer to Punch. 'You might want to start thinking in plurality.'

'Eh?'

'You see you are not the custodian of *one* island, but two. And the second, as I have already asserted, is only visible two times a century. And this is where the business of burning comes in. But it is not burning as in the visible, gaseous part of a fire, it is conflagration in *words*, the inferno of literacy. Those two bicentennial occasions are on the day of our Bard's true birthdate.'

'Angus Macintyre? Mull's poet-banker?'

'No. Rabbie. Robert Burns. The Looming is only visible on two Burns Nights a century.'

'And yesterday, the twenty-fifth of January, is one of those?' Punch said, hardly believing the sound of his own voice. He and Mary *had* lost their child around Burns Night. He remembered the snow on their drive back from Glasgow. The child's seat fixed into the Ranger, which he had wanted to hide in the boot before reaching the ferry queue at Oban, or better, toss from the Rest And Be Thankful and be done with the whole business altogether. But it was Mary who had insisted the seat stay visible, in readiness for a child that could never take hold of the small Tigger sitting in its place. The Ranger too, like a giant arrow pointing at them. Haggis added to the menu on the ferry.

'And, sergeant, any child born on one of those two days is for ever cast to the island, to the Looming. I couldn't write that part. Too painful.'

'For you or me?'

The phone rang and Punch startled.

'What in God's name is that?' the man said, intrigued and sitting forwards.

Punch felt frozen in time, between the past and the present, the island and the mainland, reality and silly buggers. Though his phone ringing always had something of the future about it too; a direct line to events that had possibly already changed folks' lives.

He walked to the phone and lifted the receiver.

'Punch. Tobermory.'

'Sergeant.' It was Dave the Grave. 'I'm assuming a secure line?'

'Can't be sure Guinness isn't listening in on a string . . . but what is it, Dave?'

'Not a quote for publication as yet, sergeant, but there could be something fishy on the SS20.'

'The where?'

'Glen Bellart. The rally stage. I'm heading there now myself. Towards the Dervaig end. I've had word of a burnt-out car.'

'On the Glen?'

'Aye, according to my source.'

'Who's that?'

'My own deputy. Billy the Box.'

'Promising name.'

Punch heard Dave shuffling paper.

'Direct quote from him: *Looks fucking serious*. End quote. Excuse my French, sergeant. I said I'd notify you. Lad was out with his rally car. Marking pace notes for this year apparently.'

'Right. He's early for October.' Punch looked at the clock, which was also his nickname on the island, given he had been born with his right arm noticeably shorter than the left; though if you uttered it in his company, you could expect a night behind the thick blue door and an earful of Rod's eighties material.

‘The car?’

‘Make unclear. But a small vehicle.’

‘I’ll be there in less than thirty. Don’t touch anything, Dave. Obviously.’

Punch hung up and spun around to the room.

‘Look, joker, I need you out of . . .’

The man was gone. In his place was the tumbler, now sitting atop a note.

Punch walked to the couch. Smelled the salty scent, like an ocean had blown into the station house. Had the man’s moustache been real? The accent? He reached for his coat and took a pack of latex gloves from the inside pocket. Put them on and held the glass his visitor had been drinking from, lip marks definitely evident. He picked up the note. Another note was under it. In a cursive style, the first read:

You cannot be angry with fate, Ivor. Nor can you arrest Providence.

Punch unfolded the other piece of paper and on it was a typed verse.

What do they see, those eyes; what image now
Looms like a picture in their dark’ning cells?
Drop the mask which life’s deceit hath made thee wear.

On the couch, on the indentation where the man had been sitting, Punch saw another parting gift. He kneeled closer. It was inked on the fabric. The print of a bear’s claw.

SCENE IX

WEDNESDAY

'THEY SAY IT'S THE CAVIAR OF DUNG . . .' Duck nodded, munching on his final bacon roll.

Davud could tell the curtains to the past were drawn again.

'Pig shite.' Duck looked seriously at Davud. 'Not eating anything, lad?'

'Eh . . . no . . . lost my appetite.' Davud shook his head and forced an appreciative smile. He feared the bins were going to come up now. He had been passing them while Duck was performing. The hotel venue was near the art school. He'd already had lighter fluid in his rucksack. In the alleyway behind the art school he hadn't turned back to see the flames engulfing. He'd made for Sauchiehall Street, darted into a bar called Nice N Sleazy, where he'd run down the stairs from the entrance and straight into a dark room with a low ceiling and a band playing. He had stood sweating at the back near the bar. He had never ordered a drink from a bar. Or drunk alcohol. It had been his birthday and nobody in the city knew. The police would never find him there. He'd been so freaked out he had imagined the band were singing about Mull secret societies. He'd made a break for the exit and run through Kelvingrove Park, up past the Queen Margaret Union, past the *Dylan Is God* and *Kurt Is King* graffiti, and then up the stairs to the halls.

'That was powerful.' Duck finished the last roll. 'My head feels less like folk are digging inside it.'

Davud had only just started the Building & Compliance module, but still, he didn't understand how Duck could expect to be granted this application. He watched as Duck drained the dregs from the Coke bottle and then scrunched it up. He tried to hide being startled.

Duck held up the reshaped bottle and spoke towards it, 'Bout time the boys at Coke started adding the vodka so I don't have to. Christ – would you look!' Duck attempted to unravel the bottle. 'Robert Burns! Thought it was.' He held the bottle up to his face. 'Says here Burns is the first person on a commemorative Coke bottle. Two hundred and fortieth anniversary of his birth. Well, I piped for you last night, Rabbie.'

'Forced to home study now?' Duck fixed his eyes on Davud. 'That why you're heading back?'

'Eh?' Davud gulped and cleared his throat. Did Duck know about the bins? Did all bin-folk know this kind of stuff? The piss on the caravan floor had started soon after the jump that went wrong. 'It was my birthday too.'

'When?'

'Last night.'

'Many happy returns! Aye, aye. Heard the sirens last night. Wasn't for your birthday, was it?' Duck smiled.

'No! No. I was in my room!'

'Steady on, lad. Aye, the furore nearly drowned out the pipes at the Burns do . . .'

'Because of the bins?'

'Eh? No, the fire. School of Art.'

'Glasgow?'

'Unless they've moved it to Edinburgh?' Duck looked straight at Davud. 'You'll know it burned down. Last night. Whoorish.'

Davud put his palms on the table and reset himself in the seat. Felt a pulse wriggling on his neck, the way his father's would. Brought up the hood of his parka.

'Yeah. Yeah. Terrible,' he managed. 'That's, erm, why I'm, erm, coming . . . why I'm here.'

'Hope Victoria's nightclub's still standing. We go on Council trips, after Rangers games. Never seen so many stilettos in a room. You'd think Imelda Marcos was a blue nose. You been?'

'On a Council trip?'

'No.'

'To Manila?'

'Anyway, if they were to ask me, Hughie MacDonald in Tob's their man for the refurb. Like a cat he is on a roof.'

'Is he?' Davud was desperately trying to breathe. Could he really have caused a bigger fire? Burned a century down?

'I'm sure you'll be back raving at all the student haunts soon. Puke everywhere, no doubt. Make the Bellachroy seem like the Vatican.' Duck took a roll-up from behind his ear. 'Ever rolled a rollie?'

Davud shook his head.

'Christ, call yourself a student.'

'We're learning about designing and constructing buildings,' Davud blurted, memorised from his notes. 'To develop an independence of style and originality of thought. To find solutions for clients' living and working environs.'

'Sounds like some rollie.'

Both their attentions were taken by a woman on one of the tables near them. She looked around the forty mark and was speaking loudly and agitatedly into a mobile phone. She had blonde hair tied up in a bun, was wearing a white shirt with checks on it, and a green woollen tank top.

'Christ, the man selling us trinkets has competition here,' Duck said, addressing the speaker and then nodding to the woman on the phone. 'You see more and more of those devices about. You got one?'

'A woman?' Davud said, then realised his error. 'Eh no, I haven't.' The revelation about the art school was all he could think about.

'Fucking sure I wouldn't want my boss knowing where I was all the time. That's probably what got Clinton in trouble, eh? Woman seems upset about something, that's for certain. Posh, she sounds. Never seen such a carnival of tweed. Throw in a horse and you'd have Princess Anne.'

Davud looked to the woman on the phone, who was now standing and leaning one hand on the table. Her voice was quieter, and she was using her other hand in an attempt to keep the conversation more private. She then nestled the phone using her chin and her shoulder and took a pair of sunglasses from her bag. She looked around her and put them on. Davud saw how she glanced concernedly at the TV screen before doing so.

'Aye, I tried one of those mobile phones from a pal, Longy, in the Bellachroy,' Duck said, still looking to the woman. 'Got it somewhere. Clearly not invented for a Council man's swollen fingers. Unless you're communicating in Slovenian.'

Davud peered out the ferry window and then to Duck. He couldn't believe how quickly a person could turn from motorbike god to jumbled mess.

'Has, eh, anybody, erm, been hurt did you hear? In the fire?' Davud asked. He wondered if Duck felt like a murderer. Like a kilted killer. Was he now one too?

'They're saying no. Lucky. Brrr . . .' Duck shook. 'It's January right enough, getting a fair draft up the gunnels. Aye, aye. Maybe even snow on Mull. We might need an extra cannister of propane.'

Davud was shocked at Duck's open mention of the caravan. As though taunting him. The news of the art school too, especially coming from Duck, now felt like another loss of a secret power Davud had momentarily had over the rest of the world. Could anybody have seen what he'd done?

'Aye, Blah Blah Blah said as much on the pier when I left.' Duck nodded. 'Snow, he said, likely, on the mainland.'

Davud would always see Blah Blah Blah on the pier. A tall, stocky man, with piercings everywhere you looked, he worked for CalMac and it was his job to tie and untie the mainland, by way of the ferry, to Craignure pier. Occasionally, even when he wasn't planning to board, Davud would take the bus from Dervaig to Craignure to sit at the end of the pier to sketch the event of the ferry arriving and leaving.

'Aye. Blah Blah Blah books the gigs around the hotels, sells the CDs. Been badgering me for a Christmas album.

Says Sinatra hasn't been done by the pipes yet. I wonder if Bono gets this much grief from his record company?' Duck looked expectantly to Mull. 'Nicknames, eh? I tried to get "Duck" on my passport the one time I was away following the Gers. But not possible. Can't fight the might of Walt Disney on a Council wage.'

Davud felt sick about the art school. But he couldn't tell his mum. Not after everything she had done to get him there. In Sarajevo, she had had flowers thrown at her on a stage. Before grenades took their place. Now she was building a shell around her called 'Dervaig'. Maybe it was better than checking the sky for them.

'Will they take you somewhere else?' asked Duck. 'The college? Your lessons?'

'Em, yes. I suppose. I don't really—'

'Will you wheesht!' Duck turned in the direction of the public address, now being delivered in Gaelic. 'No wonder they sunk the bloody *Titanic*.'

Davud looked to the failed re-enactment of Olympic rings left by Duck's coffee mug. He wanted to get away from the table. To be first in line at the foot passenger alighting spot. But Bearfoot had said not to take the bus from the ferry. To do everything as planned. That the packages would be going to Fintan's. He had said there would be *consequences* if not. Davud wasn't sure his friend was still really a friend.

'How you getting home?' Duck said.

Davud took hold of his rucksack and felt the shape of his sketchbook inside. It was a kind of armour. He couldn't wait to get rid of the packages. Wondered if he should throw them over the side.

'Oh? Eh, the bus.' Davud nodded.

'Fuck the bus,' coughed Duck. 'Come with me. I've a Burns rehearsal in the Wee Theatre.'

'Erm . . .' Davud inhaled loudly. 'It's just . . . well . . .'

'Good, that's decided.'

Davud rocked quickly. Swallowed deeply. This was all too unplanned. What would they talk about if they didn't talk about what happened the week after the record jump? All the children were questioned in the aftermath; none had seen her join the line at the end. Which had been Duck's claim too. Davud had overheard all this – including the word 'manslaughter', which had confused him, because she had been a woman – in the Bellachroy, which his mum cleaned at the time. In Sarajevo she had taken drama classes in his school. Until there was more drama outside the classes than in them.

'Yes.' Davud nodded. 'Thanks.'

He wondered if Duck had meant to wear a shirt bearing the crest of Mull's Masonic Lodge. It was supposed to be a secret society.

'Aye, I've got my new limo with me, not the Council wheels. Civilian business. Though it's filled with Council petrol. My Fiesta. Aye, aye.'

They sat in silence and Davud wondered if Duck knew Dervaig was actually 23.1 miles from Craignure. Though the signage read 23 miles.

'In a way . . . she took all the future, my family, with her,' Duck said, his voice lower. 'Or I did? Of course the village pulled over a veil. She was always an outsider.'

Davud froze. He double-checked the time of the bus he wasn't taking. Duck could have been talking about his dad.

But he knew he wasn't.

'On the plane,' Davud said, 'that's what my mum said: "The future's been destroyed." I don't think she feels that anymore. Now we're living in it. It's called Mull.'

'Aye, hullo, eh . . . hullo,' Duck managed, to a passing crew member.

Davud could hear the forced smile in Duck's voice. The transformation to 'Donald'. He noticed how Duck rubbed at the Masonic emblem in the absence of the Council one, as though in need of proof of his identity, of his status. A stain had been left. He watched as Duck tried to rescue the sagging knot in his tie.

'Talk about rebelling against the comb. Christ!' Duck signalled towards the retreating crew person. He put a hand through his own hair, leaving a powdering of flour.

Duck had briefly parted the curtains, Davud thought. But now they were firmly pulled closed again.

The Gothic structure of Duart Castle came into view. Davud anticipated the glockenspiel chimes and then the recorded voice with the slight pause in the middle of the word *starboard*. Voices had architecture too.

'A woman died!' Duck said.

'At the art school? You said nobody was hurt!'

Duck shook.

'Oh . . . right.' Davud remembered the next day there had been the screaming of a woman's name, the one Duck had landed on. 'Do you ever wonder what she would be like now? It's the anniversary.'

'*Good afternoon ladies and gentlemen . . .*'

'Aw, here he goes again. Captain bloody Birdseye.' Duck

grabbed his car keys from the table. 'Quick, we'll make a getaway . . .'

Davud watched the swoosh of the kilt as, in one continuous motion, Duck pivoted out of the seat and, with a Groucho Marx lean, headed out of the cafeteria like the past redux.

Davud fought the desire to lie on the cafeteria carpet, to await the approaching revs. He picked up his rucksack and went after Duck to the car deck. He saw how Duck performed an excitable little spin as he surveyed the alighting area, as though at any moment he was prepared, if invited, to enter into a Dashing White Sergeant. He wondered if Duck was looking out for who to avoid on the ferry too. Who to be 'Donald' to, who required 'Duck'. Just as Davud was learning who to be *war* to, and who required *peace*. Just as his mother was *wind* and his father *flame*.

Duck bound down the stairs to the car deck. Davud saw the woman in tweed descending behind Duck. He followed. Counting eighteen stairs ahead of him. Each one represented a body on the ground. He didn't step on the last one.

SCENE X

WEDNESDAY

ANNIE BURNETT WAS NOT A woman who liked to waste her time, or have her time wasted. She sat alone in the little hired car on the car deck, with the feeling her life too was about to be downsized, wondering if anyone else onboard – a ragbag of islanders who looked like they were journeying to audition for Lynyrd Skynyrd, seemingly unaware the seventies had ended twenty years earlier – had noticed the ferry was running two minutes late. Certainly, the doomed band would have been safer on a ferry. Not that she was Minister of Transport anymore. Though there was now the prospect of a reshuffle. Or the sack. No doubt re-spun as Minister of *Shagging*, if the tabloids got their way.

She herded her escaping bun and fluffed up her crown. Suspected her old trouble, the alopecia, would begin its war again now. She had heard about a roll-on camouflage for the scalp but hadn't yet tried it. The redtops didn't need that gift too. Oh, to be judged as a man, she thought.

She ran a thumb and forefinger along the pleats of her

skirt. Felt her blouse tightening. She was impatient to arrive on the island and hated not being the driver in any given situation. The concept of *driver* could encompass her various current roles as – Energy Minister for Scotland, over-forties Scottish female triathlon record-holder, youngest female member of the Scottish Bar, masked player in Edinburgh's behind-draped-curtains sex games party scene, and even – if required to get this 3,000-tonne vessel back on schedule – captain on a CalMac bridge. She had sailed to Mull before, but then she had been on her father's yacht. She had noted it was the biggest one on Tobermory's new pontoon for the two days she was docked there.

Annie took her mobile phone from the pocket of her Barbour jacket and placed it alongside her reading glasses on the dash. Not quite the available space of her Range Rover. She was expecting a call. Thankfully, there was some signal, but only a few bars. Pages weren't loading. She was irritated at having to make this journey to Mull at all. A local campaigning group were kicking up a fuss, and she had been tasked with stopping it from becoming a national fuss. No doubt a pile of crusties. She had been reported variously in *The Oban Times* as a 'hypocrite' and a 'clean air salesperson'. What they hadn't reported was that she wasn't someone who ever accepted defeat, whether that be on bicycle, boardroom, bed, or at the Bar. Nor had they cottoned on to her *actual* brief. In effect she was a decoy. Her last laugh, she hoped. Travelling without special advisers so as to limit suspicion. In retrospect, despite the impending, inevitable 'sustainable energy *Vs* blot on the landscape' public debates and protestations – which she had heard were already underway on the island in the wake of the leaked wind farm plans – her escape to the Hebrides couldn't have come at a better time. If this was to be her swansong, then there were worse places than Mull. There was a body she needed to bury. She just hoped it wasn't her own.

Annie checked her phone. Nothing. She looked across the car deck. A young lad was getting into a small car, a rucksack over his shoulder. Handsome, in a European way, with a mound of black, semi-wavy, shoulder-length hair and a brooding disposition; not unlike the pictures of a young Gordon Brown she had fantasised over. Though wished she had stopped at the fantasy. Annie watched the lad's clear discomfort as another man, maybe in his late thirties, salt and pepper hair and dressed in kilt, but no jacket, collapsed into the driver's seat like an over-dunked digestive.

Annie reached down for her leather satchel and took some papers from it. Checked her phone again. It was an extension of her arm, her mother said. She was torn between needing information from it right now or throwing it in the sea. The device lit up. She grabbed it and read the text.

They've burned you.

She rocked in disgust. Dialled the number. Her spad answered.

'Wow, thanks for the kid gloves. Call that special advice? Read it out to me. Fred Flintstone could access messages better than me here. Fuck.'

'The jilted wife of controversial Scottish Trades Union leader, Denzil Docherty, only found out about her husband's affair with a Labour Party colleague when she saw it on media reports.'

'Cut the foreplay. Am I mentioned in the headline? By name?'

'No.'

'Small graces. I'll hear the rest then.'

'We reported yesterday that Mr Docherty has apparently been in a short-term relationship with an unspecified colleague. We can name her now as Annie Burnett, the sitting Energy Minister for Scotland.'

'Sitting?' Annie exhaled. 'They'll have fun with that.' She reached to turn on the car radio but pulled back. She could hear what they would be saying in any case. 'Go on.'

'Upon the breaking of the story, according to our sources, we can reveal that Mr Docherty has been sensationally dumped by his wife on Monday after admitting to a "brief" romance with Miss Burnett.'

'He's fucking admitted it! Sources!'

'It goes on, Annie: *Ms Burnett, who recently launched the Climate Change and Clean Energy Programme at the Scottish Conservation Foundation, went on the attack today to express her innocence over the revelations.*'

'Oh bloody hell!' Annie thumped the wheel. 'We went with that line? "*Clean* energy" . . . Shit! Fan!'

'We had to, Annie. They don't have concrete proof. *BBC Scotland reported that Mr Docherty had failed to tell leading government officials about the relationship despite staff urging him to do so.*'

'So his staff are throwing Denny under the bus. Nice.'

'But not you? Not totally?'

'For now. But one leg's already under . . . how long do I have? How are the photos?'

'*Newsnight* are sniffing around . . . They've one of you together at the opening of the Scottish Parliament.'

'First Minister's office?'

'They're pressing for a statement.'

'They've written it already. You can be sure of that. Any more?'

'Yes: *Fearing perceptions of a conflict of interest, union executive members reported concerns about the relationship to the Parliamentary Workplace Support Service, an independent authority with a remit to investigate workplace incidents at Holyrood.*'

'Bloody hell . . .'

'*It's understood Mr Docherty disclosed the relationship to two different members of his staff in November and December last year, with one of them confronting him about it over the festive period. Outside a press conference this morning for the launch of a new clothing factory in Lanarkshire, a visibly angry union official said he had asked Mr Docherty to resign from the senior leadership team.*'

'I'll pack my bags . . . wait, I have already.' Annie felt strangely serene. She looked to the efficient CalMac employees around her, busying like hi-vis mice. A yellow light was flashing by the ferry's mouth. Were reporters waiting on the other side? 'On the upside, this'll sidetrack the real reason I'm here . . .'

'Look, nobody knows you're making this trip. Maybe the best place to be right now. But lie low. We might have to cancel the public meeting later.'

'Purgatory.' Annie slumped down a little in her seat. It had started. The need to hide. 'Better change my fucking name to Monica Lewinsky. Any leaks from our side?'

'*Ms Burnett's relationship with Mr Docherty came to light after reports her colleagues had expressed concern about the relationship, given she sits on a joint parliamentary workers' rights enforcement committee.*'

'Colleagues?'

'*Just last week the First Minister paid tribute to Ms Burnett for her presentation of Scottish energy policy to Westminster colleagues – namely the proposed phased introduction of wind and solar farms in Scotland.* We'll keep batting approaches away for now. You know the FM has your back.'

'You'll need a statement soon: *I pay my respects to the sisterhood who have walked this road before me. And I thank the First Minister for joining us in this fight.* That do?'

She heard the inhalation of breath on the other end of the phone. More yellow lights were flashing. Camera lenses were surely next. A horn sounded.

'Shit . . .' Annie looked over her sunglasses, fearing she had been spotted. Nobody seemed to be looking at her. She put her free hand back on the wheel.

'You okay?'

'Aye. Aye. Nothing a double G&T wouldn't solve, or numb . . .'

'Look. We're working on it, Annie. It's breaking up a bit . . .'

'Leslie! Wait! Anything from his side?'

'The FM?'

'No! Denny.'

'Yes. Ends with: *Mr Docherty's friends rallied around him yesterday, offering recent examples of his leadership for Scotland's workers across sectors.*'

'In her resignation letter, *Mizz* Burnett said that she had "made mistakes" and "not exercised good fucking judgement". That do?'

'Annie. We're not there yet . . . hold tight.'

'End the statement with: *I will now reflect on this and focus on my important portfolio work, which is to advocate for the green warriors of Mull! Blair can do his own bloody dirty work up here. He really thinks an asylum seekers' camp will fly? On Mull!*'

'Wait. This just in from the First Minister's office. Not distributed yet: "*As their leader, I expect my MSPs, and MPs, especially those in leadership positions, to exercise good judgement,*" *the First Minister said.* "*At a minimum, Minister Burnett needed to disclose to me her connection to Mr Docherty and her failure to do so showed a significant error of judgement. I have spoken to Minister Burnett, and she has told me that at no stage was there any breach of the rules regarding individual committees or her work, no sharing of confidential information, and to date no one has suggested otherwise.*" I think this is a good sign? The bus has been, at least, parked.'

'Right. Okay. For now. But is it enough, Les? It reads like it's clear this could be perceived as affecting her – *my* – work?'

'His office is going down the road of your failure to disclose as being the issue, that that was the error of judgement.'

'Shit! You're breaking up, Les.'

'I said, I think this is promising!'

The call ended. Annie looked around her. A recorded voice was coming over the Tannoy. Thankfully nothing in it about the bedroom activities of the Scottish political class. Nor her visit. A beeping sound started. She almost grabbed her satchel for a vote in the chamber. She looked across to the two men in the car, thankfully positioned ahead of her. The boy was slumped with a parka hood on. The man was licking a roll-up, drumming fingers on the steering wheel. The chances seemed too unlikely. Surely? But she was certain it was him, the piper from the Glasgow Development Agency's Burns Supper of the night before. It was all she needed. And what were the chances too about their cars? Both Ford Fiestas.

SCENE XI

THURSDAY

PUNCH CLOSED THE DOOR ON the pebbledash. He still smelled the scent of the man purporting to be out of time. *Some joker right enough*. He fitted his hat on and walked from the police house towards the station next door. He was unsure how to play this one with his deputy. If he were to ask Cluny whether he had seen a man claiming to be the famed dead writer, then he would be risking ridicule. But the man had seemed so real; had he not witnessed the bottle of Tobermory go down? The indentation on the couch. And a bear claw print?

He stopped to look further up Erray Road. And then down to Creagan Park, where the first house belonged to Mary MacBeth. No sign of the man. He put his hand on his hat and ran up Erray Road, around the corner and up over the cattle grid to the golf course. Still no sign. Just a couple of cars parked, which themselves now seemed out of time. Should've been a penny farthing belonging to Old Tom Morris or some bugger. Was golf even invented yet?

Punch looked to the Highland Games field on the next level up. The sand pit, thankfully, was out of view. If anywhere could remind him of time and place, it was here. It was in that pit that he and his wee brother Charlie used to jump. He would say, *compete*. But nobody could compete with Charlie. It was at the Games, one day in the seventies, Charlie had jumped so high it was like he never came down again. It was still in the record books. Unfortunately, ten years afterwards, Lockerbie was too.

He inhaled and turned away. Jogged, then walked, back down to the station. No need to cause alarm. He pushed open the station door. The aroma of Cluny's plants met him first. A sweet smell not befitting of a custodial setting. He wondered if he should be booking not criminals, but a massage. *Could do with one.*

'It's like the Chelsea bloody Flower Show in here,' Punch said, sneezing and shaking his head. He put his hat on top of the computer on his desk. He wouldn't even know where the button was on the thing. *Invasions from the future now too.* He was still irritated at the imposter and had to take it out on somebody. He waved his left arm at the greenery. 'Next you'll be rollicking in the rain forests like Attenborough with the gorillas, but in your tiepin.'

'Sorry, Sarge?' Cluny removed his headphones and looked up from his screen; Punch saw the man's gold-framed glasses, teeth that could fill a field. A watering can on his desk and enough framed photographs to suspect the bugger was a Kennedy. *Not the ones at the Salen garage.*

'Eh, did you see a man go by?'

'On the screen, Sarge?'

'No, PC. In real bloody life.'

Cluny shook his head. 'Why, Sarge?'

'I'd an intruder in the house, or maybe not, maybe a visitor, hard to tell . . .'

Cluny jumped to his feet. Ran to the stand for his coat and hat.

'Is this a break-glass moment, Sarge?'

'Eh?'

'The intruder?'

'If you're asking my permission to destroy that overrated typewriter, then you have it. The Faces would have had it in a swimming pool on its day of arrival. Even better, Tob Bay.'

'Who? What?'

'Nothing. Stick with your Marti bloody Pellow.'

Cluny sat back down and Punch felt a pang of guilt. He knew it was wrong to enjoy this abuse. He'd never liked his first DCI, Tulloch, doing it to him at Legacy Highland Division, Inverness. Though he wasn't sure 'enjoy' was the right word.

'Could've been a prank.' Punch walked to the window. Nobody was on the street. He couldn't believe he was even entertaining this crap. He was standing on the wrong coast, but regardless, he stole a glance to the sea. For evidence of something that wasn't there before. Only Calve Island stared back. Present and correct. Too big for his cell. 'Look – call the Wee Theatre in Dervaig. I want to know if a production is running the now.'

'On it, Sarge. Do you need a plus one? I used to tread the boards myself; Mother is president of the Bearsden Dramatic Society.'

‘I don’t doubt.’ Punch turned to his deputy. ‘No, you can forget your lippy, PC. I just need to know if there are actors currently in residence.’

‘Not likely a production this time of year?’

‘Check anyway. I’m Dervaig-bound. Dave the Grave’s just off the blower, there’s something amiss out at the Glen.’

‘Kingfisher numbers? I hear they’re on the rise?’

‘Where would you hear that?’

‘I’m a member of the Scottish Wildlife Trust. Amazing access. I can add one other subscriber for free.’

‘Eh? No. It’s a car, burnt-out apparently.’

‘Left over from the rally?’

‘My first thought too. But no. Not in January.’

Punch turned again to the late afternoon gloom. *Who was next? Burns himself?* He could still hear the man’s deep voice, soft but authoritative, accent slipping in and out, spouting all that crap about an island appearing that wasn’t an island. The upside would be he could second Cluny to police it. *Legacy Treasure Island.*

‘Right. I’m off to the Glen. Radio me if you, eh, hear anything.’

‘Description, Sarge?’

‘Small. Model hard to determine.’

‘No. I meant the intruder.’

‘Oh? Fuck. Eh . . .’ Punch could hardly bring himself to speak. He daren’t imagine the commentary from Randy, Tinsel, Appy and the other bar stools, if this shite got around. *Punch is playing Hyde ’n’ seek! Flick the Jekyll on, Ivor!*

‘Should I come to the Glen with you, Sarge? Sounds odd. Not much spooks, Dave.’

'No, PC – keep a watch on the house.'

'Sarge? *Really?*'

'Aye. Really. Have you got better things to do, PC Cluny?'

'It's just, well, as an assignment it's a tad *off-Broadway*, don't you think? I'm ready for more.'

'And Bearsden's the Hollywood Walk of bloody Fame, is it? Get onto the Wee Theatre, PC. Smartish. *West End* of Mull'll do you.'

Punch grabbed his hat from the computer and spun out the door. He turned back, half expecting Cluny to have morphed into a flipchart.

'And it's not an *assignment*, it's a bloody order.'

He closed the door behind him. Took a deep breath and released it in the direction of the sea. All the oxygen in the room was being taken by the plants, he was sure of it. He knew he had been hard on the lad, that his irritability was coming from this Stevenson joker and what he had said about his . . . in truth, he didn't know what to call a child who he never knew; he wouldn't have known whether to display trousers or a dress. He was never afforded the opportunity to raise such a signal. Should the Western Infirmary have even *had* a flagpole. Arriving in Oban that day, Mary upright and stoic, Mull had appeared as both beacon and nightmare on the horizon.

He went for the Ranger, but noticed the door to his police house was ajar. He walked slowly to the entrance. *Security, Ivor, again.* Though was sure he had locked it behind him. He peered through the window. Nothing. He used his foot to quietly swing the door further open. Nothing obviously amiss. He moved slowly to the couch where the man had sat.

The notes gone. Still the smell, though. He was unsure if the couch looked indented again. He crouched to sweep a hand over the fabric. Refixed the cushion.

'Trying to put me out of business, are you?'

Punch turned. Prepared to run the fucker.

SCENE XII

'CHRIST . . .' PUNCH SIGHED.

He got to his feet and did his best to try and hide his relief with a hand over his face.

'Close,' Mary MacBeth said. 'Though his hair was lighter.'

'Uh-ha. But you had more disciples, certainly at the primary.' He remembered his daily surveillance of her around Tob playground. How, even then, she could make his arms the same length just by a reassuring look. 'Randy, Blah Blah Blah, and the rest hanging around you.'

'Hoaf! What catches. Every one with the map of Mull on their faces . . . no escape!'

'Crops up everywhere.'

'I'd be a Council or CalMac widow by now with any of that crew. No, scrap that. Mishnish widow.'

'And that'd be better than police widow?'

She looked at him. Punch could've taken down his own name and read himself the Mirandas; knew his words had come out involuntarily and hung awkwardly for them both. *You Wear It . . . Well, Bloody Clumsily, Ivor.*

'But still,' she said, 'I somehow ended up your weekly cleaner-cum, well . . .'

They each knew she was more than his cleaner.

'Uh-ha. Well, you were, erm, in demand in the playground. No doubting it.'

'Well, you know when they made the Gutenberg Bibles? It was a similar approach.'

'I'm rusty.' Punch could tell she was trying to save them, forcing a spring in her step. Stoicism on tap. Her ponytail even jumped as she crossed the room as it used to back then. 'Remind me?'

'The Gutenberg Bibles were made by monks.' She affixed her apron. 'But they purposefully made a few very small mistakes . . .'

'I'll stay with this line of questioning . . .'

'Because it would be blasphemy, if the Bibles were perfect.'

'Ah, like you? I see. Quite the big hit.' He pushed a cheekbone up. 'And *your* mistakes?'

She didn't say anything.

Fuck. Punch knew he had done it again. Made that awkward space. He felt closer to the thick blue door than the monastery.

'Anyway,' he said. 'Sorry to startle you. I was half expecting Mary bloody Magdalene next . . .'

'Eh?'

'Nothing. Nothing.'

'You got the Mary bit right. Best I don't know, I know. Better than being Anne Boleyn I suppose.'

'Uh-ha.'

'Though it looks like you've seen a ghost.' She opened the cupboard and pulled out the hoover.

'You'll need your head for the hoovering . . .'

'Cheeky bugger.'

Punch made a theatre of cleaning up the tumblers. But kept the man's one from the sink. The notes were useless for brushing, given the fellow's gloves. The shite the joker had spouted had got under his skin. The bottle of Tobermory shouted from the table, as inconspicuous as a lighthouse itself.

He kicked his boots into some form of order.

'My, my ... Ivor Punch – caught in the act? There's hope for Imelda Marcos yet.'

'Eh?'

'Her shoes. Apparently it takes her maids half an hour to put them away after Imelda's finished choosing her pair for the day ...'

'Like Rod with the hair mousse.'

Mary brushed a hand through her dark, slightly greying, hair. Punch saw how her fringe landed back where it always landed, as it did when she was the only child in his view. If it wasn't Mull on her face, it was a place he knew. *The First Cut Is the Deepest*.

'You'll be putting me out of business?'

'Aye. Can't get the staff, as I said.'

'Cheeky bugger. Twice.'

'Anyway. Security breach.' Punch motioned to the door. 'You'll have Control at Head Office after me.'

'Sorry. I was doing the bins first. Thought it was easier to keep it open. Might need the lad Duck and his lorry for the bottles ... I see you're still being sponsored by the distillery?'

'Well, this is *elite* policing.' Punch walked to the window. 'But I better whisky a go go.'

'Eh?'

‘Nothing.’ He was for ever forgetting the jet-set lifestyle was only in his head. ‘Somebody has to support the local economy.’

‘Aye, well you would be if you were actually paying for them!’

‘Perk of the job. Has to be one, given the impudent staff.’ Punch checked there was a rollie already prepared behind his ear. ‘Look, eh . . . no, nothing.’

‘What? What’s up with you today?’

‘You didn’t, eh . . .’ He stopped. Gulped. Next he would be asking if she’d seen the fictional island, or Long John Silver himself. ‘You didn’t see somebody going down the road on your way up . . .?’

‘I did.’

‘You did?’

‘Aye. Skerryvore.’

‘Right. Uh-ha.’ He paused. ‘Did he say anything?’

‘No. His head was in the sky. Still looking for his return ticket to Tiree, no doubt.’

Mary passed by Punch with a rubbish bag on her way to the door. Brushing his right arm. She placed the bag outside and closed the door behind her.

Then she moved to the couch and reorganised the cushions.

‘Och, Ivor!’

Punch turned.

‘Ink!’ She pointed. ‘No chance getting those stains out.’

Punch turned to the couch and back to Mary.

‘Pen must’ve leaked,’ he said. ‘Sorry.’

‘I think we’re beyond love letters, eh?’ Mary said. ‘But look?’

‘What?’

‘Would you look at the shape?’

Punch leaned in. The bear print was now a map of Mull.

'And last I knew you weren't a signatory on the Magna Carta.'

'Eh?' Punch looked at her.

In her hand was a quill.

'Oh? Eh, probably Guinness. The bugger's for ever making the point I need to get with the digital age . . .'

'Really? The lad's getting braver in that case! *And* a personality?'

'About as useful as the Tiree Tree Society. You're lucky you don't have to dust his photos . . .'

'Well, I don't dust yours. You don't have any.'

Punch took the quill from her. Was sure he had another evidence bag in his uniform jacket.

Mary picked up last week's shirt from the floor before he could.

'No stains on here. Your trousers?'

Punch looked down. He shook his head.

'You used to keep one of Charlie,' she said.

'A shirt?'

'Photo.'

Increasingly, he had felt too close to the Games field to keep the photo as a reminder. Too hard to look at – at a vision of beautiful flight represented by a thing so static. Like the grounded plane itself. He had added it to his mother's collection instead at Glen Iosal, the sheltered housing across the town.

'Though they'd not likely entertain pebbledash. At Hyannis Point, I mean.' Punch pointed, as though it was as close as Calve.

'What?'

'The Kennedys.'

'Salen?'

'Nothing. Forget it.'

Mary shook her head and tipped an ashtray into the bin. Buffed up the couch cushions. *Destroying evidence*, thought Punch.

'And no,' she said.

'No what?'

'No I didn't see anyone else walking down. Though there wasn't much by way of description from my source.'

'Fair point. No, it was nothing. Probably some bugger looking to waste my time. You could form a line of them all the way down to the Mish.'

'And they'd all be called Randy.'

'Uh-ha.' Punch tried to smile, but knew he'd produced the same results as his face always threw up – a smirk-cum-grimace. He stared at the couch as he moved to the door.

'Look . . .' He took a roll-up from the table and put it behind his ear. He couldn't stop thinking about the island the man had spoken about, and him up a flagpole. How could the man have known?

Mary turned to him.

'Sometimes I wish you *were* only my cleaner,' he said. 'Is that wrong?'

'No.'

'That we could erase what happened; the entire contents of the lockup along with it.'

'I know what you mean. I do.'

'Anyway. I've a fresh carcass out there I'm looking forward to slaughtering, right enough.'

'And who said romance was dead.' She tucked a duster in her pocket and started up the hoover. Deliberately, he knew.

Punch cautioned himself again. Though the slaughter was his only relaxation. Other folk could knock themselves out with bowls in the Aros Hall, propping up bars, jogging, playing this new squash craze that had beset the island, or lifting weights. He liked dead sheep; nothing was ever suspicious about a dead sheep. Inside a carcass there weren't folk looking to bother him, nor clues to be uncovered, only known pathways, expected revelations. Humans, island; these were different. His uncle, whom he'd discovered was more than his uncle and who had taught him about the insides of a sheep, had once questioned whether livestock had souls. To Punch, livestock hung in plain sight. Souls required sheets thrown over them. One day he would find the courage to show Mary. And she to look.

He motioned to her. Mary killed the hoover, removed the duster.

'What?'

Punch sniffed the freshening air.

'You're going to leave a girl hanging?'

'It's just, well . . . no, nothing.'

'I know *that* nothing.'

'Well, do you, eh, ever feel strange that, you know . . .'

'You know you pay me by the hour?'

'That there's a word for a person who loses a spouse, and one for a person who loses their parents, but not one for somebody like us, who . . .'

'I know. Widow. Orphan. And then . . .'

'Nothing.' Punch moved his ring of keys between his hands. In so doing grasping the full gambit of his jurisdictions: station house. Station. Thick blue door. Lockup. Ranger. His mother's front door. And sometimes, he felt – the gates of heaven, and of hell. 'Just a flagpole, and clothing as indicator of gender.'

'Eh?'

'Nothing. Nothing. Just case work.'

He pulled open the door.

'Ivor.'

'What?'

'Your hat.'

Punch took it from the table.

'You'll be after a raise next.' He tapped the door with the key. 'And make sure to lock it after. You're definitely *not* head of security around here.'

SCENE XIII

PUNCH OPENED THE DOOR AND stepped outside. Pulled it behind him. Locked it. Heard the hoover restarting. Life, distraction, what-could-have-beens – all going on behind a closed Mull door. *What was it Lennon said about plans?*

The cold arrived like a hardness of heart. He walked to the Ranger. Sometimes he thought he should just be done with it and show her the pram under the sheet out back in the lockup. Then other times he thought it would be like throwing the woman into a living, pebbledash-encased grave. As far as he knew, the Tigger toy was still out there too. A carcass hanging nearby.

He selected the Ranger key. As he jumped in, Punch looked to the Saltire-forming jet sprays crossing the sky. No island, though. If it were thirty years earlier, Rod and his rooster cut would be cruising at 36,000 feet up there by now. The jet running on cocaine. He did still sometimes wonder why it was Rod who had got so deep under his skin. Randy had observed how a Frankie Miller-type would have more suited him, or better still, a Tom Waits – some dark bastard like that who might use the side of a slaughtered animal as rhythm section.

But it was to Rod, his rasp and The Faces where Ivor was drawn, their dependability of bravado, of jeopardy, the fact that they were always only one lick away from something menacing about to happen, not unlike a criminal. Punch turned the ignition and pulled out of Pebbledash HQ. Drummed on the wheel. He still kept his old kit out in the lockup, also under cover. He'd slaughtered a few on that, too, in teenage cover bands in the Aros Hall.

He drove along the top of Tobermory, past the pebbledash he had been raised in, the closest house in the town to the graveyard. And then onwards, by the kissing gate into the graveyard, where the grave of the Unknown Sailor sat close by. He wondered how much was preserved of the German U-boat commander who had washed to Mull shores, who was buried and given a stone by the locals; the sea, if not the war, having stripped the man of identification. Punch made a mental note never to ponder this around Dave the Grave. The bugger would be out here after dark with a spade quicker than you could say Fred bloody West. There was talk the gravestone had come from the quarries outside Dervaig, transported as a passenger on the bus between there and Tob. Propped on the seat, they said, belt around it as though it had been charged a fare. Mull Wee Theatre now stood on the site of the quarries. Apparently the smallest theatre in the world. *Though you'd have to ask the other Guinness. The* non-*teetotal one.*

Punch pressed harder on the accelerator, away from the past, towards the Dervaig Road, and further into a new millennium. A burnt-out car was not a common occurrence, but still, it was likely nothing more than some high-speed rallying jinks gone wrong. For some, rally fever lasted all year round.

Alongside the stories spun in the Wee Theatre, Dervaig had its own share of Mull folklore; among them the tales of the famous Dervaig Bears, who all Mull children believed inhabited caves around the village, unseen to the human eye. Unless, Punch suspected, you were staggering home from a Bellachroy lock-in. He was well aware you couldn't arrest folklore. Though he was tempted to let Guinness try. Could somebody be regurgitating this rubbish on his sofa?

Eight minutes later, he had reached the high point of the hairpin bends. Naked trees clawed at the grey sky. Punch couldn't stop himself pulling over to the side of the road, by the bench that he considered *the second best seat in the world*. He peered out to the Atlantic, now visible as a sliver of sea on the horizon. It looked much as it always did. He almost handcuffed himself for stopping to look again for it. The Looming. Could he have inadvertently seen the thing before he and Mary lost their child? *Bullshit*.

Down below, sat the scattered village of Dervaig, the church tower like a finger in the air to folklore. It all comprised a hole in the landscape that looked to him like God's last bite out of earth. Everything had taken on a holy, reverential aura since the visit from the strange man. He half expected Cluny to radio through, claiming to have William Shakespeare in the station. Coll and Tiree sat out there much as Skerryvore had said, like gulls propped on the horizon. He thought of the old man, seeing cloud atlases in the sky and rowing on these waters away from an island to which he would never return. Mull's commonplace trees awaiting him like vertical treasures.

Punch was in no rush to get to the Glen. He took the prepared roll-up and made a barrier against the wind while lighting it. As a child, he'd believed his uncle-who-was-not-his-uncle had carried a lit match to the whales of the north Atlantic and back. He inhaled the Tobermory still evident in his lungs; good whisky could do this, give you another measure just when you needed it. He saw the graveyard down below, a rectangle of death. From the quarry, the gravestones had not travelled far, much like many of the inhabitants. He took a heavy draw and thought about his younger brother, Charlie, and how they used to run and hide in the graveyard next to their house in Tob, often behind gravestones, taking the shelter of the dead. Was that what he was still doing now?

He flicked the butt to the surrounds. Turned back to the winding road and recalled how – prior to him, his mum and Charlie moving to Inverness – he and his Tob school pals had used to cycle to Dervaig as the unlikely destination for cinema. The kind of cinema where films were projected onto a screen in the back room of a local resident's house. Once, a visiting cousin of Ivor's had joined them on the cinema cycle. He was a year older than Ivor and he had been excited to show the boy off. The steep incline out of the village on the way back was always a killer. Their fake revs and bike lights acting clandestinely as deterrents to their not-so-well-hidden-teenage fears of the Dervaig Bears. Most of the films had Gene Hackman in them. To the extent that he and his friends viewed the man as a Dervaig resident. Which would've been a fair catch for the Wee Theatre too. His cousin – whose mainland status was only further enhanced by winklepickers and a Beatles mop top – had been determined to get to the top of the incline before anyone else, especially his Mull cousin. They had seen a James Bond film that night and his friends had projected the glamorous Bond villain role onto his cousin, and, due to Ivor's shorter arm, the geeky, weak oddball onto him. He had expected his cousin would come to his defence, but he was in fact worse than the rest.

Punch shook his head free of the pain of the past. He puffed to the fields surrounding the graveyard; he knew he had better get on. There were no kids struggling up the hairpins, no bear roars. But there had been a claw in his house? Was he hitting the bottle too hard? Finally tipping into Philip Marlowe territory? Below, horses belonging to Hi-Pockets Lennox – a local farmer-by-way-of-gangster he preferred to keep on the right side of – were circling and kicking up a fuss as though they knew something he didn't. Clearly unsettled and almost requiring of a soundtrack. More Eno, he thought than Rod.

Then he saw what it was. What the horses, and possibly the dead, maybe even Skerryvore, were trying to tell him. On its quarry side, the village was on fire.

SCENE XIV

THURSDAY

FINTAN MACMASTER LIGHTLY DABBED THE rouge to his cheeks, on which he had already applied white face paint. The scar on his left cheek that he'd had since his late teens was now hidden. But you couldn't disguise fifty-nine years of life, nor conceal the Gorbals streets where you'd been dragged up from, and nor would he want to. Despite the vast discrepancy in his earnings, in this regard, he still felt a step ahead of all those Hollywood actors now having filler injected into their faces to get the parts; did they not realise how they would soon all look the same and would be unable to reflect the real people they were trying to portray? Or, maybe, given how the general public were following, they would. But no. Character, for him, required originality, authenticity, flaws. Though his mantra was being sorely tested, given he didn't currently *have* any earnings. He hoped the play the following evening was the first step to remedying that. But it was a gamble. Out-of-season events at the Wee Theatre were always risky. Even with the Burns toast and piper thrown in, included in the ticket price as an intermission offering.

It was Thursday morning and nothing was prepared. He would need to get off to Tob for the bare minimum of supplies soon. Would anyone on Mull even notice watered down whisky or wine? He had already wasted time with a trip from Dervaig to Tob the day before, only to be greeted with half-day opening hours. He had brought a few final posters to circulate. His main competition for available shop window and telegraph pole space being the posters objecting to the proposed wind farm. The noticeboard outside Browns the ironmongers was his Piccadilly Circus, prime advertising, where he'd compete with local whist drives and cattle for sale. Samuel Beckett, eat your heart out.

He looked into the mirror. It was surrounded by light bulbs, of which most were blown. Staring back was a concoction of Glaswegian, theatre owner, sad actor. And a hint of cattle for sale.

Desperation had led to experimentation. Both in makeup and programming. He'd tried out so many wigs it had looked like he was speedrunning through Elton John's entire career. But he feared that no matter how many disguises, he would always be Fintan frae the Gorbals, like Elton was Reggie from Pinner. The only difference was Fintan hadn't really had his 'Elton' period.

He was in heavy coat and scarf; usually he slept in them. His breath was visible. Final demand letters were stacking higher than scripts. He didn't open any letters anymore unless the envelopes were white. He knew he had to do something pronto, or the next vehicle entering the little car park he had fashioned out of the old quarry would be not punter, Hollywood agent, Elton nor *Sunday Times* theatre critic, but the creditors.

He had fashioned a new one-man show. Hopeful that some of the locals could be persuaded out, even in late January. If nothing else, it might bring human warmth. For him, *To be, or not to be*, was less these days about Danish Princes, and more about survival. Pride. Ego. He was pretty sure the Citizens Theatre, where he had learned his trade, was not skimping on light bulbs. And it *was* a trade. He considered acting, writing, directing, producing, all as components of his working life. His father had worked in the Govan shipyards and – much like his dad's welding irons and overalls – his own voice, face and body he considered as tools of his trade. That was a healthy way of conceiving of his craft. Method acting, he had left to Lee Strasberg and the like. His own methods had been learned on the streets of the Gorbals, the River Clyde standing in for the Hudson. *West Side Story* set in the ganglands of Glasgow. The Citizens had been his saviour – just as rising to union rep had been his father's – and in the nick of time. The scar was a lasting reminder of what life had otherwise intended for him. *A Glasgow Kiss* had been his breakthrough piece. A play about a gang member who was secretly gay. He hadn't had to look far beyond Ronnie Kray. Nor himself. He always felt on surest ground when there wasn't a lot of acting involved. Everyone was a part of somebody else.

After losing his father, then his mother, he had cashed in their house – they had upgraded from the Gorbals to the suburbs of Glasgow – and followed a long-held dream, and a long-held man, another actor, to Mull. He had bought his own theatre. Forty-two seats, making it worthy of a Guinness Book of Records entry as the smallest professional theatre in the world. But the man he had followed had then decided to break some records of his own, by following a visiting actor to the mainland. A woman, at least. He couldn't have written it – *A Mull Diss*. But he was damned if he was going to be perceived as presiding over failure. Word travelled fast on Mull, but it was nothing next to the Scottish theatrical village.

So now he was alone. In a relationship more with the bank than the boards. And, more recently, a loan shark operating out of Oban had been added to his cast. Aye. Picture-postcard, West Highlands tourist Mecca, Oban. You could forget trinkets and Highland rock. When he thought of the town now it was with an image of his body hanging, facing out to Mull, from McCaig's Tower. The folly wasn't situated on Battery Hill by accident.

Fintan looked at the unfinished work in the mirror. Despite the charge of the face paint, he could see evidence of his drinking. Alone, at home, rather than in the Bellachroy. Despite his well-retained gravelly tones, he wasn't sure if an appearance from the local thesp, never mind a pony-tailed one, might push the locals' patience a tad too far. Creatively, in truth he was all dried up. Even for the storyline of the play, he had been reduced to channelling somebody else's script idea; a tale of duality, it had come from a very unlikely source. And so now here he was, caught between capturing two men: Robert Burns or Robert Louis Stevenson. Both were in the play. Could he convincingly play both? He was just so short of time to try out the characters.

Every day was a battle with his failing buildings, if not his pride. Who knew it would be in a sleepy village on the edges of the Atlantic that he would succumb to the forces of commercial and creative defeat. Even in the summer he couldn't rustle up forty-two friends, let alone paying customers. People wanted whales and dolphins now, Michelin stars, biscuits and chocolate. Balamory and the Wombles. Christ, maybe even bears! He had started showing films as a sideline. But there had been so many requests for Gene Hackman he had shut the cinematic element down. Though a possible reprieve was offered in the shape of a strange proposition from Dave the Grave, the island's Masonic Grand Master and undertaker. The man was possibly unplayable. He had pulled up in his hearse and asked if he could have a production meeting. Inside, the undertaker – who had arrived with his own herbal teabag and smelling of the seventies – had suggested Fintan charge customers to watch Dave perform live autopsies, while projecting *The Elephant Man* behind him at the same time. Something scarily dark about the man and his ideas, but captivating. Like you could drop dead in a straight line just by looking at him. The kind of fellow who stared a bit too long at your limbs. Fintan had seen the type in the Gorbals back in the day. Body parts solidifying in outside freezers and the like. After waving the man off, he had checked the Mull directory for a listing under Joseph Merrick. But thrillingly, the man's scent had remained. And Fitan's Gaydar had been piqued.

The light from just one side of the mirror was giving the emerging character a gothic grandeur that Fintan knew was not really part of his own transformational talent. In truth, he was looking at not a cross between the two writers, but his mother and father. Though only the latter had sported the grey hair and 'tache. However, the ponytail was screaming of the nineties. Maybe it was time to give it the snip, to allow in a new millennium. New possibilities. New methods.

The phone rang.

Fintan used the makeup table to slowly lever himself off the stool – one of these days his right hip was going to crack mid-scene. He walked from the dressing room, a repurposed cupboard, impressed that the phone line hadn't been cut off. There were twelve advance sales, but could this be more? The *Round & About* advert paying dividends? Just thirty bums to go! Soon he really did need to get to Tob for some haggis and nibbles. Though at this rate he would be digging up potatoes from the ground and grabbing Hi-Pockets Lennox's sheep off the hillsides. He wondered might the trip provide an opportunity to try out his burgeoning personas? Get the island curious?

He picked up the receiver.

'Wee Theatre?'

Silence at the other end.

'Wee Theatre? Hello?'

'Now *that's* what you call timing, MacMaster – eh?'

Fintan shook his head and tried to chase off a sigh. He wiped his eyes and the eyeshadow transferred to his hands. Now even make-believe was failing him.

'*Pregnant pause*; I believe that's what you thesps call it? What's the matter, man, lost your script? Do I have to write phone dialogue for you next?'

'Hello. Yes, hello. Look . . .'

'Christ, you're proper respectful now. Now that I'm having to chase *you*. Again! Me, Gerry McNair, having to fucking chase up a good-for-nothing dole-scrounger like you?'

'I'm not on the dole. Played a few over the years, though . . .'

'Playing. What kind of living is that? This isn't *playing*, Redford. This is getting dangerously close to kneecap time.'

'Look, I'm genuinely sorry I'm late, Gerry . . .'

'*Genuinely*, no less?'

'I'll catch up with the repayments, it's just . . .'

'Just what, MacMaster? And call me Mr McNair. Only my mother and fully paid-up clients get to address me so informally. I'm – genuinely – about ready to remove the teeth from your mouth. Make drumsticks of your bones. Did you know that was my speciality?'

'Look, I'm waiting for . . .'

'For what? The call from *East-bloody-Enders*? Closest you'll ever come to fucking Hollywood, fella, is my rottweiler.'

Despite his alarm, Fintan couldn't stop himself marvelling at the menacing hiss down the line. It made Anthony Hopkins' Hannibal Lecter sound like a librarian.

'Why – erm, why your dog?' he asked.

'Oscar. So look, a man like me tries to be flexible. When clients are in arrears, they make themselves useful in, well, *other* areas of my empire. And you, MacMaster, can do something approaching cherry on top for me too.'

'I can?'

'First things first. You'll have taken a delivery?'

'When?'

'Promising. Folk usually ask, "of what?"'

'Of what?'

'Well, I'll put it in language you'll understand, and, as the *other* Bard had it: "One fire burns out another's burning", fella. "One pain is lessen'd by another's anguish".'

'Benvolio. *Romeo & Juliet*.'

'Exactly, Redford. Not what you were expecting of a man of the street, eh?'

'Baz Luhrmann's telling might disagree.'

'So this fella Benvolio's jabbering on about love and pain and how one person's suffering can relieve another's … Something I know a lot about.'

'Thanks for the lesson. Just not sure what it's got to do with me.'

'For *Verona* … I refer you to Oban.'

Fintan had never heard the Italian city given so many syllables.

'Ah? Mr McNair. Is the delivery another of your script ideas? I told you more experience is required.'

Fintan had been surprised to receive some play ideas from the man. Mostly rubbish in which Oban masqueraded as New Jersey. The inspiration for the Highlands version of Tony Soprano hadn't needed much guesswork. But, hard as it was for him to admit it, one of the gangster's ideas wouldn't leave him alone. That was the one he had gone with. But he hadn't told McNair.

'You made that bloody crystal clear, Redford. I might no' look like I shake a tail feather but I was fucking good in English at the school. Didn't even need Dad to, erm, *ensure* the teacher man improved my grades. So here's how you can help me. Told you I dabble in a bit of Am Dram over here. Just have to lay low when the shows go on stage. You'll understand I need to stay out the limelight for obvious reasons …'

'Look, I'm trying to raise your cash!'

'Steady on, Redford. I've scratched your back, fella, so maybe you can scratch mine. I see you have something new advertised?'

'Aye. I've got debts to pay, Mr Newman …'

'Nice work, fella!' Fintan listened as the hissing voice gave way to a smoker's cough. 'But it's my work?'

'Well, I've reworked the whole thing, Gerard. It was a germ you offered, that's all.'

'It was a full script! So, no fucking credit?'

'You said yourself you can't exactly, eh, broadcast your authorship. You'll benefit from the returns!'

'Just not sure I'm thick-skinned enough for the reviews ... Aye well, anyway, you do have my debts to repay and here's how this is gonna work. Enough playing silly buggers, pal. My girl sorted the lad out at Oban pier. You should have the goods now?'

'I don't. What lad? We said it would just be cash loans, nothing else! To help me through a tricky spot. No mention of *deliveries*.' Despite the low temperatures in the building, Fintan could feel his forehead perspiring, chest tightening.

'You're not in a strong negotiating position, fella. You've found yourself in debt to a debtor. Not spiffing. But you're in luck, pal. Keep my work on stage and we'll not be talking about your *final* fucking arrears.'

'I have to be careful, Gerry. Folk know me!'

'Folk *know* you?' McNair parodied. 'A few grouse downed on *Take The High Road* as gamekeeper does not a celebrity make.'

'Me or the grouse?'

McNair chuckled. 'That's it, Redford, play ball. So you're telling me you don't know about a wee bit of special cargo that came over on the Oban to Craignure ferry yesterday?'

'To me?'

'Aye. I'm getting more business on Mull. Seems a few folk are growing partial to the powder. You're gonna be my point of distribution. This is you repaying some of your debt, Redford.'

'I'm telling you, I've received nothing.'

'Right, MacMaster. I'm going to believe you. I'll check my carrier. Don't let me down, Fintan fella, or you can say goodbye to your own wee empire there. Fair's fair. I'll be in touch. Oh . . .'

'Look, is this coke?'

'Don't worry about that Mull copper.'

'Punch?'

'Aye. The Clock. I've got his card well marked.'

The line went dead.

SCENE XV

FINTAN PUT DOWN THE RECEIVER. He looked at the palm of his hand, expecting third degree burns. The Oban vowels, the deep tone, the roundness of delivery all hung like weights around his neck. Despite his concern – albeit buried under a veil of makeup – of falling further into McNair's clutches, he still was a sucker for strong dialect. Authentic voices. He reproduced aloud the sound of the gangster's words: 'One fire burns out another's burning, fella.' It wasn't right for the look, but it was another potential ingredient. Why had McNair namechecked Sergeant Punch? To spook him? Was it another way of enforcing his debt? Was the copper bent? And who was 'the lad' McNair referred to? Not *his* lad, dear, sweet lad, who, granted, had been spending a bit too much time at the theatre. He feared the locals had cottoned on. That was why he had refused him a part.

In any case, no packages had arrived. He couldn't help thinking he had been lured back onto the Gorbals streets of his youth. And with it, strangely, a sense of safety. Familiarity. Talk of his old mistress, coke, was a thought hard to erase.

He walked back through and eased himself down to the stool at the mirror. Could have sworn another bulb had blown. A Glasgow gangster he was not; he never had been. The origin of the spiralling mess he found himself in was a chance conversation in the Columba hotel bar when waiting on the ferry one day last autumn after the Oban Tesco shop. Anything to avoid the Mull Rally. He'd had a few too many and poured his heart out to the barmaid. A nod and a wink and before he knew it, she was slipping him a number. *Someone who can help*, she'd said, *take the pressure off, lovie*. This wasn't a Dickie Attenborough *luvvie*, no doubting it. Sometimes a sob story paid off. Or so he'd thought.

The latest draft of the script, still populated with red scribbles, sat in front of him. In truth, McNair's idea had been not much more than scribbles on a beer mat. The suggestion of a walk-on part from an Obanite gangster prophesising that his traitors would burn with 'unquenchable fire' had been rebuked already. It was when sitting in his house watching Jools Holland at Hogmanay with the local lad, and them discussing Burns Night approaching, that McNair's idea had returned to him. Several drafts later, and here it was. The lad had turned up one day not long before, asking to see inside the theatre. He had returned. Always asking questions about process. A fascination with playing dead people, with bringing them back to life. Fintan had been careful to monitor if the lad was forming a crush. And careful to keep an eye on himself too. But the lad's unlikely interest in acting seemed genuine enough; in fact, he already had a theatre of his own about him. The lad had offered to start as stagehand or set designer, but Fintan had declined. Though he had enjoyed the opportunity to pass on a thing or two, to realise he hadn't been wasting his time for forty-odd years. He had recently started lending the lad books on craft. Saying, come summer, there might be a small part.

He looked at the script in front of him. The text on the final pages faded to a white page. His last toner cartridge running out, which he had taken as an act of symbolism. Of things mysteriously disappearing. For it was local folklore that had inspired this new work. And now the posters competing with the wind proudly announced:

> THE LOOMING
> *A Man Is An Island . . . For A' That.*
> *A new one-man play by Fintan MacMaster*
> *The Wee Theatre, Dervaig*
> *7.30 p.m., Friday 28 January 2000*
> *A Burns Supper buffet will be served. Burns himself may appear too . . .*
> *£20 all-inc.*

Symbolism had become metaphor. He couldn't help fearing it was the most public suicide note ever written. It was based on some local nonsense about a mysterious island that was said to appear around Mull's west coast. Robert Burns was connected. Nobody quite knew the source, though some said Robert Louis Stevenson was attributed. Rubbish, of course, but it beat a narrative about the Dervaig Bears. He was to play the two famous Roberts; the climax being that one of them is revealed to have written the whole hoax. The audience was tasked with working out which writer is telling the truth, and which is peddling folklore. Or was it really about those gangsters who were peddling the island cocaine?

How to be two people at once? Fintan looked for the characters in the mirror. The shit you did to try and win a lover back. The theatre site had once been a church, and he had, in fuller-house times, considered himself the leader of a congregation too. Company would be overstating it. There was something of a Battlefields Bowie staring back at him. The cracked actor. It was to Bowie, Day-Lewis, Dylan, Hanks, he often wished he could go – admiring their commitment to reinvention. A life of slashing faces in the Gorbals would have been a bore, prototypical. Worse – a waste. But now it all amounted to blown light bulbs, loneliness, the architecture of a slow death. And, worryingly, the idea of unquenchable flames as a solution to his problems had proven tricky to dislodge.

'Fuck,' he said, in a voice cast adrift between the two men. He looked at his halfway creation staring back at him. The welder was harder to disguise than he had realised. He released more words: 'I have been doomed to such a dreadful shipwreck: that man is not simply one, but truly two!' He looked at the two wigs on their stands. Took the Burns wig and put it on, tilted his head and conjured another voice by way of reply: 'I learned to recognise the thorough and primitive duality of man!'

The doorbell rang. Five minutes to curtain, or to kneecap time?

Fintan pulled off the wig. Stood. Sat again, unsure whether to wipe away the day's exploration. Time to put the Gorbals-turned-thespian voice back on. He was certain the islanders expected it of him by now. Even when coming to repair his bog.

He walked out of the dressing room and opened the stage door. He stepped onto the small stage, rubbing his hands warm.

He had left one spotlight on, facing him.

Somebody was backlit out there.

'Aye, hello?' Fintan called out; even in this, projection. Only hoped it was a potential sale.

Nothing came back from the theatre floor. His cold breath caught the light.

'Who is this?'

Silence. The kind that was either an empty room or a full one. If only the latter.

'Who are you trying to be?' came the voice.

It was female, fragile, but with those five words Fintan felt scolded. Maybe it was the European accent. The words delivered at angles, landing on the theatre floor like chips from a sculptor's pick.

'Oh? Bora? Christ, right. Sorry, I forgot!'

It was his cleaner. Pride was pride. He drew a line at cleaning bogs. Which was what his father had said street fighting would lead to. Though he suspected his dad had applied that prognosis to acting as well.

'Sorry, Bora. I thought I told you I won't need you till Friday. Tomorrow?'

'I can't see *who* you are,' came the voice.

'Not until tomorrow,' Fintan repeated. 'I said I'd get the supplies?'

The scream of silence was growing from the theatre floor.

'As long as you know, lass. Sorry.'

He could see her outline. The long coat, graceful neck. Hair in a nest.

'Eh . . .' Fintan cleared his throat, aware he was striking an actor's pose now, unable to repudiate the allure of the elevated position and the hold of the lights. He felt a pathetic need to placate her with some interest in her, given he'd had to cut her summer season hours too; even that decision he'd delayed out of sympathy for her. 'Is, eh, Bora your *actual* full name, or one you comprised, when eh, you came – over here?'

He'd always felt the poor thing was so hard to reach, but he understood she didn't want his sympathy. She and her son lived in the caravan down below. The boy sometimes coming up to help her with the cleaning. He had heard of council homes on the isle of Bute being offered to refugees. There was a show in it, if he could crack the right tone. He was unsure, even after all these years, if the category of *refugee* was a step up or down from the bracket the islanders had long since decamped him firmly within: *incomer*.

'By "over here",' she managed. 'Do you mean to the theatre?'

'No. I meant, erm … from your … eh, Bosnia?' Fintan realised she had put him right where he deserved.

'I was born with it,' she said, saving him. 'My name.'

'Right.' Fintan nodded.

'You are somewhere stuck between them,' she added, from the darkness.

'Mull and the Looming?'

'No. The two characters.'

'Aye. Yes, I fear …' He pointed to the door. 'I hear you're protesting this wind farm.'

'It will take land.'

'And I'm guessing you've, eh, seen that happen before. Land taken?'

She nodded.

Fintan did his usual thing of bringing his left hand up to

obscure his cheek, but then remembered his scar was already under the cover of an emerging, *other* identity. He instead shielded the light and watched as she patted her hair, which was black and heavily parted at the side. She had thick, dark eyebrows and black eyes. Pain swimming in them. High cheekbones kept lookout either side of a boxer's nose, which, though often considered an unattractive feature, was in fact more of an alluring imperfection on Bora. He could imagine Ken Loach or Mike Leigh making Bafta-winning use of her. Maybe getting to marry her too. But realising they would never really know her. Only the camera would.

'Powerful wind,' she said.

'Sorry, lass?'

'My name. The meaning. In south Slavic languages.'

'That is very, erm, powerful.' Fintan thought of the meaning of his own name, *White Fire*; how she had the capacity in hers to cancel out his. 'Are you okay, Bora?'

'Are *you*?' She pointed behind her, back to the theatre door.

'Look, lass, I don't need you today to . . .'

'I didn't . . . didn't come to, to clean.'

'Right?' Fintan stepped forwards. The woman's full discomfort came into stark view. She was hugging herself. Eyes like olives in brine. 'Then why did you come?'

'For a part.'

'I see.' Fintan gulped.

'To play, me.'

She pointed behind her again. Raised her nose, her mouth fell open.

'Are you expecting someone else, lass? Your lad?'

'Your house. I think it's on fire.'

SCENE XVI

WEDNESDAY

'PHANTOM BLUE,' DUCK SAID.

'What?' Davud turned.

'The car colour. In case you're wondering. Aye, aye.'

They were now sitting inside Duck's Ford Fiesta on the car deck.

'Oh?' Davud nodded. He wondered if he should have been wondering. 'Thanks.' It smelled like a distillery-cum-aftershave-factory to him. He wanted to imagine he was sitting on the back of Duck's motorbike. On the record jump. Not the failed one.

'Don't be fooled by the appearance.' Duck nodded, tapping the wheel. 'Fair poke on her.'

Davud didn't feel fooled. War made fools of people, theatre owners did too, but not cars.

'Mighty. Aye, aye,' Duck enthused. 'Closest I could get to match the Gers. Blah says it sounds more like a porn film. Co-starring Appy, no doubt.'

'Who?'

'From Tob. He's on the bins too.'

'Is he?'

'Aye. Appy's short for Apostrophe. I first started that.'

'Why?'

'Because it's quicker to say I suppose?'

'No. Why would somebody be called Apostrophe?'

'In the eighties, he had a window cleaning service and was the first here to advertise his business on the side of a van. Fair fuss he kicked up. Bugger spent a fortune adding *Stewarts Windows.* On both sides. None of us were scholars but . . .'

'What?'

'The bugger was missing the apostrophe. Had his *surname* been Stewart, then the man would've been in the clear. Confusion he caused. Had Punch been in post the cell would've been troubled!'

'Did Richard Branson start out like that?'

Duck exploded into a smoker's cough-cum-laugh. Davud heard it as a fire starting up in hell.

'Good one, lad.'

Davud wondered why he kept making people laugh when he wasn't trying to. The car deck was unfamiliar territory to him. He watched Duck eyeing the efficient ferry stewards, waiting for them to signal when they could leave the vessel. He could see Duck did this in the way some people might be glued to a World Cup final. He imagined the chaos a fire down here would create.

A siren sounded. Davud gripped the door handle. 'March away in a slow walk!' he yelled. 'Heads down! Down!'

'Christ!' Duck turned to him. 'What the hell, lad?'

'Vatra and me *always* hit the ground together!' Davud was crouched in the brace position. 'The guards said you must.'

'Fuck, lad!' Duck swivelled, looking around them. 'What's the matter?'

'Your knees would hurt! From hitting the concrete ground! Ears bleeding from shells. Vatra's dead! A shell landed on him.'

'Okay, lad! It's okay. Right you are. You're not there now. No.' Duck made to put a hand on Davud's arm. But didn't. 'Christ, what a fright you gave me. It's just the ferry's mouth opening. That's all.'

Davud slowly sat up and his hair followed. He swept it back and inhaled heavily through his nostrils. Rubbed his dark eyes.

'Think I hit the horn.' Duck looked around them again. 'Did I hit the horn?'

'Vatra even *means* fire.'

'We'll be out of here smartish, lad. No more sirens.'

Silence fell between them. Davud knew Duck was running from a war himself. One waged in Dervaig. He also knew Bearfoot was spending more time at the theatre. That was why he had agreed to take the packages. To win him back. Both of them, architects of truth, blood-brothers again. In the caves. *Bearfoot* and *Leonardo*.

'You know,' Duck pointed, 'I've watched these stewards growing old over the years, but I don't know a single one of their names.'

Davud looked to Duck, engulfed in a haze of vodka and Coke. Where did his mother, the caravan, fit in? Duck seemed to be on a fast-track to old age. Vatra, on the other hand, was frozen in time. Like his father, Vatra hadn't aged at all in Davud's memory. He remembered how he had sat behind Vatra's mum on the flight to Edinburgh. A spare seat next to her. She'd kept the window for her dead son. But Davud hadn't seen her after they'd landed. *New life*, that was what everybody was telling them.

'Hands at ten to two.' Duck demonstrated. 'First thing they teach you about driving lorries.'

'Scientists are planning to add two seconds to the end of this year,' Davud said. 'To make Earth run bang on time.'

'CalMac will only bugger it up with their timetables. Aye, aye. Talk of the devil . . .'

There was a steward right outside the Fiesta. Davud calculated that this was his eleventh ferry journey, counting returns. In Sarajevo, he and Vatra had made Lego boats. He counted twenty-three cars of various makes and colours. Going by the information on the Alight Area wall, this meant the ferry was operating at approximately 28 per cent capacity. The stewards wore hi-vis clothing so that they were always noticed, but Davud knew their shy, darting eyes suggested they were not keen on being noticed. He knew what that felt like.

Davud felt the familiar, heavy nudge of the island, like an old lady's elbow. All the cars did a little dance as though being controlled by a CalMac console. It was confirmation they were no longer solely of the sea.

Duck leaned quickly to start the engine. Davud could picture Blah Blah Blah on the outside, tying thick ropes around the bollards on Craignure pier. He thought of it as like being lassoed to the island. Theirs was the only engine running. Duck operated beyond rules. Bearfoot had said that was why the jump went wrong. That it was worthy of punishment, even forgetting the piss.

'Here, pass me your ticket,' Duck spouted, flapping his own passenger and car tickets between his lips as he spoke. In a way, thought Davud, he was actually *becoming* Donald Duck. Davud handed over his ticket and watched as Duck added it to his mouth.

'Sometimes wonder if J. K. Rowling's in charge of CalMac's recruitment.' Duck wheezed, nodding in the direction of the steward, his tone rising through the words.

'Why would she be?'

Duck wound down his window and handed the total of their tickets to the steward. 'Aye, aye . . .' The steward took the tickets with no eye contact or response. Duck wound the window back up. 'Not a smile among the fuckers.'

The mouth of the ferry was now fully opened. Mull skies, daylight and the cries of seagulls rushed in. Davud shielded his eyes from the light, wondering if some of the squawking gulls had flown from Oban with them. Everyone seemed to be trying to escape one life for another. All you needed was a TV to tell you about it. Maybe that was why his mother wouldn't have one. He wondered if the boy washed up on that beach, the waves lapping at him, had, for even a single second, felt closer to freedom.

One of the stewards signalled for them to move forwards with a slow, well-practised single-finger gesture.

'Hung like a bull I suspect . . .' Duck said.

'Oh?'

'And always the poker face. Bugs bloody Bunny could drive off here and they wouldn't bat an eyelid. As long as he had a ticket.'

'I suppose you're the next best thing,' Davud blurted.

'Eh?' Duck turned. 'Right enough, lad! Good one!'

Davud felt his heart skip, like he was under Duck's

motorbike again, Duck's spell. The Fiesta revved louder, creating the impression the final car in the line was about to be crushed.

'Home, eh?' Duck said, as they left the ferry and moved onto Mull.

Davud took it simultaneously as a question but also as a directive he should follow; that he should feel about Mull – about life, football, islands, war, peace, hi-vis, bin collection – as Duck did.

'Aye, aye. When you've driven through a village on a bin lorry, you'll never go through those streets in the same way again. You think *Punch* knows folks' secrets!'

Davud took in the snow.

'You'll have a team yourself, lad?'

'Sorry?'

'The football? Did you have a team back, you know, before, eh . . .?

Davud gulped. Nobody could ever finish that sentence.

'Yes. FK Sarajevo. I went with my dad.'

'Right. Aye, aye. Good.'

Davud thought of the books that had always sat above their fireplace in the apartment in Sarajevo. Some were football annuals. They rubbed shoulders with his dad's old football trophies. His mother had teaching certificates, graduation rolls. But showing them was not something his mother did. Davud knew if she showed them then she was in a way showing herself. There had been a Bible too. Were Bibles not supposed to be indestructible? He never found out. Next to the Bible there had always sat two other books, by a writer called Robert Louis Stevenson. *Treasure Island*, and another about two men who his mother had said were really one. It was impossible now to think of those books, that island, those two men, in ashes. Just as it was his father's trophies. All transformed to rubble, to dust. Represented by an empty window seat.

'I'd been called "Evel" after the record jump,' Duck said, staring ahead. 'But only for a week. The week later even my father had replaced the *e* with an *i*.'

Davud saw Duck's eyes were watering. Duck gestured to show it was the light's fault.

'The *i* happens to me every day,' Davud said. 'It's the *u* people want rid of.'

He watched as Duck waved to people. The man's identity seemed to be returning to him. Increasingly, Davud was documenting things like this in his head, rather than in his sketchbooks. Figuring nobody could burn his memory. He wondered if he could mention the bins now. Maybe even the packages. But how could he explain the lighter fluid still in his rucksack? Bearfoot had suggested if all went wrong with the plan then he could set the evidence alight. Did he mean Duck?

He said, 'I have to sort of represent a country, a war, that people only know from the news.'

'Matching up to a father who runs a bloody village is enough for me.'

Davud turned to Duck, who was looking ahead. How could he explain the burning man? That he might have to do the same to Duck?

'Especially,' Duck croaked, 'when I killed my own mother.'

SCENE XVII

THURSDAY

THE TWO CHARRED BODIES ARE lying in front of me. I hadn't accounted for feeling watched. No doubt about it, the eyes become more prominent when the teeth are removed. Centre stage. Even in death. The textbooks don't tell you that.

I drove them from the Glen. Then, one after the other, by moonlight, I dragged them in here. Into the deepest bear cave. I can hardly believe it. I finally have company. The kind that won't leave me. And they *are* bear caves. Hidden in the village. Don't let anyone tell you different. Folklore is everything on an island. It's passed down for a reason. *The Headless Horsemen* in Tobermory. *The Dervaig Bears*. *The Maiden of the Cairn* at Lochbuie, *The Granny Inside the Whale* at Uisken, and *The Legend of the Water Horse*, also on the Ross. Stories are blood and oxygen long after bodies are dust. Smallness, the local, is not parochial, it is right. Fintan said that. An incomer. Why doesn't the rest of the mainland know it?

Leonardo is always a willing follower. We said we would kill Duck if we had to. In the olden days they used to believe that death can bring back life. And I have two here for the price of one! One body is to return Leonardo's dad, the other is to return my dear, dear Grey Lady. We both had our reasons. We never said it aloud, but we both knew we would stop at nothing to find truth in everything. The kind of truth beyond what other people accept as reality. Beating our chests like we are twelve feet tall!

I sit with death. But my heart drums like never before for life.

I am bear. I am here. I have done it. It is even more exhilarating. He is not here as arranged. Leonardo?

So, have you considered we might be the same person?

SCENE XVIII

THURSDAY

PUNCH USED THE EXTINGUISHER TO kill the last of the flames. It had looked a lot worse up on the hill. He always kept an extinguisher in his boot. Usually a box of Tobermory next to it; luckily, one landed in the Ranger every month out of the distillery's back door. He hoped he'd acted before the fire brigade boys came hurtling down the hairpin bends with all the bells ringing like a Van Halen solo when a simple Ronnie Wood lick was enough. Randy in their number. Bugger wasn't happy just screwing up the Forestry's hygiene protocol.

The theatre door burst open and a man appeared. Looked like he'd seen, or *was*, a ghost.

'God!' Fintan said, rushing forwards and then stopping to take in the damage to his house.

'Not quite, but close,' Punch said, lowering the extinguisher. He didn't recognise the man. Though it wasn't easy to see the actual person under the disguise. Looked like he needed a good foam spray himself. He'd heard there was a strange artsy type out here. 'This your place?'

'Yes! Yes, sergeant!' Fintan rushed to the side of the house.

Punch saw the man's ponytail bobbing. *Worthy of arrest alone.*

Fintan returned with two pails of water. He threw them onto the smoking porch. Unnecessary, thought Punch, given it was the same area he had just extinguished. But drama was drama.

'Christ!' Fintan dropped the pails.

'Getting warmer,' Punch said.

'Seems to be the last of it! Thankfully . . .' Fintan turned full circle to make sure there wasn't any additional threat. 'Lucky! Lucky, I think?'

'Certainly advise doing the lottery at the weekend.' Punch stepped out of the porch.

'The real tragedies in life are the ones that blindside you on an idle Thursday – don't they say that?'

'Speak for yourself. Idle, I mean.'

'None taken.' Fintan stared at his house. Given what McNair had implied at the end of his call, he was unsure if the presence of the sergeant was good or bad news; was the copper here to imply Fintan was safe, protected, operating as a drug pusher on the inside of the law? Surely that would get his ex's attention?

Punch looked at the battered Fiesta parked nearby.

'Lucky your car didn't get in on the act.' Though, looking at the state of the thing, he couldn't be sure it wasn't the torched one Dave had called in.

'Indeed. Thank you again, sergeant.'

Punch looked at the red door of the house, mostly black now. Was sure the effects of the flame had left the outline of Che Guevara on it. He looked to the bigger building the man had emerged from: so that was it. He had never been inside a theatre.

'Any idea what could have started this?' Punch said. He had half a mind on the Glen, which he still hadn't got to. He put down the extinguisher and took a roll-up from behind his ear. It was amazing what you could fashion while navigating the winding Tob to Dervaig road.

Fintan shook his head and produced upturned palms. 'No idea, sergeant. They say it's the silent killer.'

'Smoking?' Punch puffed. 'Or fire?'

'Well, both really . . .'

'Uh-ha. Just as well it didn't spread to your theatre, your business.'

'Can only think it was the wiring? The house is old. An old manse house.'

'Well.' Punch inadvertently waved his right arm. 'You certainly had somebody on your side. God trodden your boards recently?'

'Can't afford him.'

'Uh-ha.'

'Name?'

'God's?'

'No.'

'Oh, mine? Sorry. Fintan MacMaster.'

'Marcel Marceau?'

'Sorry?'

'The rigout?'

'Oh? No. No.'

'Tob panto with my mother is the closest I've been.'

'To Marcel Marceau?'

'To Hollywood. Had a few ham actors in the cell right enough. As long as the buggers can't mime their way out, eh?'

'Sergeant, this was extremely good fortune . . .' Fintan gestured to his house, taking this as his opportunity to test whether Punch *was* open to corruption.

'You should have seen the production.' Punch had even found himself mentioned as Mull's most eligible bachelor.

'No. That you were here. I'm entirely indebted.'

Punch knew to play a bit daft and loose at first with certain people, to keep them on their toes. Cluny got that bit wrong. The approach usually resulted in folk leaving a window ajar in their narratives that they hadn't meant to. Setting them up nicely for the conversational equivalent of the thick blue door to close in on them.

'You were, eh, close by?' Fintan asked, instinctively making to cover his cheek. He was reminded of how strange he must look. Though 'Punch' struck him as a kind of stage name itself. The sergeant would likely know of McNair. What had he got himself hooked up in? After the production, he needed to get rid of the McNairs of the world.

'Aye, certainly lucky I was approaching the village.' Punch puffed towards the larger building. Tulloch in Inverness had said policing was about *going with your belly*, which Punch had evolved into a mantra of his own: *right place, right time*.

'Mid-character, eh?' Punch gestured. 'That what they call it?'

'Something like that.' The man signalled to Punch for a smoke.

'Thought it was the silent killer?'

'Mid-character. Qualifies as research.'

Punch handed the man the emergency roll-up from behind

his other ear. Used his left arm to provide a light. 'Should I have a look inside? You know, to make sure Guy Fox isn't part of the equation?'

'What equation?'

'I'm assuming the theatre is connected to the same external power supply. Better to be safe?'

'Safe from what? Thanks, sergeant, but despite the actor's hands, I'm the son of a Clydesider. I'll check after you've gone.'

'Best see that you do.' Punch took a deep draw. 'You know, I've never said a line that wasn't my own. But we do have one thing in common.'

'We do, sergeant?' Fintan was trying to think if he had ever played a cop. He had once written a one-man production called *Scotland's Yard*, but that was about the demise of the shipyards, an attempt to appease his by then dying father.

'We both live next to *the shop*.' Punch puffed. 'Except folk pay to go into yours. In mine, people pay to leave.'

'Seen it that way around too, sergeant.'

The theatre door slowly opened. Punch looked to a woman emerging in black, almost gliding as if about to *cuckoo* the time or visually represent a weather prediction. Patti Smith came to mind. She was familiar, from the Bellachroy he thought. Not a Dervaig native for certain; 'bears', they were referred to in the olden days. She was white, but darker skinned; European-looking.

Punch removed his police hat.

'Oh?' Fintan turned. 'Sergeant, this is, erm, Bora ... Sorry, I don't know your last name, Bora?'

'From-away,' she said. Her raised cheekbone wasn't lost on Punch. Timing, you either had it or you didn't.

'Aye, well.' Fintan puffed. 'Bora helps out.'

Punch nodded. 'Acting?'

'No, eh, no,' Fintan said.

Punch suspected the woman wasn't so sure.

Bora folded her arms. Looked like she was holding her insides, stopping them from pouring out. Come the slaughter season Punch would be doing the same with sheep carcasses hanging in his station lockup. Gallbladders on the concrete floor, as they would be on the moors; birds never took a gallbladder.

'Did you not notice the burning?' Punch asked, looking beyond Fintan.

'Wiring, sergeant,' Fintan said, realising Bora didn't know how to respond. 'Didn't we decide on that?'

Punch clocked how the man nodded to the woman as though the discretionary tone was required for *her*. She was silent as a moon.

'Did we?' Punch puffed. 'Must've missed the script in the post, eh?'

Now Skerryvore's talk of burning came to mind. But from Dervaig? Eight miles away? At this rate he *would* be including this bloody Looming nonsense as part of Mull's Lima Bravo division.

He watched the woman walk away, arms still folded, looking to the earth.

'You're local?' he asked.

She turned, but kept walking. 'Not yet . . .' she said.

Punch had the strange sensation he'd been voodoo-ed or something.

'Can I drive you anywhere?'

'She lives in the caravan, sergeant,' Fintan offered. 'Just a few bends away.'

Punch watched the woman descend to the main road. He wasn't sure from what or where, but he could tell there was noise around her.

'She on her own?' Punch asked.

'You mean, does she have a man?'

'Family?'

'Just, eh, a lad. Aye. Think he's away now. They keep to themselves mostly.'

'Right.' Punch fixed on his hat. 'I'll let you get back to the boards. I hear the Oscars are approaching.'

'Thanks again, sergeant. I was halfway through my acceptance speech.'

'Uh-hu. Elton's after-party in the Bellachroy no doubt.' Punch gestured to the house. 'Don't suppose you'll be up for Best Special Effects.'

He walked to the Ranger and opened the door.

Fintan watched him, unsure if he had missed some unspoken prompt or piece of information relating to the McNair business. Could the sergeant really be in on it? He was relieved not to have lingered too long on talk of the local lad.

Punch threw his hat on the passenger seat. Lowered himself into the Ranger. Closed the door. He watched the man make a fuss of the burned Che Guevara. Maybe all of life was bad acting. He put the Ranger in gear and drove off, troubling the gravel for effect. A couple of details were troubling him about Gielgud back there – had the pails been a bit too handy? And why hadn't the fire boys been alerted? Randy's aftershave alone wasn't a good enough reason.

'L747 to L519. Do you receive? Over. Do you receive? Over.'

Punch took the radio handset from the holder. Before Cluny had been imposed on him, such feed-throughs would come from a control room officer, or McColl, the senior shift sergeant in Oban. At least with McColl there was a bit of craic, and maybe a tale or two on the latest Clan McNair escapades, the kind that didn't turn up in *The Oban Times* Courts section. Buggers would still be carrying shields and swords, biting the heads off squirrels, given half the chance.

'L747 to L519. Do you receive? Over. Do you receive? Over. Sarge?'

Punch pressed on the talk button.

'I've told you before, PC Cluny, whatever Tulliallen drummed into you, you don't have to keep using shoulder numbers. And you missed an "over"!' Punch released the talk button. 'And fuck.'

Mull fell within Legacy Strathclyde's L division, which dropped down to LB sub-division, accounting for Argyll & Dunbartonshire, encompassing the towns of Oban, Lochgilphead, Dunoon, Campbeltown and Rothesay. Sometimes it was more colloquially referred to as 'LB Dal Riata' by the divisional sergeants, after the old Gaelic Kingdom. At least on this closed channel his deputy couldn't bother the rest of LB Div with the price of a Chianti, or squirrel, for that matter, in Waitrose, Milngavie.

'Sarge, I've had Dave on the phone. He's on the Glen now. At the cars. Over.'

'Plural?'

'That's just it, Sarge. There are two apparently. Over.'

'Right. Wonder why we were told only one?'

'Next steps, Sarge? Over.'

'Radio Control for Forensics. Possibly jumping the gun, but better to be safe than sorry.' Punch checked the dash. 'They'll make the last ferry. Give them co-ordinates and explain I haven't been at SOI as yet, but am on my way. Over.'

'Scene of crime? Over.'

'Scene of *incident*. Lower grade for now. And, PC?'

'Sarge? Over.'

'Did Dave waste police time talking about his new mobile phone again? Over.'

'Says he had the first on the island, Sarge. Over.'

'Bloody man.'

Punch fixed the radio into the holder. He leaned into full lead foot. The radio had fallen silent apart from the crackle-cum-expectant-breath of his deputy.

'Over! Arthur C. Clarke! Over, man!'

Silence again.

'Over!'

'On it, Sarge. After the last ferry, we're on our own. I remember. Hope it's okay but . . .'

'What? Over.'

'I already called for Forensics. I did it when you left. Something was telling me there was more to come. Over.'

'Okay. Over.' Punch released and then engaged the talk button again. 'That's called using your noggin, PC. Police work is noggin and belly, not hard drive. Over.'

'I'm heading to Craignure now, Sarge. Over.'

'No. Have PC Monteith do it. She's already at Craignure?'

Silence again.

'Christ. Over.'

'Remember she's on leave this week, Sarge. Back home on Morvern. Family wedding. At the big house at Drimnin. Over.'

'At least we can keep an eye on her. Over.'

Punch cleared his throat, throwing his Adam's apple into a caravulkin. His-uncle-who-was-not-his-uncle's word for a somersault. *Monteith was on leave?* That was why uniforms shouldn't have families. Because then planes exploded over Borders towns, and uncles were revealed to be really fathers, mothers got dementia and girlfriends such as Janice the teacher in Inverness emerged with talk of kids, of buying a house together and attending classical concerts at the Edinburgh Festival, resulting in his leaving of Highlands division. All mounting evidence as to why it was best that Mary MacBeth remained his cleaner; that they barely acknowledge their family that nearly was. It was the uniform's job to protect not the public, but himself.

Punch shook his head and replaced the handset again. He reached for the tobacco from his breast pocket, had a strong word with the bend. Were the burnt-out cars the work of a local prankster, or something more? The jury was still out. No doubt its members swimming somewhere between the mainland and the island. And why had Dave withheld information?

Right place, right time? He wasn't called the Clock for nothing. He felt the hands starting to turn.

SCENE XIX

WEDNESDAY

'As I suspected. Boys are late with the gritter,' Duck announced as they progressed up the pier slip. 'Snow's lying. Unless it's a poorly executed cocaine heist.'

'Eh?' Davud turned quickly to Duck; he'd wondered if drugs were what he was carrying. Surely bombs would be heavier?

'Aye, Blah!' Duck thrust a Hitler-esque salute over to Blah Blah Blah up on the pier, who returned it. 'There'd be your first suspect. Bugger's nostrils are like buckets.'

Davud kept his gaze on the emerging Craignure buildings. Why was Duck mentioning a suspect? Did he know something? He saw the scarlet sky that night just before Duck landed on his own mother; Duck was silhouetted against it.

Duck turned right, in the direction of the Salen road, from there they could access the Glen to Dervaig.

'I'm back on the bins the morrow. Awe fuck!' He pulled over outside the Ceilidh Place. 'Shit!'

'What?' Davud asked.

'Slap in the chops, Donald!' Duck shook his head and inhaled through his angled nose. 'I've forgotten my jacket, to go with the kilt. Left it at the posh do in Glasgow last night. Not good.'

'Oh?'

'Nor is this weather. Snow's keen.'

The bus passed them and Davud wished he was in his usual seat. He looked across to the lines of cars now being signalled by Blah Blah Blah to progress towards the ferry. The passengers with towns and cities already visible on their expectant faces. He wished he was one of them. But was there now no art school to attend? What had he done? He ran through his memorised schedule: *Oban (12.11 p.m.), Taynuilt (12.34 p.m.), Loch Awe (12.50 p.m.), Dalmally (12.55 p.m.).*

'That'll teach me for blowing my pipes elsewhere . . .' Duck said. 'For taking the big money.'

Davud saw that Duck's stomach was forcing the Masonic emblem almost up to his chin. The unknowable, helmeted version of Duck, in his red leather jacket with Bruce Lee on the back, must have been in there somewhere. Duck was nothing like Evel to him anymore. He was more like an unmade bed. He'd just prefer it wasn't his mum's. An image of his mother on her knees, beating the ground came to him. She on the hot Sarajevo pavement. It was the same image he had spied of Duck, after leaving their caravan late one night. The next morning his knee marks were still outside.

'Better see what I've got in the back,' wheezed Duck. 'It might be just the Wee Theatre, but still. I've never been. You?'

Davud shook his head. Knew why he was lying. He had thought about setting it alight too. The ponytailed man there was bringing his mum to her knees again.

'Burns *and* a show apparently. Seen the posters?'

'I've been away.'

'*The Looming*? Don't know why folk can't stick with what they *know* to be true. With what *actually* happened. Not fucking hearsay! Gossip!'

'People know it was an accident. That you didn't mean to . . .'

'My brother doesn't! The father couldn't have given a toss about her. But pretended he did.'

Davud knew Bearfoot had been hanging around the theatre more and more. He was starting to feel like his friend was trying to get him to do his dirty work. That Bearfoot wasn't a *real* architect. He was going to do as instructed with the packages and then be done with it. Ask his mother never to go there again. In Bosnia she had been on TV. Won acting awards. Trained students.

'Still,' Duck said, bundling himself out of the car in instalments, leaving the door ajar. 'This Fintan fellow better be good for a hundred and fifty notes.'

'It should be her,' Davud said. But knew he hadn't been heard.

He felt the burden of the rucksack, the packages and lighter fluid, even more now they were on Mull. He gazed to the sky; was he imagining it? A cloud shaped like a sleeping bear. He shook his head. He had drawn a bear claw print in his sketchbook. Bearfoot had asked him to draw it. Said it was part of their pact. Like a symbol of truth; an acknowledgement of who they had lost.

'Rabbie . . .' Duck croaked from the rear of the Fiesta, 'accept my apologies.'

Davud turned back and, when the boot came up to obscure Duck, he leaned to zero the milometer. The boot closed. Davud turned to see bagpipes spread-eagled across the floor like road kill. The entire rear of the car was a graveyard of Tennent's cans.

'What do you reckon to this?' wheezed Duck.

Davud turned to see Duck now wearing a black jacket, with a blue and gold badge on the pocket, not unlike the Brazilian national football team colours. The emblem read: *Isle of Mull Masonic Association*.

'It's all I could rustle up.'

'Isn't it supposed to be a secret society?'

'Smart enough, though – eh?' Duck rolled up the cuffs.

Davud didn't know what he thought. He always stuck to the dark blue parka and black skinnies, even in summer. It was a kind of armour against the prospect of buildings collapsing. But now they were burning down again.

'Granted it's maybe a tad New Romantic . . .' said Duck. 'Not sure about Burns being the *biggest* Spandau fan . . . No bugger will turn up anyway. I told the man that.' Duck manoeuvred himself back into the car. 'I can always knock out "Gold" on the pipes if requested.'

'The boot's still open,' Davud said.

'Christ . . . you're right, lad! I'll be fucked? Do you have this weekend's winning lottery numbers on you too by chance?'

'No,' said Davud. 'Why would I? It's an independently monitored live draw.'

Duck put a CD in his mouth. He wrestled the jacket off and threw it to the back seat. Davud had spotted the hand-written CD labelling: *As Duck Would Have It*. Duck slotted the CD into the player and Davud looked to the others strewn on the dash. *Bad Duck, Best of Duck, Better Duck Next Time* and *What's Duck Got To Do With It?*

'You're indestructible ... always believing ...' Duck sang. 'Waiting on the second verse, lad?'

'Sorry?'

'The boot?'

'Oh? Right. Yes ...' Davud opened his door. He considered grabbing his bag and getting back on the ferry, but the woman in Oban had said his *family's safety depended on him*. His family only meant one thing: his mum. He walked to the boot and noticed another case of Tennent's. Also a can of petrol. He gently closed the boot. He felt like a lit match.

The Fiesta was now pumping out very fast ceilidh music.

Davud winced as he sat back inside.

'You're hearing me on the pipes and drums!' Duck drummed with the music. 'When the extra snare comes in that'll be me as well! Might as well tie a symbol to my clangers and be done with it. Randy on percussion! Appy on accordion!'

Davud did his best to listen for a moment.

'Bursting for a squirt!' Duck announced. 'Want anything? I'll trouble the Spar for a fruit pastille or two.'

'No. No, thank you.'

Davud watched in the rear mirror as Duck ran towards the shop. He had the look of an extra from *Braveheart* taking the wrong turn into a Marx Brothers revival. Then Duck waved to a car that tooted as it passed. Raised his kilt.

Davud stared ahead to the snow gathering on the windscreen. Lowered the music. Moved his leg away from the rucksack. Duck reappeared in the wing mirror, cradling another large bottle of Coke; a bag of fruit pastilles hanging from his teeth like he was a dog. *Teeth*, thought Davud, multipurpose.

'What a relief.' Duck slumped back into the Fiesta, swiped his gelled and now snowy hair to the side. Davud noticed it was peppered with silver streaks glistening at the sides. Like Duck had been dragged headfirst along the trail of a giant snail.

'There goes my student following . . .'

'Eh?'

'The music?'

'Oh.' Davud gulped. 'Sorry.'

Davud remembered Dervaig plunged into mourning. And with it, Davud's new friend, who he would soon know as Bearfoot.

They took off to join the main road. A heavy jolt came from the driver's side. They slid sideways towards the petrol pump. The car stopped before it.

'Aw, Christ!' Duck unpeeled his chest from the steering wheel. 'Bastard! But I'm okay. I'm okay! You okay?'

Davud attempted the brace position. But his action was interrupted by the seatbelt. He heard the sirens again. He felt his chest burning.

They had hit the side of a car, which had now pulled over in front. Hazards flashing. Davud gripped one hand in the other. Needing flesh. Bone. Something not to slip away. He pulled open his rucksack.

'Lucky!' Duck shook, turning to Davud. 'What you doing?'

'Documenting the crash.' Davud was sketching. 'You might need it.'

‘Ah? Okay . . . keep the Tennent’s out of it.’ Duck gazed in front. ‘Another Fiesta? Though I don’t recognise it . . .’ He looked to the scene emerging on Davud’s page. ‘Bloody hell, lad. That’s good.’ He unfolded himself out of the car. ‘I’ll survey the wider damage. See who we have here.’

‘VT57 6SR,’ Davud said.

‘Eh?’

‘Your numberplate. In case you need it.’

‘Oh aye. Good.’

‘VP94 5PM.’

‘Eh?’ Duck turned again.

‘The other.’

Duck slammed the door and Davud flinched. He watched Duck walking to the other car. It was slate grey, like a reflection of the sky. Duck began a discussion with the driver. Davud saw it was the blonde woman dressed in tweed from the ferry. She was wearing sunglasses now and seemed uncomfortable interacting with Duck. She pointed to the road and nodded efficiently, her actions making it clear she knew the accident was not her fault. Duck removed napkins from his sporran. She produced a pen and they exchanged details. The woman turned away and eased herself back into the car. A hired car, Davud noticed.

The driver’s door opened. Duck flopped inside.

‘Christ, my skull feels like William bloody Wallace has submerged his cleaver in it.’ Duck concentrated on breathing deeply, slowly, as though checking he still could. ‘Okay. Three Hail Marys and a voddy and Coke required . . .’

‘You were at fault for the accident,’ Davud said, closing his sketchbook.

'It was seven fucking years ago! And not my fault.'

'No, no! I meant now.'

'Aw, right. Right. Okay . . . aye.'

'You broke the law by accelerating forwards while looking backwards: *Driving Without Due Care and Attention*.'

'Jesus. Punch can hang up his badge. Actually . . .' Duck looked around them. 'Hope the Lighthouse isn't kicking about. We're on her beat. You know they have a cell here too?'

'A lighthouse, at Craignure?'

'PC Monteith. Legs on her like John bloody Cleese.'

Davud felt like a hypocrite for talking about rules.

Duck read from the CalMac napkin he had scribbled on: 'Mary Shelley, she calls herself. Looked like somebody had pulled her wrong udder.' He threw the napkin to the floor and took hold of the can. 'Let's get out of Dodge before she notices the name I gave her.'

'What?'

'Robbie.'

'Burns?'

'Williams.'

'But you're *not* Robbie Williams.'

'I didn't write "Angels" either, lad, but we might need a few to wing us out of this!'

'Rules matter. For example, they stop one country invading another!'

Duck peered into the thickening snowstorm. Steered them safely onto the road. The other car was still there. Hazards flashing. That surprised Davud, the woman had looked so keen to get away.

'You're hellish jumpity . . .' Duck said.

'I was only in the primary school for one year,' Davud blurted, looking to the coastline. 'We would do field trips to collect shells; you know, at the shore after the church. But I would ask to stay behind. Shells meant something else.'

He gazed to the concrete sky, now fully cloud, imagining they were Sarajevo, and not Dervaig-bound. He had heard his mum screaming in the night. The caravan rocking. Thuds on the walls. Like a war on bricks. And pipes, or had he imagined the pipes? Maybe the scrunched-up napkin made sense. He *did* feel like a monster for what he might be forced to do next. If it did away with himself too, then so be it.

He felt the car being caressed through the gears, echoing the twisting bike throttle. The soundtrack of a mother about to die. He needed to make sure this time it wasn't his.

SCENE XX

THURSDAY

PUNCH PULLED OUT OF THE theatre driveway and swung a left onto the Glen. The task at hand had been hiked up a notch or two by the news of there being two burnt-out cars, both similar sizes by the sounds of it.

The Mull Rally was three months past, but still he was slightly spooked to be driving the Glen in this direction, against the flow of competition traffic. He remembered being taken for the first time to watch the night stages by the man he had thought was his uncle. He was seven; Charlie was not long born. He had grabbed a school jotter to log the cars. It was pure excitement. His uncle had got the start times wrong and when they inadvertently drove in their Ford Anglia 307E across the finishing line of the stage at Dervaig, past the stewards frantically waving, they were actually entering into the live race. Only, in the wrong direction. The intention was to find a spot to park up and spectate on the roadside. Sandwiches, flasks and torches had been packed. Suddenly, the full beams of a car came at them. With the engine's superior roar as accompaniment. It could only mean one thing: they had come face-to-face with a Dervaig bear! Ivor remembered his uncle immediately killing his headlights. Throwing the Ford into reverse and backing up into a quarry. When it was in fact the blurred, otherworldly glisten of the rally leader's car that flew past, Ivor had been deflated.

Punch looked to the radio. His deputy, along with the rest of the world, briefly silenced, held between that void of news and no news. A void he was expected to fill. With reason. Motive. Truth. Culprits. Consequences. To make everything okay again for the island. That was the deal. And why he wore the sergeant's three-stripe chevron on his upper left arm. The longer one. Punch felt not the presence of his uncle next to him, but *she*, or *he*. The lost, almost child.

Dark skies hung above, like the child had gone mad with charcoal. No floating islands evident, nor scent of burning. He checked in the rearview. Briefly, he saw his uncle's Ford in the mirror. A hunched driver. Sideburns. And evidence of a boy in the passenger seat. The head in a book. He recalled how some five years later, a revelation came from his uncle in the old slaughter shed behind the house beside Tobermory graveyard. It was the most words he had ever heard the man use, and those words left him feeling bigger than an ocean. '*I didn't tell you something, lad. I didn't tell you because your father, that prick, was still around. Or in Oban at least. Just a ferry away. What I didn't tell you is . . . I'm your . . . dad. Both of you. But keep calling me uncle. Right.*' Punch looked ahead to the wilderness, expecting hung carcasses, unsure if he had turned the handset completely down or not. But he didn't check. *Over*. It was all. *Over*.

He flew around a corner and hit the brake. Dave the Grave's hearse was parked ahead on the grassy roadside. Gleaming in the gloom. About twenty feet in front of the hearse, there they were. Parked, as Dave had reported, alongside each other and just off the road.

Two burnt-out cars.

The cars were near the opening of a quarry. Punch recognised it as *the* quarry. As with everything of childhood, it was smaller than he remembered. It was there that they had stayed for hours, spectating on the full night stage. All he remembered were the first few cars, then waking up in his bed the next morning and, as if by magic, all the car number plates had been documented in his book, but not by his hand.

Punch pulled in behind Dave's hearse.

Dave emerged from the vehicle. Punch could see the undertaker's trainee sitting in the passenger seat. Still head. *Not too bloody still*, Punch hoped. There were rumours of Dave transporting the dead in this way.

'Sergeant,' Dave acknowledged, making a small drama of ensuring his black raincoat was securely, correctly buttoned. His black trousers had the usual silk seam down their sides. His black shoes, despite having walked the scene already, were as reflective as a monarch's mirror. Punch observed Dave's bald head as somehow even more noticeably egg-shaped.

'Dave.' Punch took a roll-up from behind his ear and used his hands to shield the lighting of it. Increasingly, the length of his roll-ups was reflective of whichever Mull road he had travelled.

'Oaf, come-come. I see you're still discolouring your lungs, sergeant?'

'Aye, Dave. Have you any spare?'

'Well, I do keep one or two in the freezer, sergeant. But not an easy procedure. Though this World Wide Web helps. Slow on the dial-up, though.'

'Christ, Dave. I was joking.'

'Teeth too. Dentistry's easy enough in fact.'

Punch looked at Dave, inhaled deeply. He pointed his smoking hand to the cars. 'Guinness updated about there being two of them. Anything else amiss?'

'No.' Dave shook. 'Just as well, coffin supplies are low. Heavy winter. But whatever's happened here, somebody didn't want so much as an eyelash left behind. I've had a decent scour.'

'Fiestas, I'd say,' Punch said.

'Oaf, I'm not so sure, sergeant. Maybe best not to jump to conclusions.'

Punch decided to let the comment go, but he had noted it. He walked towards the cars. 'Nothing's been touched?'

'No, sergeant.'

'How's the lad?'

'Billy? Oaf, a bit – what is it they say nowadays – *anti-social*. Been quieter these last few weeks. Wasn't exactly Stephen Fry to begin with.'

'Think he'd been hit by a tranquiliser dart . . .' Punch turned seriously to Dave. 'He hasn't, has he?'

'Eh?'

'Dave?'

'No. No, sergeant!'

'Right. Uh-ha.'

'He's promising on the cryogenics though, the lad. Does a lot of study in his spare time.'

‘The what?’

‘It’s the practice of freezing an entire human body after death, sergeant. In the hope of later restoring to life. Oaf, it’s all the rage on the mainland.’

Punch shook his head as he walked around the cars. ‘No hint of identifying colours, markings?’

‘Not a sausage.’ Dave arrived alongside Punch with both arms straight down by his sides. ‘You’ll be arresting Ansel Adams, sergeant.’

‘Both registration plates totally charred.’ Punch puffed. He looked around at the surrounding landscape. Thankfully, the snow hadn’t settled. He peered into one of the cars. ‘Talk about travelling light.’

‘Shells. Both of them. I’ve seen bodies look like this, sergeant. I’ve had a scout up the hill and into the woodland. But nothing.’

‘Appreciated, Dave, but I can’t have you disturbing anything.’

‘Gracefully done, sergeant. Got the memo.’

‘Both handbrakes are engaged,’ Punch said, now looking into the other car. ‘And no skid marks evident. Doesn’t look like any form of accident.’

‘And both facing the same way, sergeant. Quite the dance.’

‘Uh-ha.’ Punch walked around the cars. Looked again to the horizon. Thursday night wasn’t far from falling.

‘Christ,’ Dave said, leaning closer to the charred bodywork. ‘Here? Sergeant?’

‘What?’

‘Do you see what I see?’

‘What, Dave?’

‘A face.’

'Eh?' Punch removed his head from the car.

'Francis Bacon. On the driver's door panel?'

'Who?'

'The artist. His famous self-portrait as if recreated? Made by fire. Do you not see it?'

Punch shook his head. Had no idea what Dave was talking about. He took a deep draw, feeling a little inferior; next thing, Dave would be seeing Fidel Castro.

'No more distractions, Dave.'

'Right. Right.'

Punch was never sure what was going to come out of the undertaker's mouth next, but the man seemed jumpy, jumpier than usual. Though Dave knew how to effectively clean up a body better than anyone else he had ever worked with.

Punch kneeled to look underneath one of the cars.

'It's almost as if the bodies are *invisible*, sergeant.'

'Why do you say *bodies*, Dave?' Punch stood, kicked around the ground with his boot. He looked to Dave, who was also Grand Master in the island's Masons, as well as president of the one-man band that was the Mull Historical Society.

'Because there's two cars, *Ivor*?'

'Aye,' puffed Punch. 'Remember I'm in uniform.'

Dave stuck his head into the second car. 'Can't help thinking it's a metaphor for life, sergeant. Or death.'

'I give up . . .'

'All you're left with is the steering wheel.'

'Some don't even get that.' Punch took a longer draw. The lockup came back to mind. The image of a dress or trousers floating in the sea.

The radio erupted from the Ranger.

'Oaf, it's the understudy!' Dave said, spinning to face the police car. 'Still trying to upstage the leading man, eh, sergeant?'

'Given half a chance, Dave.' Punch nodded as he passed the hearse, the theatre terminology not lost on him. 'You'll discover the same, no doubt.'

'Not so easy to "shift-erase" our deputies, eh?'

Punch had no idea what Dave was on about. He leaned into the Ranger and took the radio from its unit. New compliance laws from Head Office were now requiring all officers across Strathclyde Legacy Division to keep their radios on their person for entire shifts. He had no doubt Cluny kept his under his pillow. But for as long as Mull, sub-division of Strathclyde Lima Bravo, was under his jurisdiction, he would do things his way.

'LB sub-division! Do you receive? Over! L747 to . . .'

'Come in, PC! What's going on?'

The radio signal crackled expectantly.

'Christ. *Over!*' Punch's only relief was that the rest of Lima Bravo weren't in on this word salad.

'*Sarge. It just went to answerphone at the theatre, but I did some additional digging. There* is *actually a production coming up. Tomorrow. Friday. Over.*'

'Right? Over.' He wasn't about to tell Cluny he had just been there; had seen the poster on the theatre door. Also, that he knew how to recognise the days of the week.

'The Looming. *About the relationship between man and island, if I can fathom. Over.*'

Punch walked back to the cars, and Dave, who had returned from the roadside and was doing up his fly. He watched Dave's Adam's apple rise and settle, like he was housing the internal workings of a toilet system.

‘It’s a very satisfying thing, sergeant, to direct urine successfully.’

‘I better get on, Dave. I’ve two cars to find homes for.’

‘Of course. I’m on the mobile if you need me.’ Dave made a small theatre once more, this time of waving his new device. ‘Oh . . .’ He moved to Punch and handed him a card. ‘Now updated the business cards with the number.’

‘Right. I hear there’s not much signal to be had in any case. Better with two cans on a string they’re saying.’

‘Oaf, a mere pimple on the backside of progress, sergeant.’

‘That’s one name for Ben More.’ Punch nodded to the hearse. ‘He’s chatty? You taken on Harpo Marx?’

Dave the Grave shook his head. ‘Oaf, he’s running a fever. I’ll get him home with me. Get some immune-system-enhancing drops inside him.’ Dave leaned to Punch, lowered his voice. ‘Seems an overreaction, to be honest.’

‘Well, I’ve cuffs if you need them.’

‘Also looking at some tattoo laser removal kit for him, sergeant. Off the World Wide Web. From Utah, by Christ!’

‘Didn’t have Donny Osmond down as a tattoo man.’

‘Ah, the use of humour, sergeant. Helpful as you try to secure the guy ropes for the rapidly changing, billowing tent that is contemporary Mull.’

‘Sure the uniform helps. Though my mother’s dementia wouldn’t agree. Sometimes I could strangle her.’

‘You know the evidence of strangulation shows up in one unexpected place?’

‘I was kidding, Dave. Christ.’

‘The eyes.’ Dave looked to the burnt-out cars.

‘Right, Dave.’

'We'll *dare to be honest and fear no labour*,' Dave said, turning back to Punch.

'Eh?'

'Burns. Will you be attending the production tomorrow, sergeant?'

'Something tells me I might be busy.'

Dave dipped into the hearse and Punch saw the undertaker turn and say something to his deputy as he applied his seatbelt. The vehicle pulled away. A right-hand indicator blinked, followed by hazards. A tad overblown, thought Punch; the man was to red tape what Gazza was to off-licences.

Punch looked into the emerging gloom. There was something that Dave hadn't mentioned, possibly a missing piece in the puzzle that was bothering him. Billy's rally car was nowhere to be seen. Maybe the lad had gone to Dave and back out again. Strange though, if he was unwell.

He walked over and into the quarry. Saw something on the ground. It had clearly escaped Dave. It was positioned where the old Ford would have once purred and a boy of seven, jotter on his lap, having noticed the moon for the first time amid thoughts of seeing roaming bears, succumbed to golden slumbers. Was it really it, still here, after all these years?

SCENE XXI

WEDNESDAY

A THUD.

'You bastard!' Duck dropped his Coke bottle and criss-crossed his arms on the wheel. The car swerved and skidded.

Davud bolted back in his seat. Gripped the seatbelt. Waited for the outsides to cold wash his skin. Saw his father's clothes become flame. Felt his legs frantically searching for concrete. His mother lifting him away. He folded into the brace position. 'Standard procedure in any accident! Standard procedure in any accident!'

The Fiesta slid off the side of the road to a stop. The music still blaring.

Davud slammed it off.

'What. The. Fuck. NOW!?' Duck held his ribs, swivelled around. 'Think I hit something? Did I hit something?'

Davud looked up to see not snipers, but Duck. Coke dripping from his chin. Up ahead, on the side of the road, he saw an irregular white lump in the snow.

'A lamb.' Davud pointed.

'A lamb? Christ . . . Fuck this journey for a caper!'

Davud saw not the lamb, but Vatra. He had recently looked for his friend on the tube in Glasgow. He hadn't told his mum about it. That he'd seen the tall woman, dressed in black, walking the carriages with a hat outstretched. She'd been gently lowering it towards people. A fellow passenger had dropped coins into it. When she'd got to him, he knew her. It was Vatra's mum. But she looked different, dirty and like she was still in the war. She'd quickly withdrawn the hat from him. Then got off at the next stop.

Davud took his sketchbook from the rucksack.

'We're fine. Fine.' Duck eased himself up in the seat, caressed his sides. 'Could be a rib. What's next? Eddie the Eagle had more fucking luck.'

Duck made a brief attempt at rubbing the stains off his kilt and then swung his bare legs into the cold air. Davud remembered Duck had been wearing jeans for the jumps. *Lees*. Everybody wore Lees.

'One of MacTavish's flock no doubt,' Duck said.

'Why do you keep coming to the caravan?'

Duck looked ahead. Gulped and shook his head. 'Early season for a lamb, is it not?'

'To me the night you killed her was like Vatra had been crushed. All over again. My mum even went along with it. We walked down to the football pitch to make sure, but the route was blocked with police tape. Flowers were already there. I thought bomb craters might be on the football pitch; the main street nothing but rubble . . .'

Duck rubbed around his back. 'Kidneys took a hit I think.'

'On the way back we passed your motorbike outside the

Bellachroy. Then soon after I saw your Bruce Lee jacket in the caravan.'

'Somebody said a kidney stone can be passed quicker if you ride a rollercoaster!' Duck managed. 'Right enough.'

He exited hastily and slammed the door closed. Davud watched him stumble up the side of the road, keeling forwards, the Sound of Mull in the distance. Duck's thick socks were gathered at his ankles like an Olympic hammer thrower. His calves white as the snow. Davud watched as the light made a halo of Duck's head. That was how he had once thought of him.

He checked the milometer: *4.9 miles*.

Maybe Duck was trying to kill *him*? Maybe he was working for Bearfoot too?

Davud looked to Duck's kilt having a dance with the wind. The motorbike hero was now the size of his index finger. Reduced, like Lismore lighthouse. Davud had never felt so powerful, so ready for action. He watched as Duck bent down to the lamb. It was time. He needed the goods in place. Davud removed the four packaged blocks from his rucksack. He held one up to his ear. No ticking. Each one had ties attached to it. He'd thought instead about putting them in the boot. Would them being closer to the petrol be a bonus? But he'd better do as he'd been told.

He manoeuvred himself into a kneeling position on the floor. He reached and fastened a block underneath each of the car seats. He brought his head up. Swiped back his hair. Duck was still up ahead, facing the other way. Davud stretched into the back and put the other two blocks under the mats below the back seats. He got back into the passenger seat. His forehead was sweating.

He had managed to keep it secret from Duck, but he'd been well aware the piper would be performing in Glasgow the night before, near his halls. He had been tipped off by Bearfoot. He'd stood outside the hotel venue and heard the pipes even from the entrance. He had made sure to be on the same ferry.

Given the threats he had received, he told himself he was only doing what was needed to keep his mum alive. Following truth. Being an architect. Bearfoot had said it would get Duck's piss off his floor. To make room again for his real dad. Their old life.

The bombs were now in place.

SCENE XXII

WEDNESDAY

'CLANDESTINE ENOUGH?' Ludo Merriweather pinched his suit trousers at the crease as he eased himself into the car. 'So, I purposefully avoided you on the ship, but stopped just short of disguises. Freezing!'

'So, no Wee Jimmy hat?'

'Wee, what?'

'Ah, don't worry. And they call it a ferry.' Annie refixed her sunglasses. 'Happy Wednesday.'

'Maybe kill the hazard lights? Or am I being paranoid? I feel like James Bond.' Ludo placed his overnight bag on his lap. 'Nice to see you.' He gripped her hand at the gearstick. His fingers in ski gloves. 'But not so happy for you. How you holding up, dear?'

'The upside is I think you're safe enough with me today. As in, to take away any potential Westminster, or local, heat, suspicion, that our visit might arouse . . .'

'Oh, Annie – was there not *another* verb?' Ludo turned sympathetically to her. His expression worthy of a pantomime.

'I asked for that. Didn't see alpine skiing on the itinerary?'

Ludo raised his large gloves. 'Bond. Remember?' He turned away. 'So I heard the headline of the affair on *Today* in the limo up to Oban. Frightful timing. Or . . .?'

'Safe place to hide . . .? I hope so. But does that make me Miss Moneypenny, or Q?'

'Surely, you're a Bond girl?'

'I'll take that. Talking of which, how's Liv?'

'Sends hugs. She's still on maternity. No sleep for either of us . . .'

'I hear kids will do that to you.' Annie looked around the pier, now tranquil after the bustle of the ferry arriving and departing. It was to be her second attempt to leave Craignure within ten minutes. 'Well, there's been a few, my dear Ludo, but this one takes the biscuit for days you wished your parents had practised birth control. Bloody hell.'

'Gosh.' Ludo buckled up. 'I'm sorry this has befallen you, dear Annie!' He took her hand again. 'Let's try and cheer you up.'

'Toilet stop?'

'Taken care of on the ferry. Once a civil servant, always a . . .'

Annie indicated and drove the car onto the main road.

Salen 11 miles.

'So you've seen the tabloids too?' she said. 'Never been so terrified to enter a ferry shop.'

'Enough of that rubbish. Unless you need to talk?'

'Nope.'

'Have you gone through the Mull report?'

'*Asylum: the Nuclear Option.*' Annie nodded. 'I did. Remind me not to leave it lying around the island's tearooms.'

‘Hmm. Yes, I did argue for a, let us say, more *forgiving* title.’ Ludo made fine adjustments to his silver quiff as he looked to the glistening sea. ‘My secretary checked if I could fly here . . .’

‘There’s a private airfield. I flew in once years ago. *Lussa Falls*. Not far from here, if I remember rightly. It’s got a habit of losing planes.’

‘In any case, the Highland air is a welcome distraction. As secret missions go, the location could not be finer. London feels so strangled in winter.’

‘Thought we could’ve been here and away in a day. But frankly, given the headlines, I’m now quite thankful of the night away.’

‘Flight from London was delayed, then a wretched sleep last night in Glasgow. Were the, what do you call it again, the Glasgow footy teams playing each other or something? Frightful din all night.’

‘The Old Firm. No. And “footy” isn’t advisable. Nor “rugger”.’

‘Memo received. Though I’m a cricket man. Afraid I tick all the clichés. Boarding school. Oxbridge. Father was a civil servant too.’

‘Aye, a Wee Jimmy hat wouldn’t be next on that list. You haven’t heard?’

Ludo turned to Annie and shook his head. ‘There’s more?’

‘No. Not me this time. Glasgow School of Art. Burned down last night. That was the commotion you heard.’

‘Really? I didn’t hear. Must have dozed off in the car?’

‘Aye, after you heard the juicy bits . . .’

‘Arson?’

‘They don’t seem to know yet.’

'On the upside . . .'

'It keeps the heat off me? Copy that. Well, at least bumps me further down the headlines.'

'Isn't it awful how we're trained to think? Or was it always in us?'

'Nurture or nature?'

'One way of describing Tony and Gordon.'

'Getting brave now you're six hundred miles away?' Annie swept a hand through her blonde fringe. Looked in the direction of the mainland, its bulk lurking like paparazzi on the other side of the Sound of Mull.

'First Minister?'

'He's saying all the right things, thankfully. For now.'

'Right. Good-o.'

'Funny – people always suspect I play for the other side . . .'

'We're not still talking foo—?'

'Not football.'

'No.' Ludo patted down his coat. 'We miss you at Westminster. But devolved you are!'

'Devolved, to Mull now, yes.'

'My first time in the Hebrides.' Ludo looked around. 'Different light, for sure. Ah, a golf course. Never played. You?'

'I might be playing more now . . . and getting my triathlon time down.'

'It'll blow over. Events, my dear, will come to the rescue. Always do. The FM likes you?'

'He does. Jury's out on Blair, though. I know Gordon better is the problem. Pinned my clothing to the wrong mast.'

'I like Gordon. He's a decent man. Blair is of course surface level, but hugely gifted strategically.'

'Not that I'm complaining now – but remind me why you needed me here and not my spad?'

'You need to see the planned site, Annie. Tony is keen on the policy. Or at least in us sounding it out. If Devolution is to work, both him and Gordon want to see the administration owning it. We would set the policy at Westminster, but you folks will be responsible for running it.'

'I can never tell if we're sailing closer to Independence or further away.'

'Yes, the *settled will* and all that. Poor John Smith is buried up this way, of course. I was thinking about him on the ferry.'

'Lovely man. At peace among the saints. Iona is in the opposite direction. Though I don't think Columba was navigating in a Ford Fiesta.'

'I sat on the upper deck, as instructed.'

'At least you didn't call it "chamber".'

Ludo took in the surrounds, his expression turned pained. 'I hate to pull the wool over these folks' eyes. If these are the protests for a wind farm, can you imagine the stick for an asylum seekers' camp?'

'My point exactly.'

Ludo checked his phone.

'Good luck with that.'

'Flicker on the ferry, but dead as a doorknob now . . .'

Annie slowed down as they approached a car which was angled off the side of the road. She wasn't about to offer help for fear of drawing attention. Her mug on the front cover of every bloody Scottish newspaper was more than enough already. Thank God for the art school conflagration. As she passed the car, she saw the man who had shunted her earlier. He was walking back to his vehicle. Fair to say Take That were not known for traditional Highland dress. Two could play that game. She'd plucked the nom de plume she'd given him from her reading pile. Trying to get through the classics again. Though now she was starting to see it as some form of premonition.

'My first kilt spot!' enthused Ludo. 'All I need now is Mel Gibson and I've won the office sweep. Should we stop?'

'Eh, best we don't, don't you think?'

'Oh? Quite right. Yes.'

Annie stole a glance to the man, who acknowledged their passing.

'Did that man just wave to us with a sheep in his hand?' Ludo asked, turning to her, mouth ajar.

'We had better talk policy,' Annie said. 'If we're to be convincing at the public meeting. Before we see the site too.'

'Right-o.' Ludo removed his gloves and opened his bag. He took out some files and rested them on his lap, being careful not to interrupt his trouser seam.

'Schoolboy error,' Annie teased. 'The overnight bag.'

'I see. Rucksack would've been more *not-from-the-civil-service-about-to-mess-up-your-island* chattel?'

Annie stole a glance at his paperwork. *Office of the Minister of State for Asylum and Immigration: Barbara Roche.*

'So I'm doing Barb's dirty work, eh?'

'Welcome to devolution . . .' Ludo turned to her and smiled; he waved a hand. 'The Home Office have been leaning rather heavily, mercifully.'

Annie angled her head. 'So . . . send the Scottish Minister for Pubs 'n' Hooses, who has no power to make policy, but all the willingness to play Jenga with the Mull locals?'

Ludo turned sheepishly to Annie. 'But the PM will be *so* appreciative.' He performed a well-honed jut of his head to lower his reading glasses from the top of his head to his nose. 'And so it goes: *Sending asylum seekers to holding camps on the Scottish island of Mull and removing them to "safe havens" in third-party countries such as Turkey, South Africa and Kenya, is among the "nuclear options" considered by the Cabinet.*'

'And by "Cabinet", we mean Blair, Brown and Alastair fucking Campbell.' Annie kept her eyes on the road.

'Now-now. It goes on: *This "big bang" solution has been muted following PM's expressed frustration that "ever tougher controls" in northern France have failed. At Cabinet, he insisted, "We must search out even more radical measures to tackle the growing number of asylum claims."*'

'Remind me of the numbers?'

Ludo turned to her, peering over his rims. 'To the end of last month, they've reached six thousand two hundred. Higher than projected.'

'When we first had the brainstorming session with the government advisers last spring, I honestly thought it was an April fool. An asylum seekers' camp on Mull? And made only worse now that the locals think it's a renewable energy policy? Wait till the Mulleachs find out plans are afoot to detain people here till they can be returned.'

'Well, they themselves have jumped to that conclusion, in fairness. The Attorney General's office is behind it, Annie.'

'We've never been strong here, but even if it doesn't become policy, if word gets out, we can forget ever getting a candidate over the line here again.'

'Mulleachs, or Mullahs?'

'The premise being, given Mull is an island, people who come here by sea will have by definition already passed through a safe country?'

'Exactly. And very few of those who apply at airports are genuine refugees.' Ludo removed his glasses. '*Salen*, *Tobermory*,' he read off the signage. 'I'm under great duress from my kids to bring home something with a Womble on it.'

'*Refugee* Wombles next. CalMac as Border Security? Fuck! And I read the PM made reference to the successes of the Australian system, to them holding asylum seekers in camps before returning them?'

'I haven't said this aloud as yet, but I seriously doubt that it is going to work because of the NIMBY factor . . .'

'Not in my back yard.' Annie waved to the surrounds. 'Or croft.'

'No, the landowner is keen.'

'It'll deepen his pockets, that's for sure. Though masquerading first as an environmental policy. Really? I seriously question this tack, Ludo.'

'Wind farm is a long way from refugee camp. I know, I know. But baby steps is the advice— '

'From whom? Putin?'

'It's proposed the land will indeed be reworked into an environmentally friendly policy. That's how we're selling it. And it's true.'

'File under "Guantanamo . . . " This could seriously backfire up here. This is now SNP country.'

'Look!' Ludo pointed, as they exited Salen. 'Two ruined boats. Liv has always wanted to live on a houseboat on the Thames. Perhaps I could sell her this. We do adore Powell and

Pressburger's *I Know Where I'm Going* – it was filmed here.'

'There's the tagline for the camp.'

At a sign for Aros Bridge, Annie carried on straight, following the signage for Dervaig.

'*Dervaig*,' Ludo read. '*Eleven miles*. Getting close. This is the bellwether test. When policy either jumps off the page or is consigned to the Cabinet shredder. Would you believe we've gone so far as commissioning work to look at tagging, detention?'

'Won't fly.' Annie wiped around her eyes.

Ludo turned to her: 'Do you love him?'

Annie let out a deep sigh. She pushed her sunglasses to the top of her brow. 'I don't honestly know. It was . . . I'm just . . . numb.'

'At least there's no children involved.'

'Look, the main problem with removals is the courts.'

'Exactly. They will not let us return them to countries where they might be at risk.'

'How about *regional safe havens*, managed by the UNHCR?' Annie waved to the wilderness. 'Then we would be able to return Iraqi asylum seekers to a centre in Turkey, Zimbabweans to a centre in South Africa, Somalis to a centre in Kenya . . . Bosnians to Italy, and so on.'

'I'm sceptical that such host countries would be willing.'

'Ludo, we'd almost certainly lose this case when it got to Strasbourg.'

'But we'd have two to three years in the meantime when we could send a strong message into the system about our new tough stance.'

'I get it. *He-man* Blair.'

'Big pants an' all,' Ludo said.

'He'd have to borrow Gordon's.'

'You speak from experience?'

'Despite reports, I'm a good Catholic girl . . .' Her phone bleeped. Annie leaned down to her handbag. 'Talking of which. My mother. Again.' She dropped her phone in the bag. 'Here's hoping for no signal. *Ever. Again.*'

Ludo gestured to the snowy hilltops. 'Who knew we would turn wind into money?'

'Remind me of the croft owner's name? The one we're about to dupe here on behalf of our salesman, I mean, our PM?'

'Lennox. A Mr Len Lennox.'

SCENE XXIII

WEDNESDAY

DAVUD WAS ALONE IN THE car with the bombs. Each now hidden and in place. But when, and how, did they go off? Bearfoot hadn't explained that part. Had he missed the instruction from the girl in Oban? Despite the cold, his palms were sweating. He'd lost the spit in his mouth. The pulse in his ear sounded like it was coming from his conscience. His mum.

He saw Duck, out ahead, holding the carcass by its neck. Duck quickly circled as though about to toss the lamb. But he didn't. Davud could tell Duck was embarrassed he hadn't been able to do it. Maybe also worried about passing traffic seeing him. *You are never that far away*, his mother had said when he first went off to the art school. But he knew she hadn't meant from Dervaig, or the island.

Davud thought again of the day after Duck killed his own mother; school had still been on. All the children had been taken into rooms to make sure they spoke about how they felt. Before the home bell, he'd gone to the football pitch, this time on his own, sneaking through the woods to avoid the police tape. He had waded through rock pools, dunes and hideaway places where his mother would pick winkles by the ocean. It was then he'd seen the boy in school who he had never spoken to but whose face that day had itself been like a flame. The boy who would become Bearfoot. He was turning a corner further around the coastline. With what looked like long sticks in his hands. Even from a distance, he already spoke a language Davud understood. Not English, nor Bosnian, but a kind of *truth*. Davud had recognised something else in the boy – death now surrounded him too.

Davud racked his brains for any other detonation instructions the woman at Oban pier might have given him. She had been behind the counter at one of the shellfish cabins. That was where Bearfoot had told him to go. 'Collection point,' he'd called it. She had looked to him like all Oban girls: otherworldly, Roman-nosed, porcelain-skinned.

'Can I help, lovie?' she'd asked, after unlocking, then opening the cabin door. 'Buying, or . . .' She'd looked him up and down. 'Deliveries?'

'Toilet,' he'd blurted, before he could stop himself. He had meant to go on the train.

'Use the station ones.' She'd signalled, her bangles performing a landslide. 'Then come back and see me. Okay?'

Davud had nodded and then done as instructed. He'd thought about just running for the ferry. But he had said he would do it. Needed to do it. A pact was a pact. Architects were all about delivery. He'd returned to the cabin and knocked on the door again.

'Right?' she'd said. 'Come away in. Name, hun?'

'Eh, *Leonardo*,' he'd offered, again, as instructed. 'Bearfoot said I'd to say that.'

She'd smiled, nodded. 'Deliveries. Overseas.' She'd ushered him inside and locked the door behind them. She'd looked impossible to shock. Like you could tell her your dad had been burned alive and she would just flash her fake eyelashes back at you.

'Your first time, Leonardo?'

Davud nodded. Then grew more alarmed. 'What? Is this sex?'

'Awe . . . cute. But no. Rightio . . .' she sang into a computer screen. 'Okay. So I see you have a bag already, so we're in business.' She spoke so quickly Davud had felt it was like a whole orchestra was falling out of her mouth. She had gone to a back room and then returned with four packages. Then motioned for him to put his rucksack on the counter.

'So you know where these are going, don't you?'

Davud had nodded.

'And you know it's very important they get there, don't you?'

'Yes. Yeah.'

'But what you might not have been told is that if they *don't* arrive at their destination, you can forget ever walking again. Your friend provided your proper name and your address. We know who you are, *okay*? And where your caravan is. Okay, lovie? And we know who lives there with you. Your ferry is waiting. Safe travels.'

'Are they bombs?' he'd managed.

'If that helps you take extra good care of them, lovie, then yes. Remember what I said about the, eh, *consequences*, David.'

She had unlocked the door and he'd darted for the ferry. It was there, as expected, he'd spotted Duck's car in the ferry queue.

Davud looked to Duck, now walking towards him with the dead lamb. He remembered there had been a gathering outside Dervaig village hall the night of the death. Police cars parked at angles. He had never seen a village attempt to become a city before; he had expected everyone to be speaking Bosnian, and he wondered if he still could. His mother had only spoken English to him since they had left, which felt like another act of war. Then, soon, the Bruce Lee jacket was part of the caravan.

The next morning, the headteacher had said that anybody feeling sad could go to a teacher, *must* go to a teacher. And Davud had wondered why that was never said to him before. He had heard crying coming from a corner of the playground. The boy he would later see around the coastline from the pitch. He would discover this boy also saw patterns and order in the things most people on the island seemed to ignore; a boy who in fact ran not with sticks along the coastline, but with animal bones. And with whom Davud would fall face down on the sand by the caves, trying to make the shapes of bears. The boy who said he knew what it felt like to lose somebody special too; and that Davud could even call him 'Vatra' if he wanted to. Soon after, he and Bearfoot formed their own club to reach the dead. Because that made them feel less guilty about being alive. *Architects of the Post-Truth World.*

The boy would tell Davud that he didn't like how his father had treated his mother. The island, too. That he could never forgive his dad, nor his brother. So he and Davud – Bearfoot and Leonardo – might have to design their demise.

Davud looked to Duck, now slowly jog-wobbling towards him. A car passed. Duck gestured to it. It was the woman's car. The one pretending to be the author. But it didn't stop. The dead lamb's neck hung with all the dignity of a white plastic bag from the village Spar. For a second Davud saw it as the motorbike helmet. He realised that was part of the mystery of the memory of both jumps: Duck hidden in the helmet. Removed. Like a jousting knight. Davud watched as Duck took a roll-up from behind his ear. The caravan toilet always had stubs floating in the bowl.

The driver's door opened.

'No damage to her.' Duck leaned on the outside. 'The Phantom Blue, I mean. The lamb, not so lucky.'

'Okay.' Davud rubbed his eyes and pushed his heavy hair back. He had run the night before from the music venue on Sauchiehall Street to the student halls at St George's Cross, to grab his rucksack. And from there to Duck's hotel. Then to Queen Street station, to await the first train to Oban.

'I'd better survey the back . . .' Duck said.

Davud watched as Duck moved slowly around the outside of the car in a crouched position, like a matador might size up a phantom blue bull. He drew a single tree in the condensation on his side window. Making it blend with the forest alongside the road. Tears were running down his face. He felt completely disconnected, out of proportion with his surroundings.

Duck collapsed back inside. Pulled the door behind him. Yawned and closed his eyes.

'I hope I have a course to go back to,' Davud said. He looked to Duck, who was so still. He nervously reached to touch him, to check all this was real like a dog assessing a statue. But then he pulled away.

'It was the next morning in school, you know, after. That I first spoke to the boy, to *anyone*,' Davud managed. 'He became my friend. Said the dead body wasn't Vatra. It was his mother. That he was . . .'

'My brother.' Duck slowly nodded. 'Fuck.'

'That his name was William, but I was to call him something else.'

'Billy.'

Davud wanted to say 'Bearfoot', but he knew he couldn't break the pact.

SCENE XXIV

THURSDAY

'CAME JUST AS SOON AS my body was embalmed, sergeant.'

'Eh?' Punch scanned the undertaker up and down. '*Your* body, Dave?'

'Oaf! Now that would be macabre!'

The two men had reconvened back on the Glen, beside the burnt-out cars.

Dave elaborated: 'I received a delivery last night. Still got a bit more to do on the fellow. I prefer their faces to be smiling, you know. Best way to arrive to St Peter. A tourist down the Ross. Keeled over outside the church.'

'Considerate.' Punch took a deep draw. Kicked at the snow, barely settling. 'I've heard nothing my end about that. Though Monteith's been off, otherwise she'd be all over it. We'll need to do the paperwork.'

'The Lighthouse on her hols?'

'Longest wedding in history. You'd think the Corleones were native to Strontian. And fuck.'

'So you wanted Forensics, sergeant? I'm here.'

'Aye, well, you know we'll need to go down official police lines too, Dave. But I think there's more to unearth here.' Punch wanted to check whether Dave was withholding information. 'Control have suggested a different approach, given the terrain. I've sent Cluny to collect a Professor Strathclyde from off the ferry at Craignure.'

'None taken, sergeant. Strathclyde? The noted botanist! Oaf, I've already read up on her.'

'Her?'

'I perused her profile on the World Wide Web. Have you been on?'

'Next they'll be solving crimes on *Gardener's World*.'

'So – it's a crime scene? Official?'

Punch was struck by Dave's response. The poor attempt at alarm. He looked to the fading light. He was frustrated at having no real leads. What he had thought was a jotter hadn't been his. What he had found at the quarry was a sketchbook. Intricate drawings, the work of quite a talent, but with no obvious indicators as to who it belonged to. Buildings, ferries, train times and a man on fire. Maybe some superhero CalMac gubbins. Certainly niche, but you never knew these days what shite folk could get off on. Some mumbo-jumbo on the first page about, *Architects of the Post-Truth World*. The book had been photographed, wrapped in an incident bag and readied for brushing. Guinness was good for something. Finding people's mistakes was what solved crimes, not what weeds they had stepped on. Next they'd be giving Monty bloody Don three chevrons.

Cold cases kept him awake at night, drifting into nightmares of being left behind holding Rod's tartan-themed luggage on runways.

'Sergeant?' Dave pressed. 'The Internet? You been on?'

'Eh? No, no, Dave.' Punch gazed to where the moors became sky. He could always tell when the mainland was coming. As though the light adjusted by way of warning.

'Oaf, the net certainly brings Oban closer ... no doubting it.'

'That's the first mistake Bill Gates made.'

Punch looked to the charred cars. Numberplates and all other forms of recognition erased. Like two bodies rendered soulless. He followed his cold breath towards the quarry.

'From what I can gather, her method is to use the evidence of plant life from the scene of a crime to reveal leads,' Dave said. 'I've read she'll stand at a crime scene and close her eyes to try and *smell* the evidence. The woman is to forensic botany what Hugh Grant is to bumbling bookworms.'

'I think we're closer to funerals than weddings here. All you're missing is a violinist and a bouquet of flowers, Dave.'

An engine approached. Both men momentarily succumbed to the familiar expectation of a rally car about to fly over the brow of the hill. Punch remembered how that sense of excitement only grew in his later childhood years, when he and Charlie – by then old enough to accompany them – would sit on the bank of a hill in the cloak of night out here with their uncle, who by then Ivor knew was not their uncle. One of those times, they had the visiting cousin with them again. The same boy who had humiliated him on the cinema cycle. It was on that visit Ivor had become aware, when overhearing a conversation between his mother and uncle-who-he-was-not-to-call-his-father, that the lad was not in fact his cousin. On the hillside they had sat in the darkness surrounded by drunk men who could not be seen but only heard and smelled, keenly awaiting the first, faint impressions of headlights, of engine roar. The men would recount tales of the Dervaig bears, goaded by Ivor's cousin, who he was beginning to further resent for somehow getting between him and Charlie by showing off his nascent moustache to the younger boy by torchlight. 'Taller than the Bellachroy!' the men would claim. His cousin – by then sporting a Led Zeppelin mane – had then stood to loudly reenact the animal, clawing Ivor as he fell on him. Ivor had wet himself in the darkness.

Punch shook his head free from the past. Relieved to be in the uniform of the present. He was one of those men now.

The white, yellow and blue of Cluny's Ford, not Anglia, but Ranger, appeared around the bend like a vision of the future, slowing down as it approached the men and the two cars. Punch noted the passenger alongside his deputy.

'Kingfishers, sergeant . . .' Dave said.

'Eh?'

'Numbers are on the rise this year out here in the Glen.'

'Right. I've my hand on the cuffs, Dave.'

'I mean, this woman will be able to link that to crime numbers, just watch.'

Cluny engaged his hazard lights as he pulled over.

All overblown, thought Punch. He preferred to impress by doing less than might be expected of him in any given situation.

The blond flash of Cluny jumped from the Ranger and jogged around its rear. Punch suspected the lad was about to put a nail in the coffin of feminism's second wave. All that was missing was a red carpet rolled under his arm. Cluny opened the back door and Punch saw a woman with grey, bobbed hair step out. He had her in her early fifties, nimble, slim and in a black, close-fitting outdoor pursuit jacket. Boots up to her knees. Helen Mirren wasn't a bad shout.

'Professor Lydia Strathclyde, Forensic Ecologist,' Dave purred into Punch's ear. Not an actress, then. 'Saw her quoted in *Kidnapping & Ransom Monthly*. Been a fan, I mean, subscriber, ever since.'

''Pete's sake, Dave.'

'Oaf, it'll be a suite in the Western Isles Hotel for this one, sergeant. None of your room-in-the-Mishnish gubbins. No toasties and chips here. Soupe de poissons à la bretonne!'

Punch moved uncharacteristically quickly towards the woman and an emerging Cluny. His immediate concern being if he didn't, then he might have to issue Dave a restraining order, followed by a night of Rod's eighties material.

'Eh, hello,' Punch said, standing about five feet away from the woman, deciding against extending his arm. Always a dilemma.

Lydia Strathclyde smiled forcibly at Punch, her heavily kohled eyes barely open. He was about ready to write up a caution to her cheekbones.

She walked towards the cars.

'Lydia needs quiet, Sarge,' Cluny said, holding a black bag that presumably belonged to the woman. 'Often tricky to come by at a crime scene. Prefers not to speak at first. I'll take Crime Scene Manager?'

Punch looked searingly to his deputy-cum-bellboy.

'Crime Scene Manager presents Forensics with analytics and photographic evidence,' Dave spouted, in the direction of Cluny. 'Your sergeant here assumes that role, man. Place. Remember your place.'

'And he doesn't mean Bears-bloody-den,' Punch puffed.

'Right. Right.' Cluny gulped.

Punch saw the woman glance sympathetically at Cluny. He considered knocking his deputy's head clean off. He had a promising exponent of this art in his ancestry. A towering coal-merchant-cum-coffin-maker-cum-postie, who would fell disobedient horses on his rounds with his fists during the era of Victorian Tobermory, which had given rise to Ivor's nick-name-as-surname. The man himself had tragically lost his head in a masonry accident relating to the building of Tobermory Clock. The Clock, again.

'Got her here safely from the ferry, Sarge. Located her the second she stepped down the gangway.'

'Uh-ha,' Punch said. *No amount of 'Baby Jane' would be enough.*

'Look at the eyes closed, lost in thought,' whispered Dave, now busy perfuming Punch's other shoulder. 'You could be forgiven for questioning whether science or raw instinct was unfolding before you, sergeant.'

'Palynology,' Cluny said. 'That's what she studied, she said.'

'So she *has* a tongue?' Punch puffed, watching the woman circle the vehicles, her gaze to the ground.

'Trained as a botanist, first, she said.' Cluny nodded. 'Then worked as an environmental archaeologist using her skills to evoke ancient landscapes – she's worked with every police force in Britain.'

'If ever *Mastermind* comes calling . . .' Punch said. He blew smoke to the surrounds.

'Her speciality is ancient pollen,' Cluny enthused, 'apparently the kind left at archaeological sites.'

Dave nodded. 'Looked her up on the net. Took all bloody day to load the page, but worth it. That's her all right.' He stared straight at Cluny. 'Left the dial-up running all night, constable. Not cheap.'

'I'll have you both in the back of the Ranger on charges of stalking,' Punch growled. 'Enough. Wonder if snow is an issue for her . . .'

'Oaf, I wouldn't mind inspecting her interface, it has to be said!' Dave chortled.

'Neckringable, the pair of you. You can use your web to order some bog roll for the cell.'

'Eh, excuse me, sergeant,' Lydia Strathclyde called over; she was crouching, her face positioned inches from the rear of the cars. 'Can we refrain from smoking. Yes? Despite what it's doing to your insides, and ours, it is also potentially destroying evidence. Thank you for your cooperation.'

'Masterly,' Dave said.

Punch angled his head towards the Atlantic. He used his thumb and index finger to propel the butt of his roll-up into the air. He had a puff of smoke still in his lungs and, in trying to deny its release, convulsed into a fit of coughing. He brought his hand to his mouth, cleared his throat several times. *Disaster*.

'Absolutely not!' Lydia Strathclyde stood, motioning her arm towards Punch, but not looking at him. She pointed a trowel in the direction of the flicked butt. 'The cigarette butt needs to go too.'

Cluny moved quickly.

'Leave it!' Punch instructed.

Cluny stopped in his tracks. Had the look of an actor who had stepped onto the wrong stage.

'I clean up after myself. And f . . .' Punch hissed. 'Can't risk this going back to Mary MacBeth . . .'

Lydia Strathclyde raised her head; Punch couldn't be sure if it was at the hint of the swear, or the female. He detected her accent as a mixture of Scottish and English. One of those that could grate.

Dave took his gloved hands from his black mac and stepped towards the woman, then stopped abruptly. Punch was sure he heard the Blue Stratos settle.

'Oaf, it's only David MacIntosh,' he said, thrusting a business card towards the woman. '*Sorry For Your Loss, Inc.*'

Lydia Strathclyde took the card. She looked at it and returned it to Dave.

'Lorox,' she admired. 'The font.'

'Powerful!' Dave blurted. 'I'm the island's custodian of the dead. Sergeant Punch here takes care of the *living*. He's the island's lock and key. On t'other side of the card you'll find my local historical work.'

'I know,' she said. Her gaze was still fixed on the ground by the cars.

'You do?'

'I'm aware of your work, Mr MacIntosh.'

Punch could see Dave was all but expecting kittens, behaving like a child tossing laundry from a basket; whereas he felt seriously on the back foot.

'What I'm doing firstly here, Mr MacIntosh, and well . . .' Lydia Strathclyde spoke from the side of her mouth in Punch's general direction, 'to *all* of you – is looking for pollen. There is pollen even in winter. But you have to be careful because last year's pollen will be evident as well. The wind swirls up the fallen leaves and they waft pollen back into the air, causing secondary circulation, secondary deposition.' She looked directly to Dave. 'This is something a forensic scientist must keep in mind – recirculation.'

'Recirculation,' Dave recirculated. 'And *David*, please.'

'The snow – what's left of it – isn't our friend here?' Punch attempted. *Foliage as fingerprints, for Christ's sake?*

'Nothing is our friend in the wild, sergeant. And nothing must be disturbed unless totally necessary.' Lydia Strathclyde stood and surveyed the wider landscape. 'Whoever committed this crime, they might have left their mark on the place, even if very, very subtly.'

'Crime?' Punch said.

'So, I believe you're looking for faint impressions, like a tracker?' Dave said. 'In leaves, broken twigs?'

'Like the old Indian tracker?' Cluny added.

'Affirmative,' Lydia said. 'And that's a nice association, Jonathan-Ambrose.' She moved to take her bag from Cluny and rested it on the bonnet of Punch's Ranger. She pressed a button and the bag fell open in two, impeccably organised sections. From one side she removed some brushes, a smaller trowel and clear bags.

Punch considered charging rent.

'You have to imagine a landscape as it *was*,' she spoke, 'from a piece of microscopic evidence, before it was disturbed.'

Like The Faces dressing room?

'Reverse engineering, if you will.' Dave beamed. 'Oh?' He sidled closer to Cluny, lowered his voice. 'Remember, that offer of an operation on that cocked leg of yours over at mine is a live offer.'

'Right, erm, thanks. Thanks, Dave.'

Punch watched as Lydia kneeled by the back wheels of the car closest to him, taking samples from the surrounds.

'Plant profile, that's what we're after, gents. And then you can see a landscape in your mind. And if you can get to pollen, then you know what plants are there. You can't always get to species, but pollen gives you a stronger idea. Then you look for the same pollen elsewhere. On bodies, evidence, surrounds . . .'

'I've read of it even on coffee cups, cigarette ends?' Dave nodded.

Punch felt the burn.

'And if you get to plants,' Lydia Strathclyde said, 'then you can guess what the soil is like, which leads us to timeline, the climate even, if required.'

'Timeline?' Punch said.

She nodded as she worked an implement carefully along the ground. 'And if you've got the soil then you can imagine what the geology was like; if you've got the geology map then you can eliminate places and suspects straight away.'

Punch decided it was time to play good cop.

'So are you seeing anything, professor?'

'All of a sudden a pattern emerges, sergeant, and you think, gosh, yes, I can see this place. When you're looking for bodies this is a great help. Geology determines place, and place has the trace of a criminal.'

'Bodies?' Cluny said. 'Would charred bodies carry pollen?'

Punch wasn't altogether hating the intervention, had been thinking the same.

'Yes, Jonathan,' Lydia said.

'Let's not get ahead of ourselves,' Punch said. He heard his radio activating from the Ranger. Signalled to Cluny to address it. 'Likely Control looking for confirmation Professor Strathclyde has arrived. Or expecting the case closed already.'

A blond flash took off for the Ranger.

Punch turned away from Lydia Strathclyde's apparent braille reading of the undergrowth; he walked to the quarry, paying newfound attention to the earth. He was out of eyeshot of the others and could only barely detect Cluny's Ferrero Rocher tones. From the top pocket of his uniform, in the position where Legacy Strathclyde's recent directive would have had his radio, he removed a small hip flask. He unscrewed the top and released the sweet smell of liquid amber, eighteen-years matured, into the wild-scented Glen Bellart. He took a glug. It hit the back of his throat like flame. Daylight wasn't on their side. Here he was again, where, forty years before, he had not been able to fight the sledgehammer of sleep; and where, several years later, his cousin attempted to stand twelve feet tall and roar into his face. Even his mother had seemed keen to see the back of the lad.

He walked further into the quarry, away from the road. He sat on the rocks where the gravel met the beginnings of the grassy incline of the hill. Took another swig. Two sheep scampered, causing him to flinch. He wondered if they recognised in him a warning sign: *Fucked if we'll be hung in that bastard's lockup!*

Punch looked to his left. Beyond bigger rocks he saw a stone circle. Evidence of a firepit in the middle. Could this be a trace, some forty years later, of his uncle having sat out here that starry October night, while the young boy lay comatose in the Ford Anglia dreaming of sharp-fanged bears? Would his uncle have been wondering if it was the right time to tell the lad he was his father?

Punch walked to the embers. Put his hand on them. The fire had been recent. He bent closer. What had appeared to be sticks were something else. Bones. And beside the bones. Teeth. And beside the teeth. In the earth. A bear claw print.

ACT II

SCENE XXV

WEDNESDAY

'TERMINAL. THE LAMB,' DUCK SAID. 'Thing could've done with brushing up on the Green Cross Code. Poor bastard never even made it to the Bard's plate.'

'What?' Davud warmed his hands with his breath.

'Or maybe the fellow at the theatre could make use of it for his do?'

'I'm not going there! Why are you saying that?'

Duck looked to Davud. 'Did I say you were? Steady on, lad.'

Davud was to give it to Bearfoot, who was going to bring it to the theatre, to the man, Fintan, who treated his mum like shit. He could easily see that place go up in flames. But Bearfoot had implied that Duck should burn instead. It seemed like a war between them, the two brothers. Because of what had happened to their mother. Maybe, Davud thought, blood-brothers were different from real ones? He was relieved to be an only child.

'Starving.' Duck ran a CalMac napkin over his head, removing the snowflakes. 'Okay! Let's get the hell out of

Dodge before the Lighthouse arrives with her speed gun!' With the engine came music. Duck threw the lamb to the back seat. Davud felt it brush his parka and flinched. He turned quickly to see the carcass had landed on top of the bagpipes. Davud wasn't sure if that might set the bombs off. Should he run now?

'Don't think even Bill the Pill could save the poor fucker now!'

'Or a rollercoaster,' Davud said.

'Ha! You're right, lad! But we didn't half give it one. We'll make a personality out of you yet. Aye, aye! Shit. Left my tobacco out there.' Duck pushed the driver's door open again and lurched outside. He slammed the door.

Davud shook. He was alone with the dead animal. He felt Duck kicking the tyres and took it as him being kicked. William had said people thought his older brother had killed their mother, but that it was really his father too. Hi-Pockets Lennox. That was why Davud had stopped going to the horses. He watched the flumes of smoke now coming from Duck. Shook from the cold. Felt trapped. He thought about how important space was, and how you had to design and refine the things that fitted into them, the spaces. The size of war felt like all of him.

He turned to the carcass, which had settled on Duck's jacket and looked like it was issued by the Brazilian Football Confederation. He leaned down to see if he could detect ticking. No. Then he looked at the lamb again. He felt he knew who it really was. No lambs were born in January.

'Sorry I didn't save you, Dad,' he said. 'Are you here to save me?'

He turned to face forwards. Needed logical thinking. Irrefutable data. He knew for a fact in the district of Argyll & Bute it had been snowing intermittently since the afternoon of 16 January. He knew for a fact Vatra was dead. That his dad was dead. That a little boy had washed ashore. That Bearfoot's mother had died. That Duck, her older son, had killed him. That it had been deemed an accident. That Mr Lennox also might have something to do with it. But why did the man at the theatre need bombs?

Duck opened the Fiesta door and whooshed back inside.

'Almost landed on my arse. I'd have this lot covered quicker than you could say Gary bloody Barlow.'

'What?'

'Grit.'

Duck moved them off the verge and back onto the snowy road. He opened a packet of Wotsits and a cloud of orange appeared. Davud was relieved the music was off. They passed the turning down to Fishnish, where you could catch the smaller ferry to Lochaline. *The other way*, everyone called it. Which always confused Davud because he knew there were more than two ways to leave an island. Though there was definitely only one way to leave a war: *cowardice*. War didn't observe winter and summer timetables.

'Why did you go to *last-man* position?' Duck said, gripping the wheel more tightly. Davud turned and Duck had tears running to his mouth, becoming orange on arrival. 'She wouldn't have gone there if you weren't there!'

'But I never knew her! I never knew that she was even there.'

'She was trying to protect you.' Duck turned to Davud. '*The Grey Lady*? Everyone knew her!'

'I didn't!' Davud pulled his hood up again. He began rocking. 'I had heard of the Grey Lady, but I didn't know it was her. Or why she was there!'

'I made it clear that all primary folk were to go to the front positions! Like the week before.'

'All you wanted was a new record! It was getting too dark!'

'But what the fuck? A grown woman lying on the pitch? In a fucking dress! Dad's dealing ruined her. She lived like a bag lady!'

Duck sped up. Davud heard the motorbike throttle. Remembered the feeling of being alive. Duck's spotlight approaching. The children all laughing and hooting. And him too. Finally he was one of them. Accepted! Everyone going quiet. The engine growing louder. He was wanting to get up. To run back to the front of the line. But he knew it was too late. Then feeling a new presence. A hand holding him down. The whack on the ramp. The wheels right above his head. The spray of dirt. Him stealing a glance to the hand for reassurance. Her looking up with an expression he had never seen on a face before. Rushed. Alive. Thrilled. Thrilled by Duck. Thrilled to be under her son.

Thrilled by death?

'Slow down!' blurted Davud. Duck pushed heavier on the pedal. They passed the island's abattoir. Davud lowered into the brace position. He noticed Duck's Wotsits wrapper on the floor, opened the wrong way up.

'The Grey Lady! Ruined!' Duck shook. 'Skin pale! Fucking druggie!'

'She didn't make a sound! I didn't see you land!'

'Reduced to scavenging around the coast by the pitch . . . and in a dress all year round. Fucking embarrassment!'

'And then everyone screamed! Scattered!' Davud sat up. His hair fell from his hood and he swiped it backwards. Duck slowed down into Salen. 'Did I go to the end because I wanted to die?'

'Or did she?' Duck thumped the wheel. 'I'd a helmet on. Never heard a thing ... She used to take the bus to Tob to beg, for fuck's sake! Harry on the bus never charged her. Bigger embarrassment was, she'd even try to flag us down on the bin lorry. Hi-Pockets cared more for his horses! For his "customers". Until she became one. Now Billy's getting involved. I'm sure of it.'

'Then I saw William.' Davud said, lost to his version of events. 'It was the day before I actually knew his name. Lying further down the line ... near the ramp.'

'Course he was! I made sure of it!'

'Said he wanted me to call him "William". Because that's what she had called him.'

'Drugs.' Duck spat. 'I didn't kill her – coke did! *Dad* did! Hi-Pockets was happy to see his wife die. Otherwise, her addiction was going to link him to McNair.'

SCENE XXVI

THURSDAY

'THE QUESTION IS, DO THE bones and teeth have plant detection consistent solely of the car site?' Lydia Strathclyde asked of herself. 'That's first on the menu.' She was sitting in the cell, the door wide open. PC Cluny had moved a table and chair in, having fully disinfected the area. She inhaled deeply through her nose. Took in her surrounds, then peered into the microscope. 'So we start here. Though it's a tad *analogue*, it has to be said. But maybe no worse for it.'

'None taken,' Punch said, standing at the thick blue door. 'First time I've had a key to an autopsy suite, though, has to be said.'

'Indeed, sergeant.'

'I'm guessing the "solely" part is most of note?'

'Yes. It's about localising detection.'

'Most secure place, I thought,' Punch said, gesturing to the cell. 'You know, to avoid contamination. We're light on *customers* in January and we can secure it each night. Safest place on the island, now I think on it.'

'But you'll let me out at night, sergeant?' Lydia Strathclyde said, looking over her glasses.

'Uh-ha. We usually reward good behaviour.'

'So few teeth . . .' she said into the microscope.

'Inconclusive?'

'Hmm. Not my area. But let us see.'

'I'll run them by Dave too.' Punch had all but had to taze Dave back at the Glen, suspecting the man was close to proposing. The jury was out on whether it was to the suspected human remains or the forensic ecologist. Were it not for the Bunessan body sitting on his table, mid-embalm, then Punch knew Dave would be here now, so close to the action the set of teeth would be in his mouth.

Cluny arrived behind Punch like a red setter waiting on a walk. Punch was tempted to add a collar to the man's paraphernalia. *Ears up for walk, tail up for toilet.*

The professor was in white gloves, and surrounded by the found materials; making up the party were sample bags, magnifying glasses and other implements. Punch could hardly believe she had all this in her two bags. He and Cluny had performed as much fingerprinting as was possible in and around the cars. But deeper work had been requested.

'Thank you, J-A. For the cushion,' Lydia said. 'Very considerate. This toosh has lain on enough hard ground over the years.'

Punch was ready to turn the key on her if she attempted his Christian name. *But then, how would that feel?* In any case, it didn't seem forthcoming. He had waited for ten minutes on his own with the remains before alerting the others. He had no clue whether that was to do with the shock of finding them, or with where they had been found. Or possibly, more accurately, it was that thing that always happened when he stumbled upon evidence of potential serious crime, the desire to be alone with a discovery before including colleagues or the wider force. It had first become evident in Inverness, when he would withhold information from Tulloch, often going solo, realising that when he did so there emerged a deeper focus in his crime-solving.

Cluny scampered off to his keyboard. Punch had noted the lad had turned ghoul-like upon the discovery of the remains, possibly losing a few points gained with Lydia Strathclyde. But none of them could deny she had called it first. Or smelled, or *read* it: Death.

'Aye, we'll need to have the mainland process the findings as well as, eh, your work here,' Punch said. 'You know . . .'

'None taken,' Lydia Strathclyde said, her head in the microscope. 'Though I didn't have you down as a man wedded to, "by the book".'

'Appealing to my propensity to take the road less travelled, Miss Strathclyde? Dangerous.' Punch put a search team on his ear, for the roll-up already prepared. 'If it is a Miss?'

'It's a Professor.'

'Uh-ha. PC Cluny is setting up Forensics with Control now. Things can take a bit longer on an island, but no less effective because of that.'

Professor Strathclyde looked up at him, her glasses poised on her nose. She waved a brush in her latex-gloved hand. 'I've got my big girl pants on, sergeant. You're in danger of *becoming* door frame.'

Punch took the cue. Walked through to the station office,

convinced his eyebrows were singed, or his arms the same length now.

Guinness had his head in his screen. Punch and the professor had returned with the bagged evidence directly to the station. Cluny had taken his instructions to secure the scene of crime.

'Guess this makes you incident scene manager,' Punch said, troubling the kettle. He saw Guinness's blond head jut from his screen.

'Right. Really, Sarge?'

Punch knew when to throw a dog a bone. It was all insurance, points in the bag.

'I added the Wotsits bag to the sealed evidence, Sarge.' His deputy had recovered it from the surrounds of the cars.

'Right. Never know, could be a DNA trace. That's if the kingfishers don't have a penchant for them . . .'

'Maybe debris from the rally?'

'A possibility. But the marshals are pretty thorough on the cleanup. Worth a try in case there's any correlation with the other found materials.'

'One thing, Sarge. The Wotsits were opened the wrong way up.'

'And?'

'Just saying.'

'We'll be pulling in Willy Wonka next. No calls from the public?'

'No, nothing, Sarge.'

'Not having much to go on with the cars is the problem.'

'Should we start asking about?'

'Not yet, PC. Clearly the island is not alarmed. Mull, I mean.'

'What other island could it be?'

'Nothing. None. Eh, but catching people off guard is good policing, PC.' *Right place, right time*. 'Let's us be in control of the Mull rumour mill. As best we can.' Punch knew the talk of him and blow-up dolls was harder to contain. Though putting a pin in Randy would be a start.

'DCI been on?'

'Affirmative, Sarge.'

'We'll keep Control in the back pocket for now. If this is nothing, we don't want grief coming down the LB wires. Paperwork'll be up the gazoo.'

Punch watched as Cluny removed his glasses and took a cloth from his pocket. He cleaned the round rims and replaced them. 'But Lima Bravo are sending additional help, yes?'

'No! Hold off. Monteith will be back from Costa del Drimnin soon. Don't want too many bodies around yet. Other than those who own the teeth, the bones . . .'

Punch saw his deputy flinch. 'You okay?'

Cluny nodded.

'Plenty folk on this island without teeth, mind, so it could still be some prank.' Punch bent to the emergency supply of Bell's under the sink. Stayed crouched as he poured a drop into a mug branded, *Sorry For Your Loss, Inc.*

He shook his head, reflecting again on the fellow pretending to be Robert Louis Stevenson, how the joker had drunk him dry of the good stuff. Pinning that on MacMaster would have been ideal. But 'Stevenson' was clearly not him, taller and, going by the accent slips, not Glaswegian. Though were they not all supposed to be capable of transformation?

'Has he been back again, Sarge?'

'Stevenson?'

'Who?'

'Eh, nothing. Who?'

'The old fellow. Erm, the lighthouse? The resident of Hayfield Hotel?'

'Oh, Skerryvore? No door, no bell. No. Likely bar-side at the Mish having epic conversations about gallbladders and waiting for somebody else's wages to spend. And fuck.'

'When he said about the burning ... do you think he could have been talking about the cars? But how?'

'Not unless he has the nose of Gordon bloody Ramsey on him. No.'

'Oh, and the garage in Salen did call about towing the cars?'

'I know. I called them. I can trust them. Cars need to stay where they are for now, though. Control will support if we need further checks. We can only contain what we can. I've got a special constable around there now on guard.' He nodded towards the cell. 'I'll go back and check on Kim Wilde.'

'But she's a famous *singer*?'

'That too.' Punch gestured to the dishes in the sink. 'Save the mugs.'

'The mugs?'

'For the tea leaves.'

Punch walked to the cell. The professor was brushing the bones, stopping periodically to seal small, clear plastic wallets. He daren't spark a smoke, knew that much.

'I provide a toilet seat.'

He saw the sides of her mouth curl.

'Can only hope I *make* it to my hotel room ...' Lydia said.

'A cup?'

'No, thank you. Though maybe a drop of whatever that is you're having, after I've been around Tutankhamen here.'

Punch acknowledged her powers of detection with his eyebrows. 'Distinctly lacking in years matured, I'll warn you now. Plants *and* grain detection?'

'I'll be charging you double.'

'Well, it was you or the dentist. He's more expensive.'

'This is not deep work, sergeant, but I'm trying to establish if a potential primary source can be identified; what I'm doing are presumptive tests to establish if there is a specified biological presence – semen, saliva, blood, urine, etc.'

'In the cell? Very possibly.' Punch feared he had used up all his best lines.

'If positive samples are detected by my preliminary work here, then they will be submitted for analysis to the lab in Glasgow, where confirmatory tests and further tests are performed.'

'That's in line with our thinking.' Punch was next to the switch to activate the fan heater in the cell; had considered turning it on for her. 'So, eh, this pollen thing is handy I'm guessing?'

'Snow doesn't help. Too early for its real flowering, but yes, certain contamination still shows. Bacteria decomposes pollen. We might have to take the cars to bits and analyse everything.' She addressed him over the rims of her glasses. In the style of *Mirren-meets-Miss-Jean-Brodie*.

'Yes, we've started that ball rolling too, though it's second phase procedure.'

'No cars missing? No clues as to their owners?'

'Fingerprinting has gone off. But not holding my breath. No people missing. No cars reported either. Small cars are ten a penny. But I've got PC Cluny trying to draw up a *database*, that's what he calls it.' Punch was keen to follow a more analogue hunch of his own, relating to the sketchbook, but he wasn't up for leaving Guinness on his tod with the botanist. Bugger would need tied up by a lead. 'Tricky not being able to run searches on the cars. Seen more branding on a crab.'

'This is my way of getting close, sergeant. Or closer. Though I know it rubs with your training, your methods.'

'Tulliallen? Granted, they teach you to be objective, procedural, but emotional involvement with suspects and those affected by them is about hours on the job.' Punch looked away. 'The island.'

'Empathise, be intuitive,' she said. 'Even more so here. I get it.'

'A fellow Tulloch taught me that.' Though Punch wasn't about to mention his former sergeant's other pastimes.

'Until you're standing in a gym in Lockerbie with rows of dead bodies to be identified lying in front of you . . . then *everything* changes.'

Punch coughed. Leaned on the door frame.

She looked up, then dropped back to the microscope.

'You were, eh, part of that?' he managed.

'We were taken into a room after that day in the gym and top brass asked us, "Is everyone all right?" As if any of us, mostly men, would have admitted to being otherwise. Lo and behold!'

'Eh?'

'I've detected a profile I recognise. A very species-rich moss . . .'

'Elton John's hair?' Punch was still in the Borders town.

'Floor moss habitation.' Using tweezers, the professor handled the contents of the glass plate under the microscope. She hunched over it again.

'Surely just moss from the quarry or surrounds?' he asked.

'No. The nature of the quarry floor,' she pointed towards Polaroids she had taken of the incident scene, 'as well as the fact there is only the road between the quarry and cars suggests another habitat. These teeth and bones have been a-walking . . .'

'As Bacharach and David *almost* had it.'

She looked up excitedly. Punch saw the little girl in her. Akin to a boy of seven noticing a moon for the first time. Imagining it was a different one that the man he still believed to be his father – who had left them not long after his birth – looked at over in Oban. The man he would go on to realise was in fact his uncle.

'You can tell all that from *moss*?' Punch moved closer to her findings. He wasn't used to somebody else doing all the work. Could see how Tulloch in Inverness had got used to it.

'It's all there, *always* there,' Lydia Strathclyde said, gesturing with her glasses to what lay beyond the thick cell walls. 'Solving crime is not a loud voice in my work.'

'Was, eh, Lockerbie your first?' He wasn't sure if he could go there, but he couldn't resist.

'No. My breakthrough case was in Aberdeenshire. A body in a huge field with hedges all around. "*We'd like to show you where we think the body was*," the DCI there said to me. I said, "No. If you will please allow me, I would like to tell *you* where it *is*."'

'And you did?'

She nodded, her head already back on the microscope.

'So—' He used the mug to gesture to the remains on the table in front of her. 'Are we suggesting they weren't in the cars? Or didn't start out in the cars?'

'Or were removed from the cars, taken somewhere else, and then returned.'

Punch tried to fathom the movements required for the scenario the professor had painted. The palm of the island usually held the answers; he just had to wrestle them free before it closed on him or punched him in the gob.

'This plant profile right in front of me feels significant,' the professor enthused, leaning back in her chair. 'I was sure we would need more powerful apparatus.'

'One name for Dave.'

'Dear man.'

'How long we talking?' he asked. 'That these teeth and bones have been out of a body? Weeks? Days?'

Lydia Strathclyde inhaled.

'Not my department, sergeant. They could have been on yesterday's ferry. The mind boggles.'

'Can we use your evidence to prove that the cars, or one of them at least, was in a mossy field?'

'No. Sorry, sergeant.' She leaned forwards again, as though addressing the crime as having happened on her specimen plate. 'Were the cars not toast already, then that might have been possible.'

'And we have pretty meagre tyre tracks to go on . . .' Punch said. 'That the source of your moss then? The verge?'

'No. Not in that open terrain. This species of moss only grows in more moist, often coastal, but always sheltered, areas.'

'Like where?'

'Dwellings, usually.'

'What?' Punch considered the bear prints. *You can take the man out of the seven-year-old boy . . .*

'Well, animal habitats being one.'

'Sarge!'

Punch turned to the blond shock of Cluny.

'Just had a call come in from Monteith, Sarge.'

'Monteith?' Punch pointed across the Sound of Mull. 'She's not back in uniform until next week? Though it's been tempting to get the binoculars out.'

'Came back over yesterday, the other way, Lochaline to Fishnish. Unmarked car, of course. No uniform. She saw them on the Craignure to Salen road, just as she was driving up to join it from Fishnish.'

'And?'

'Two cars.'

'Sightings of folk?' Punch said.

'Colours?' Lydia Strathclyde said, standing.

'The people?' Cluny frowned. 'Oh? Right. No she said it was hard to see in the blizzards. One car was smaller, maybe light blue or silver.'

'She on her way here?' Punch said.

'No. She has her grandkids with her. Back on duty tomorrow she said. Didn't think too much of it. Thought maybe it was connected to a job, a death.'

'A death?' Lydia Strathclyde said.

'Think too much of what?' Punch asked.

'The smaller car was being towed by a hearse. Dave's.'

'Eh?' Punch rushed through for his hat. Took his keys in hand. He returned to the cell door. 'Tell Monteith she'll need to ditch the crumb-snatchers. I'll be in touch about meeting her at Dave's. Need her back on duty sharpish.'

'But shouldn't you do it, Sarge?'

'No. Eh, did you not want more authority?' Punch hoped he'd gotten away with it; they were both privately terrified of Monteith.

'Right, Sarge,' Cluny said. 'But surely Dave couldn't have had anything to do with it?'

Punch motioned towards Lydia Strathclyde's evidence table. 'Look, you're the expert . . .' He caught her eye and then looked away. 'Just a hunch, but . . .'

'I'm listening,' she said.

'These bones and teeth didn't come from a human body?'

He didn't say it aloud, but thoughts of bear teeth, bear bones, they were now in his head.

SCENE XXVII

PUNCH JUMPED INTO THE RANGER. In his rear mirror, pebbledash.

He pulled away from the station, going over his own theory in his head about the origins of the teeth and bones. He had another hunch. One that took him away from boyhood fables. The Glen was big deer territory. Often you'd see them killed, folded by the roadside in rally season. Some had done entirely for title contenders. But there wasn't much to go on – a few teeth and bones. And it was tricky now to consult Dave on the matter. Could the man really be involved? Something was fishy about him earlier, discounting the man's gills, he'd been sure of it.

Punch had left Lydia Strathclyde to continue her work; Guinness no doubt plaguing her for badminton singles. He had also tasked his deputy with contacting CalMac for car and passenger records. As well as leaning on Control about the fingerprint processing. Short of going down to MacKay's garage and compiling records of the identities of every small car owner on Mull, he was operating on slim pickings. No reports of missing folk had come in. Human remains couldn't be ruled out. If word started to leak out, then roaring and other piss-take noises down the station telephone line weren't out of the question.

He had instructed Cluny to leave Dave to him. Stating if the man did call in, as he often would, then not to provide him with any case information. A call to Monteith hadn't provided much more than the earlier reports. Children screaming in the background. They were brave around her. She had a cell too, after all, and with it as much Coco Chanel and Celine Dion as any criminal, or offspring thereof, could handle. *Another reason the* Titanic *went down.* On Mull, they prided themselves on being jailers *and* police officers. Craignure was also the best place for Monteith to facilitate any support required either from Oban, or further into L div.

Could Dave have been transporting the dead body from the Ross end? Strange he hadn't mentioned anything. Had he been assisting somebody off the ferry? But he wouldn't have come via Craignure from the Ross to get to his house-cum-funeral-parlour at Ulva Ferry. Punch questioned if he was giving Dave too much free rein. Whatever the answers, a case inspector visit was increasingly likely now. He was following the sniff of a lead. On the passenger seat sat the sketchbook. On closer inspection he'd spotted several drawings of potentially recognisable locales. Though the text, *In war everyone should carry a glockenspiel*, was a puzzle enough in itself.

He passed Mary MacBeth's orderly front garden at the beginning of Creagan, somehow, even in January, offering the hope of spring. Soon he was out of Tob and making light work of the Gally Goo. His destination was Dervaig, but he was intentionally going the long way. Snow was evident on the fields, but the roads were clear. He passed Aros Mains and then down to Aros Bridge, where he turned right off the Salen road for the Glen. If one of the cars Monteith had seen was of note, then it would have entered Glen Bellart here. He needed to see the road in the same way. Monteith's sighting traced them as having likely passed here just one day before. The sketchbook carried impressive drawings of buildings; some, more disturbingly, were set alight with people running through the pages. There were transport timetables, though, frustratingly, no correlating dates. There was one other image of significant interest. A bear claw print.

Punch sped on, watching the roadsides as he travelled, knowing he was doing that thing again, going solo, rogue-style, needing to be alone with the evidence, because for some reason unbeknown to him – though he suspected the events of Lockerbie, 1988, if not the confusing actions of adults who were or were not his parents circa 1955, were contributing factors – this way of proceeding made him a better police operator.

The landscape on the Glen was not screaming murder, human suffering or anything new; it was the same mix of the barren and the forest. He leafed open the book as he drove. A roll-up already fired. Sergeant Tulloch's words – before the big fellow went useless – rang in his mind: *go with your belly*. As well as the print, there were three other sketched pages of particular interest. One was of a long caravan, set on bricks, and drawn so realistically that Punch had expected he could open the door. Another was of a sequence of bodies lying down like sardines. Names had been assigned to each one but were subsequently heavily scored out. The final body was in flames. The last of the three drawings was clearly more haphazardly depicted, but was potentially the most significant, and had caused him to put a request into Control for a database search. It was of a crash scene. Two cars. Each Fiestas. And next to them, a male standing alongside a female. The male was in a kilt. The female in dark glasses. The numberplates visible.

He progressed down through a dip in the road and then upwards into a corner. He wished to be transported back to 1970, but in uniform, so as to take to the hillside and handcuff that taunting cousin of his.

He slowed down when he saw them. The burnt-out cars. Now sitting like two old women at a whist drive in the outer edges of hell. He had driven in their tracks, but still he was not in the occupants' heads, nor in the *right time, right place*. It was like searching for a page that had been torn out and lost.

The rural setting, coupled with the desolation of the vehicles and the police tape surrounding them, now conjured some form of ghoulish art installation. Guinness had done a decent job of the gift-wrap. There was another car parked up nearby, out of the cordon.

Punch engaged the brake and wound his window down.

'James,' he said.

'Ivor.'

'Sergeant. When I'm in uniform, Jamesie. Which is always.'

'No bother, sergeant. Sorry.'

'You got here ahead of rush hour?'

'Aye, just a few deer jostling for the tube. But I'm discovering – even for a lowly *special* constable – the world moves aside. Tagged onto the extra pay I'll be seeing each month, it's a bonus.'

'Christ, you didn't have the blues out on your first week, Jamesie? Warned you about that . . .'

'No. Only jesting, Sarge.' The man stroked his beard. 'Though the wife's enjoying the perks of my job-share.'

'Uh-ha. It's been known for the uniform to come in, eh, handy . . .' Punch blew out a breath, his eyes set on the two cars. Tried to imagine the pencil on the page.

'At least I knew the Rod back catalogue.'

'Helped with the interview, no doubting . . .'

'Any leads?'

'Christ, you've got all the lingo. No. Not much.'

'You'll not mind me having a puff on the job, Sarge?'

'If it helps you stay alert, no. You never know when a kingfisher might pass, so to speak. Anything transpires, just radio the station, okay? Closed LB channel. Don't need Lochgilphead, Oban and the others hearing about our dirty laundry. And fuck.'

'Got it, Sarge. *Harry Potter*'s been on already. Power crazy. I hear there's a *plant whisperer* in our midst too?'

'Uh-ha.' Punch took a draw. He was suddenly embarrassed at his close proximity to hocus pocus, but also quietly impressed he was entertaining such millennial methods. There was no doubting the woman had a track record of results. He hadn't been expecting Lockerbie on her CV. Didn't know what to do about that. 'Cluny's arranged Dan Craignure to take over from five p.m. Monteith's back on tomorrow. Today if I have anything to do with it.'

'You're brave.' James nodded his police hat to the cars. 'So, no owners yet?'

'No. Not yet. Any ideas?' Punch kept the teeth and bones

to himself. No point freaking the whole island out. You engaged the public when folk were *definitely* missing. Not before.

'No. Christ, I hope they're not local. And are they Peugeots, Golfs, Fiestas . . . who knows? – and that's the bother.'

'Fiestas is my bet. Worst part of the job, you'll discover.'

'I'm all ears.'

'Somebody always knows more than you do. Right.'

Punch got out of the Ranger and walked to the cordon. He ducked under and circled the cars again. There was something he was looking for. *Bingo*. He stepped closer. There was a small dent on the driver's door of one of the cars. Had it been there before? He couldn't be certain. It was on the same side as the dent on the illustration.

He walked back to the Ranger. Stepped inside. He nodded to the flask on the passenger seat next to the man, raised a cheekbone.

'I suspect it's light on nectar?'

'Wouldn't be so sure, Sarge. The day job's still the distillery after all!'

'Christ. Don't get me in trouble, Jamesie. But keep the supplies coming.'

'All good, Ivor. Sarge.'

'Right, SOCO.'

'So what?'

'Scene of crime officer.'

'Promotion already?'

'Keep the bottles coming.'

Punch wound up his window and drove on, past the quarry, picking up speed. Seeing the cars again in the wilds made Lydia Strathclyde and her methods seem all the more relevant.

But he wasn't about to order flowers. She'd only consider them case notes. The sky was charcoaling. No moon to report. The book pointing the way. He had the feeling he was living within a world depicted by pencil, like those buggers in *A-ha*.

Soon, he'd reduced the remainder of the Glen to two roll-ups. He was getting close to Dervaig.

'Call out to Lima Bravo. Sarge, are you reading? This is PC Cluny. Over.'

The succinctness was promising, thought Punch. If not the trans-Atlantic disc jockey timbre. He was tempted to request 'Do Ya Think I'm Sexy?' just for badness. If nothing else, to make sure Jamesie back there was staying awake.

'Come in, PC Cluny. Over.'

'Fingerprints are dud. As we suspected, Sarge. Over.'

'No surprise there. And CalMac? Over.'

'Being a bit funny about releasing records, Sarge. Something about transitioning to a new operational system. Their booking system is undergoing new software. Data migration. Over.'

'Eh? Bullshit. Alan bloody Turing'll be in hi-vis next. Tell them I've instructed this. Raise the paperwork. Have McTeal, the DPO in Oban, lean on them too.'

There was silence.

'Over!'

'Affirmative, Sarge. On it. Over.'

Punch replaced the radio on the holder.

'Control to L519. Do you receive? Over. Do you receive, sergeant? Over.'

'Like fucking Piccadilly Circus ...' Punch reached for the handset again and tuned it to the wider channel. Amazing how you could accept the world with just a button. Reject it too.

'Lima Bravo sub-division to Control. This is 519. I read you duty officer. Over.'

'*Sergeant – we have those two numberplates you requested. Ready to receive? Over.*'

'I am, DPO.' Punch swung the Ranger to the side. Imagined the oncoming headlights. He grabbed a pencil from his top pocket and the notepad from the passenger seat. Thing had already been brushed in any case. 'Please proceed. Over.'

'*As you suspected, sergeant, both vehicles identify as Ford Fiestas. Over.*'

Punch had kept that bit to himself. Though a call around the garages had been next on his list.

'*One is silver, and belongs to GoTravel Cars, a car hire company operating out of Glasgow airport. Over.*'

'Got it, thank you. And the other? Over.'

'*Blue in colour. Bit more complicated. Over.*'

'You've an audience. Over.'

'*Newly purchased. Arnold Clark's, Anniesland, Glasgow. But – frustratingly – not registered yet with the DVLA.*'

'That possible? Over.'

'*This is the Hebrides we're talking about . . . Over.*'

'Uh-ha. Insult taken. Can we try the dealership for description, any scraps? Over.'

'*On it, sergeant. Over.*'

'The first car . . . any hire details? Over.'

'*So, it was hired yesterday morning, to a Miss Mary Shelley. Looks to be a fake address, though. Edinburgh. Over.*'

'Bugger. Right, thank you, officer. I'll keep lines open and will likely have follow-ups. Signing off for now. Over.'

'*Anything else we can support with here then lines are open.*

Signing off L519. Over and out.'

Punch flipped the channel to LB. Local. Pressed the receiver.

'Come in, PC Cluny. Over.' Now he felt like he was calling into one of those call-in radio shows that were all the rage just now. Frasier Crane on the other end. People needing everyone to know what they thought all the time. Maybe plants were a better study than people, right enough.

'Sergeant. Station Tobermory, receiving. Over.'

'When CalMac start playing fucking ball, PC, have them run a check on a possible passenger name. Mary Shelley. That's S-H-E-L-L-E-Y. Over.'

Cluny verified the spelling, using the NATO phonetic alphabet. Punch almost threw the handset out the window at the second mention of 'echo'. Leave it to some deer on the Glen to make sense of his deputy.

'Sarge! The name! It's the same as the author? Over.'

'Who?'

'Dracula. *Mary Shelley. Over.'*

'Uh-ha. Right.' Punch let go of the receiver. The only books he knew were the ones about naval ships. 'I, eh, got that too, aye. But there can't be just the one of them, PC. Fairly common name. Run the check. Over.'

'On it, Sarge. Over. Oh, sergeant? Over.'

'Uh-ha? Over.'

'Look, about the name . . . we can all get the Michael taken out of us. Over.'

'The Clock?'

'No, I meant the Mary Shelley one. It's how you recover that counts. The criminal never accounts for that.'

'Right, Rebus. You forgot to say over. Over!'

Punch pressed on. Pissed off he'd mentioned his nickname over the wires. But he was relieved Robert Louis Stevenson had been left out of it. He was nearing the end of the Glen stage. He checked his pace-notes-turned-incident-notes, flicking through the sketchbook. The night before he'd been sure he'd seen an island drawn on the horizon in it. But today the page was not there. *The dent on the bottle of Tobermory was, though.*

He found the page of interest. Glanced at it. Slowed down. Looked between it and the scene coming into view. He was here. He had driven onto the page in the book. Bear territory. The Ranger was well-named.

He pulled over, left the engine purring, ready to pounce. He was never sure of the usefulness of half of the good-for-nothing shite he stored under his hat that Guinness would call a 'database' – but somehow he had retained this matching image. Just the one he needed. When he needed it.

He was outside the long green caravan on bricks, exactly as depicted on the page on his passenger seat. *Go with your belly.*

SCENE XXVIII

PUNCH KILLED THE RANGER. Spat the rollie out the window. Lydia Strathclyde wasn't here to tell him to do otherwise. This was *his* page.

He took hold of the sketchbook, hid it behind his back, then jumped out of the Ranger. He walked up off the road to the caravan door. Steps below it. Rusted. A few plant pots that had seen better days. In the illustration they were depicted as healthier. Summer maybe. The usual array of gas canisters and a washing line. Wellies hung upside down at the door. All tidy enough. A bicycle discarded in nearby bushes. Something about it requiring closer inspection. Haphazard was not usually the friend of the innocent. *Steady on, Ivor.*

He knocked. Imagined Jim Rockford might answer in his chequered slacks. The unlicensed pistol stored inside the cookie jar. He had purposefully left the handset in the car. He fixed the book inside his uniform jacket in the small of his back. No point in freezing up folk's tongues before they might spout something he could use. He wasn't feeling this as a full-impact occasion of hat on and protruded pigeon chest. Though it was a tad late for Rockford's plainclothes and tan. *Badger temples an' all.*

He heard creaking inside. Looked to the bricks doing their job. Imagined them as the final bricks on Skerryvore lighthouse. Children's clothing on the washing line. He turned quickly to the road, to the fields giving way to streams and rock pools as signifiers of the earliest hints of the Atlantic Ocean. It started drizzling. Giving the impression that thousands of invisible fingertips were breaking the water's surface. A winter sun broke through, amber and pink streaks on the sky. Arctic terns circling within it all. *Fuck your kingfishers.*

The door released. He turned to it.

It was her. Patti Smith. The woman who had been at the Wee Theatre, along the road.

'Uh-ha. Sorry to bother you.' Punch removed his hat. 'It's you.'

Bora was standing in the same black clothes. Same angled head and narrowed eyes. Punch cottoned on this was a greeting.

'Aye,' he said. 'We met earlier, over at the theatre.'

'Yes.' She nodded. 'Who were you expecting?'

Punch hadn't been expecting a question. Her accent arrived more heavily now. Eastern European or thereabouts. That way of making English sound more intellectual, pronounced and less everyday than it really was. Authority. That's what she carried. *Quietly, mind.*

'Well, I'm here because I, eh . . .' He stopped; for some reason he needed another starting point, another page. 'Just wanted to clear up the fire. You know. At the theatre. Nothing amiss in your estimation?'

'I'm sorry?'

'Anything odd? In your, eh, thoughts?'

'I know what you mean, what you meant, officer. I'm just not sure what, why, you think I would know.'

Punch was happy to leave 'sergeant' out of it. The lass was fidgeting with a wooden spoon.

'Well, eh . . . it's just not every day a house decides to set itself on fire, is it?'

'Fintan likes to keep himself to himself.'

'Not ideal for a theatre?'

She waved the spoon slowly back and forth, implying it was capable of replacing speech.

Punch was aware of Dervaig's creative community, not exactly San Francisco in '69, but if a hippy was to be found on Mull then here would be your best bet. He was fairly sure he had only once or twice set eyes on this woman before their meeting at the theatre. It was possible to do that on Mull. Less so, unfortunately, with Randy.

Punch was trying to fathom a line of questioning. 'Look, can I pop in for a moment. Just a quick chat?'

She stood aside and nodded to the steps.

Punch went to remove his hat, then realised he already had it in his hand. He stepped up and into the caravan.

It was dark. Two closed doors led off a short corridor. There were some canvases on the walls, not in frames. Punch was no art historian, but they were very possibly from the same hand as the sketches in the book. One was of the woman. It was stunningly lifelike. Even capturing her discomfort at being depicted. The same uneasiness he was feeling from her now. Maybe the book was hers? And she had dropped it walking the Glen when out capturing the wilds?

She closed the door to the poky bathroom and Punch saw

a shower in there too. Two towels. He followed her into the main room, windows all around. There was a kitchenette and inbuilt soft seating around the edges of the eating area. Bedding was stacked near the window. A pot simmering on the cooker. The smell of soup that he'd first detected at the entrance.

'Sit. Please sit.' She indicated with the spoon. Punch sat down and wondered if there was anything the woman *couldn't* make happen with that spoon. 'Can I get you anything?'

'Soup?' Punch was embarrassed; it had come out as though he was asking for some.

'It's not ready. I was thinking tea.'

'Yes, uh-ha. I know you were.' He rested his elbows on the table that was fixed to the seating. Glad he hadn't stuffed a bib down his uniform collar.

'So, would you like tea?'

'No. No, thanks.'

She attended the simmering pot. She then turned to Punch.

'Been here long?' he asked.

'We've been in this caravan since we came to the island.'

'*We've . . .*?'

'There is my son and I.'

'Right. Right. His name?'

'Davud.'

'And you came from?'

She looked to the window. The light streaming in now. Punch watched her serious eyes, how they made him feel confined. The box of cornflakes caught his eye, stored neatly away on the counter. Opened the wrong way up.

'Who's the cornflakes fan?' he asked.

'Sorry.' She turned distractedly. 'Why?'

Punch pointed. Longer arm.

'Ah, my son. Yes.'

'Right, your son. And what age will he be?'

'Look, is all this about the fire?'

Punch caught her eye. She looked to the window again. Used an elegant hand to brush her thin lips. He was no expert, but her hair appeared more hauled than parted. He remembered there was a roll-up behind his ear, which he felt uncomfortable about now. While she was still looking away, he removed it and stuffed it into his pocket.

'Had you just arrived?' he asked.

'When? Now?'

'No. When I saw you at the theatre. After I'd put the fire out.'

She turned to address the pot.

'Not long before you.'

'Did you see the fire, you know, on your way in?'

'Look, why would I want the theatre to burn down, officer?' She spoke with her back to him. 'It is one of the ways I make money. Well, not much. Less in winter.'

'Uh-ha.' He tapped his hat on his knee. 'But that's not, eh, exactly what I asked.'

She stirred the pot.

'So you work there? Acting, is it?'

She made a fake laughing sound. 'No. Well, yes, actually, in a way I am – I clean. In the season. Cook for visiting companies too. Bosnia.'

'Eh?'

'You asked where I came from.'

'Right, thank you. I think I did know that, maybe read something somewhere.' Punch wiped his palm across the table. 'Just seemed odd no one was in a hurry to call it in.'

'What?' She turned to him, again with the spoon. 'The war? Did you not get reports?'

'No. No.' Punch felt immediately responsible for his failure in policing the BBC's editorial output. Wanted to say he didn't have a TV.

He pointed to placards facing the wall, handles pointing up.

'That, eh, what these are for?'

'No. For the planned wind farm.'

'Was there not supposed to be a public meeting about it last night in Dervaig Hall?' Punch had given the brief to Cluny, figuring the PC had enough hot air in him.

'Cancelled. Supposedly the weather. Says everything. Just more of powers that be treating us like second-class citizens. Community here have been very good to me. So I like to do the same for them.'

Punch couldn't imagine old Skerryvore among them. 'Would folk not *want* a cleaner environment?'

She killed the burner. Turned and looked straight at him. 'At the expense of your landscape? Land *is* your country. A country.'

'Of course. Sorry.' The book was bothering his lower back. Would it be weird to produce it now? 'Just,' Punch gestured, 'I'd have pinpointed Dervaig as having a greener mindset more than most on the island. In Tob we'd sell our soul to the devil. Well, Morvern anyway.'

'It's about balance, and placement.'

Punch saw several leaflets on the kitchen counter. *Bora* handwritten on them.

'Lennox will do what he wants,' Punch said. 'Talking of bad actors.'

'Did I say I was a bad actor?'

'No! No. I meant something else.'

Punch considered jumping into the pot. Just his hat floating on top. He wondered if he should simply produce the book and be done with it. But something was telling him to hold off. She didn't seem the type to hang her own self-portrait. Could her son be mixed up with the cars?

'Presents problem for me,' she said.

'What?'

'Mr Lennox. The land. My son likes his horses. In a way they have been healing him.'

'Right. Of course. Hi-Pockets good for something. Who'd have guessed it. No, it's more that I felt something at the theatre was amiss. Wondered how recently the fire had started. I'd seen it from up on the hairpin bends. If you had just arrived, then why didn't you see it too?'

She allowed her hair to drop and then wrestled it back into position. Turned to the pot, then realised she had already killed the flame.

'Look. He told me not to say anything.'

'MacMaster? About the fire?'

'Well, no. Not that day. But that he might have to do something. Something he didn't want to.'

'What?'

'He never said. I know he is struggling . . .'

'Money?'

'Yes. Maybe confidence too.'

'Talent?'

She shrugged.

'Has he said anything else to you? That he was planning such a thing?'

She shook. 'Really. No. He hasn't.'

Punch leaned back on the padded seating. Looked to the bedding.

'I'm imagining the wind farm could mean work for the area?'

'Am I in trouble, officer? I have not done anything. If I find a coin on the street I try to find its owner!' She gestured with her hand, then used it to hold up her jaw.

'No. No,' Punch said. 'I'm trying to help here.' He stood. The book fell from his back.

The woman kneeled for it. She leafed through.

'Why would you take my son's book?' she said as she looked around the room. 'When did you do that?'

'I . . .?'

'*Why* would you?'

'I didn't take it. I found it.'

'Where?'

'Outside. Outside the caravan.' Punch pointed outside, turned quickly and tried to fake buffoonery. 'Christ, what with the fire, I clean forgot I'd picked it up.'

She held it to her chest.

'That your son's work too?' Punch motioned to the entrance. 'Talented lad. He in the high school?' He wondered what unimagined fate was going to befall this woman. He had experience in this field himself.

She exhaled and sat down. Punch sat again, opposite her.

'Something stronger then?' she asked.

'Sorry?'

She stood and reached for a bottle of Bell's. Punch saw there were two glasses already next to it. She brought them down and poured into both.

'*Medicinal* you say?' She tried to smile, her lips tightening to a line.

'Uh-ha.'

'You want to move forward,' she said, sipping from her glass. 'You want to live in tribute to loved ones lost. I thought that's what life here was going to be about.'

Punch pulled the glass towards him. Took it to his nose and then his lips. Felt the heat through his gullet.

'My husband. It was normal to fall in love with him. He was always trying to do the hard thing. Fighting for the right thing. Others – the easy thing. War made me feel like I was somebody else. Now Mull does that.'

'You arrived when?'

'In ninety-three.' She nodded. 'Davud was eleven. War made time stand still. Funny how that made Mull seem faster.' She rubbed her hands over her black top; Punch could see specks of paint on it.

'Your husband?'

She shook her head, gulped and looked away, chasing the sunlight.

'I'm sorry. Hellish.'

'All my family.'

Punch clasped his hands in one another. Some of the pages in the book were starting to make more sense.

‘Your lad. Where is he now?’

‘Glasgow. Studying.’ She looked, trancelike, to her glass.

‘Drawing, is it?’

‘Architecture. I really do know nothing more about Fintan. But I can tell you I saw flames. So what you thought you saw, you saw, officer. I just could not say anything about them. I saw my husband. I saw my city alight. I froze. I only went up there . . . huh. Hopeless.’

‘What?’

‘I used to act, or taught acting in our community programme. In Sarajevo.’

She made the place seem more real to Punch than any news report he had seen or heard. The island never stopped surprising him.

‘But . . .’ She sipped. ‘How can you pretend anymore after . . .?’ She put both hands on her lap. ‘Death. Sudden death, makes . . .’

‘Bad actors of us all,’ Punch said. ‘Worse. Fools.’

‘They say war equalises everyone. It doesn’t. Death does that. He misses his father. More than I know. Friends.’ She put her hand to her mouth. Gulped. ‘Grandparents.’

‘I’m very sorry. When did you last hear from him?’

‘My husband?’

‘Eh, no . . .’

‘Oh? Davud calls the phone box below Bellachroy every Saturday. He lives a lot in his head. Worries me. First year we were here he saw bombs landing on Dervaig Main Street.’

‘Christ. Poor lad. And has he settled?’

‘An island asks a lot of you.’

Punch sipped, nodded.

'When you are not used to living on one.'

'When you're born on one too.'

'I am particularly worried, sergeant. Tuesday was his birthday and we were to speak specially.'

'The twenty-fifth?'

'Yes. But he did not answer.'

The Burns Night birthday had registered with Punch. Shook his head free of the nonsense.

'There was no beauty here,' she said. 'At first. Grief came in waves. Hitting against the island. But now I think I can never leave.'

'Why was it to Mull?' Punch helped himself to another hit. Wasn't sure, but hoped he was still policing. The teeth, the bones, were sitting a lot heavier on him. *Please, Mull, don't ask me to deliver them to this woman.*

'In November ninety-three, Refugee Council together with British Red Cross set up a programme to receive and settle Bosnian refugees. That was our new title. One thousand Bosnian men, to come to the UK, with their families. Some like us, with no man. Flew into Edinburgh.'

'And then here?' Punch now recalled when he had been posted on Bute, before Mull, he had been aware of this programme there.

'Fourteen thousand Bosnians applied for asylum. Some forcibly expelled from Kosovo. The *politic of staying* they called it. But in our case, we had nothing more to stay for. Red Cross, Refugee Action and Scottish Refugee Council organised evacuees. I feel bad about it, but up here I don't have to see them. Other refugees. We can just be people here.'

Punch was feeling the weight of this woman's situation on him. Like it was his responsibility to police not an island, but hope.

'So you heard from your son on Saturday?'

'Yes.'

'Everything all right?'

She nodded.

'Is he a driver? Have a car?'

She shook. 'Why?'

'Where is he studying? You must be very proud of him.'

'I am. I'm hoping it is his saving – his talent.' She nodded to the walls. 'The Glasgow School of Art.'

Punch stood. 'You haven't seen the news ... shit! Pardon me.'

Bora looked at him quizzically. Shook her head.

'Look, I've not seen the headlines, but apparently there's been a fire at the school of art. But no casualties. So they're saying.'

'What?' She stood.

'Sorry, I should have made the connection sooner ... can you reach him?'

She raced off around the caravan and appeared with a bag. 'I call his halls from village phone box! He's not good with flames!' She rushed to the door.

'I'll drive you! I can put the word out on the channels.' Punch took hold of his hat. Made sure the woman's gas was off. Ran to the door. 'I'm sure we can assist with information!'

She turned to him, her hair stuck to her face. 'Look, things are complicated right now in village. With the protest. People taking sides ... don't want to seem like I am ...'

‘Right. Will you call into the station? When you know?’

She rushed outside, leaving the door ajar.

Punch noticed a hi-vis top hanging behind the door. An Argyll & Bute emblem on it.

SCENE XXIX

FRIDAY

SHOW DAY. WELCOME TO CAVE LIFE. Welcome to post-truth world. Dervaig-style.

Leonardo ballsed up the plan. So he paid for it. Duck too. Couldn't have him crossing Fintan's threshold. Taking my applause. Don't poke the bear!

A fire is burning now. The reflections of the flames flicker on the faces of the bodies. Making them almost alive. They're on *my* land now. Hi-Pockets can forget it. And fuck the horses. They can all burn in hell for what they did to my mum.

She once told me Dervaig used to bury their own, not in the ground, but in these caves. Where they'd mummify in the moisture. That was what she wanted. To be given to the land. Well, this is the next best thing. Two bloating faces and soon mummification in their hands and feet. Death as life. That's how I keep Mum alive.

WE ARE BEAR is chalked on the cave wall. I'm taking control. Of her legacy.

Teeth are teeth. But one thing I've discovered that everyone should know is you mustn't catch eyes with the dead. Oh no. Whether they are charred or not. Then they imprint on you. Awakening conscience. Making you – *theirs*. Fuck that.

I watched Punch earlier. Asking questions around the theatre. Trying to make sense of his presents – virtually gift-wrapped just for him – of the cars. The two cars represent me and Leonardo, in a way. Blood brothers. Stripped down to no-logo. Free of corporations and other people's designs for life. We both knew we were different. We connected by having parents taken from us. Like all good duos. Just look at Lennon and McCartney. You have to lose something big to live in a new way. To design your own life, to be free to be yourself. But he failed me. Wanted the glory for himself. I had to take his from him.

Punch will be waiting on forensic analysis. I spied on him from the forests. Some woman sniffing around like a dog trying to assess another dog's shit. And that idiot Dave! You don't get your hands on the bodies this time, Dave!

Mummification takes cave-time. Embalming is a quick fix, artificial. I'm providing the correct conditions for the skin and eventually the soft tissue beneath to become desiccated. The bodies will ultimately take on a dark, leathery appearance. In olden times, this was considered bearlike. It was a sign of strength. Until all skin and soft tissue breaks down to the bare skeleton.

The Lennox empire is going to be mine. Bearfoot Inc.

SCENE XXX

THURSDAY

THE PHONE WAS RINGING.

'Wee Theatre?' Fintan said. And then, more hopefully – 'Box Office?'

'Redford.'

'Oh. Mr, eh, McNair.'

'Like pulling teeth for you that, eh, fella? Heard you've been speaking to the local law enforcement, if that's what you can call him. Can't have you disclosing our wee "sideline", now, can we?'

'*Our?*'

'Aye. You're in my game now, lad. On *my* stage. Christ, it's even my idea!'

'The packages haven't arrived!' Fintan shouted.

'I don't believe you, MacMaster.'

'Why are you calling me? I have nothing. I'm telling you!'

Fintan was fighting every urge not to be excited by the apparent, impending arrival. A return to the intoxicating eighties. To the drug like a seducer rushing up his nostrils.

That over the decades became a thief. Thousands sniffed away. Lover-man had helped him kick it. If not the island. He knew how lucky he was to still even have what he had. But now he feared a return. An escape. To the old abyss. Maybe that was the *real* Looming.

'I've already been to deal with Lennox. It's my patch now.'

'Deal?'

'I don't believe you, MacMaster. That's why I'm here.'

'Where?'

'At your door, man. I want a part. I've a score to settle. I've brought script notes too.'

Fintan dropped the receiver. Looked out the theatre window. He saw a man at the porch of his house. Dressed in breeches and frilly shirt. Leather boots up to his knees. His black hair was shoulder length, clearly a wig. The mobile phone an anachronism in his hand. All he was missing was a match.

'What the fuck?'

*

Punch sat in the Ranger outside the caravan. He had thought to go after the woman, Bora. But decided to give her some space to make her own discoveries about her lad. He couldn't tell whether the case, if it *was* a case, was getting colder or warmer. But somebody was being careless with a match or two. And he knew fine well that on an island it didn't take much for one spark to ignite another. Just as he knew you didn't wait for the wind or the sea to bring news, or answers, from the mainland; they were usually right in front of your nose. Though a few gossips on the CalMac ferry probably did the same job. Maybe the theatre fellow had been up to nothing much more than an insurance claim – but Punch didn't like the proverbial being taken out of him. And now there might be a lad missing. Possibly connected to the cars, to the theatre.

He turned the Ranger around. Bora was not visible in his rearview mirror. He hoped she didn't have more grief ahead of her. He was starting to feel responsible for the island's status as an apparent safe haven. Was that not what Blair, and Major before him, had promised these folk? Was it really up to him to police government policy, to ensure its safe passage through the House of Hebrides? Next he would be fiddling his expenses, servicing Edwina Currie, arresting fucking bears.

He reached for the handset as he progressed back along the Glen in the opposite direction to the village. He turned the volume up in case he was being missed anywhere. Nothing came through other than a low-level gurgle, which could have been Guinness watering his plants. Before arriving at the woman's caravan, he had passed the Wee Theatre sign at the roadside. An impromptu billboard had sprung up by way of a wooden box with the title enclosed within it: *The Looming*. Could Stevenson be MacMaster? The connections seemed too strong to be anyone else.

He arrived again at the sign – at least it was a step up from inky scribbles on cardboard – and turned up the gravel drive into the parking area. Surprisingly, a Mercedes saloon was parked. *Andrew Lloyd Webber?*

Punch stepped out of the Ranger. Made a mental note of the model and numberplate. Next to it was MacMaster's battered Fiesta, making for quite the contrast. Success, and failure, represented in engine capacity, on wheels.

He walked to the theatre door and knocked. It released inwards. He thought better of removing his hat. He fully activated strutting-pigeon-chest-mode, and walked into the little foyer. In faded lettering there was a sign reading: *Welcome to the Famous Mull Wee Theatre – the smallest professional theatre in the world! Please take one of the 42 seats!* He was surprised to see another sign, even more faded, stating that the theatre was *a proud sponsor of the Tour of Mull Rally*. He had no recollection of the theatre being represented on the sides of the cars of his youth, alongside the sponsorship of local hotels. But he could still smell the rally stickers. He tapped his breast pocket for his notebook. Saw the production poster. What rubbish the man claiming to be Robert Louis Stevenson had spoken; a performance definitely worthy of MacMaster. He felt sure he could employ a thousand monkeys on a thousand typewriters and come up with better material. *Can't imagine the amount of shit, though, right enough.*

He heard an engine starting outside. Wheels spitting up gravel. He moved to the side window. But the vehicle was already out of sight. A loud voice was coming from the other side of a red door marked: *Auditorium*. He couldn't help thinking the promise of the signage was a tad overblown, but, regardless, opened the door into a room the size of a small church. He was standing at the back. At the front of the room there was one man on a low-rising stage.

'I already asked you to leave, man! I want nothing more of it!'

'That how you treat all your audience members, Mr MacMaster?'

Fintan stepped out of the light. Shielded his eyes. 'Oh, Christ. Sorry.' He looked searchingly beyond Punch.

'Close. He had longer hair. Not keen on his ending either. Who were you expecting?' Punch could see the man had undergone quite a transformation from the day before. He was sporting a shirt with a melange of frills populating his Adam's apple. Heavy sideburns.

'Nobody, sergeant. I was in character. Just, eh, trying things out.'

'Hopefully a sale?'

'What?'

'The Merc?' Punch pointed behind him. 'Tickets?'

'Oh? Aye, aye. At least there'll be some in. You're back again so soon? After a part?'

'Hamish MacBeth at your service. Guessing I'm too late for Cinders? Or was that nearly your house? Your clientele is going up in the world, by the looks of it. Sorry – the door was open.' Punch walked closer to the stage. The seating in the venue could best be described as quirky. Church pews long ripped out by the looks of it. 'Nerves getting to you, eh? Opening night just a day away?'

'More like repossession . . .'

'That an admission, Fintan? The fire?'

'No. Eh, no.'

Punch took in the full higgledy-piggledy-ness of the seating; each one, he saw, was a repurposed car seat.

'A gift-by-way-of-tradition that I inherited from the previous owner,' Fintan said, standing beside one of the two wooden chairs facing outwards on the stage, which was otherwise empty. 'The Mull Rally has always been associated with the theatre. A driver each year donates a seat. I know, quirky, and surprising for *my* types.'

‘Types?’

‘Come on, sergeant. I saw you all but take my *cravat* in for questioning yesterday. Old lady in the Spar asked me outright the other day if, I quote, “I was one of those pansies?”’

‘The millennium might take its time to arrive around here,’ Punch said.

‘Which one?’

Punch shrugged. ‘So, do you hand out steering wheels at the intermission?’

‘Nice thought.’

‘Nervous?’

‘No. Past that.’

You were certainly assured earlier. In the station house.’

‘What?’

‘Stevenson. Come on, man! Who are you now?’ Punch outstretched his arms; aware it was putting him at a weakness. The elevated position of MacMaster didn’t help either. The closest he had got to being called a *luvvie* was picking his mother up from the whist drive in Tob.

‘Can you not tell?’ Fintan said, stepping back into the spotlight.

Punch saw the man grow six inches. Looked him up and down. He was wearing knee-length boots, breeches and a waistcoat. *Have I been hitting the bottle too hard again?*

‘I’d say a Bay City Roller?’ Punch offered. ‘But then the breeches would be tartan, and a little more flared.’ He was surprised to be feeling so unsettled; *was* it the same man as had sat on his couch? ‘Bear claw’ cocktails served at intervals? Was there one on every seat?

Fintan MacMaster gestured with his palms towards himself,

then mimicked the movement of a writing implement in his hand, followed by that of digging a spade in the ground. Punch saw it all as quite the dance; he could see the man had more confidence, more assurance, in another's identity. He still hadn't seen the fellow in his own flesh, as it were.

'Burns?'

'Bingo.'

'Uh-ha.' Punch moved around the front of the stage, glanced back at the tired-looking room. The only royal box inhabitants fit for here were hanging on the slaughter hooks in his lockup. 'So it *was* you?'

'What?'

'In my station house?'

'No. I saw you here, sergeant.'

'Masquerading as, eh . . .' Punch couldn't get the name out. How did the man know about the almost child?

'Sergeant?'

Punch needed a puff and reached for his ear, then pulled away. 'I was passing and wanted to check if there was any more bother with the fire.'

'The one you already put out?'

'Aye. I wasn't sure if everything was okay. What with the lass being here too.'

'Bora?'

'That's her.'

'Everything is fine, sergeant. Thanks for looking in.' The man strode between the two chairs with intent. He produced a quill from his pocket. 'Yes, welcome to the inner sanctum of Mull's Wee Theatre, sergeant! Part of your island principality you might think, but which one?'

Punch took the roll-up, sparked a match and puffed; he was getting close to sticking cuffs on the clown, though it had to be said, the accent was believable enough. Next, Skerryvore would be treading the boards.

'The space you're standing in is famous for being the smallest professional repertory company in the world. I am *the Bard*, at your service! Tell me, on your way in, sergeant, did you perchance see an island in your peripheral? One that, ahem, *hadn't* been there before?'

'Enough! Joker! One mention of that fucking flagpole again and I'll kick your arse into my cell.'

'Sorry, sergeant? Is dressing up now an offence on Mull?'

'No. But breaking into another property is. Especially a police one!'

'No idea what you're talking about.'

'What's the story with the woman along the road?'

'Bora? No story. She helps out cleaning when we're in season.'

'Not sure she sees it that way. Don't have a part for her? That below you?'

'So, you're a casting agent now, sergeant?' Fintan gestured with the quill. 'Look, she doesn't exactly set a room alight.'

'And you do, Mr MacMaster?'

'I *do*, sergeant.'

'That what you did next door? The fire? Money job?' Punch was careful not to drop the Bosnian woman in the shit. 'Cars, on the Glen now, too?'

'What the hell are you implying, sergeant? Look, her son is a pest,' Fintan said, sitting on one of the stage's chairs, becoming agitated. 'She and him are always after something.'

'Like what?'

'Well, *she*, acting, and he for set designs and the like. I keep telling them I have nothing to pay them.'

'Would he need paying? Seems the lad is talented.'

'He wants, eh, *more* from me, sergeant.'

'Meaning what?'

Fintan looked towards Punch.

'I may not exactly wear my sexuality lightly, sergeant, but I'm not in the business of corrupting young boys.'

Punch raised a brow. 'This is only your script of course?'

'I've nothing to hide, sergeant. I'm frankly bored of you walking in here and implying otherwise. The lad has more to worry about with Lennox's lad if you ask me.'

'Hi-Pockets?'

'Yes. You see the two of them around. Walking the Glen. Strange pair. Codenames and drinking each other's blood is the word locally.'

'High praise coming from you. Tell me, does the Bosnian woman work on the Council, too?'

'No. In the Bellachroy, and I think she does some reading in the primary. Look, if you don't mind, I've a show being staged – hell's bells, tomorrow! A script to learn and . . . and . . . casting. Christ. And I didn't make it to Tob today!'

'How are sales?'

'Slow. But there's a wee Burns Supper thrown in. Three days late, but I hope it's a crowd puller. Piper too. Hopefully get a few from Tob.'

'Is Robert Louis Stevenson in the production?'

'I'm sorry?'

'Is he?'

'No. Is my "Rabbie" *that* bad?'

Punch hated to admit it, but the fellow seemed genuinely baffled. But then maybe he was a better actor than he, or anyone, knew.

'I really need to get on, if there's nothing else.' Fintan refixed his wig. 'Or is this where I ask if you have a search warrant?'

'No. This is where I find out why a man sets fire to his own house. You've a sideburn on the loose.'

Punch turned and walked down the aisle. He progressed back through the small foyer. He noticed a bottle or two of Bell's in what passed as the bar area. Cheap shite, undeniably so, but he did consider it. He arrived into the cold. Nightfall was on the next page. Cluny and special constables out there somewhere as stagehands. Monteith in makeup.

He fell into the Ranger. Took the handset and placed a call to Control. The numberplate. Better get it in for searches before another vehicle went up in flames. *Shit*. Punch couldn't be certain he had remembered it correctly. Decided to call it in anyway.

MacMaster had referred to Billy the Box. Had that been the real reason why Bora had said the wind farm was 'complicated' for her? Was her lad being corrupted by the Lennox boy?

Something else was troubling him. Unless, without him realising, MacMaster had dropped *The Looming* for a new production: *The Strange Case of . . . the Missing Seats*.

If MacMaster's gaff was really the smallest theatre in world, and famous for forty-two seats, then why had he counted forty-four?

SCENE XXXI

THE SKY WAS LIKE A darkening blanket being pulled over him. His mother busy stitching stars. *Celestial pace notes*. If only she was still capable.

Punch pulled away from the theatre. The Bosnian lad was troubling him; he also didn't fully believe MacMaster's denigration of him. He had radioed Monteith – who'd sounded like she was one grandchild short of a promotion – asking her to check in on the Bora woman; hopefully to confirm she had reached her son. Why was the hi-vis in her caravan – how many jobs exactly did the woman have? How many did she have to *do*? Was this the country, the definition of peace, she was promised? Or sold?

Punch turned right out of the theatre exit and onto the Glen. Soon he was passing the caravan. No lights on. He expected he might see the woman walking, but nothing. He passed the primary school and then, at the junction entering the village proper, he slowed down. He remembered how the stone wall opposite was always a good crash site for spectators. Often the colours of the vehicles were left on the wall all year round. Like sheep wool caught on a barbed wire fence. A left turn would take him towards the Old Byre, and further, to Calgary beach guarding the ruined village of Invea, where, last year, he had buried an effigy of Charlie. The morbid thought arrived as to whether Lydia Strathclyde had seen his brother's *actual* remains. He shook his head free. But feared only Ledaig eighty years matured could handle the job.

It was his intention to take the Atlantic coastal route past Calgary and further around to Ulva Ferry, to Dave the Grave. He needed to understand the undertaker's towing arrangements. Did Dave know more about the cars than he was letting on? Had the man corrupted young Billy in some way?

Punch was about to swing a left when he noticed Bora in the telephone box to his right. It had been there as long as he could remember, just a few of them remained on the island fighting a last stand in red cast-iron against perceived progress masquerading as cultural homogeny. Not even Mary MacBeth knew he kept a little tin of red paint in the boot of the Ranger. Further up the hill, parked at the Bellachroy, he spotted Randy's forestry Jeep. That was the turn he took. He peppered the brake as he passed the woman in the phone box, but didn't want to intrude further. She was facing the other way.

He pulled into the Bellachroy car park. The signage claiming it was Mull's oldest hostelry.

'Sarge. PC Cluny at the station. Over?'

Punch was struck with the lack of Tulliallen-speak coming out of Guinness's mouth. A slight tremor in the timbre too.

He killed the ignition and lifted the handset. Selected the LB channel.

'Receiving, PC Cluny. Any calls from the public? Over.'

'Nothing, Sarge. Anything of significance from Dave? Over.'

'Not as yet. Professor Strathclyde received anything further from Forensics? Over.'

'No, Sarge. She's retired to the Western for the night. But can be contacted at any time. Over.'

'Uh-ha. Craignure Dan, the special constable? Over.'

'Has taken over the night shift at the cars, as you instructed. Over.'

'Plans are underway to tow them in? Over.'

'Affirmative, as instructed. Over.'

'Good work, PC. We'll need to supervise this, of course. I need you to come to Dervaig . . . no. Scrap that. Monteith is meeting me at Dave's. Contact her and ask her to stop in at the green caravan outside Dervaig on her way around. It's located just below the turn to the theatre. A lad who lives there with his mother – a woman called B-O-R-A – could be in trouble. Missing, even. Studying at the Glasgow School of Art.'

'Caught up in the fire? Over.'

'No. Well, I don't know. Over.'

'I'll action all of the above. Over.'

'And stay put in case of updates from Control, or calls into the station. Somebody had to be driving those cars. Over.'

'Will do, Sarge. One strange thing. A weird man. Entered the station. Said he knew you were out. Over.'

'Skerryvore again?'

'No. He was even more, erm, out of . . . time?'

'That's saying something.' Punch let go of the talk activator, blew out a breath, then engaged it again. 'Who did he say he was?'

'Robert Louis Stevenson. The writer? Over.'

Punch thrust the handset home.

'*Sarge? Sarge?*'

Punch opened his driver's door and stepped out. Slammed it behind him. Put his hat on as he passed Randy's Land Rover, pushed out the full pigeon. Now he knew it was impossible that MacMaster was playing the joker. *Go with your belly.*

He opened the door into the bar. Clocked Randy with two Dervaig locals. All three with their backs to him. Facing him was a TV screen mounted onto the wall next to a dartboard. The sound was down, but the subtitles relayed news of a scandal involving a Scottish MSP. The tagline read: *FIGHTING FOR HER JOB*. The story changed to footage of the Glasgow School of Art. Presented as a smouldering pile. No causalities confirmed. *Relief, for something*. He felt more personally connected to the story now. Had he done his job? Played any part in ensuring the lad's safety? It seemed the world was on fire.

Punch walked to the bar.

'Aloha,' Randy said.

'Wish you'd stop fucking saying that,' Punch said.

'We're the surfers' paradise, are we not?' Randy smiled, a roll-up between his teeth.

'Mixing us up with Tiree, man. And fuck.'

'Islanders stick together. Yip yip.'

Punch saw how Randy was doing his usual channelling of Axl Rose, had the long-haired singer worked in the Mull Forestry.

'You're a long way from Tob, Ivor? You usually get a nosebleed by Loch Torr.'

Punch sniffed.

'They got you through customs at the hairpins okay?'

'Shut the hell up, Randy.'

'Just strange to see you over here. Like if Robert De Niro *hadn't* been in *Raging Bull* . . .'

'What?'

'Well, just . . . wrong, I mean. We saw that film over here, remember? Maybe why it came to mind. Cycling like little bastards! You bringin' up the rear.'

'Crime doesn't stop at the village signs. If I'm here then I'm here. And fuck.'

'*Crime?*'

'Does everything that comes out of your piehole have to be bullshit?'

'*Two* city boys we've got here now, eh?' one of the other two men said. Raising the brow of the other. 'Come for another football thrashing like in the primary? Or a whipping at the clay pigeons?'

'Aye, lads,' Punch managed. 'Gluttons for punishment.'

It was Longy, and his cousin, Langy. Abbreviated from the more official monikers, Longitude and Latitude. They were Dervaig natives given their nicknames due to their powers of navigation in helping each other stagger home come closing time most nights, though usually to somebody else's home, and occasionally to the surrounding undergrowth or a coastal cave. Often they were considered an extra stop on the bin lorry rounds.

'A Coke, please,' Punch said, in response to the open smile of the lady behind the bar who fell into the island category of *know her, but really don't know her*. He realised Bora was well short of even that.

‘Don’t worry, we’re fine, yip yip,’ Randy mocked. He nodded towards the music coming from the speakers in the corners of the room. ‘The new CD. *Randy Doodle Dandy.*’

‘It was only a matter of time,’ Punch said. ‘Of all the bars . . .’

He noted an extra dram alongside Randy. Maybe belonging to the woman behind the bar.

‘Aye, waiting on a round from Punch is like watching paint fade. Yip yip. More like Sergeant Pinch!’

‘It can be arranged. Minus the fan heater. Or bog roll. And fuck. And remember . . .’ Punch put the glass to his lips. Was close to clamping his mouth around one of the spirits dispensers. ‘It’s *sergeant,* when I’m in uniform. Out of it too.’

‘Sergeant Punch, eh?’ Randy goaded. ‘Wee Ivor all grown up. Well, on one side. Yip yip.’ He forced Longy into a fist punch.

Longy looked worriedly towards Langy.

‘Haud yer fucking wheesht, Randy. You want the thick blue door?’

‘Sergeant,’ Longy acknowledged.

‘How’s tricks, Longy?’ Punch managed.

‘Ach, alphabetical.’

‘Right.’

‘Aye, everything’s in order.’

‘Uh-ha.’

‘You’re just in time, sergeant. Langy here questions whether sheep can touch their tongues with their noses.’

Punch jutted his hat to the screen. ‘Shame *Prime Minister’s Questions* was yesterday. You’ll have to wait till next week to pose it again, Langy. Neckringable.’

The door to the Gents opened. Punch saw a skipper's hat appear.

'Sergeant!' Skerryvore said, scurrying around to the stool next to Punch.

'Skerry.' Punch nodded. 'Funny way to arrive into the village?'

'Eh? Did I not row?' Skerryvore looked back to the toilet door, confused. 'No, I caught a lift with Longy and Langy. Yes. I remember.'

'Fortnightly Co-op shop in Tob,' Longy and Langy said in unison.

'Thanks for putting me out of my misery, lads,' Punch said. 'Pit stop in Macgochs?'

'Anything for a free drink, that right, Skerry?' Randy said. 'Yip yip.'

'Though talking of *arrivals* . . .' Skerryvore enthused.

'Here goes . . .' droned Randy, into his glass. 'Our correspondent from the Hawaii of the North.'

'Have I told you,' Skerryvore persisted, 'when I rowed into Tobermory Bay surrounded by all that lushness from my native Tiree I thought the bottle had directed me to Scandi-bloody-navia?'

'About a thousand times, Skerry,' Randy said, leaning away from the old man. 'Tiree. The island deodorant forgot.'

'You're a walking tourist industry right enough, Sker! Hayfield Hotel!' Longy said.

'No door no bell!' Skerryvore chimed. 'Though not easy being measured against a lighthouse, boys . . .'

'Virginia Woolf had the same problem on Skye I hear . . .' Punch said. *Who knew Janice's bedside reading would count for something?*

'Every morning between nine and ten o'clock,' Skerryvore continued, lifting his big hands up before his entranced eyes, 'as a boy I watched a ball being hoisted at Skerryvore lighthouse to signify to the folk back on Tiree that all was well. And should the signal fail to be given, then a ball was raised at the signal tower at Hynish to enquire if anything was amiss. If no reply was received then the schooner was hurried from its wet dock and steered towards the lamp.'

'Now we know how to get a round out of you,' Randy said. 'Yip yip!'

'Before that of course it was the old semaphore system of hand-held flags and paddles,' Skerryvore informed them, whether they cared or not'.

'Instead of trousers or a dress?' Punch said.

'Eh?' The old man turned, gums on display.

'Eh, nothing,' Punch said. 'Nothing.'

The identity of the hi-vis was preying on his mind. Word would be getting out about the cars soon. Though he noted no mentions from the bar stools were forthcoming. Media briefings were on the cards if he wasn't careful. Inviting every conspiracy theorist this side of Ullapool to pitch in. The eyes would be on him, expectant, waiting for him to make sense of it all.

Skerryvore turned to Punch. 'So now we know!'

The child's sex, Skerry?

'The burning!' Skerryvore went on, taking his dram in both hands.

'Eh?' Punch said.

'From yesterday. Seems it was a spot of bother at the theatre.' Skerryvore nodded towards the door.

'Uh-ha,' Punch said. 'You'd have to have some conk on you, Skerry. Surprised you never called in the art school blaze.'

The seats from the cars were playing on his mind, too. Why the theatre's increased capacity? Didn't seem likely MacMaster was going to need them any time soon. Not unless Christopher Biggins was coming off the next ferry as Widow Twankey.

'Bugger there has a new *production*,' Langy said, as if on cue, reinstating his combover and licking froth from his top lip. 'Who'd have thought wee Dervaig would trouble the Book of Guinness, eh?'

'Instead of their distillery?' Longy offered.

Langy exploded into laughter.

'He's tackling *the island*, I hear . . .' Skerryvore hissed, toasting his glass to the west. 'You know. Burns and all that. Twice a century.'

'Like you getting a round in old fellow!' Randy said.

'Grandfather used to talk of it. Thon island.' Langy nodded. 'Spooky business.'

Punch was still with the image of the child's clothes blowing. He wasn't sure how to explain the professor having been in the station house to Mary MacBeth. They were in that awkward, not knowing stage again. Like being between two islands. *How could a lockup contain all that?*

'He'll no' tackle the bears, though . . .' Randy said. The 'bears' had been placed in finger quotations. Punch had arrested folk for less.

'Shut up, Randy!' Langy reached for Randy.

Longy took hold of his cousin. 'Don't take the bait, Jacky.'

'I'm just sayin', boys,' Randy goaded, 'school stories should stay there – at school.'

'I've fucking *seen* them!' Langy said.

Randy shook his head and adjusted his sleeve. 'Maybe one of those *furries* you saw. People identifying as animals. Walking on all fours and the like. Dervaig no doubt has a few.'

'Tob boys acting all superior again, Jacky!' Longy thumped his fist.

'Take it easy, boys,' Punch warned. 'Or you'll be identifying a thick blue door. I've pulled you in before, Randy, remember, to give Edna a break.'

'Thon time I put my birthdate down as 1756 instead of 1956!'

'Aye,' Punch said. 'You're not bad on the box but you're not Mozart. And fuck.'

'If I said I saw them, then I saw them!' Langy said, coming off his stool.

'Aye!' Randy mocked. 'Along with the Headless Horseman, the Grey Lady, Xander Lowry *and* Lord fucking Lucan!'

'Randy!' Punch said.

'The Grey Lady . . .' Longy shook his head. 'That one we *do* know about. Poor Duck. Hi-Pockets should be hung for what he did to his wife.'

'Keep the horseman out of it too, eh, Ivor?' Langy said, throwing daggers to Randy and nodding to Punch in recognition of the sergeant's ancestor. 'Forever embalmed in Mull folklore.'

Punch checked his handcuffs were part of the equation. The Grey Lady incident had been before his time on Mull. The nature of Hi-Pockets' wife's death had never been convincingly laid to rest locally. Case records had her documented as death-by-hypothermia. Which was a funny name for a husband, a drug habit, or being landed on by her older son.

'Family of them I saw . . .' Langy nodded, wiping his whiskers. 'Claws on them like two-ton peckers! One reared up to me and I swear it could've swiped snow off the top of Ben More! All 3,169 feet of the bitch! Don't mind saying I was shit-arse scared!'

'What you reckon, Mhairi?' Randy pressed. 'Need to cut these boys off? Yip yip.'

The barmaid smiled. Turned to wash glasses.

'Aye, anyway,' Skerryvore said, 'just the cloud formations to solve now, eh, Ivor?'

'I've got a CID unit on it as we speak, Skerry. Aye.' Punch downed the remains of his Coke. The bottle of Tobermory behind the barmaid practically had its hands around his throat.

'So, what brings you to these territories?' Punch said, turning to Randy. 'Never saw you as a protestor.'

'Eh?'

'The wind farm.'

'Posters are everywhere,' Longy said. 'Would you believe there was a march down Main Street here? People from away and everything!'

'Quite right too.' Langy nodded. 'Leave our wind to us.'

'Och, it'll not come to much, yip yip,' Randy said. 'No,' he added as he turned to Punch, 'I'm here for a wee practice. For the Burns thing at the theatre the morrow. I'm on the box. Hope thon fellow over there is good for a few quid.'

'You and . . .?'

'Dervaig Duck. Off the bins. Yip yip. Supposed to meet here, right enough?' Randy checked his mobile phone, which Punch could see now had an image of Pamela Anderson on it. In uniform of red swimsuit. 'Don't know why we have these things. Signal's blocked everywhere.'

'Maybe something to do with your choice of screensaver. And fuck. Eh, does he have a phone?'

Randy shook. Ran his fingers through his scraggly red strands. 'Said we'd meet here. He was away playing at a posh affair. Burns do in Glasgow. You'd think he was driving the bin lorry back . . .'

'He's not, is he?' Langy said; the man was still staring ahead, Punch noted, as though seeing claws on the barmaid.

'No. Took the Phantom. Yip yip.'

'That being?' Punch said.

'His new Fiesta,' Randy said. 'Fresh out the wrapper.'

Punch turned to him. 'You didn't cut through the Glen from the Forestry, on your way here?'

'No. We're on a felling job up the Kilmore standing stones, yip yip. Thought I'd kill two birds with, eh, one stone. Course, talking of which, Duck could've stopped off on the way . . .' Randy nodded to the door. 'To the caravan woman.'

'Don't go talking about that nice lady!' Langy reached for Randy again.

'Here, Jacky!' Longy grabbed his cousin's hand and moved it back to his glass.

'What?' Randy said. 'Not enough of her to go around, boys?'

Punch moved quickly between Randy and Langy. 'Stop, you buggers! I've got enough on my plate without bar stool brawls.'

He sat down again.

'You're not going to let a man with one wing shorter than the other get the better of you, lads?' Randy needled.

'Shut your gob, Randy,' Punch warned.

'Just sayin' . . .' Randy smirked. 'Aye, maybe Duck's got himself in a lorra *Bora* . . .'

'Right!' Punch moved off his stool, knocking it over. In one single action he grabbed Randy off his perch and threw him towards the door. He picked him up by his overalls and used a boot to wedge open the door. Then he shoved Randy into the night.

Punch wiped his frothing mouth and straightened his jacket as he turned to the bar.

'Sorry,' he said, with a gesture in the direction of the barmaid.

Then the door opened behind him.

SCENE XXXII

'FUCKING HELL, RANDY!' Punch pivoted to run, but stopped.

It was Bora. She rushed to the TV, trance-like. Then turned to the bar and caught Punch's eye. 'Could not get him!' she said.

The barmaid walked around, righted Punch's stool and moved to put an arm around Bora. 'What's the bother, Bora lass?'

'Where does Duck live again?' Punch said to the others, lowering his voice.

'*Well . . .*' Longy gestured his pint glass towards Bora.

'Right. Right.' Punch took his hat and walked towards the women.

'No casualties,' he said. 'Sure the lad is fine.'

'What have you all done to him?' Bora said, windmilling her arm to the room and then wiping her eyes, her hair falling out of its hold. 'Davud! His name means *paradise garden*.'

Punch stepped back. The lad's name conjured Lydia Strathclyde's work. He hoped there was no connection. He looked at Bora, then gazed to Mhairi for saving.

'What have *we* done to you?' Mairi said into Bora's face, while rubbing her upper arm. 'Scotland.'

Punch walked out of the pub. Thankfully Randy had done a runner. *Off to commiserate with Slash, no doubt.* Should he go back to the cars? But what could they tell him that they hadn't already? Tomorrow they would be taken in for questioning of their own. He was trying to put the information in some order; was he really reduced to Lydia Strathclyde running the bristles of her brush over the island? He needed to hit the stage. But was it Rally or Theatre? Maybe the explanation for the strange events was more *local* than he had thought. He decided to put Dave on ice.

He turned out of the Bellachroy and down towards the junction. From under the visor he took a roll-up, already prepared. He hit full beam. Full roar. Swung a left and passed the primary. His lights discovered the sign for *Caution: Deer*. He saw bear. He peppered the brake at the caravan. No lights. No Fiesta. No Duck.

Punch threw the Ranger around, back towards Dervaig. He put the lead foot down and grabbed hold of the handset. Selected a closed channel. Talking of formidable women, it was time to further involve PC Monteith. *Leave or no fucking leave.*

At the Bellachroy, he swung a left along Dervaig's Main Street. It was known on the island as *the sleepy one*, but he feared the place was about to get a wake-up call, big style. He progressed past the pitch entrance and out towards the coast. When he came to a slew of corrugated barns he swung the Ranger into the farm entrance. Slowed down to take in the placards and protest signs fixed into the ground. *You'd think it was Parliament bloody Square*. He progressed up the gravel driveway and pulled up outside the farmhouse, alongside several horse boxes. An orderly enough scene.

He killed his engine. Detected a beeping noise. Hadn't been here since trouble with the inhabitants' fishing permits. Small fry. Acting as visible warning of bigger catches.

No rally car. No Merc saloon. But Hi-Pockets' four-by-four was parked out front. He saw the source of the beeping. The driver's door was open.

Punch exited the Ranger. Noticed the front door of the farmhouse was also ajar. No lights on. He reached into the Ranger and took hold of the handset. Left the hat.

He walked slowly to Hi-Pockets' vehicle. Nobody appeared to be in it. The key in the ignition. He used his backside to bump the door closed. The immediate beeping had been dealt with, but now there was a fainter alarm sound. He turned on his touch and shone as he walked towards the house. The alarm getting louder. No obvious signs of anything amiss on the ground. All well maintained, for farming folk. Rounds of thick rope in orderly circles. A few creels. Buckets of animal feed.

He pushed the front door with his boot. Thought the better of calling out. Smelled burning. He walked into the kitchen. The beeping was now extreme. Every surface cluttered. Milk carton and a bowl on the counter. An Aga was centre stage. His light revealed a pot on the stove. Smoke rising from it. The pot completely black. Punch took it off the heat, closed the lid. Looked to the ceiling for the offending alarm. Jumped onto the counter and reached to press the flashing green light. *Silence*.

He took a knife from the rack. Noticed one was missing.

He shone into the hallway. Nobody. Checked the living room. Horse portraits all over the walls. None of people. The horses offset an evident masculinity about the place. He saw a chair was turned over. The glass table smashed. A copy of *The Oban Times* discarded on the floor. A story about the wind farm. Punched kneeled but saw no trace of blood.

He put on gloves and progressed slowly up the stairs, knife ahead of him. More horse portraits. At the top, his torchlight presented a mess of wellies. He could smell the aroma of farm. He stepped into one room, checked under beds, in cupboards and behind the wooden shutters. Nobody. Just overalls on the floor.

He opened another door. A mattress with no bedding on it. A hi-vis vest on a chair.

He walked out and approached the final bedroom. Turned the knob. Inside he saw posters of rally cars on the walls. Bands too. Some dark metal shite. *Billy's room*. He scanned the room, but there wasn't much more than a bed, a chest with a mirror and a chair. Racing leathers discarded on it. Two large gloves on the floor. Ski gloves. Too big for rallying. Punch turned for the door. Conscious of not contaminating anything.

He kicked the door to the bathroom. He held the knife aloft and pulled the shower curtain aside. Nobody. Though he suspected the farm animals used it too, going by the state of it. As he turned to leave, he saw evidence of a finger scrawl in the mirror above the sink. He leaned closer and blew hot breath on the glass. The words emerged:

Architects of the Post-Truth World.

Punch left the bathroom and headed for the stairs. He put a call into Cluny to get here smartish. The whole place was going to need going over.

Outside, he noticed two lines in the gravel. They led from the end of the path to where the vehicles were. Hadn't noticed it before.

He ran to the Ranger, put the knife under the seat. Fired up the engine and spun around. Billy's boss knew more than he was letting on. It was time for the House of Dave.

Punch had the feeling again. As though the waves were at his throat. When there was nobody left to trust on an island, it was as good as a prison itself.

He turned left at the temporary signage and sped back towards the village. At the Bellachroy, he took the hard right, then flew down past the empty phone box and onwards past the church. The Atlantic glistened to the west, a line of hazy promise on the horizon, as though restating: it knew. Now he was making up his own rally stages: Calgary, Treshnish, Burg, Kilninian, Ballygowan, Lagganulva. He thought of Bora. Felt the responsibility for policing the moral compass of an entire country. Twenty-two thousand officers, and he was just one. What had the Bosnian woman's boy got caught up in? He couldn't be in the art school fire, or the book wouldn't have made it to the Glen. Could the Duck lad, too, be involved? And what was he to Bora?

Punch worked the Ranger to the max through the windy bends. This was the road he was still to travel. He suspected it led to Hi-Pockets Lennox's other son. Billy the Box. Which led back to Dave.

The phone box was a red blur as he sped past it. He wound down to Calgary beach. From there, it was up and around the coastline. No barriers between him and the rising tide. Sea and only sea for company. Like he was the last person alive on this island.

The look on Bora's face back at the pub was an image he couldn't shake. When one tear, one *war*, would have been more than enough, he feared the island was about to cry the woman a river.

SCENE XXXIII

WEDNESDAY

'I KILLED MY OWN MOTHER,' Duck said, hitting the steering wheel as they vacated Salen. 'My wee brother's mother!'

'You didn't kill her,' Davud said. 'It was an accident. She wasn't supposed to be there. You said it yourself – drugs did it.'

'No.' Duck peered into the snow. 'I said my father did. All his shit! To think some folk think he's a crofter.'

'You didn't kill Vatra either. War did. I know that now.'

'I've spent my time since hurtling around like a runaway asteroid.' Duck put his hand through his hair. 'I wanted to drive the bloody motorbike into the sea. That's the truth of it. Never rode it again.'

Davud remembered how it had been parked for weeks at the Bellachroy.

'Everything was divided into the before and the after,' Duck said. 'Look around us.' He gestured with both hands. 'We're all led to believe we're living at the end of a rainbow here. But are we?'

'Hands on the wheel, please.'

'*The Bowline Bowline. Essential knot*,' Duck said, slowing into the corner that had the pair of children's shoes hanging by their knotted laces from a line above. Everyone on north Mull knew those shoes. '*Show me how you work the Bowline Bowline!*' That's about all he ever said to me. My dad. Rope was more important. Horses.'

'Maybe she's in a better place?' Davud said; he had had this said to him and knew it was a lie.

Duck laughed through his tears, which Davud only noticed just now. 'Like a ball of rubber bands she was! Before the drugs . . . Mum. Totally different person. Always on the horses. House clean as a whistle. Pulling open my shutters first thing. Worse than Yoko Ono with the shutters! Sometimes I wonder if that was what Mum saw that day at the pitch . . .'

'What?'

'Me on a horse. But I was always into bikes.'

Davud didn't know what to say.

'I don't like myself,' Duck said. 'Never have. Terrible that, to admit it.'

'My mum likes you.'

'I wondered, what did she want with a guy like me?' Duck said. 'Bora. She always seemed so *out of reach*?'

'That's what I thought about you,' Davud said.

'And I don't just mean the bit of age difference. Anyway, lad.' Duck wiped his face. He leaned down and picked up two cans of Tennent's. 'Help yourself. Your birthday week. We'll make a student of you yet . . . aye, aye.'

Davud took the can. He was relieved Duck had slowed down. Stole a glance at the dashboard.

12.2 miles.

They passed the grounded boats, then the Salen show field, where last year Davud had attended with Bearfoot. Who he was starting to think of as William again.

Duck accelerated them straight on at Aros Bridge, no indication, taking the Dervaig road. Otherwise known as the Glen.

Davud still hadn't opened the can. He was pretending to sip from it. The bombs were on his mind. Now he wanted to remove them.

About ten minutes into the Glen, the car began to stutter.

'What?' Davud turned to Duck.

'Shite!' Duck rocked back and forth, willing the car up the incline. 'C'mon, Phantom Blue, you fucker!'

'What's happening?' Davud sat straight up. He felt his head touching the roof.

'Bastard'n engine! Can't be playing up!'

'What's going on?'

'Driven faster sewing machines! C'mon, Donnie!'

Davud closed his eyes. Expecting a giant ramp. Evel. The Grand Canyon below. Distant cheers from crowds. Sideburns. A soft landing that wasn't earth.

Duck pulled the car over by a quarry. Immediately, the engine gave out.

'Calls itself a new bloody car?' He puffed. 'Shite!'

'You didn't mention this would happen,' Davud said.

'I didn't factor sending a bloody lamb to its maker, nor entering the Official Scottish Album Chart at number 389 either, but shit happens.'

They sat in silence. Duck reached back for his holdall. Shook the carcass off. Removed his phone. 'Motherf . . . battery's dead.

No signal likely anyway. Waste of notes the thing.' He tossed it back in the bag.

'What we going to do, Duck?'

'We'll wait for something passing. Where *is* a member of Take bloody That when you need them?' Duck waggled the gearstick. 'I can get a tune out of most things, but . . .'

They sat in silence. Visitors in the wild, as though they'd interrupted a play by fairies.

'In the days after, we found Billy around the coast.' Duck was staring straight ahead. 'That was when I lost him. Blamed me ever since.'

'Easier than blaming your dad.'

'Hi-Pockets had convinced her to start shifting the drugs. The land was failing us. Told her it was the only way to keep her horses. Then that became all she wanted. Oban, the McNairs, weren't far enough away. Hi-Pockets even had me delivering the blow around the island on the bin lorry. Could've lost my job,' Duck said. 'He and McNair were in the same class at Oban High. Some bad shite between them. But I got out.' He performed a cat's yawn, then drank from the can, grimacing, as though swallowing flame. 'I can only think she was larking about. Nobody could be bothered with her by then.'

Duck moved to touch Davud on the shoulder, but given he was holding the can Davud felt not Duck's hand, but the can. Duck pulled it away and took another gulp. He rubbed his face.

'And now he's part of it too, Billy. Gangsters on Mull, wee Dervaig – who'd have thought? And Punch turns a blind eye, sure of it. Hi-Pockets resented that I wouldn't do it. Fucked if I was losing my council wage for that man.' Duck turned to Davud. 'They haven't got you caught up in it, have they? I see you up at the horses, you know?'

Davud felt his body going stiff. He was sitting on it. So was Duck. He shook his head. Maybe his friend really wasn't his friend.

Duck tried the ignition again. 'Nope. Starter motor, I'd hazard. Can happen any time in fairness.' He looked out to the blackness. 'Be lucky to find a house. Baltic. Starving.'

Davud now felt he was betraying everyone. He couldn't tell Duck anything about the bombs. If he were to remove them then he wouldn't be doing what Billy had asked of him. Keeping their pact. Billy had said Davud could have the horses for himself if he stuck to the plan. He zipped up his parka and pulled the hood over his head. Blew hot air on his hands. It was almost dark now outside. Billy had said if he didn't go through with it then he would tell everyone it was Davud's idea. That he wouldn't be a post-truth architect anymore. He would be in Punch's cell.

'I did sixteen bodies. The week before.' Duck turned to Davud and, with an equal measure of pride and sadness, he flashed his teeth.

'I was proud to be one of them.' Davud looked through the condensation to the blackness outside. His ears were numb. He tucked his hands into the pockets on either side of the parka. Warmth *and* symmetry, he thought.

Duck narrowed his eyes into the rearview mirror. 'Lights!' He pointed. 'Finally!'

'An engine!' Davud swivelled.

The lights were coming from behind them, from the Salen

end. The car came slowly around the bend, flooding them with light. Hazards were engaged as it passed them. Duck and Davud tried to see into it. The car pulled over on the verge in front of them. It was towing a smaller vehicle.

'Of all the folk . . .' Duck swallowed. 'Now we're in real shit. But what's with the towing?'

Davud also recognised the hearse. It was too late to run. He watched, terrified, as the driver's door of the hearse opened. Would it be Bearfoot? His rally car being towed? Here to properly finish the job on Duck himself.

SCENE XXXIV

THE FIGURE WALKED TOWARDS THE rear of the hearse. Opened the back door, becoming obscured by the towed car. Was there a coffin? The person appeared with a warning triangle. Walked it past them and placed it on the middle of the road. Then walked back to the Fiesta. Tapped the window.

Duck wound it down.

'Grand Master! It's Duck!'

'I know,' Dave said.

'Thought we'd be here all night!'

'Oaf, a bit cold for that business, Donald.'

'You've got the hearse out late? And breakdown service is it now?'

'Oaf, a client from the Ross end. Broke down. Easier if I got him myself. So it looks like a hitch-hiking arrangement?' Dave bent to identify Duck's passenger.

'This is, eh . . . I was giving him a ride home from the ferry. A local lad . . .'

Davud, reluctantly, pulled off his hood. Forced a smile. He wasn't sure he had been called that before. A local. He'd noticed Duck's tone was different with the undertaker.

'Wearing the Order's jacket on civilian duties?' Dave said, gesturing to Duck. 'The Grand Lodge of Ancient Free and Accepted Masons of Scotland will consider this a breach, will it not?'

'Eh, early start in Glasgow it was, got dressed in the dark. Sorry, Dave.'

Grand Master, thought Davud. He watched the clouds of breath leaving Duck's mouth, becoming night.

'I mean Grand Master,' Duck said.

'A new automobile?' Dave said.

'Aye. Can't believe it.' Duck pointed to the towed car. 'Maybe the unusually cold conditions are causing the bother. Gulf Stream, my arse.'

'Will a maître d' show me to my table?' Dave said.

'Eh?'

Dave nodded his dome-shaped head to the lamb in the rear. 'I'm assuming a Burns Supper? I've a Burns book in the hearse. For funeral services, you know. Good to have the Bard to hand for emergencies.'

'Aye, aye, Dave,' Duck said. 'I keep a burner in the boot right enough.'

'Oaf here – let's bring the subject closer. I can tell it all about my Michelin stars . . .'

Duck reached back and handed the lamb to Dave. Davud watched as Dave held the lamb aloft.

'Like a bad episode of *MasterChef*, Grand Master,' Duck said.

'Or a good one of *One Man and his Dog*,' said Dave. 'And I'm guessing it's not the lamb who's gone a tad heavy on the aftershave. The booze, too?'

Dave reached inside his black mac and produced a scalpel. He pulled up his sleeve to his elbow. Then slit the lamb's fleece and manoeuvred his hand inside the body. Davud watched blood stain Dave's white cuffs.

'Sorry about that, Dave,' Duck said.

Dave reached in further. 'This is the contents of the stomach,' Dave announced, withdrawing from the lamb. He was holding out a bloody mass of gunk. 'Much the same gig with a human. Not for eating, though.' Dave tossed the lamb and its inners backwards, into the night.

Duck passed Dave some CalMac napkins. Dave admired the clean sweep of the paper cloth on his bloodied sleeve. Then on the scalpel.

'Not a bad napkin?' Dave said. 'We haven't met? David.' Dave said, leaning to shake Davud's hand.

'Davud?' Davud managed, shaking the hand, his nostrils flaring.

'Ah! We're brothers. Okay. Jump in the hearse the two of you. The body won't bite.' Dave slipped his scalpel into his mac and strode back to his gleaming vehicle.

'Body?' Duck said. But Dave was already off collecting his warning triangle.

Davud wanted to run.

Duck opened the door and the light came on. He took hold of his bagpipes and holdall. He surveyed the inside of the car for a final time. Davud picked up his rucksack and glanced at the front seats. It was too late to do anything. Oban would not be pleased. Nobody would be. At least Duck was safe. But what about the consequences for his mum?

He closed the door and the car turned black.

They walked to the hearse. Davud progressed uneasily, saw the moon reflected in the vehicle's rear window. He spotted the coffin and felt a sinking feeling in his stomach. It was hard to tell in the night, but the towed car looked similar to Duck's, only greyer.

Duck opened the passenger door.

'Not free,' Dave announced from the driver's side.

'Oh fuck!' Duck stepped back. There was a person in the passenger seat. 'Eh ... okay ... sorry, sorry, pal. Dave is this fellow dea—'

'Company,' said Dave. 'It's a long drive from the Ross.'

Duck closed the door. Took several deep breaths. The person hadn't so much as flickered acknowledgement.

Davud bent to see if it was Bearfoot. It wasn't. There was a very pale, perfectly still man, with a moustache preened like a musketeer, belted in the front seat. He had heard stories from William about the undertaker transporting the dead in this way, but thought it was simply intended to spook him. At least it wasn't William in the car. He knew Duck was thinking the same. William had said one day soon the undertaker's empire would be his. Like his father's. That his mother would have wanted it that way.

The passenger still hadn't moved.

'Oaf, there's room enough in the back for both of you,' Dave said. 'Either side of the coffin. Mind the flowers, boys.'

Duck and Davud manoeuvred themselves slowly into the back of the hearse. Davud's view of the milometer was obscured. No way of measuring.

The corpse sneezed.

'Oh good God!' Duck erupted.

Davud recoiled halfway up his seat. Reached for Duck's outstretched hand.

'May I?' the passenger asked, in a chocolate-toned English accent, signalling his camel leather glove towards the tissues on Dave's dashboard.

Davud reached for the door, but it was locked.

'Oaf, calm down in the cheap seats!' hissed Dave. 'You'll make a ghoul of our guest.' He turned to the passenger seat. 'Apologies, my friend.' He frowned with disdain in the rear-view mirror. 'Must have been Paco Rabanne in the back there . . . Not part of the rescue plan. Let's light another incense stick.'

Duck gripped his pipes. Davud was still pulling at the door handle in the darkness.

'Central locking,' advised Dave. 'Becomes operational with a moving vehicle. Even the dead can't escape. I mean, come to any harm. And mind your Ps and Qs.'

'Why can he . . . *talk*?' Davud said.

'Because he's a man for a' that. Like you and me, lad. As the Bard himself once was.' Dave sniffed. 'Oaf, I've, erm, moved into assisted dying, that's it. Aye. Not enough dead on the island. We all have bills to pay.' He turned sharply to his passenger. 'Eh, again, apologies.'

'None taken,' the man said, nodding as he raised, then lowered his glove to the rear.

Davud noticed how Dave touched the man's knee.

'This is Robert,' Dave said.

'Rab.' The man smiled.

Davud was delighted the man hadn't offered a hand. Was he in the Order too?

Duck looked reassuringly across the coffin to Davud.

The flowers spelled: *R O B E R T*.

He leaned over the coffin and whispered to Davud: 'At least it doesn't spell *our* names …'

Davud tried to smile.

'And don't worry lad, I can see the milometer. I've got you. Your reading.'

Davud felt embarrassed.

Could he tell his mother the truth? Maybe one day he would be known as a *real* architect. But would she live to see it? He brushed his heavy fringe to the side. Looked to the suspicion of mountains.

'Okay, David,' Dave said, 'gently on the accelerator. Easy does it. Extra cargo.'

Davud felt the vehicle gradually picking up speed and moving through the gears. Closed his eyes and saw flame again. Felt it welling up in him. The urge to burn something. He had to get out. He pushed his feet hard to the floor. What trace had he left back in the cars?

'Stop!' he yelled.

'Eh?' Dave hit the brake. They all heaved forwards.

'I want out!'

The central locking disengaged.

'Davud!' Duck shouted.

Davud grabbed his rucksack and flung open his door. He rolled out onto the road.

'Go!' he yelled. He slammed the door. Slapped it like it was a horse's backside. 'Gee up!'

Before Duck could object, the locks reengaged and Dave thrust them forwards.

Davud looked at the lights of the towed vehicle fading, disappearing around the bend.

He walked to the quarry. There was a small circle of stones. Evidence of fire. He took his sketchbook from his rucksack and threw it on the ground, inside the stones. He poured lighter fluid around it. Took hold of the matches. He sparked one. But couldn't throw it. He knew now you couldn't erase the past like this, not with flames. The match fizzled out.

He walked out of the quarry and onto the road again. His breath like a beacon clouding in the night.

'You were my hero,' he said, in the direction of the hearse.

Bearfoot, who was William who was Billy, wasn't a good person. Could he be out here watching him?

Davud turned to the abandoned car. Didn't know whether to wait for the explosion. Behind him a rustling noise. He turned.

'Vatra?'

He saw a lamb bound off onto the moors.

SCENE XXXV

THURSDAY

'SERGEANT!' DAVE THE GRAVE SAID.

'Christ!' Punch nearly went for his cuffs. He took a step back.

'What's the matter?'

'The mask, man. Remove the mask!'

'Oaf! Sorry, sergeant. Sometimes I clean forget I've got it on.' Dave lowered the fencing sword. 'Was just practising down the hallway.'

'Right.'

Punch was standing at the undertaker's front door. Even here – or, given the greater exposure here on the island's west coast, *especially* here – pebbledash. He suspected folk might actually find comfort in being received by St Peter, as Dave liked to refer to himself, in a building like their own. He wasn't sure the police cell had the same effect.

A rally car was parked beside the hearse. Strangely, no sponsorship or identifiable text on it. He had already despatched Cluny to the Lennox farm. The two lines in the driveway were about a human gait apart, he was sure of it.

Dave put the sword down inside the door. 'Welcome to Ulva Ferry.'

Punch took a rollie already prepared from behind his ear. The moon was fighting through and making something interstellar of Dave's hairless head.

'Oaf, sergeant, even for you I can't have tobacco in the house.'

'No bother, Dave. Quick puff out here.' Punch turned to the ocean, high in the sky and, to his eye, currently free of mystery islands. The small isles of Ulva and Gometra were down below, acting as brokers.

'My mother always said it was like a backscratcher. Rest her soul,' Dave said. 'A Lewis woman. Oaf, she'd lost two sisters to North America.'

'What was?' puffed Punch.

'The Atlantic. If you stare at it long enough then you start to itch.'

Punch took a deep draw. He thought of Charlie. Lockerbie. If only his wee brother had not scratched.

'Even the cockerel's not allowed to be with the hens on a Sunday,' Dave said. 'Lewis.'

'Randy wouldn't survive a week.' Punch gestured to the driveway. 'The lad's rally car?'

'Aye. Keeps it here sometimes does William.'

'No advertising?'

'No. A "statement" apparently. I joke it's because he drives so fast. Though the lad's increasingly full of them. Statements.'

'Right. He here?'

'No. No. Day off. I'm solo with the body from the Ross. You here about that? It's just PC Monteith called too.'

'Kind of.' Punch took a long draw. Turned to the scattered

pebbledash nearby, situated out here in farming country just along the winding single-track road from Ulva Ferry primary.

'Did I tell you I had Kennedy soup up the hearse?'

'Fair poke on her?'

'Monteith?'

'We might have a line of questioning, Dave. For you.'

'Me? Why me?'

'I'll come in, Dave.' Punch knew this wasn't going to be easy. He felt he owed it to Dave not to question him at the station. The undertaker was definitely more Classic FM, than Rod.

He took a final draw and, at the last second, managed to stop himself flicking it to the wind. The Strathclyde woman was with him even when she wasn't. A worry.

'Here.' Dave motioned for Punch to put his stub into the company mug. 'Come away in.'

Dave stepped to the side. Punch removed his hat but gestured for Dave to go first. Dave took up the offer. Punch grabbed the fencing sword and threw it away. Closed the door behind him.

'A herbal tea, Ivor? I make my own.'

'Eh, no.'

'If required, I can be clumsy with a malt.'

'Your own?'

'Yes.'

'No thanks, Dave.'

'Now let me help you with your bearings, sergeant.' Dave rotated on his heels. 'That-a-way is embalming.' He pointed to a door which Punch suspected led to the garage extension he had noticed outside. 'The office is for Masonic matters.

Kitchen is surgical. Front room for historical affairs. Bedroom for the information superhighway – from the German: *infobahn*. Oaf, I can hook up with Thailand in there. Brides on the shelves, the lot!'

'We'll keep that from Legacy Strathclyde. Professor Strathclyde, too.'

'Welcome to Sorry For Your Loss, Inc.'

Punch looked to a wipe board fixed on the wall, with the heading:

The 5 Procedural Steps of the Embalming Process.

'Sure they supported Jethro Tull once. And fuck.'

'For William's benefit,' Dave said.

Punch followed the heady trail of Blue Stratos to the kitchen. The hallway was immaculately presented, the walls adorned with photographs of Thai women. He strained to read what looked to be a handwritten note framed above the kitchen door.

'Invea,' Dave said. 'Census info. Wish I'd buried every last one of them. From the dead we learn, sergeant. Not the living!'

They turned through a doorway and Punch had never seen a more spick and span kitchen. Both men sat at the table. Classical music was playing quietly.

'How's Mum, sergeant?'

'Ach. You get used to reaching only half a person. Sometimes less.'

'Oaf, it's a hellish business that illness.'

'Uh-ha.'

'Same on my table. But know they're always reachable, Ivor. People think it's simply about applying a touch of rouge, straightening a tie and consulting the poetry almanac, but the undertaker's raison d'être is about more. William's still to pick that up.'

'Look, Dave.' Punch placed his hat on the small table. The spread incorporated a large Masonic emblem. 'That's why I'm here.'

Dave tapped the table. 'We refer to him as the *Architect of the Universe* in the sanctity of the lodge room, in Tob.'

'Billy?' Punch thought of the words in the sketchbook; the same as those that had also emerged in the Lennox bathroom.

'No! God. The letter "G" in Freemasonry is meant to remind us that all our lives and actions are performed in the presence of God. The Grand Architect. It bridges the gap between the material and the spiritual, the scientific and the divine.'

'I've heard the pitch already, Dave. Look, this is quite a serious matter.' Punch stood. 'I'll come right out with it. The hearse was spotted towing a vehicle on the Craignure to Salen road.'

Dave fell silent. Punch wished he'd known the formula all along, could bottle it.

'You never mentioned this, Dave? Reported as a small car.'

'*Reported?* Oaf, this all sounds a bit official, Ivor.'

'Call me "sergeant" when I'm in uniform, Dave.'

'Aye. Of course, sergeant. Am I allowed to ask who reported this?'

'I did,' came the voice.

Both men looked to the door.

A tall lady, short black hair, had entered. Red lipstick and blue eyeshadow.

'Rachel?' Dave said, his mouth ajar. 'We didn't hear you, lass.'

'"Police constable" when I'm in uniform, Dave.'

Punch nodded approvingly to the tall, sleek figure of PC Monteith, her hair Vantablack, and then to Dave, now rubbing his bald head with both hands.

'Who were you towing, Dave?' Punch asked. 'One of the cars?'

'Erm? I'm a bit tired . . . hazy . . .'

'Come on, Dave! This from the man who knows which body he buried on the third Tuesday in April 1978!'

'The morning of . . .' Monteith chipped in. 'Point being, we think you bloody well can remember what you were doing yesterday.'

'Right. Well, yes. I was.' Dave wiped his hand along the table cover. As though, in that pattern, he could recover his authority. 'I'd the corpse on the way back from the Ross.' Dave pointed towards the garage. 'I told you that, sergeant!'

'But you never mentioned towing, Dave.'

'You do a *car service* for the dead now?' Monteith said.

'It was Billy's car. I said he was practising his rallying. Lad broke down. The Glen. Oaf, that was it. I told you that as well!'

'I didn't see it as a rally car, Dave. No marketing, not that I could see.'

'His car doesn't *have* markings!' Dave shook. 'Oaf, and it was snowing. Look, what is this?'

'But she saw you *before* the Glen, Dave,' Punch said.

'Eh?'

Punch sat back at the table. Happy to take up the role of good cop.

'I saw you from the Fishnish road, Dave,' Monteith said.

'Oh? How was the wedding, Rachel?'

‘Forget that! So you’re saying the lad had been rallying the dual bloody carriageway?’ Monteith said, moving behind Dave.

‘And *did* you then take the Glen Bellart?’ Punch followed up.

‘I feel like I’m being hung like one of your sheep, Punch!’

‘You’d offer to tow somebody even when you have a body in the vehicle?’ Monteith asked. She hadn’t removed her hat, Punch had noted. The woman was terrifying, even to him. He’d had men ask to be transferred from her cell to his.

‘You need to be totally straight with us now, Dave,’ Punch said.

‘The Order’s surveillance is everywhere, sergeant! The lad was always on at me, wanting to join!’

‘Billy?’

‘Yes. William. But I told him it wasn’t possible on Mull. Colleagues cannot join the same order. That was when he started going to Oban. Even offered him sponsorship on his rally vehicle.’

‘Hi-Pockets is in the order?’

‘I’m not supposed to . . .’

‘Dave!’ Monteith pressed.

Dave nodded. ‘Though I think father and son are fighting over a different order . . .’

‘Meaning?’ Punch said.

‘All drama. Not sure what the fuck they’re caught up in. Excuse my French, Rachel.’

‘Drama?’

‘William attends in Oban, the Order. Actually, the same night he goes to an amateur dramatics class over there. So he tells me. Boy's dramatic enough if you ask me. He's a worry getting ...'

Dave looked down to his polished shoes. Brushed his hand on the tablecloth. 'If this is it for me in the Order, then every old horse at some point has to be taken off to the glue factory. But not my business, no?'

'Time for more straight answers,' Monteith said. 'The boy's here now?'

A bell sounded. Punch noted it wasn't the one he had pressed outside.

'Sorry, folks!' Dave said. 'A customer.'

'Book themselves in now, do they?' Monteith said.

'No. It's the alarm from the embalming room. The visitor fellow to the Ross is at the correct temperature.'

'I need to see in that room,' Punch said.

'Best you don't, Ivor. It'd be like me entering your cell.'

'It can be arranged,' Monteith said. 'In Craignure.'

'Look, Dave.' Punch stood. 'You're getting yourself in bother, let me get you out of it. Concealing evidence won't help with that. And fuck.'

'Evidence?'

'Dave!' Monteith said.

'Fuck. I told the lad he was going too far!' Dave rustled keys from his pocket. He got up and both uniforms followed him back down the hallway to the 'embalming' door. Dave turned to them both: 'I want it on record this was me just covering for the lad. He drove it here. Sweating. Forced me to comply! Talked about a new order. Wanted us to merge. Truth *Architects* or some gumpf!'

'Open the door, Dave.' Punch gestured with his left arm.

'The door, he said!' Monteith added.

'Heart attack he said.' Dave turned the key in the lock. 'I thought I was next is the fucking truth!'

The door opened. What had looked from the outside like any other pebbledash garage was a concrete room painted entirely white. Punch saw Mull's version of heaven. The walls had various coffins racked up on them. Two freezers at the far end of the room. A white coat was hanging, and at the opposite end of the room, a long table. On the table was a black sheet. The sheet was concealing something. Around the object on the table were various implements. As though a dentist had taken a career swerve into beauty consultation.

Punch heard Monteith inhale through her nose. Dave was standing with his head down.

'Dave,' Punch said. 'Who's under that sheet?'

'Fellow who keeled over at the Ross. Like I told you, Ivor. Just, eh, waiting on his people to make contact.'

'Prove it,' Monteith said.

'What could I do?' Dave turned to them. 'Said it's his empire now! But does he mean here or the horse farm?'

Punch walked to the covering. He removed latex gloves from his inside pocket. Put them on both hands. He lifted the sheet.

'Bloody hell,' Monteith said.

'Knew it,' Punch said.

Dave put his hand to his forehead.

'Hi-Pockets,' Monteith said. 'Christ.'

'Sergeant?' Dave said, his watery eyes halfway down his cheeks. 'Am I in trouble?'

Punch turned away from him. Removed the gloves and

darted to the door.

'Jury's out, Dave,' Monteith said, dispassionately. 'But status when it falls, falls hard. Especially on an island.'

'You know, even Burns himself had once to bid farewell to his Masonic brethren!' Dave said, slumping into despair.

'*Ye favoured, ye enlightened Few*,' Monteith recited. 'You might need more than poetry, Grand Master. Are the principles of Freemasonry not based upon honesty and transparency?'

They heard the front door closing. Punch returned to the room.

'Rally car's gone. He was here the whole time, Dave?'

'Aw, fuck!' Dave said, sinking yet further. 'Knew the tattoos were trouble! Drugs! Said he wanted me in on it. Said nobody would suspect a hearse. But I wasn't involved. I wasn't! Ivor? Rachel?'

'I have to ask you, Dave, did you kill this man?'

'No!' Dave shook. 'Ivor, I did not.'

'Are there drugs on these premises?' Monteith asked.

'No. Again! Look, the lad arrived with Lennox like this. Said it was natural causes. I hadn't had a chance to check his story when you arrived!'

'Need you to get your sense of loyalty in order here, Dave,' Monteith said. 'Like, sharpish.'

'He won't have gone back to the farm,' Dave said, his voice close to a whimper. 'Said something about meeting his "boss". *I'm* his boss, aren't I?'

'Constable Monteith will be staying,' Punch said. 'I won't read you your rights, but you're effectively under house arrest. Until we know more.'

'Scratch "effectively",' Monteith said. She moved to handcuff Dave. Walked him to the hallway. Pressed him down into a wooden chair inside the front door.

Punch walked outside. Monteith quickly followed, keeping the front door ajar. It was now dark outside.

'Poor bugger,' Monteith said. 'Can't imagine he's capable. But it never fails to shock what folk do in Mull pebbledash ...'

'It all happens behind pebbledash, Rachel. Keep your channel free. I'd go after the lad but I can't help thinking he's got an unfair advantage.'

'Age?'

'That too.'

Monteith took her radio from her pocket. 'Right I'll organise checkpoints at the ferries. We'll need to clean sweep this place. Can you imagine the fingerprint job?'

'I've already got units taking positions at Oban and Lochaline. I knew it was odd the lad's rally car wasn't anywhere to be seen on the Glen when the cars were reported. But where would he go now? Cluny and the specials are scouring the north of the island.'

Monteith gestured behind her. 'Think Dave might need a heavier touch?'

'*Some Guys Have All the Luck*?'

'It's a place to start,' Monteith said with a nod.

'Hi-Pockets? My God. Dervaig just got a lot quieter ...'

Lights were approaching. From the direction of Dervaig. The sound of an engine growling. Dan, the Craignure special constable, swung into Dave's driveway and pulled over alongside the two Rangers.

'Night watchman,' Monteith said with a tilt of her head. 'Prearranged backup.'

'Good work. Frees you up. Still, in all this, no evidence of an actual crime. Yet.'

'Let's check if the constable saw the car.' Monteith said. 'Media briefing?'

'Inevitable now.'

'What we need is the island to talk to us. Otherwise, when the teeth are shut the tongue is at home.'

'Young Billy's aspiring to box his own bodies now.'

'And inherit his "family business". Motive?'

'There's enough,' Punch said.

'Duck's the best of them.'

'Another thing . . .'

'Sarge?'

'The lab results are in.' Punch looked to the dark sky, then to the glossy blackness of Monteith's hair. 'They think they're animal bones. But human teeth.'

SCENE XXXVI

WEDNESDAY

WELCOME BACK TO CAVE LIFE. Two dead bodies. It never seemed possible. Like Michelangelo sculpting *thought*. But even he could not mix body parts between species.

Punch and his beanstalk are sniffing around now. And the flower arranger too. Does the man need a woman to do everything for him?

Leonardo has failed me. I even bought him a new sketch-book. One of us designing buildings, the other death. He was supposed to follow a plan. I need to go find him. Scene-stealer!

Then there is Fintan. Getting all impressed by the mainland. Well, he is one of them. Truth is, he needs McNair and his coke fix more than he needs me. Old habits die hardest.

'I'm an actor,' I told him. 'Not yet,' he said.

But the bastard wants me for other reasons. I thought I could convince anyone of anything.

So, I need to take myself deeper into character. Method, Mull-style. Beyond truth. One said he would get me to the Citizens – Fintan MacMaster. The other that I could join his

'Order' – Gerry McNair. But they were both bullshitting. Just hoped for the fool my dad is in me. *Was*. Like I'm not a valid person. Just as Duck and Dad treated my mum.

This cave is my stage. The island! Oban is the support act.

My curse upon your venom'd stang,

Tearing my nerves wi' bitter pang!

Mum – this is my final performance. My final stage. I'm coming to join you soon.

SCENE XXXVII

FRIDAY

SCRATCHING. SPINNING. CASE NOTES. Scenes-of-crime. All circling in his head. Dave. Billy the Kid. Hi-Pockets. MacMaster. Bora. Possibly her lad. Maybe Duck. The Grey Lady. Bad actors. All singing to somebody's tune. Somebody's else's script. Not his. Not yet.

Punch rubbed at his eyes. What a couple of days. Somehow he'd made it to Friday.

Wasn't he supposed to know everything that was happening on the island? It was like somebody had thrown a pack of clues into the valuable Hebridean wind.

It had been a stormy night. One of those when you expected to wake with no power. No badge. Just badgers. The three chevrons blown from your shoulder. Stuck with your own thoughts under candlelight. Locked in your own cell, rendered civilian. Like demoting Rod to assistant tour manager.

He and the unit had searched the Lennox farm and surrounds until daylight struck. No more leads had emerged.

He had come back to the station house for grub and must have dozed off.

Dave's place was now being given the once-over. The undertaker still under house arrest. Punch suspected by the time Monteith and Celine were done with him Dave would rather be laid out on his own embalming table. Hi-Pockets' body was already on the mainland. Before Lydia Strathclyde could get her brushes on it. Booked into the autopsy lab. Though Punch suspected Pathology would consider it low-level lab work. The heavy bruising around the neck didn't leave much to the imagination, but he wasn't expecting a quick response. Forensics were stripping the cars.

Punch felt burned out too. He daren't look at the liquid line on the Tobermory. He rolled off the mattress. Walked slowly towards the scratching sound. To the offending vinyl. Lifted the needle. Dylan? *Time Out of Mind.* Now he remembered putting it on. The final track. 'Highlands'. Dylan doing Burns. All sixteen minutes of it. The words circled his head; he felt stuck inside not Dylan's cage, but the island, if not the cell itself.

He picked up the phone. Dialled the number. His daily early morning check-in. One that always trumped any current case leads. The line ringing out unanswered never failed to feel like a new form of torture. Too many rings set his imagination running wild. He consulted the clock: *1.30*. The nurse would be well gone. He considered hanging up and just jumping in the Ranger across town.

'Glen Iosal, 2057?'

He closed his eyes in relief. And promising, Punch thought, given the numbers were in the correct order.

He reached for a measure and thought against it. For now.

'Mum, it's me. You're there then?'

'Well, of course I am if I've answered. You've slept in.'

'Aye, I have. Well spotted. That's good. You sound out of breath?'

'The hallway's like the Glen-getting.'

'Why the Glen?'

'Why not? It's long. A reference we both know. It's called a punchline. *Punch*-line!'

Punch heard the familiar cackle down the line.

'Are you preparing your sermon?' she asked. 'I like your sermons.'

'No. Remember, Mum, I'm in the police. Reverend MacLean does the other beat. I'm just your *chauffeur*, to God. Every Sunday.'

'What?'

'You govern the heavens, Mum, I'll take care of the earth.'

'Why are you telling me this now?'

'Because you implied I was a minister.'

'I didn't say that; I asked if you were preparing your sermon. What have I done wrong this week?'

'Right. Right. Guilty as charged.' Punch reached for the remainder in the glass. Took a warm hit. *Fuck the liver*.

'Hairy arms anyway. Not a proper minister.'

'Eh?'

'MacLean. You can see them from the front pew!'

'I've handcuffs if you need them. Wasn't Jesus himself in need of a haircut?'

'And while I'm on the subject, don't you think the newsreaders have hairier hands these days too? On the TV?'

'I'll prepare the cell. Better still, Monteith's.'

'The men too.'

'You okay, Mum? Your voice sounds a tad off.'

Punch feared a stroke. All he needed. *Nobody even to bury her*.

'My old knees.'

'Stiff this morning?'

'Uh-ha. You see, son, the thing about getting older is you need to know all this ageing is worth it. On days like this I'm not so sure.'

'I see the way you motor down the aisle at the church, Mum. And remember, I don't *have* a TV. Your voice is . . . sure you're feeling okay?'

Punch looked to the spot where there might have been a TV, were it a normal house, a normal life.

'Anyway, lad, I called you about the not insignificant matter of a person's teeth.'

'Remember, I called *you*, Mum?'

'They're not in my mouth! I've had these teeth thirty years and then . . . *nothing*!'

'Right.' Punch knew instantly where this puzzle sat in his pecking order. 'Both sets, Mum?'

'Just the bottom. Those *pizza* things in the Co . . . hard as nails.'

'Christ.' Punch took a glug straight from source.

'Language! Leave my son out of it!'

'You're meaning Charlie, I think, Mum. Can't be me anyway.'

'Where is Charlie?'

'Remember we lost him, Mum.' Punch felt his gullet closing. Cleared his throat. 'Look – about the teeth . . .'

'It's not my fault, Ivor!'

'I know. It's the Co's. I know, Mum. But I thought we'd decided to give the pizzas a wide berth?'

'No! It's this head of mine!'

'I know, Mum. I know.'

'You picked the messages up! I thought you'd know.'

'Why does everyone think I know everything? Anyway, that's why I'm calling you. Your weekly shop . . . I'll check for the teeth when I bring it over. The usuals?'

'Is it that time again? Your uncle used to measure time in sheep fleeces, you know, during the slaughter months . . .'

'Any specifics?'

'Pizza.'

'Really?'

'Yes. I like this new invention.'

'Right. Look, I'm busy with a case but I can head down now. Then I'll check your bin.'

'No need, son. The nurse. I think she took them. Made a puppet of me!'

'No, Mum . . . I'll double-check when I've done the shop.'

'A gossip? She doesn't leave the phone alone. She adds years to me. Oh, son?'

'Mum?'

'She visited yesterday. Always has a tear in her voice. I think you know why.'

'The nurse?'

'No. Mary MacBeth. Fix it.'

The line went dead. Punch replaced the receiver. The only person on the island he could take orders from.

He checked his radio handset. Volume was up and it was set to receive all channels. Control would notify about the post-mortem as soon as it was in. Two burnt-out cars, a village in protest, and an all-nighter search of Hi-Pockets' land had reaped nothing. Dave was undoubtedly a dark bastard, but was he really capable of conspiracy to murder? *Not likely*. Manipulated by his protégé? *More likely*. Cluny had been instructed to get out there at first light. The DCI had insisted on two officers from Oban coming off the first ferry to assist. But assist what?

Duck still hadn't transpired. There had been nothing from Bora. He couldn't trespass on her again unless he had something more concrete.

Punch moved to the window. Saw just his own Ranger parked at Dodge. Monteith and the two special constables had policed Lennox's leaving of the island, met by a Forensics team from Legacy Strathclyde at the other side of the water. Punch had passed on another item to them. Thankfully it had escaped Mary MacBeth's kitchen sponge. *Stevenson's* tumbler.

He needed time to try and piece it all together. Too many roads and not enough signs. He was dangerously close to having to stoop to asking Randy to raise a team. This was when TV coppers usually stuck photos and Post-it notes on walls, attached them with pins and string. Punch preferred to find order, those potential connections, in his head. But his mum needed him. That took precedence.

He emptied the glass. Looked at the bottle with a mixture of regret and further regret. In equal measure alarmed at his overnight consumption, and how little he had left for later. Tonight was MacMaster's show. If folk would even attend now. Or maybe the macabre was a draw. Fact more powerful than fiction.

He took hold of his bunch of keys and hat. Locked the door behind him. He jangled towards the Ranger, unlocked it and jumped in. Driving down the Western Road he passed the town's only palm tree. *Not technically an offence.* Then the Western Isles Hotel, where Lydia Strathclyde would about now be putting her organic eggs under the microscope. He took the sharp turn onto the Back Brae. Always vital to make the turn in one continuous movement. Cluny had already disgraced himself with the locals to this end. The task completed, Punch progressed down towards the seafront. He saw Sonia Hislop walking ahead, the painter-cum-barmaid in Macgochans. She was going in the direction of the seafront, walking with her usual air of grief. As if being a widow wasn't hard enough, she too carried that condition that came without a name; she too had lost a child. Albeit in more tragic circumstances.

Punch drove past her. Promoted a cheekbone by way of recognition.

The bay glistened, boats swung. Punch turned right at Tackle & Books and along the Main Street. Friday. Full-day opening, but quiet, with the air of the working week limping to an end. He would happily be invisible, unbranded, rid of the Ranger's fluorescent stripes. Guinness was forever making his vehicle too clean. The man hadn't yet realised that police work was about *not* being noticed.

He pulled in and stepped out of the Ranger.

'Hello, sergeant.' A voice, almost lost in a purple woolly hat. 'Goodness, I always want to call you Ivor, lad. Still see your mother in you, even in the uniform. And, eh, of course . . .'

She stopped, but Punch knew who she was referring to. Not Charlie. But his uncle-who-was-not-his-uncle.

'Uh-ha, Jessie,' Punch said, crossing the road to the Co-op entrance.

Punch watched her move off and then stop to attend to her yapping dog, which she had tied up outside. She spoke without turning to him.

'You're a good lad getting the supplies in. Say hello to Jane. Like pulling teeth in there . . .'

'The pizzas?'

'Eh? No, the lad on the till. You'd get more chat from Chaplin.'

Punch walked into the shop. Being in the Co, and uniformed, always felt to him like he imagined Rod would feel if he were to walk among the fans on the venue floor before the show. He made his way speedily up and down the few aisles. He arrived at, not the *teeth* section, but the frozen foods. He lifted two pizza boxes up to his face, trying to determine which had the thinner crust.

'I've heard of police surveillance, but . . .'

Punch turned and his hat slid in the process.

It was Sonia Hislop. Her hair bleached now, in the Western Isles Hotel uniform.

'Oh?' Punch said. 'Aye. Sorry.'

'For what?' She smiled.

Punch was glad to see the lass a bit brighter. And paint evidenced on her. A good sign too.

'Do you need in?' he asked.

'No. You're okay. Thanks again.'

'For the pizza inspection?'

'No.' She laughed. 'For the Christmas tree. And for painting the sign on the rock face this year. Again.'

'Wasn't sure if I should stop?'

'No.' Sonia smiled, briefly clasped 'thank you' hands, and moved off.

Fuck, Ivor. Steady.

He selected the least offensive pizza and dillydallied a little until he was sure Sonia Hislop would have vacated. Poor lass, only buying for one, when she had once been three. He grabbed a few of the other weekly essentials. Luckily, no queue.

Punch forced a smile to the lad at the till as he began scanning his items. He didn't recognise him. He counted at least eight piercings on the bugger. Each item was transferred from the basket to his other hand, and from there to the bagging position. Punch noticed the items piling up. The pizza was the last to be scanned.

'Do you have bags?' Punch asked.

The lad said nothing. But produced a handful of carrier bags and placed them on top of Punch's items. Punch had to look to the register to know how much it had cost. He couldn't decide whether he admired the lad's cheek or wanted to give him no bog roll and some third-rate Rod for the night. He paid and the lad placed his change by the bags.

'Don't get up,' Punch said.

As he turned to exit, he couldn't resist checking the logo on the lad's shirt. For a bear claw instead of Co-op? But no.

He took the bags in each hand. Made sure to level out his arms. He moved to cross the road. A car horn sounded. Punch stepped back. A Fiesta pulled in and parked on the new double yellow lines. The only ones on Mull.

Punch was starting to wonder if Fiestas were taking over the world. If not red tape.

The driver opened the car door.

'You know you can't park here,' Punch said.

'Morning, officer.' The person signalled to the shopping bags. 'Oh, so you *do* eat? Shop? Like the rest of us.'

'It's sergeant. And do you not see the yellow lines?'

'Oh? Do you observe them?'

'You'll need to move.'

'More infiltration from the mainland?'

'You said it.'

'I'll just be a jiffy, sergeant, a few supplies for the do tonight – that okay?'

Punch noticed the Mull Wee Theatre sticker on the driver's door. He looked closer at the man. It was Fintan MacMaster, as God intended. He hadn't recognised him out of the powder room.

'Oh? It's you? No, you'll need to move.'

'Really? What an irritation!'

Not as irritating as your ponytail.

Fintan shook his head. Got in his car and reversed to another parking place. When he returned, Punch detected makeup still around the man's temples.

'What?' Fintan said.

'Wine. Potatoes. Haggis. But I'd forego the matches.'

'I know! On my list! You make them sound like suspects.'

'Any other visitors to the theatre?'

'Sorry, sergeant, I don't log every customer that pulls in.'

'No? You're not exactly employing a parking valet though, are you?'

'Not sure any of this is an offence, sergeant. I need to get on.'

'How's Burns?'

'As prepared as he can be, I suspect.'

'Still a one-man show, is it?'

'Yes,' Fintan said. 'Likely.'

'Likely?'

'Yes. Bloody yes!'

'Setting *the stage* alight this time, eh?'

'Sergeant, I must get on.'

Fintan MacMaster walked off, manbag slung over his shoulder. He petted a dog before entering the Co. *Seeing this man twice a century would be twice too many times.* But an actor-director, or whatever the bugger was, who didn't confidently know his cast list on the day of the production, surely that wasn't the norm?

Punch walked to the Ranger before he could be accused of having a can of yellow paint in his boot. He spotted the rear of a man in an off-white, ballooning shirt. Dark hair and long boots. Walking behind the clock. Punch saw the man disappear up the lane between the Co and the Captain's Table. Punch dropped the shopping bags and walked quickly to the lane. The man was out of sight. Punch ran up the lane. Turned right onto the old Tobermory Main Street. Expected Kirsop plumbers' vans, but instead a car came speeding towards him. Punch jumped out of the way. *Was it open fucking season on attempted hits on him?* The car screeched around the corner. It was the Mercedes, red wine colour, the same one he had seen at MacMaster's. It flew out onto the Main Street and careered right. Punch sprinted after it, his hand on his hat. He hadn't properly seen the driver's face. But he was sure it was him. Couldn't bring himself to believe it. The dead writer.

He ran out onto the street. The Merc was already out of sight. Only evidenced by a distant roar. He ran to the entrance of the Co-op. Nobody was outside. Just another dog barking; that was the extent of his witnesses. He turned one-eighty. Ran to the Ranger, threw the bags in the back seat, jumped in and sped off. He put the lead foot down as he headed up the Ace Brae; the Merc would be well ahead, but it was worth circling the town. Along the top roads there was nothing. He considered searching out the Salen or Dervaig roads, but he needed to make a pizza delivery first.

He pulled into Glen Iosal sheltered housing. Took hold of his handset and called the Mercedes numberplate into Control. Took the ribbing about whether his memory was failing: *have you definitely got it right this time?* Little did they know his nascent fears. They'd get back to him, they said. Nothing through on Lennox yet. Lydia Strathclyde would be at the station soon, where he'd arranged to meet her.

He took the shopping bags from the back seat and kneed the door closed. Walked to his mother's red brick home in among the many other red bricks. The house next door belonged to the old twins, Tinsel and Tonsils. Neither were evident. Just the scattering of wooden swords outside.

He rustled his keys and fitted the correct one in the door. Tried to turn the key. But it was already open.

Punch slowly turned into the small kitchen. By now he would usually have announced his arrival. He put the bags gently on the counter. Stepped lightly along the corridor. Past the framed photo of Lady Di. The door to the living room was open as always. He poked his head around the corner.

His mother was sitting watching the TV with the sound down. Punch scouted the rest of the small room. Looked through the patio doors to the patch of garden. All clear. He went back along the corridor. Chairlift was at the bottom. All as expected. He walked up the stairs. Her bedroom and ensuite all clear. Damn sight cleaner than the Lennox gaff.

He jogged back down the stairs. Into the kitchen. Took the cold items from the bags and put them in the fridge.

He ran to the living room.

'You want the sound, Mum?'

Nothing.

'Mum?'

Nothing.

'Mum!'

'Oh!' She turned to him. 'Are you leaving, son?'

Punch blew out. 'Eh, no. Just arrived, Mum. Christ. You okay?' Punch leaned to her, worried she might have stroked. 'Front door not properly closed again. Must be catching.'

She jolted when she saw the uniform.

'I don't have any!' she said, pushing herself back into the armchair.

'Steady, Mum!' Punch moved away. 'Any what? It's me! Ivor.'

'Drugs!'

'Drugs?'

'That was my husband's game. Gangsters! All of them. Except his brother there. All talked with their hands, of course. The only good egg among them.' She pointed to the empty armchair opposite, where Ivor's 'uncle' would sit, albeit in the old house.

'That's why we moved to Inverness! Still not far enough away.'

'Eh, Mum? Settle down. That's it.'

Punch had never heard any of this out her mouth; but he couldn't believe much of what she said now in any case. Last thing he needed was the island becoming flooded with cocaine, but he wasn't expecting Glen Iosol to be a focal point for narco-traffickers. Though Eric Clapton had once been spotted in Macgochans.

She sat up straighter. Gulped several times and took a tissue from under her cuff. She was watching some game show. *Folk acting like arseholes.* Punch plumped up the cushion and placed it back behind her.

'Your teeth!' he said.

'What about them?'

'You found them? You've both sets. In your mouth?'

'Yes. Where else would they be?' She settled again. Faced the TV. 'The nurse said he's going to a Burns Night later. All right for some.'

'He?'

'Aye.'

'But your nurse is a woman. Linda? Remember?'

'Whoever it was, they put my teeth in my mouth. And said they're going to a Burns Night later. Are you questioning me?'

'No. No. Where's the Burns do?'

'Dervaig. That tiny wee theatre.'

'Look, have you ever, eh, heard of the Looming, Mum?'

'The what's-that-when-it's-at-home?'

'An island. Only appears, eh, every so often . . .'

She shook her head. 'That like the one the fellow Bergerac's on?'

'Eh, aye. Something like that. I need to get on, Mum. Will I flick the kettle on?'

'No. The man got me one already.'

Punch leaned to put his hand on the cup by her side. *Still warm.*

'What man? The nurse?'

'A man came to my door. I thought he was selling Bibles at first. Nice fellow. Old fashioned. In fancy dress or something. Had me searching for guineas.'

'What did he look like? *Did* you give him money?'

'No. Said he was an actor. Like the nurses on *Casualty* I thought?'

Punch inhaled. He noticed a note on the table. It was in the same cursive handwriting as the notes he had found on his sofa.

Ye favoured, ye enlightened few. But it's my turn now, Ivor. And fuck.

Next to the note. A drawing of a bear roaring.

SCENE XXXVIII

FRIDAY

'TALKING OF WILD HABITAT, I'd be careful running your brushes in here,' Punch said, turning the key in the station house. He was still reeling from the note left at his mum's. He'd instructed Jamesie to keep watch outside her house. Had to fetch the bugger from the distillery.

Punch had a date to keep. He pushed open the door and stood aside, motioning Lydia Strathclyde to go inside first. He stepped in behind her and looked with some embarrassment at the calamity in front of him. One of the two Oban uniforms was next door in the station, leaning on Dave. He figured it might reap more rewards if he and Monteith weren't involved. Dave had looked like a man about to lose his IP address. Still maintaining he had nothing to do with it. Though Monteith had extracted some evidence of questionable activities relating to euthanasia.

The other Oban copper was out looking for the Merc. Checkpoints widened to main road routes now too.

'You didn't say you were, eh, *so* house proud, sergeant.'

'Uh-ha. Look, we'll, eh, need to be quick here. Several new leads have opened up.' Punch had left his mum's smartish. Having made sure the actual nurse sat in with her. He'd knocked on Tinsel and Tonsils' door to check if they'd seen a Merc. Half expected their doorbell to be a roar. But no answer. The old fellows would already be up and scouring the golf course for balls, no doubt. He'd flown around the town a few times, but no sign of the mystery saloon. The number-plate search had been a dud. It wasn't even registered. Home-made job.

'Need to get that nice boy of yours to lend a hand in here,' Lydia Strathclyde said.

'Guinness?'

She chuckled. 'Didn't notice it on his name plaque, but nice.'

'I hear there's nothing yet from fingerprinting?'

She shook. 'Bones and teeth are at the lab too.'

'Separate labs?'

'Not necessary. So you ready for the flower show? Haven't done an all-nighter like last night in years.'

Punch's hunches were lying elsewhere. Monteith was investigating potential Masonic Order connections between Dave, Hi-Pockets and Duck. The piper was still unaccounted for. As was the Bosnian lad. He suspected Bora might only speak to him. Not that he had done a thing to help her. Calls had been placed to the art school investigation. Definitely no bodies had been found. He was starting to think the phone box in Dervaig knew more than he did.

He looked to the record player. It was spinning again. Maybe it was Dylan, moving in, taking the place of Rod. What was Bob trying to tell him? Punch glanced at the couch.

No markings. He scouted out the rest of the single-storey house. Nothing. No jokers.

He arrived back to see Lydia Strathclyde leaning over the turntable. She part sung, part recited several lines from the album.

'So it's not been all just plants, eh?' Punch said, taking the empty bottle and putting it behind the bins.

'Mostly, I'm afraid, but everyone makes space for Bob. It's an endless vocation; you know there are just over seven hundred and ninety species . . .'

'Of Dylan?'

'Of plants, sergeant. And that's just up until last year. They include sixteen species of bramble, six species of rose, thirteen species of eyebright, thirty-six species of hawkweed, twenty-five species closely related to the dandelion and fifteen species of pondweed.'

'And I thought Bob was prolific.' *Fairly sure Randy accounts for the pondweed.*

Lydia Strathclyde moved towards the discarded record sleeves.

'May I?'

Punch nodded. Though the clock was ticking. *The Clock was thirsty.*

'Rod?' she asked, leafing through.

'Mostly.'

'Ah?' She held one aloft to him. '*Brandenburg Concerto* has found its way in, I see. Not The Faces version, I assume?'

'Forgot about that one.' It had been a gift from Janice in Inverness. She who had tried to identify his species a bit too closely. 'Like taming the wild' she had called it, as though it was an assignment dished out by Legacy Highland Division.

'We'd better get on.' Punch yawned, motioning towards one of the chairs by the breakfast table. He moved to remove the discarded trousers from it before they did so themselves.

'Okay.' Lydia sat on the seat and Punch cleared the cereal bowls off the table. 'So, I've brought all my case files. I might have a steer.' She took her papers from the wallet and carefully placed them around the table. She produced two books. 'Thank you for dropping these in to me.' She read both titles: '*The Plant Life of Mull* and *Natural Mull*. Good. These were helpful.'

'Duncan in Tackle & Books must think I've given up battleships for plant beds.'

'Not to mention hocus pocus.'

'Remind me what we're looking for?' Punch dropped into the other chair.

'Profiles of pondlife *and* honeysuckle.' Lydia Strathclyde took a pencil from behind her ear. Allowed her reading glasses to fall from the bridge of her nose. 'To some in this game they're seen as giving off mixed signals. But *huge* honeysuckle. No.'

'And that's what you detected on the Glen?'

'Yes. But if something *were* to correspond in here, it must be coastal. That's not so common, which is why I thought this was worth a try.'

'Uh-ha.' He couldn't help thinking Dylan, with his heart in the honeysuckled-Highlands, had gotten even here, first.

'You paying attention, Ivor?' She turned to him. Mascaraed eyes like slits. 'If I may?'

'Aye.' He brushed his unshaven face. 'On it.'

'Look, I just wanted to say, to acknowledge, how incredibly, well, *open* this is of you. You know, open to trying new methods. Convention, the norm, the traditional – well, it is hard for anyone to surrender. *Especially* within Legacy Strathclyde. And here I am, here *we* are, having gone even deeper into the division, to Lima Bravo, by Jove. You should be very proud of yourself.'

Punch was ready to handcuff himself for even thinking about going *deeper* into Strathclyde.

'I've been looking at the records. There was a coastal death on Mull in the early nineties.'

Punch had still been propping up Bute at the time. But, of course, he knew she was referring to the case involving the Grey Lady. Now her man, Hi-Pockets, had gone too. And both her sons apparently missing?

'Is she still a cold case?'

'Not exactly,' Punch said. 'Well, no. It was determined at the time to have been an accident; that is all I know. Tragic really. Her son landed a motorbike on her. She wasn't of sound mind.'

'Good God. Really?'

Punch nodded: *yes, really*. 'But it could be related,' he told her. 'Before my stint as I said, but there was a lot of rubbish spouted at the time about the woman. Even now you hear it. Folklore gone bloody mad.'

'I can only access so much of the notes.'

'She had a drug habit.'

'But I read other accounts. Some quite, well, *out* there.'

'That's the thing with folklore – you can't lock it behind a thick blue door.'

'That's exactly it, isn't it?' She removed her glasses and swung them in her hand. 'Caves. Bears. Bite marks that couldn't be explained.'

'Look, this is Mull, professor, not Montana.' Punch figured it wasn't the time to go full-on Christian name.

'Yes, you need artefacts . . . shoes . . . clothing . . .' she sang. 'I get that. But . . .'

'I've given you two cars! And fuck.'

'Generous.' She looked away.

'Sorry. It's been an intense couple of days. Nothing worse on an island than the past interfering with the present.'

She put her hand on his. Smiled. Her eyes twinkling. 'I get "goldfish bowl". Sherlock *Combs* they called me in Aberdeen.'

If he could, Punch would have laughed.

She took her hand away.

He was starting to suspect the two *brothers* might be more relevant. It was well known the Lennoxes were a family pulled apart. But he had never had anything to pin on them. Drug-running had always been known, but not known, and on an island people spouted lots of shite. The sergeant before him had warned him it was best left alone. That one big, known dealer was better than a hundred little fish swimming under the surface. The MacTavishes, the other crofter-cum-rally-driving family with 'extra-curricular' activities, on the other side of Salen, were an easier read.

The professor reached for one of the books Punch had provided. Pages had been noted with yellow markers.

'Okay, so . . . Mull . . . coastal . . . pondlife . . . honeysuckle . . .'

Lydia Strathclyde spent several minutes with the text, taking more notes as she went.

'We drove through Dervaig, am I right?' she asked.

Punch nodded.

She selected the other book. Punch, growing irritated, looked to the door. The answers were out there now. Not in the pages of books. Nor in the sky. He'd tried both those options already. He didn't need this woman pulling an Angela bloody Lansbury on him.

'Look. Let me know who does it . . .' He reached for his keys. 'We'll be weeding next.'

'Wait! Coastal . . .' she said. 'Coastal!'

'The Glen?' Punch stood. 'Couldn't be more landlocked on Mull.'

'I mean the trace is coastal.'

'Are you saying somebody returned to the cars with the teeth and bones, having been at a coastal habitat?'

'I wasn't saying that, sergeant. But I like it.' She leaned forwards and tapped her page with the pencil. 'Anyone in mind?'

'The woman's other son is currently a person of interest. He was reported at the scene when the cars were first discovered. He has access to the dark side, put it that way.'

'They live where?'

'Around the coast from Dervaig.' Punch sat again.

'Interesting. So this is not high science, possibly not even mid-range, but I might as well tell you I've identified one of the few coastal areas with honeysuckle. The hardier version. Full-on coastal exposure freeze-dries the flower – so the Atlantic is not our friend here. But inlets and pondlife in the vicinity are kinder.'

'Where is it?'

'North Mull, along the west coast.'

'So – including Dervaig?'

'That's near where the lady was found?'

'Are we looking at current crimes here, or historical?'

'I don't need to tell you all crime is crime, sergeant. Criminals usually stay criminals. Some even like to get caught.'

There was a double knock at the door.

Lydia Strathclyde looked over her glasses.

Punch turned. Knew the drill. A short period of waiting. Then the key would turn.

Punch looked to the mess. Back to the door. Then to Lydia Strathclyde. *Some would view her as part of the mess.*

The door opened.

Mary MacBeth stepped into the station house. She was carrying a row of shirts on hangers. Each shirt with one sleeve turned up, just once.

'Oh?' Mary said, turning to the room, its inhabitants.

'Aye,' Punch said.

'It was locked,' Mary said. 'The door.' She used her arm to signify the door as though it was *her* crime to have unlocked it.

'Uh-ha,' Punch said. 'Cluny has been on overdrive. The station is, eh, occupied.'

'Guinness?' Lydia Strathclyde said. In a single act, she smiled, looked to Punch as though he was not of the species she had logged him for, and moved towards Mary MacBeth, extending a hand.

'Professor Lydia Strathclyde,' she said, smiling efficiently.

'Oh?' Mary said. 'Mary … eh, Mary MacBeth. Creagan.'

Punch could tell from Mary's expression, the hang of her head, that she wished for some other line of profession to disclose; for prior warning, too, of this exchange; and certainly for information that would have resulted in her not choosing to wear her tracksuit. Her hair was tied up like it was in the primary school playground. Punch himself approved, but knew Mary would not.

'Erm, Professor Strathclyde here reads plants,' Punch attempted. 'This lady here.'

'You mean there's others?' Mary blurted. 'Here?'

Lydia Strathclyde laughed; Punch wasn't sure if it was in a sisterhood way. He could see Mary was embarrassed at her outburst. Again, his fault. *This is a form of personal and career suicide.*

'Right,' he managed. 'We better get to it. Could be, eh, *barking* up the wrong tree, but I've a hunch.'

'At least you didn't say *roaring*, sergeant,' Lydia Strathclyde said, packing up her papers and the books.

Punch realised their exchange had made an outsider of Mary. He tapped his pockets for his keys. To the Ranger, not the Ford Anglia. *Get a grip, man.*

'In front of you,' Mary said.

Punch grabbed the set of keys.

Lydia Strathclyde nodded politely to Mary, who, Punch noted, did her best to return the act of theatre.

Punch opened the door and Lydia stepped outside. He turned to Mary.

'Oh, you might've seen a print, on the couch . . .' He felt like their prisoner, if not Dylan's. *Like the island or something else was pushing back the Clock.*

'I imagined it was a drinking session. Randy's date? Took

extra elbow grease, but it'll pass.'

'Sorry,' he said.

'For the room?' Mary said.

'That too.'

SCENE XXXIX

WEDNESDAY

DAVUD WAS NOW REGRETTING JUMPING from Dave's hearse. For the first time he really felt the cold. He wondered whether Duck should have put up more of a fight for him to stay. Would Petar have?

He pulled the hood tighter around his head. Walked in the darkness, through clouds of his own breath, back to Duck's car. His teeth almost jumping from his mouth. Wednesday night would soon meet Thursday morning. And would he be stuck out here on the Glen? Frozen alive.

He tried the handle, but Duck had locked it. Did this make it the only locked car on Mull? He looked inside. Now feeling like he had been visiting another planet in there, powered not by NASA's space food laboratory, but by Tennent's. Nothing seemed real, but at the same time he felt so weirdly calm and aware of everything. He was being used, for one thing. But by whom? Were the Architects of the Post-Truth World ever real at all? Or even the invitation to partner Billy in this year's rally? If not, then that was one thing he could stop worrying about. Especially if he drove like his brother.

He bent to scoop icy crystals of snow into his mouth. The world was completely silent. Not an engine's roar around him. There was an otherworldliness about it all. Like he had stepped into another solar system; as though another universe was saying to him: *Welcome, first human, come, explore, design, build – but don't fuck me up like you did your last one.*

He urinated into the snow, a dramatic spoiling of its pristine surface. It was the most private public thing he had ever done. The coldness, like his suspicion of hunger, now felt more like numbness.

He heard a single note, growing louder. An engine. Revs. He looked behind him. Lights revealed moors. Was it Bearfoot? Had he come to save Leonardo?

A car appeared. Davud shut his eyes against the lights. What would he say to him? Was their cave-life together nothing more than some piss-take? Or were the authorities searching for him? About the Glasgow fire? The packages in Duck's car? He didn't want lights beaming down on him. He longed for the usual sensation of not being noticed.

The car stopped alongside Duck's.

Davud turned his head away.

The window wound down. The driver's side.

'Are you okay?' a woman said. 'Can we help?'

Davud moved to look at her. For some reason, sunglasses were propped on her head. A blonde bun. Davud wondered if he was on Trauma Island now.

He saw it was the woman from the ferry. The one Duck had bumped into at Craignure.

'Are you broken down? Can we drive you somewhere?'

'Erm . . .' Davud looked down.

'I'm Annie.'

No you're not. He saw the dent on the passenger's door.

The woman leaned back by way of introduction to her passenger.

'Ludo,' the man said. 'Happy to be of any assistance we can. You must be frightfully cold out here?'

You're Mary, Davud thought. *Creator of monsters*. None of this was part of his plan. But he was too frozen to object.

'Okay.' He shivered. 'Thanks.'

He walked around the front of the car. Opened the back door and placed his rucksack inside. He sat on the back seat and closed the door behind him. The heat was like a tropical sun on him.

'Gosh, the chill's coming right off you!' Ludo said, turning around to Davud.

Davud tried to smile. He smelled food. Realised he *was* starving. He was trying to stop himself shaking.

'Can we drive you in our direction?'

'Yes,' Davud managed. 'Please.' He was starting to worry about what he was going to tell his mum. Would Duck be there? What if their stories didn't match?

'Let me crank up the heat,' the man said.

'Are you local?' she asked.

'I am. Yes.' Davud realised it was the first time he had said that.

'The next village is Dervaig, we believe?' Ludo said.

'Yes. I'll jump out there. Actually . . .'

'Yes?' she said, looking for him in her rearview mirror.

'There. Yes.' Davud didn't want to draw attention to where he lived.

'We're staying at the Bellachroy. That suit?'

'There, please. That's fine.'

'Good to have some local knowledge!' Ludo said. 'Are you hungry?'

'He must be,' Annie said. She pointed to the floor. 'We stopped at the . . .'

'Salen Hotel,' Davud said. 'I saw your car.'

Davud realised they didn't know he had lighter fluid in the car. He had that feeling again. Power. Control over events.

Ludo handed back a carrier bag.

'Chips okay?' he said. 'Still getting used to these Scottish portions!'

'Thanks,' Davud said, meaning it. He took the carton out of the bag and opened it.

'A bottle of water there too,' Ludo said. 'Afraid the burgers are gone.

'And sauces,' Annie added.

'Right. Right. Thanks.'

Davud was worried they might offer a menu; was this what a drive-through was really like? He started to eat the chips with his hands.

'Car broke down?' Annie said.

'Yes.' Davud was relieved she hadn't realised he was with Duck earlier.

'Coming from the ferry too?' Ludo said.

'Erm.' Davud felt he was giving too much away. 'Yes. And yes.'

'Do I detect another *accent*?' Ludo said.

Annie's hand nudged the man's knee. Davud could tell the woman thought the man was prying too much.

'Yes. I'm from Bosnia.' It felt good to say it.

'Bosnia?' Ludo said. He quickly turned to Davud, then the woman.

'Really?' Annie said.

'Why would you think I'm lying?' Davud put the empty carton and bottle into the bag. 'Why do people lie all the time?'

'Do they?' Ludo said.

'Even you,' Davud said; he caught Annie's eyes in the rear-view mirror. 'The first thing you said to me was a lie.'

'I didn't, did I?' Annie said.

'Your name,' Davud said.

'My name *is* Annie.'

'Or Mary?' Davud said.

Ludo looked quizzically to Annie.

'Oh?' The woman's eyes darted from her mirror. She ran her hand over her hair. Davud saw strands come away in her fingers. 'That was the car that hit me, back there? You were in it too?'

'Yes,' Davud said.

'Where's the driver?'

'Ah . . .' Ludo said. 'The kilted fellow?'

'He's . . . not here.' Davud wondered if all lies could be righted with lighter fluid. If that what the bins were about.

'How did you end up here?' Ludo asked. 'If I may?'

'Because the car broke down,' Davud said.

'No. From Bosnia?'

'We were given a new home,' Davud said. 'Some fled to

Austria via Hungary. For them, Austria became a second home. Like Scotland is for us.'

'I'm so sorry . . .' Ludo said.

'Us?' Annie asked.

Davud saw Ludo's finger tap hers on the gearstick.

'Oh . . . I'm sorry. I didn't mean to pry. Sorry.'

'I don't like people to hear about it. When they hear my story, they feel they have to, erm, stand there and start crying or show that they feel sorry for me. Some laugh. People laugh when they don't know how to respond.'

'That must be . . . very hard,' Ludo said. 'Did we get your name?'

'It's Davud.'

'Hello, Davud. Pleased to meet you. I'm Ludo, this is . . .'

'Annie,' Davud said. 'I know.'

'I'm very sorry I told you *Mary*, Davud. I'm having a bad day, a bit of a horror story of my own. And then the accident . . . it threw me. I'm sorry.'

'It's okay. The *us* is me and my mum.'

'So, she is with you here?' Ludo asked. 'Your mum.'

'We had to start from scratch. We shared a tiny bed in Edinburgh in a block with other refugees from Bosnia, Croatia, Serbia and Turkey. Mum always said at least we had the roof over our heads, like we should have been thankful for that. We shared the toilet and shower with strangers. No kitchen. I was used to my mum's cooking. Dad singing his old songs in the shower. Now we have somebody else in our shower.'

He realised he had made them silent.

'Have I said something wrong?' he said.

'No,' Ludo said.

'Not at all,' Annie added. 'That must have been very difficult.'

'Do you mind me asking if your mother is okay?'

'I think so,' Davud said. 'Wait, do you know more?'

'No. No,' Annie said.

'I like your pencil,' Davud said.

Ludo had one in his mouth now. Like he was thinking of using it. Davud saw he had opened up a large wallet. Papers scattered on his lap.

'It's from the HB graphite grading scale,' Davud continued. 'It's used to determine the hardness and the darkness of pencils. The "H" in the HB scale stands for hardness. The higher the number next to the "H" then the harder the pencil lead inside is. Eh – sorry.'

'No. You're very knowledgeable.'

'What does the "B" stand for?' Annie asked.

'Black.'

'Right.' She nodded.

Davud still didn't want to mention the art school. Somehow Bosnia, war, even, were easier. His memories of Sarajevo were mostly clad in concrete.

'But would I even know the place now?' he heard himself saying.

'Sorry?' Ludo turned.

'Nothing. It's just for a while I thought I came from a place called "genocide".'

Annie blew out. Ludo turned to her.

'Why are you here?' Davud asked. His mother had told him it was polite to ask people questions, that he shouldn't talk all the time about his own things.

'Well . . .' Ludo shifted in his seat. Davud saw how the man's eyebrows rose. He scratched his head. 'We're . . .'

'. . . here to look at an area of ground, Davud,' Annie said.

'Where?'

'Dervaig.'

'Why?'

'Because we work for the government. And people in the government might have plans for this piece of ground.'

'The wind farm?' Davud asked.

'Do you know what the government is, Davud?' Ludo asked.

'Yes.' He looked at them both. 'Of course.'

'Fine. I just wanted to check as I know it might be called something else in Bosnia.'

'Mum says it will be a blight on the horizon. The posters say that too. I helped draw the posters, so I know. I'm learning about solar panels too. Solar is the cheapest, easiest renewable energy to build. If I designed the world, I'd have solar on all new buildings. It's like growing your own food.'

'Right . . . quite right.' Ludo took his pencil from his mouth, scribbled notes.

'Hope you're warm enough now.' Annie put the car in gear and prepared to pull away.

Davud nodded, but kept the parka hood up.

'So, a lot of the land we're taking out of production is land that doesn't make money, Davud,' Annie said. 'It might produce some low-grade feed for cattle. If it made money, they'd carry on farming it.'

'Will you tell that to the horses?' Davud said.

'Fuck!' Annie stalled the car, put her hand to her chest.

'What the . . .?' Ludo managed.

Davud looked out the windscreen.

In the headlights was a person.

Bearfoot.

He had a knife in his hand.

SCENE XL

FRIDAY

PUNCH CLOSED THE DOOR ON the pebbledash. Turned the key. Making a prisoner of Mary MacBeth inside. He ran to join Lydia Strathclyde in the Ranger. Half expected she might be in the driver's seat. As he drove them off, he wondered if the woman had ever accepted a door being opened for her, or received a bouquet of flowers? *She'd probably end up telling you who had their throat cut next to them.*

'Wasn't sure whether to leave the handcuffs and grab a trowel,' he said.

'Quite, sergeant. You'll need to add *pollen tracker* to your shoulder.'

'At least the Ranger is well named.'

Lydia Strathclyde leafed through the files on her lap. 'The irregular combination of plantlife detected definitely points to somewhere coastal.'

'To Dervaig.' Punch shook his head at his lack of options. Like he was twisting a kaleidoscope. 'Need results on Hi-Pockets, sightings of missing folk. Media are circling.

Briefings going out today to the public. Just wish I knew what actual crime I was telling them about.'

He sped them across town and then up by Rockfield. Further ahead, he swung them hard left towards Dervaig and the Atlantic coast.

For most of the winding eight miles he listened to her humming what sounded like small breakthroughs, and heard her scribbling notes. He, too, turned the case notes over in his head. Cluny was still deployed at Lennox's place, in case Billy the Box returned. Seemed the best place for him. Special constables were located at Fishnish and Craignure in case anybody under suspicion tried to leave.

They reached the top of the hairpin bends and began the descent into the village. Punch looked at the second-best seat in the world. For some reason he couldn't conjure the Ford Anglia 307E and the small boy, nor another island out there. Maybe the world had become all too adult.

Lydia Strathclyde removed her glasses and rubbed her eyes. Sighed deeply. She took all the materials on her lap and weighed them in her hands. 'Hardest thing is always . . . should all this amount to anything *like* the real picture, the fact that then people's lives will change forever. Mostly for the worst. Even if the truth is uncovered. People will suffer.'

'That's the job spec.'

'I find giving evidence is the hardest thing, you know, especially with extreme crimes. I hate courts.' She patted her bob, adjusted her glasses back on her face. 'Seeing the accused next to the families of young women who have been raped. They have the *real* guts. But then everybody deserves a fair trial. Otherwise the house collapses in on itself.'

'Islands too.' *Or they float away. Children's clothing with them.*

Punch wound them speedily by the old graveyard and down into Dervaig, passing the houses adorned with the various buoys and boating paraphernalia he'd seen all his life.

'Dervaig. Well named. *Good inlet*,' Lydia Strathclyde said. Nervously, Punch could tell. 'Taken from the old Norse.'

'This, the anomaly of policing – especially *island* policing . . .' Punch swung a right at the Bellachroy onto the sleepy Main Street.

'Sergeant?'

'How to do the necessary and discreet investigative aspects of the job, in a vehicle with fluorescent stripes.'

They passed the village hall where he had once performed in a teenage covers band called TRAX, with the Spar adjoined. Was certain at the time Kenney Jones had never been subjected to such disrespect, whether he was drumming or larking about atop a polo horse. He drove them up to the end of the street and slightly beyond, where he pulled over on the verge. The Lennox farm lurked further out, under protest from officialdom and placard.

'This is as close as we can get.' He killed the Ranger.

By the time he had got around to her side the professor was standing waiting with her bag and materials.

'This way to the coast,' he said.

She followed him around the failing deer fencing and down through the scraggly pathway between the tufts of dunes and rocks. They came to a tree-lined area that opened out onto a football field, rusted white goals at either end. Here, in school, his Tob side had once lost 47–3 to Dervaig. Longy and Langy among the victors. To their right, rock pools succumbed to the Atlantic Ocean, glistening like a million fluid arms in the air. Punch felt he knew who one of them was, imagined the flagpole.

'This might be it? Honeysuckle.'

'That what you call all the girls?'

He watched her stride towards the coastal end of the pitch, following scent he couldn't detect. It was quiet, save for the lapping of waves and the questioning squawks.

I know, we don't belong here. Tob people.

'Finding a path!' she shouted. 'That's the golden ticket!'

He followed her into the undergrowth. All he could see were nettles.

'Two pathways,' she said, walking carefully back and forth. 'But one full of rotten twigs. The chances of detection are minimal.'

'Detecting what?'

'Trace,' she sang. 'Consistent with those found on the bones, the teeth, and around the cars.'

Punch arrived behind her, careful not to step onto a page she hadn't yet drawn. He was starting to suspect there had been two visits to the burnt-out cars.

'Promising ... promising ...' she said. 'Nettles ... see how they're trodden. And there, on the other trail.' She pointed her gloved hand to the pathway leading inland, away from the coast. 'Recovery.'

'In other words, regrowth?'

'Exactly, sergeant. When you tread on a plant you disrupt its hormonal flow from its tip to the rest of the plant.'

'Right. Same with Cluny.'

'Now . . .' She kneeled to the ground and crawled alongside the path that was not more than a scruffy wad of nettles to Punch's eye. 'When you disrupt that flow, all the side shoots are no longer controlled, and so they start growing and then their own tips start supporting others at the back of those. So, I'm seeing a disruption, but also estimating – I emphasise estimating – a timeline.'

'Timeline, really?'

'This is a well-worn path. And the disruption here is too high for livestock, deer and the like. Though our animal bone guess is still not out of the running.'

'To have been taken from here?'

'It all factors.' She pointed. 'Grass, nettles and hedge woundwort.'

'Sure they played Woodstock . . . So, this could be where somebody has been coming and going?' Punch looked ahead. 'But going where?'

She was already off ahead of him again, stepping through rock pools. The expanse of ocean now came into view. The woman was nimble, no joke. Punch suddenly felt watched; out there were the Treshnish Isles encompassing the Dutch Cap and Staffa. The treeless Coll and Tiree keeping guard further beyond.

He followed her along the coastline. As it curled in front of them, he saw caves. Some had the sea washing into them and some were on higher, grassier ground. His heart was beating faster.

'Hair on a twig or branch,' she called out, now behind him. 'That's what we're after. That's gold. But . . .' The professor pointed, almost bursting into song, 'we might just have silver . . . *Lonicera Fragrantissima*!'

'Eh?' Punch turned to see her framed by the sea; was she implying the Spanish Armada had instead sunk here?

'Winter honeysuckle!' Lydia Strathclyde turned to review the direction travelled. 'And the potential approach route!'

'Fingerprints might be along this path,' Punch offered. 'But good luck brushing . . .'

'Exactly. But now I hope you won't have to.'

Punch stepped up onto the higher ground, nearer the rock facing. The wind was testing him. The island too. Darkness was falling. He reached down for the professor's hand. She accepted. Even he had spotted they were now standing on a floor of moss.

'Here . . .' Punch wiped sea spray from his face, turned to the widest cave opening. He walked into the cave and the world fell silent. The cave floor was carpeted in the same moss, though dryer and thicker. A stone circle in the corner, evidence of a firepit. 'Christ.' He brought his sleeve up to cover his nose and mouth. Stumbled back. Outstretched his arm to the cave wall, felt his left hand make contact with the chill of damp stone. There were two of them. Positioned on the ground. Two charred bodies.

'My God!' Lydia crouched behind him.

They were both looking at what had once been a male and a female.

'I've seen a few dead bodies in my time . . .' she said. 'But . . .'

'Teeth.' Punch pointed. 'Removed.'

'Waterloo teeth,' she said.

'Eh?'

'The tradition of removing teeth from deceased individuals, particularly for use in dentures. Prevalent during the eighteenth and nineteenth centuries.'

'From who?'

'From whom? From the fallen, sergeant. During conflicts like Waterloo, Culloden.'

'Clearances too, now I think on it.' Punch crouched to the bodies, put his hat over his mouth. 'I heard a programme about it. It was a Celtic tradition. Of extracting teeth from corpses, primarily for landowners. Sometimes from a poor wretch who simply needed money in hand more than teeth in mouth. We could be there now.'

Punch leaned over the corpses. A decomposed, scorched combination of bone and flesh. Straggles of hair.

'Could be your wife or brother, and you wouldn't know it,' Lydia said.

Punch felt vomit arriving at his gullet.

'Look.' Lydia pointed to words chalked on the cave wall.

Punch turned.

WE ARE BEAR.

Punch spotted a book lying beyond the bodies. He walked over and kneeled to it. It was another sketchbook. He flicked through the pages, but it was completely untouched. The exact same kind as the one he had found on the Glen. An empty Spar plastic bag lay alongside. He picked it up. No receipt inside.

'Good work,' he said over his shoulder, reaching for his tobacco. 'Led us to the bear pit.'

He stole another glance at the pile of former humanity. The fingers had already part mummified into curled, gelatinous talons.

'Sergeant!'

Punch turned. Lydia Strathclyde was holding a helmet. It only confirmed what Punch had already determined.

SCENE XLI

PUNCH'S HEADLIGHTS TORE DOWN Dervaig Main Street. Decided on no sirens. No need for the blues. He was alone again. Undetectable. How he liked it.

It was 7.30. Showtime.

Lydia Strathclyde had stayed at the football pitch. She had been joined by Cluny, relieved from his station at the nearby Lennox farm by the Oban detectives. Cluny was also going to sound out the Spar manager. Had the Bosnian woman's lad and Billy Lennox been working together on something? The words of MacMaster were starting to make more sense.

Punch swung a right at the Bellachroy and sped down towards the junction of the Glen. He took the left for the theatre and tore on past the school. Could he smell burning? More of Skerryvore's shite? It was too dark to look for islands in the sky, or in the sea. The smell was getting stronger. Smoke now evident. He turned the corner.

Flames were lighting up the night. Punch pulled onto the verge of the Glen. Killed the ignition. *More burning! Since when did an island become flame?* He jumped out of the Ranger. Ran to open the boot, took hold of the fire extinguisher and the protective gloves. Left the knife. Ran to the driver's side and leaned in. Grabbed the handset and radioed for the fire brigade.

He sprinted around the Ranger and up the banking until he was behind the caravan. He began spraying from downwind. An explosion was likely. Given the propane. He got as close as the heat would allow. Stumbled off the banking and almost landed on the caravan. He sprayed down one side of it, revealing the door was closed. The insides were blacked out with smoke. He worked around the rear again, the smoke and heat frequently forcing him to turn away. Then down the other side. The structure split in two, metal melting as the caravan folded in on itself. It collapsed on either side of the bricks, sending flames rushing to the sky. Punch leaped away. Landed in the undergrowth. It was where the bicycle had been. He turned to look for it nearby. No sign of it.

He got up and continued to spray wherever he could. The caravan was once again engulfed. He saw flashing lights. Turned from the furnace to see a Ranger pull up behind his own. Monteith.

'Work from your side!' he yelled to Monteith. She was in a face mask, and now also brandishing an extinguisher.

'I'd a tip-off! Alerted the brigade! Anyone inside that we know off?'

Punch couldn't bear to think about it.

He heard a siren. The fire engine swung into view and pulled up. Punch dropped his extinguisher. Ran towards the road. Could only hope people were out of the hellish thing.

'Knowledge of anyone inside?' one of the brigade yelled at him.

'Undetermined, Appy,' Punch replied. 'You take it from here!'

He saw Randy and several others of the brigade crew now rounding on the caravan. Hoses being tag teamed. Bursting into life like giant canvas snakes.

Punch jumped into the Ranger. His face still held the flame's bruise. He turned the ignition, hit the accelerator. He flew along for half a mile. Pulled onto the verge again. Killed the engine. He removed only the car key from the ring. Stuffed the rest under the driver's seat. His next move was going to be tricky enough without broadcasting his presence. Lydia Strathclyde had told him solving crime was not a loud voice. He just wished he always had the choice.

He grabbed the radio from the handset and fixed it to his uniform. Turned down the volume. It was only coming along for the ride because of its red alert button, should last resorts be needed.

He jumped from the vehicle. It was the roar of the crowd he heard now. Or more of a ripple. MacMaster had clearly beaten expectations. Would Bora be among them? He could only hope. Though it seemed unlikely with her son still apparently unaccounted for. He felt bad now about withholding that information. His only hope was that when the embers burned out, there weren't going to be more bodies. Drugs were bad enough. But could Mull survive more burning? More death amid flame?

He shone his torch on the makeshift billboard. *The Looming*. He ran up the gravel driveway. He'd already planted shadows by way of two plain-clothed special constables in the audience, where they could legitimately pass as genuine members of the fee-paying public. As unlikely as that prospect sounded to him, given MacMaster's pish.

He was going purely on instinct. The roads had led here. He was trying to order events, chart human failings, work to his own methods. *Off grid.*

He came to the top of the short driveway. It was strange to see cars, and so many of them, now parked at the theatre. He couldn't help wondering if recent events – that was if they had reached the grapevine at all – had helped MacMaster pull a crowd. Art imitating life and all that.

He turned to look, surprising even himself. The Atlantic part of the blackness. If there *was* a mystery island out there, it wasn't making itself known.

Punch turned to scan the cars. No sign of the Merc or the rally car. He refused the theatre building for now and turned instead to the house. It might be the only time he could be sure MacMaster would be out of it. Otherwise, he would be in search warrant territory. It was *real* showtime.

He arrived at the door of the house. The insides of the porch were still black with soot. He made light work of the lock.

Inside, a lamp by the door was on. First impressions were of a chaotic life, with plenty of the mumbo-jumbo he would've expected from an actor-cum-hippie type. Books, papers and scripts were strewn over fusty furniture. Posters of past productions hung at irregular angles. Accompanied by applause from the main building across the way.

He took latex gloves from inside his jacket. Put them on and walked from the doorway along a short corridor. Several coats were lying on the floor, a cravat, waistcoat and long leather boots; likely evidence of a last-minute creative impulse or a second guess. The same long boots? Ivor had only one remaining hunch as to why a man dressed as Robert Louis

Stevenson was roaming Mull, and goading the island's law enforcer as he did so. But the playing pack was still too scattered, and the centuries too distant, to believe it possible. But he knew it wasn't Fintan MacMaster. Possibly the man himself wasn't even aware he had competition in depicting dead Scottish writers. Whoever it was, he had a bit of money in their pocket, going by the Merc. But suspects were running out. Dying, in fact. Was it drug money? Matters of the Order? Or family? But then, people who so visibly put themselves in the island's police house – as well as on the island's stage – were not exactly choosing to hide their potential guilt? Or was it double bluff? *Go with your belly, Punch. Go with your belly.*

From the corridor he walked into the kitchen. A light above the cooker presented more chaos. Bottles of red wine, some corrupted by candle wax, lined the wall. Punch noted two glasses on the table. Two chairs pulled out. He got busy with the drawers. Rummaging and turning things over. He checked the fridge and freezer. MacMaster made the station house look as well stocked as the Co. There were cookbooks stacked within a tall wooden shelving unit. He leafed through them, checked inside all the dockets. Nothing but ticket stubs. He turned back to the table. What appeared to be a religious script was on it. Wine circles on the pages. As though the clergyman had returned. The dialogue caught his eye: *Unquenchable Flames. Those who have been condemned at the final judgement . . .*

Punch turned out of the kitchen and opened a small door to his left. He took the torch from his chest. An iron and a drying rack came to light. The carpet was raised at the edge. He lifted it further. Nothing. He closed the door behind him. Walked the corridor. Pushed open another door by the entrance.

Walked in. A small living room. This was where the sermons would have been concocted. The room was not big enough to swing a golden Bafta mask, let alone a Bible. A red light was flashing in the far corner. Punch walked to it. A phone. Positioned on the carpet, by the foot of the curtains. A message trying to reach MacMaster. He pressed play. A crackly recording. Female voice. Hard to detect. He played it again. *Get petrol quick . . .* Maybe? No mention of matches.

Punch walked to the fireplace. Put his hand on it. Cold. The curtains were drawn. He turned on his torch again. Shone it onto the two sofas. Then under them. He could see an object. Reached to pull it out. It was a tin box, the size of a small shoebox. No markings. He took the lid off. It was a mould of some kind, sitting face down in an ink base. He lifted it out, the shape immediately recognisable.

A bear claw print.

He got up. His torchlight revealed a bunting of theatre masks high up on the back wall of the room. Each face linked in the chain by the words 'Comedy' and 'Tragedy'. One side of the chain was flagging. He closed the heavy-set door fully. Reached with his long arm, and, with the aid of the torch, managed to disrupt the chain. Something fell to his forehead and Punch stumbled backwards. He had gone with the beanie rather than police hat. He, too, was capable of disguise. He steadied himself and shone to the carpet. It was a key. He put it in his trouser pocket.

Punch opened the door and walked back into the corridor. Clapping came from the other building. MacMaster getting what he wanted, needed. The man was at work. But Punch was too. Just hoping for a bit of *right time, right place*.

He stepped onto the creaky stairs. A thinning red carpet on them. Symbolically threadbare. On the stair walls quotations were scrawled, page numbers noted, and what looked like some possible title ideas. At the top, *THE LOOMING* was written.

A bathroom opposite. Door wide open. Punch turned to the small landing. Here, a closed door faced him. He gently pushed the door. It didn't budge, so he slowly turned the doorknob. The door released. Inside, it was pitch black. His eyes adjusted a little. With the aid of the light from downstairs he could see the bed. He stepped towards it. His thumb primed on the red. He took hold of the covers and pulled them away in one deft movement.

Punch stepped back. 'Christ!'

SCENE XLII

SOMEBODY WAS LYING IN THE bed in the shape of a star.

'Who the hell are you?' Punch barked.

The person was fully clothed. Arms and legs tied to the four corners of the bedframe. Punch directed the torchlight to the head. A dark blue parka. A shock of black hair escaping from it. The mouth gagged. Sounds a baby would make.

Punch pulled the bandana from the eyes. It was a lad in his late teens. Wearing terror on his face. Shirking from the blast of light.

Punch reached down and pulled the ropes, making sure they were securely tied. He kneeled one knee on the boy's chest. Didn't want to risk getting lamped for his trouble. With his hand that wasn't holding the torch, he pulled the blocker from the lad's mouth.

A gasp and a heavy inhale.

Punch moved off him. Killed the torch.

'Who are you?'

The lad was frantically bucking his upper torso.

'Steady yourself!'

The bucking lessened.

‘Don’t kill me!’ he said, staring away from Punch to the wall. ‘Don’t kill me! I didn’t do anything!’

‘I’m Sergeant Punch. Do you know where you are?’

‘Code name, Leonardo!’ he shouted.

‘I’m not going to harm you, lad. Did Fintan do this to you?’

Leonardo shook his head. Sweat claggy on his face. Hair stuck to it.

‘Here.’ Punch leaned for a glass of water on the bedside. ‘Open your mouth.’

The lad sat up as best he could. Punch poured water slowly into his mouth.

‘I think I might know who you are,’ Punch said. ‘Are you . . . Davud?’

A nod. A grimace. Punch saw that Davud’s wrists were bleeding.

‘I’m going to search you, lad. All right?’ Punch patted the body and parka down. ‘I’m going to untie one hand.’

‘I don’t know anything! Nothing about anything! Or why they asked me to do it! Is my mum okay?’

Punch took out his Leatherman and sliced the rope fixing Davud’s right hand to the bedframe.

‘Is she okay? He said he was going to burn my family!’

Punch could hear the slight accent now. ‘Steady on, lad! Take some deep breaths.’ He untied the lad’s other hand. Briefly considering that these were talented hands. It was best to keep the caravan out of it for now. ‘Fintan said this?’

‘No. No.’ The lad still wore a caged expression. Punch had seen it before. In the boy’s mother.

‘Then who?’

Davud shook his head.

'You're in Fintan's bed, in his house. Does he know you're here?'

'Yes.' Davud sat up. His feet were still tied. 'Bearfoot didn't do the things he said he would. He said we were both architects! Said we were blood brothers – that we'd look inside things. Look deeper. But he used me. Just wanted to see inside bodies!'

'In the caves?'

'Yes.'

'Have you harmed anyone, son?'

'No. Yes. Maybe. I don't know yet. I think he was jealous that Mr Lennox liked me. That he wished I was his son. I think I set it alight, too.'

'The caravan?'

'No.' He shook. 'No! Why?'

Punch turned and moved the curtain a little to the side. No sign of anything out there from the direction of the caravan.

'Is my mum okay?'

'I'm sure she is. Yes.'

'The art school!' Davud said in a sudden rush. 'I can never go back! Nor can anyone else now.'

'You did the cars too?'

'No. He drove back out the Glen last night. Said Fintan would stop loving him if he didn't. Said it was another person doing it to him, and to Fintan too!'

'Steady, lad. So, who's let you down? MacMaster, is it?'

Davud shook once more. 'No. I expected that from him. He's let Mum down too. Promised her this and that!'

'I think I know who, Davud. Take those deep breaths for me.'

'Bearfoot.'

'Billy Lennox?'

Davud nodded, then tried to free his legs.

'He did this to you?'

'No. Another man.'

'You said Billy drove out to the cars?'

'Yes. But it was just one car. Duck's car.'

'Right. Both Fiestas, though?'

'Yeah.'

'So, who tied you up? The other man?'

'Yes!'

'And Billy burned the cars?'

'I don't know. Are they burned? He said he'd do it, but I thought he was trying to scare them.'

'Why would he do that? Burn the cars?'

'The evidence? To keep our prints off them? Bearfoot wanted the seats too.'

'Billy? Why?'

'Because, before he drove off, I told Billy the packages were where he'd wanted them. Fintan was to cut them out. I don't really know why. I ran!'

'Bearfoot, I mean Billy, wanted to scare who?'

'The people. Because they'd seen him. But I was worried. He was obsessed with seeing dead bodies. Duck had got away. I thought I was next!'

'Calm it, lad. Whose car?'

'The government people.'

'What people?'

'They're to do with the wind farm!'

'How many of them?'

'Two.'

'A man and woman?'

'Yes.'

'Did you get their names?'

'Erm, Mary.'

'Mary?'

'No. No! Wait, Annie. Yes, Annie. And . . . and . . . Ludo. Yes, Ludo. I'd never heard that name before.'

'Right. Keep telling it to me straight. Last names?'

'I don't know. Are they okay?'

'No. No, I don't think so.' Punch switched a little. 'Do you know anything about a Mercedes? Do you know what one looks like?'

Davud nodded. 'Of course.'

'You saw one?'

'No. I know what one looks like. But I didn't see one.'

Punch took the key from his pocket. 'Do you know what this is for?'

Davud shook. 'Is Mum safe? The caravan?'

'Look – *you're* safe, lad. I think she might be.'

'Oh!'

'Listen, though, you have to help me if you're going to help yourself. Your mum too. What is this for?'

'It's where he keeps it,' Davud said at last. He rubbed each wrist. Wiped his brow with the back of a hand, leaving a smear of blood.

'Who? The person who let you down? Billy Lennox?'

Davud shook. 'Fintan.'

'I'm going to release you, Davud. And I want you to show me where this key fits, okay? Can you do that for me? For your mum?'

Davud nodded to the bare mattress, cast his eyes down. 'But she said she would hurt my family.'

'Who?'

'The woman in Oban.'

'She gave you the packages?'

'Yes. Yes.'

'Okay, lad. Steady.'

Punch cut both the ankles free. He stood back.

'That's it. You lead me now.'

Davud slowly rolled off the bed.

Punch stood back and prepared himself for a runner. To knock the lad into next week, onto fake islands floating offshore, if required.

'I don't know if I should . . .' Davud said, standing. 'I'm not supposed to.'

'Well, this uniform says you are, Davud. Don't worry. You're not in trouble if you don't bring any more trouble. I know you're a talented lad, that's what your mum wants for you, not this.'

'Should I be in handcuffs?' Davud said. 'What is *Corpus Delicti* . . .'

'Why are you asking that?'

'Bearfoot told me about it.'

'It means "body of the crime".' *Thank fuck for Tulliallen.* 'A crime must be proved to have occurred before a person can be convicted of committing that crime. Right now, as it stands, lad, you're on the right side of that equation.'

'But arson?'

'For now, leave the art school to me, okay, Davud?'

'He keeps it . . . downstairs,' Davud managed.

'Okay.' Punch stepped aside. 'Show me.'

He followed the lad out of the poky room and back down the stairs. The boy was tall, brooding and smelled of the wilds. They took the corridor to the kitchen and then through to a small, porched laundry area. Suits were hanging. A dress. Punch saw it gently blowing, before a huge sky and sea. There was a small fridge on the floor. Much like the one he kept for meat in his lockup. It was padlocked.

Davud stepped aside and pointed at the fridge.

'You stand there.' Punch motioned for the lad to move to the back corner of the porch, where he could keep an eye on him. He kneeled and turned the key in the padlock. It fell open. He braced himself for body parts, or any other possible revelation of actorly high jinks. Though had a clear hunch of what was inside. He opened the door. He was staring down multiple hefty slabs of cocaine.

Punch looked up at the lad, who seemed as caged and pale as the faded paintwork he was leaning on.

'Tell me your part in the story of how this stuff got here, will you?'

Davud cowered into the corner.

'More I know, Davud, the more I can help. You. Your mother too. Who was this woman in Oban?'

'I was to meet her at the pier. Billy said. Fintan arranged it.'

'And you did?'

'She had packages for Fintan. But I think they were for Billy too. I didn't call him Billy. Is Bearfoot okay?'

'Not sure. And the car seats are in the theatre now?'

'Yes. Will they explode?'

'No. No, lad.'

'I thought they were bombs! Billy wanted rid of Duck. Or their dad did. I don't know. He made me say I did too. That Duck would take Mum away from me.'

'Right. The woman. Would you be able to recognise her?'

'Yes. She said everything would be okay if I did it. That you knew about it.'

'Me?'

Davud nodded.

'Right. And where is Duck?'

'I don't know. We broke down. He went off with Dave.'

'Dave the Grave?'

'Yes. He was passing, when we were stuck on the side of the road.'

'And the person who's forcing Fintan. Who tied you up. You've seen him?'

'No,' Davud said. 'But he's a man. I heard his voice. He said there was a final act to show you.'

'Me? Not Fintan?'

'You.'

'Is he on the stage? This person. If we go over there will you point him out, by voice?'

'I don't know. I don't like too many people. Don't know if I can. I want to go see my mum.'

Punch nodded; he understood. 'Have they harmed you in any other way?'

'Like what?'

'You know, physically . . .'

'No. Just threats. I saw his feet. Black boots. Boots high up his legs. I only did one thing, officer! I set fire to the bins! I didn't mean for . . .'

'Where?'

'Glasgow. Behind the art school.'

'Christ.' Punch stood. 'Does your mum know you're caught up in any of this?'

'Doesn't even know I'm back here.' He looked around, distraught. 'She's worked so hard to get me into halls. I've let her down. My dad. Our country. Oh, please help!'

'You're not responsible for war, lad. I think you can do this. You know right from wrong, don't you?'

'So, you just need me to tell you the person?' Davud said, sweeping his hair back, composing himself with the gesture.

'Yes. But I want you to hear something first.'

Punch exited the porch and Davud followed, unsteady on his feet. They travelled through the kitchen and back to the front room.

Punch played the answerphone message. They both listened several times to the distorted voice.

'That the Oban woman?'

'Yes,' Davud said.

'*Petrol quick* – was that for the cars? The art school, or the theatre?' Punch was keeping the caravan out of it.

'That's not what she's saying,' Davud said.

'What is it then?'

'*Petrović*, she's saying *Petrović*, Davud said. 'It's my last name. She's saying to get *me*. My name, it means son of Petar.'

SCENE XLIII

PUNCH OPENED THE DOOR OF the theatre house. He stood aside to let Davud step outside first. A smell of smoke. He doubted it was detectable this far away from the caravan. Hoped it was still emanating from the porch. He looked at the theatre building. *Right time, right place.*

'Davud. Wait outside for me. Right here, where I can see you.'

The boy nodded.

Punch took his radio from the holder. Selected LB.

'PC Cluny, do you read? Over.'

'Sergeant! Where are you? Over.'

'Theatre. Look I only have seconds. Davud Petrović – that's Davud Petrović – son of Bora Petrović, resident of the caravan outside Dervaig, is safe and well. And helping the investigation. I think suspects are inside the theatre. I'm preparing to go in. Over.'

'Sergeant! Been trying to reach you. It's about William Lennox. His rally car has been found out beyond his farm. And he's inside it.'

'And?'

'Dead. Suspected suicide.'

'Fuck.' Punch released the button. *Four bodies.* He sighed, the night absorbing his breath. 'Lucky we have Forensics on the island. They on their way to the caves? Over.'

'Affirmative, sergeant. Never, eh, seen anything like it, Sarge. Any leads head office can work with? Over.'

'Any word as to why the public meeting last night was cancelled? About the wind? Over.'

'Official word was the snow storm, Sarge. Over.'

'Have Control run some checks. I only have Christian names. Though the male one is uncommon enough. They might be government or company officials. A Ludo and an Annie. All we have. Maybe they were due to appear at the meeting. Over.'

'Got it, Sarge. On it. Over.'

'Right. Okay. Any news on the caravan fire? Bora Petrović? Over.'

'Still a missing person, sergeant. Over.'

'Shit. PC Cluny?'

'Yes Sarge?'

'You okay?'

'Affirmative, Sarge. Over.'

'Okay. Hang tight. Keep the channel open, constable. Over.'

Punch turned the volume down before listening for a response.

He stepped out of the porch to join the lad. There was no point in derailing him with any of this. Punch was impressed the boy hadn't run for home.

'Okay, Davud. As we discussed. All right?'

'Yes. Okay.'

They walked the gravel towards the theatre. Davud pulled his parka hood on. Punch saw a light flickering in the little foyer. No one around.

'Follow me through, into the main room. We'll have to be like mice. Like mice. Okay?' Punch instinctively reached for a roll-up, but no. 'Anyone asks. You were just late for the show. I gave you a run.'

'Okay.'

'We'll stand at the back of the room. If you see the person, you point to them, or whisper to me. Okay?'

'Okay. I can do this.' Davud nodded more times than strictly necessary.

'You can. And you might not see the person till the show ends. When folk leave. Need to piss or anything first?'

Davud shook.

Punch opened the theatre door. He held it ajar while ushering Davud inside, then gently closed it. Folk's coats were hung around the walls, making the foyer seem smaller. Remnants of wine in glasses and beer in bottles. *Intermission been and gone*. Punch walked to the red door. Gazed to the claim above it: *Please take one of the 42 seats!* Clearly somebody on the Glen had taken this literally. *Billy Lennox?* This mystery person? He had seen only MacMaster and the Stevenson joker wearing those long leather boots.

He crossed to the red door. Ushered the lad closer. Heard the odd cough from the audience. A voice started booming.

Punch raised his eyebrows expectantly to Davud.

No. Davud motioned.

Punch put his forefinger to his own lips. He opened the red door. Davud moved through it. Punch followed, again closing the door gently. *Act I, completed.*

They each had their backs to the rear wall. The room was dark. Warm from human bodies. Live ones. Multiple backs of heads in rows in front of them. Two spotlights pointed to the stage. Each positioned on either side of the room, about halfway down. The space seemed bigger, its smell more of people than it had been the day before when Bora had commanded it.

He looked to Davud. Gestured for the lad to lower his hood. Didn't need anyone thinking Liam Gallagher was in the house. *Though his presence would explain the drugs . . .*

Two voices were coming from the slightly risen stage. They were projected so loudly Punch wasn't sure if the lad was going to be much cop at this. The jury was still out on this cop, too. The same two chairs were positioned on the stage as they had been during MacMaster's rehearsal. Punch looked to the owner of the current voice. It was MacMaster. Doing Burns. *Third degree.*

Punch glanced at Davud, who was facing the stage, but not giving any indication of recognition.

'*Under the wide and starry sky*,' MacMaster as Burns recited. '*Dig the grave and let me lie.*' It can be arranged, thought Punch. He was surprised to see MacMaster reading off a script. As though handed lines to read. At least the man had done away with the ponytail. '*You will have heard it said, good people of Mull, that a man is an island.*' He faced the audience, addressing them: '*Have you not*?'

The room was silent.

'Have you not?' MacMaster pressed.

There were several outbreaks of laughter; folk clearly didn't know what to do. Punch detected MacMaster was among them. Several folk at the front spoke up, the kind that want to be part of a performance, not content being a spectator. The room rippled with more laughter.

Punch took it as a cue of his own. He signalled to Davud to stay put. Then moved back out the door. Crossed the foyer to the outside. He ran behind the building, to what would be the rear of the stage. There it was. As he suspected. The Mercedes. *Fucking gall.* Lab tests were not yet in on the whisky tumbler. But Punch was doing his own analysis. He needed to see the man again. Really see him to believe it. The past redux.

He peered through the Merc windows. Nothing evidently amiss. Clean as a whistle. Hanging where there might have been an air freshener tree, Punch saw a bear claw pendant. *Company logo.* He moved away from the car. If accuracy counted for anything, the man Stevenson would more likely have parked up a penny farthing. On the ground in among weeds he saw a mechanical saw. Punch crouched to study the teeth. Fresh metal shards evident. For removing the seats? He investigated further. No bones.

He stood. Walked to a door at the building's rear. Turned the handle. It opened. *High security, MacMaster.* The man had clearly been on Mull too long.

Coming from inside, Punch could now hear the second voice from the stage.

'And this man, this island, he charges his soul to seek a life beyond this enchanted island . . . to another island . . .'

'We call it the mainland!' a voice shouted out; the audience laughed and clapped and hollered.

Punch moved in further. *Stage door* in front of him. Just a wall between him and the actors. Was surprised to feel a strange privilege. Like he was trespassing on the present. He saw a small room, door ajar, opposite the stage.

'Oh?' came the voice from the stage. Punch recognised it as Burns. *'You do. Yes. But what are we saying if the island he stands on and the one he has become, are not the same? And he has streams of desire that are not charted on any map. Desire for another man's woman!'*

'Far over seas is an island,' Stevenson's voice said, *'and whereon when day is done, there shall I go, methinks, When I am done with all. To take it over! That time is now!'*

'But is it island itself, or island of the mind? When life shall prove unkind?'

'Up, sluggard soul!' shouted Stevenson. *'We shall not police such an island. It will be one of happiness! Instead of mine of sorrow!'*

'Try Iona!' came the audience call. More laughter.

Punch stepped into the room. Realising it was a makeshift dressing room. There was a mirror with just a couple of bulbs lit. On the table below the mirror, alongside makeup pots, brushes and wig stands, were the keys of the Merc. Next to the keys was a bank card with two lines of white powder visible alongside it. Punch bent to the card. An inscribed name was scored out. New text had been written next to it.

~~UTTERSON~~ *OTHER SON*

Punch walked out of the room. He crossed to the stage door. Gently, he took hold of the handle. Slowly, he pulled it towards him. The door came away from the frame with not a sound. He opened it just a few inches. Put his face to the crack. The second voice. As he'd suspected. Robert Louis Stevenson. Dressed exactly as he had been in the station house.

On his hip, a gun now strapped. The audience clearly bending to the belief it was fake.

'*And now I am here, my truths I seek!*' Stevenson said, thrusting a quill to the audience. Punch noted how Stevenson was not reading from a script.

'*Or nigh' enchanted island, steer, down the weak . . .*' recited Burns, still reading from the script. But MacMaster was shaking his head, clearly at odds with the text.

'*Do not allow police to our answers seek!*' Stevenson proclaimed, more theatrically.

'*The evidence would seem to indicate that we are expected to believe in another island,*' Burns said.

'*We'll call this island a man. Utterson,*' Stevenson said, ham-fistedly shortening one arm. '*Or, Other son, and Utter scum!*'

'Punch!' came the call of recognition from the audience.

'*Well quite,*' beamed Stevenson, circling the back of the stage, just several feet from Punch. Ivor could almost have grabbed the gun. '*But with no jurisdiction, one island can steal from another. Just as a man, a boy, can take a father!*'

Punch studied Stevenson more closely.

'*He had allowed in restlessness which would assail him in a place so distant from all the friends and scenes of his past life,*' Burns read, dropping the Ayrshire accent for that of the Gorbals, and then dropping the script to the stage floor. He looked to the audience: '*Does this make any sense?*' he asked.

There were murmurs from the audience.

'*Here leads another son to call upon those resources of the spirit and of the imagination that are the mainstay of man in whatever abode,*' Stevenson said, leaning his hands on the back of one of the chairs. *'And he tells himself . . . Redemption is God's business. Rehabilitation is man's. Or better still, the island's! But which island, which son?'*

'*To The Looming one must indeed go hence? Twice a century,*' Burns attempted, *'a brother must roar his rightful belongings . . .'*

'From one brother's weakness! From another father's roar!'

Punch saw Stevenson was a pool of sweat, entranced.

MacMaster put his head in his hands. 'Utter pish more like!'

There were embarrassed murmurs from the audience, no laughter now.

'Refund!' somebody yelled.

'*Erm, of course I had a man kidnapped nearby, on Erraid?*' Stevenson said, more evidently ad-libbing. *'Did I not? Could that be yet another island? Another son? The one blown out of the sky?'*

Punch studied the man. The reference to Charlie was too close. He imagined the Stevenson character without the fake moustache. In the teenage clothes of the sixties. He recalled the time in the shadows of a hung sheep when his uncle-who-was-not-his-uncle had told him about his brother; about 'what a shit he was'. This the man Ivor had believed was his father until that moment. Who was in fact living on the other side of the universe. In Oban. It was also the first time he had heard the man's name.

Steven.

Punch heard a whine behind him. He turned, letting go of the door. There was a man in a kilt and jacket. Holding bagpipes. Who he recognised as Duck off the bin lorry.

'Backup, Sarge,' Duck whispered, his mouth on the blowpipe.

'Caravan? Bora?'

'She's fine.'

A note escaped from the bag under Duck's arm. Punch heard the audience gasp. A blast. A gun going off? Screams. The sound of feet on boards. Punch grabbed the stage door and Stevenson emerged at speed through it. Duck put a foot out for him, deftly and automatically. Stevenson tripped, stumbled to the floor. The gun spun across the carpet. Punch booted Stevenson on the side. Jumped onto him. Stevenson rolled him off. Struggled to his feet and ran back onto the stage. Punch followed. The audience were now a scattered mass. Screaming as they ran, pushing and panicked, for the exit. The special constables stormed the stage. Punch felled Stevenson from behind this time. Sat on him with his knees on his shoulders. Burns was cowering in the corner. The special constables fixed handcuffs on Stevenson.

'Him too,' Punch said, nodding to MacMaster.

Punch shielded his eyes from the spotlights and looked out to the room. Saw Bora rush in. Searching for, then finding, her son. He saw her mouth make the shape *Davud* just before they embraced. Duck was standing a few paces back. His pipes discarded. He walked to the stage and handed the gun to Punch.

Ivor looked down on his captive.

'Gerard.' He nodded. 'Been a while.'

SCENE XLIV

SATURDAY

PUNCH TOOK THE CUP OF TEA from Constable Monteith. Aware he was in her jurisdiction, her station now. Craignure. Thankfully she was laying off the Celine.

'Next of kin?' he asked.

'Notified. The Merriweathers are in London. Hers in Edinburgh. Bloody terrible.'

'They'll want to visit.' Punch puffed. 'Understandable.'

'And she in the parliament?'

'Couldn't say I recognised her. Teeth help, mind.'

'Ivor!'

'More bodies off to the mortuary. We'll be getting discounts . . .'

'Well, if this doesn't kill off the wind farm . . .'

'It took four bodies,' Punch said.

'Poor couple had nothing to do with it. If only they could have gone to the production. Might've lived then, you think?'

'Think they got off lighter by *missing* the production.'

'Christ, Ivor!' Monteith tried to fight a smile. 'Can't believe the gall of the man though. Stevenson! McNair.'

'Best place to hide is in plain sight. I suppose the political class do it all the time. Obanite drug barons, less so.'

Punch saw photos of kids on the side of Monteith's mug. 'The grandchildren?'

'Aye. But "suspects" wouldn't be altogether inaccurate ...'

'Christ. I almost saw a tear well up there ... they're kept in line?'

'Little buggers. Always wanting to see Granny's cell.'

'Talking of which ...'

They stood, and he followed her down the corridor. Punch was only glad it wasn't *him* who was being shown to it. The reverb on Monteith's snare drums alone would force anyone to crack. Cluny was back with the Oban coppers at Pebbledash HQ. Behind the thick blue door, there was a bigger fish to fry. A fresh catch waiting for Punch.

Monteith unlocked the cell door. Fintan MacMaster raised his head. His body was slumped, still in his Burns rigout, breeches and boots, but without the wig. Thankfully, the ponytail had remained tied up. *Small mercies.*

Punch walked into the cell. Monteith followed.

'The handcuffs?' he said. 'An updated character note?'

'We'll have to stop meeting like this, sergeant.'

'Lucky you only have a bullet hole on the stage wall. Though musket might've been more in keeping with the historical period.'

'Didn't know I was in the actor's studio?'

'Okay, MacMaster. Crimes against literature is one thing ... But let's try again to see if you can separate fact from fiction this time.'

'You and Billy Lennox were an item?' Monteith said.

'Both using the Davud lad to transport drugs to Mull?' Punch added.

Fintan shook his head. Then dropped it into his hands.

'McNair has told us everything,' Punch said. 'Forced his way onto your stage, did he? Literally.'

'The theatre company was a mess,' Fintan managed. 'Only way I could get myself above water . . .'

'Was to become his Mull-based drug runner?' Punch said, stepping nearer. 'Billy Lennox too close to his old man's operation? So you became patsy? That it?'

'Look, I met his girl purely by chance at the Columba in Oban.'

'Hi-Pockets' girl?' Monteith said.

'No,' Punch said. 'McNair's.'

'Poured my heart out to the lass,' MacMaster told them. 'Might just as well have walked to your door with my hands held out.'

'Who killed William Lennox?'

'*He* did.'

'McNair?' Monteith said, towering over the man.

'No. Well, yes! But no. Billy killed Billy. Wanted to be like me, then his dad. Totally changed. Then wanted to be like McNair. Unhealthy regard for death. For even *higher* drama.'

'And who killed Hi-Pockets?' Punch said.

'I honestly don't know.' Fintan sighed. 'Either one of them did it. The joke is I came to Mull to get away from this kind of shit.'

'None of this is a joke, MacMaster.' Punch walked to the cell door. He turned back to the man. 'The car seats? Simple audacity?'

Fintan angled his head. 'Aye. And a bit more wedge into the bargain. The Gorbals had to stand up to you Teuchters, after all.'

'I hear fellow inmates are always up for an acting class.' Punch exited the cell. 'And fuck.'

Monteith followed.

'You carry on here,' Punch said. 'But I think he's too bad an actor to be telling us porkies.'

Monteith nodded. 'Right. I'll keep you posted. Good luck in the bright lights.'

Twenty minutes later, Punch was pulling the Ranger into Pebbledash HQ. Tobermory had never appeared so grey. Just how he liked it. It looked like a Tulliallen convention going by the number of Rangers out front. He drove up the lane between the buildings and pulled over outside the lockup. A carcass was inside, slowly drying out, getting to the correct temperature, ready for the slaughter. Before that, though, was the human slaughter in the cell. The final act. The body there had been kept at the correct temperature too. He'd instructed Cluny to keep the fan heater off. Bog roll only on request. *Probably wasn't any way to treat family. Except the killing kind.*

Punch stole a moment in the vehicle. He'd managed to keep his connections to Oban mafia a secret from the island for long enough. His mother had never been exactly proud to broadcast it. *A mainland problem*, she used to say. It was the ghost of his father-who-was-not-his-father, following him. He didn't know any of them from Adam, thanks to his mother cutting off ties after his supposed father walked out, when Charlie was born. *For Ivor and Charlie's betterment*, he had heard his mother telling his uncle-who-was-not-his-uncle, his father's brother, who evidently, thankfully, was nothing like him. But still, Ivor had always known had he not taken his mother's side's name, and then their given nickname, that it was by rights another family name – that of a well-established Oban dynasty, no less – that would have been printed on his uniform.

Sergeant McNair.

Punch opened the door. Put on his hat and engineered full-on pigeon chest. He walked to the back door of the station. Selected the key from his chain. Turned the lock and walked inside. He heard the voices from the incident room. Cluny in round rims came charging at him like he was expecting Voldemort.

'Ah! Sarge. Sorry! Thought it was our prisoner.'

'It's okay! Stand down, PC.' Punch straightened his hat. Best that both badgers were fully covered. 'Good work.' Punch looked to the thick blue door opposite. 'I'll take this one.'

'Right, Sarge. We've left him alone. As instructed. Hit the red if you need us.'

'Uh-ha.' *This one is personal.*

'Oh, sergeant?'

'Aye?' Punch turned, the key selected.

'It's just . . . you always make me feel like I use too many words.'

'Think of each one as a criminal.'

Cluny walked back down the corridor.

Punch reached for the fan heater. Decided against it.

He turned the key.

Inside, the man pertaining to be Robert Louis Stevenson was sitting on the floor. Still in all the rigout. His arms chained to the bars.

'Was it about controlling the Order, or the island?' Punch said.

'Watching another man shit isn't beyond you, I reckon,' McNair said, holding his side, nodding to the toilet.

'We encourage guests to bring their own seat. Like MacMaster.'

'Luxury right enough. Family's family.'

'Which were you after, Gerard?'

'Neither. It was about taking back what was mine. A father.'

'Method acting, is that what they call it?' Punch gestured.

'Well, it fooled you, hook, line and sinker.'

'Skerryvore, the old fellow – bribed him with drink, did you, to play silly buggers at my door?'

'Don't know what you're talking about. Anyway, it must be all of thirty-five years, eh, Ivor?'

'The rigout fair suited you. Forgot you were an unlikely bookworm. And that you liked to act when we were kids.' Punch put the cherry on top: 'The prick, that is.'

'Didn't need to stretch my acting chops too far either. Gullible fucker.'

'Bond villain became reality, eh? You're far from a twelve-foot bear now. Maybe you'll work your way up to prison librarian.'

'All I could do to get some of the spotlight off you and Charlie. He was my dad, too. I'll never know what he saw in a wimp like you. Pissing yourself all the time.'

'What is it, Gerard? You think I've had the better life? Clamping down on your crimes? What you don't realise is I did all I could to let you bastards reign. Still, your boys are never out the papers. You know I was offered Oban? Had to turn it down . . .'

'Long time since I've been *Gerard.* Since I watched a puny wee cripple trying to cycle up a hill.' He sneered. 'Feared of bears and Gene fucking Hackman! It's Gerry. Gerry McNair. A proper surname. You'd know, if you'd joined the family business.'

'I'll stick with my stage name. If it's all the same to you.'

'Still.' McNair cradled his side. 'You've a firmer boot on you than I'd have credited you for.'

'Prison guards are even tougher. And fuck.'

'Charlie was twice the fellow you are. Poor Charlie.' McNair held Punch's gaze, unflinching and cold. 'Hellish what happened to him.'

'Leave my fucking brother out of it.'

'But that's just it, though, Ivor, isn't it? He was my brother too. But he wasn't allowed to be.'

'Half-brother. Different mother, thank fuck.'

'I know which half I'd take. Him over you.'

'You don't deserve to be in the same sentence. What the fuck happened to you?'

'Could ask you the same. At least your whisky was decent.'

'Your first mistake.' Punch felt the moment of small triumph. 'I had the lab look it over. Who knew DNA stretches all the way to Oban.'

'I had to leave you a chance, bro!'

'The girl in Oban. Your daughter?'

'Girlfriend.' McNair's expression was smug. 'I duped you for long enough. Leave the scripts to me, Ivor.'

'Except I get to write this one, Ger. Never knew you were capable of this. You're going down for years.' Punch gestured to the man's clothing. 'You should be up for parole around

1894. Wait? You died then.'

'Had the lad held his bottle I'd be running cocaine through your fucking station!'

'His old man lost his bottle first, though. Hi-Pockets.'

'All those protests about his land and whatnot . . .'

'So you took on his lad instead?'

'Aye. Fresh blood. Just didn't realise what a dark little bugger the fella was. Tattoos only the start.'

McNair showed his arms. Punch felt like he was back on the hillside.

'Bear prints?'

'Company logo, Ivor. I remembered how much you'd pish yourself!'

'Let's stick to the present. So the lad took it all too far?'

'Was obsessed with his caves. Codenames. Thought I'd use him to balls up your empire.'

'Funny name for an island.' Punch had to ask. 'And MacMaster?'

'A bonus. Also, he has what I always wanted.'

'A ponytail?'

'A stage.'

Punch shook his head. 'The caravan? Could've been another innocent life.'

'Your mother fucked up mine!'

'Leave her out of this, you sick prick.' Punch motioned towards McNair's face, then pulled away. Rested his arm on the wall. 'Visiting an ill old woman to confuse and intimidate her. Pathetic.'

'You, she, all of you, got to have time with him – with Dad!'

'Christ, he didn't say much . . . just that he'd escaped. I always thought he meant from the whaling.'

'I had the shitty version. His brother. Who'd hooked up with *my* mother. He pretended he was *my* father. You have to admire the symmetry. Couldn't write it!'

'Aye. I thought only rock stars got up to this kinda' marital merry-go-round. Maybe we all got what we deserved. We were kids, for fuck's sake. Not our fault.'

'After Charlie was born,' McNair said, 'that's when my visits to Mull stopped.'

'I didn't know why.'

'The man told me on his death bed. Steven, I mean. That he was in fact my uncle. *Our* uncle. But it was too late. Dad was dead. I don't even know if he knew. I suppose you were always heading for the outside of the cell, Ivor. Me, the inside.'

'None of us are angels. But have you no conscience? Don't you think what you do to people with this stuff? Oban has, what a population of eight thousand? Ten recent victims of drugs buried there. The youngest was twenty-one. I get to see the figures!'

'Christ. I know, Ivor! I was only eleven when the nightmare began. Not long after my last trip to Mull. Woken before dawn by the doorbell. Men with baseball bats taking the man I called Dad away.'

'This. This is next level, Ger.' Punch sighed. 'It's not a bit of mischief, we all got up to mischief.'

McNair looked to Punch, and it was almost as if they were both teenagers again. 'I loved the rally. The banter. But it all changed. I resented your life. Your family. Began to dabble with shifting cannabis. Then the class As. Soon crime was all I knew.' He raised his eyebrows, shuffled as if he might get more comfortable. 'The house I grew up in was near Oban bay. I'd see the CalMac ferry. I'd see Mull! I could imagine what you had.'

'I can't protect you, Ger. Not from this.'

Punch thought of those nights with his uncle-who-was-not-his-uncle, out spectating on the rally with his cousin-who-was-not-his-cousin. How Gerard, as he was then, had been so much more outgoing than him. Flamboyant. Almost as riveting a show as you got from watching the rally. Had it all been a show, an act?

'But you almost had me,' Punch said.

'It felt good . . . to have a real dad. Even if just for a night.'

'Look. You're not you anymore.' Punch stood, wanting to be done with this. 'And I'm not me.'

'That what you tell yourself? Don't bet against blood. Or a brother's heart. I'll keep looking for it.'

'Brother?'

McNair shook.

'Heart? Father?'

'Island.'

'Welcome,' Punch said, 'to the Looming.'

SCENE XLV

PUNCH EXITED THE CELL. Closed the door behind him and turned the key on McNair. He reached for the fan heater and switched it on.

He exited the back door and sent a search party behind his ear. Sparked the roll-up and took several deep, abrasive hits. He flicked it away and walked around to the station house. Selected the key and opened the door.

He was met by one of the Oban uniforms.

'Thanks, PC. I'll take this from here. There's a butter beer next door waiting for you.'

'Right you are, Sarge. I'll certainly enjoy it more with McNair behind a cell door. Oban'll be quiet.'

Punch closed the door behind the officer. He turned to the room. Not to evidence of a band on tour, but to a man in a cell of his own.

'Dave,' Punch said.

'Sergeant. Oaf, how bad is it? The shit I'm in?'

'Upwards of neckringable, Dave. I'm not going to kid you on.' Punch had never seen the man so dishevelled, so disorganised in himself. Even the shirt hanging out.

'I appreciate the discretion of the house setting.' Dave waved to the room. 'As opposed to the cell. The Order will run me out of town if this gets to head office.'

'God?'

'Him too.'

'What gets out? Euthanasia? That's about all I have on you, Dave. Though covering for Billy Lennox needs a moment more exploring.'

'Oaf, it's not euthanasia, goddammit, Ivor.'

'No?'

'The man is my lover.'

'The fellow from the Ross? He's not dead?'

'No. He's the editor of *Ransom Monthly*. Though if ever a time I needed him . . . If I hear from him again it'll be a miracle. Wasn't sure how the island would react, you know?'

'This is the twenty-first century, Dave. I think it would have been okay.'

'There speaks the privilege of a man who has been able to live his life how he wants.'

'The photos of Thai women?'

'Cover.'

Punch exhaled. Got up and walked to the sink. Reached under it for the emergency supply.

'Want one?'

'Aye. Aye, lad.'

Punch returned to Dave, who was rubbing his bald head. He placed two hefty measures in front of them.

'So – Billy killed his father for making his mother a drug addict? Or because he wanted his drug beat?'

'I've genuinely no idea,' Dave said, downing his measure.

'He called me in a blind panic, saying he was bringing his father's body over. That he had collapsed in their living room.'

'Did you think the lad capable of this? Did you know anything about some Architects truth pact?'

Dave lifted his glass as if it might have refilled itself. 'No. On both accounts. He certainly appreciated the theatrical element of the undertaker's job.' Dave shook his head. 'But too far, too far, lad. Can I ask where you found him?'

'In the rally car further around the coast. Out by Quinish Stone Row. Alongside a scattering of deer remains. Some dark shit. I thought *you* were on the edge, Dave, but . . .'

'It pains me. The country-boy visionary who wished for, then inherited, a small, failing croft-cum-burgeoning-distribution-business . . .'

'That turned him into a drug dealer, a murderer.' Punch assessed his own empty glass. 'And fuck. There's going to be aiding and abetting to navigate here, Dave. Accomplice liability.'

'Murderer? Oaf, when could he have planted the bones, the teeth, for Christ's sake?'

'Two visitors, Dave. He extracted their teeth. Took their bodies to the bear caves.'

'How did he first come to you?' Punch asked, refilling both glasses and taking a hit.

'Bloody hell! Who on earth were the visitors?'

'Can't disclose.'

'Hi-Pockets got in touch. Said the lad was leaving school. Had no real interest in the croft, or the horses. Said I'd give him a go. You know, a favour from one Brother of the Order to another. The lad was so keen. I was delighted with him. But what did I create?' He shivered. 'A monster?'

'You didn't. I thought the boy was the usual teenage bag of awkwardness, too. But no. And I assume the lad put the call in about the vehicles on the Glen as a deterrent?'

'As in, "why would he do such a thing if he was involved?" Yes, I think you're right, sergeant.'

'In actual fact, he'd been there and back already. And fuck. Even lit himself a campfire.'

'Christ, I do remember his fascination with exhuming his mother. I warned him. Saying I was inclined to believe there would be more than bones, that it would not be a pretty sight.'

'He wanted to dig her up?'

'Exhume, yes.' Dave drank, breathed out whisky fumes. 'Said he wanted to prove whether his brother or father had intended to kill her.'

'How could he do that?'

'I told him the same! Then I found him one day in the embalming room. He had an empty coffin on the table. I was outside the door; it was open. He didn't know I was there. He had that other lad with him. He was telling the lad about unscrewing a valve in the coffin to let any trapped decomposition gases escape. About how the room would quickly fill with the overpowering stink of death. To be truthful, after they left, I had to check the contents were not actually the woman's remains.'

'You never thought to tell me this, Dave?'

'How could I have known it was more than a curious, grieving boy, Ivor?' Dave took another glug. 'You know I saw the file records?'

'Whose?'

'The Grey Lady's. The boy's mother. She suffered at least

three death-dealing injuries that would have killed her before she took another breath: a broken neck and a grotesquely mashed rib cage and a crumbled pelvis. Likely died so quickly she might not have had time to imagine it. Mercifully for her. But that's what they all had to live with. Duck mostly.'

'The other lad you're referring to is the Bosnian, Davud?'

'Oh?' Dave put down his empty glass. 'He was in the car with Duck? On the Glen? I thought he was familiar . . .'

Punch went for the bottle.

'But the strangest thing . . .'

'What, Dave?'

'When I was closing the lid on the empty coffin that day, after the lads had left – there was a dress in it.'

SCENE XLVI

TWO WEEKS LATER

HE HAD BEEN DRIVEN INTO TOWN. But now he was on his own. Standing outside Tobermory police station. The police car was parked out the back. Davud could hear music, maybe from the vehicle. He was aware of his body shaking, his nails digging into his palms.

He checked around him. Nobody seemed to be watching. He pulled his parka over his head. Started walking up the lane in the gap between the station and the house next to it. Clouds of his breath left an unwanted trail. The music seemed to be coming from a lockup. The door to it was closed.

Inside the lockup, Punch hoisted the carcass up onto the hook. The meat fridge had been preset to the correct temperature. 'Stay With Me' was blasting out. He had no capacity for 'The Killing of Georgie' neither part I or II. He needed full-on Rod stomp. The only threat of danger coming from a case of JD's and Rod's swinging microphone stand.

He'd had a few days to process the paperwork, if not the events, of the past week. Maybe he would need to take up

Cluny's suggestion of media training. Four bodies. Mull had never seen anything like it. Two Lennoxes had been put into the earth in the graveyard outside Dervaig. Duck had piped them in. Face pale as the sky. The folk who *did* come left the plots saying the buried had escaped justice. That the earth knew. And lying next to them, the Grey Lady. An undertaker from Oban filled in for Dave, who had been advised by Punch to stay away from Burns.

Ivor wanted peace now, and the warmth of his hands between the linings of the cut fleece and the animal's skin, that his real father would allow him during the annual slaughter. Slaughter season, like rally season, being the only times he ever saw under the skin of the man.

He took the knife in his hand. Steadied the carcass with his other. Remembered his dad would call him 'Smit'. His mother called Charlie 'Lamb'. Livestock, everywhere. *Who was to know a black sheep was lurking across the water.*

Davud walked to the lockup door. Imagined a live band was playing in there. He looked behind him. All clear. He took his hand from his parka and knocked on the door. Nothing. He knocked harder. The door partly swung up from the ground. The music stopped.

Punch turned to the door. Questioned whether to put down the knife. Decided it was best in his pocket. He swung the door fully open. The Bosnian lad was standing there. Something of an impending slaughter on the boy's face too.

'Mum said . . .'

'Uh-ha?'

'That I had to apologise.' Davud pushed his hood back. 'Well, more than that . . . probably.'

'You did well in the questioning. But you'll have to testify in the court hearings. To give evidence. Your role will be looked at by the criminal assessor. I said to your mum I'd put a word in. Nothing will happen quickly. Lucky she left the caravan.'

'She cycled out to the Glen to look for me.' Davud couldn't look up. 'I know it's still serious.'

'It is. You'll be offered counselling too.'

'Mum said that's good.'

'I hear you're moving to the farm?'

'Yes.' Davud raised his head. 'The horses.'

'Right. Anyway. I'll put a word in.'

'Okay.' Davud saw what was beyond the uniform. Averted his gaze to the ground.

'You need to keep out of trouble now. You hear?'

Davud gulped. 'Do you think I'll go to jail?'

Punch shook his head. He gestured behind him. 'Maybe the hook.' Then regretted saying it as he saw Davud's face pale to the colour of sheep's wool. 'Look, stick to the things you're good at. I was fairly taken with your ferry drawings. I like battleships myself.'

'I'm doing lighthouses now,' Davud said, the faintest glimmer of pride. 'I'm going to walk down to the Tobermory one later. Anyway.'

'That's right. Keep your curiosities to the page.' Punch wasn't sure why the lad hadn't walked away.

'Did you kill it?' Davud asked. 'The sheep?'

'Uh-ha.' Punch needed to shift the subject. 'If you, er, like lighthouses, look up the Monarch Isles lighthouse. Aye.'

'Right?'

'Comes with a mystery too.'

'What?'

'Well, eh, my dad . . . he was a whaler. He used to take me out to watch the rally. For the night stages. One of those times I was struggling to stay awake. We were waiting for the first car. So he told me this story about the Monarch Isles. They're out beyond the Uists.'

'What did he tell you?'

'It wasn't safe for a lighthouse keeper to be out there during the war. So Monarch lighthouse was closed down in 1942. But before that it was still manned. No signal had been registered from the two lighthouse keepers in weeks . . .

'Oh?'

'And a boat carrying inspectors went out to check. Not an easy task with the waters carrying German U-boats. There were people still living on the Monarchs then, but my dad said they daren't set off a warning flare.'

'In case they alerted the enemy?'

Punch nodded, realising he had never said 'Dad' aloud. 'The inspectors entered the lighthouse and walked up the winding steps and then into the lantern room . . . still nothing. Nor in the service or watch rooms. But in the kitchen they found two places set at the dinner table. Half-eaten food on the plates. Cutlery still forked into two cold gannets.'

'Gannets?' said Davud.

'Seabirds.'

Davud pulled a face. 'Had the men been taken?'

'Their oilskins were hanging on the back of the door. But they were never found. In the logbook the final entry was in German. My uncle said for all he knew the lighthouse keepers ended up in a concentration camp. Anyway.'

'You said your dad?'

'Aye. You don't miss much, right enough.'

'I heard you singing,' Davud said. 'About kicking Rita out the door?'

'Wouldn't call it that . . .'

'Is she your girlfriend? Sorry, sorry. . .'

'No. No she's not, no.' Punch thought how alien the concept sounded; then questioned why the lad hadn't said 'wife'?

'My dad used to sing at football,' Davud said, brushing his hair off his face. 'Mum said that was the best place for it.'

'That's why I keep sheep. They don't complain. Or can't.'

'My dad told me stories too. But I can't remember many. He said never go through life with a closed hand. I didn't know what he meant. But now I think maybe he meant if your hand is closed then you can keep everything, protect what you have. But nothing new will come in. If your hand is open, you will lose some things, and it might be messy, but new things will always enter.'

'I think that was good advice, lad. And your studies?'

'There's a temporary building.'

'Right.' Punch could see something different in the lad. 'Make your mother proud. And . . .' Punch reached for the door. 'Stay away from matches.'

Davud's face twitched, like he didn't know whether to smile. He realised the sergeant had shown him it was there all along, waiting for him. The next page.

'Oh?' Punch turned to the lad again. 'I take it you were told if all went tits up with the drug run, then you could blame it on him. Dervaig Duck?'

Davud nodded.

Punch looked to the section of sea visible between the police buildings. 'Then I think it's him you're due an apology to.'

Davud turned away; he still questioned why Duck didn't come back for him on the Glen when he'd exited Dave's hearse?

'Also.' Punch reached for the roll-up supply behind his ear. 'If you're still interested in lighthouses . . . you might not know Tob lighthouse is one foot taller than the original drawings done by the architect. Don't forget that.'

'What?'

'To carry yourself taller.' Punch reached up for the door. 'And so go and be one.'

'A lighthouse?'

'An architect.'

Davud heard the lockup door closing. And then music.

He walked back through to the front of the station. The bin lorry was purring.

Davud saw Duck at the wheel, scratching his stubble. Elevated. Again.

Duck wound the window down. 'Well done, lad. Jump in.'

Davud walked around the front of the lorry. He opened the passenger door and climbed up.

'Your mum will be happy. It go okay, lad?'

'Think so. Not sure.'

'Punch is all right. He knows how Mull works.'

David thought about apologising to Duck, but didn't think he would right now. Duck didn't seem to need one.

'So, if you're riding up front here I might need you to run out for the odd bin, lad. I won't be sharing my wage, though.' Duck shifted to face Davud, smiled.

'Me? *Bins*?'

They both laughed.

'Eh, look, lad . . .' Duck faced ahead again. 'I came back out to look for you on the Glen, but there wasn't so much as a trace of you. Imagined you'd gone to, well, Billy's . . . Poor bugger. Christ. And I didn't say anything to your mum because I didn't want to worry her. I didn't know what you'd got yourself caught up in. All I knew about was the art school.'

'I know.' Davud stared out the front windscreen, too. 'And I know that you wouldn't have . . . wanted to worry her. And to protect me.'

'Then I was out on shift early the next two days. Down the Ross. I'd no idea you were . . . what was . . . even happening? That I was becoming . . . an orphan?'

'I went to the theatre.'

'Thought you were in your scratcher. First I heard I came tearing to the caravan. Then the theatre.'

'I went there to try to be rid of it all.' Davud wiped his face. 'To explain.'

'I know. I know, lad. Look – I've a group of kids I teach the pipes to in Tob, aye, aye. We practise in the winter in the hall and on summer nights on the pitch.'

'I've heard you.'

'Aye. I like to point the bum notes at the mainland. Anyway, it keeps the kids off the drink and the screens and whatnot . . . but there's a little lad, wren-sized, pipes dwarf him, he's bloody good, best I've seen, but he's struggling a bit with things at home. You might know the family. He has just his mother. The wee bugger's bright, you can tell, but he's like a ship without a compass. I'd like you to speak with him.' Duck turned the key in the ignition. 'You could do that?'

'Me?'

'I think you'd be a help, aye.' Duck sniffed.

'Two atoms,' Davud heard himself say. 'Sometimes that's what I felt we were.'

'Who?'

'Me and Bearfo— I mean William. Billy.'

'You've lost a friend, lad. A muddled, tragic, messed-up one. I'm feeling that loss too. But he *was* your friend.'

Davud couldn't say anything.

'Maybe come to a game sometime? The Gers? I could let you know when I'm down?'

Davud nodded. Though he didn't know if he would.

'That's if you haven't burned down the stadium first, eh?'

Davud looked at the Council ID on the dash. *Donald Lennox*.

'Joking, lad. Look, I'm not trying to take his place. I'll do better now.'

'Billy's?'

'Your dad's.'

Davud felt the bin lorry pull away. He had a sense his life was balancing on scales: the art school on one end, Mull on the other. Or maybe it was war, and peace? Two fathers? He didn't want to be measured against anything.

He closed his eyes and it felt like every thought turned off. Like he was a shape that didn't need to be filled.

SCENE XLVII

'I FEEL SO SORRY FOR the boy. Cases stay with you.' Lydia Strathclyde sighed to the bustling Craignure pier before her. 'Especially returning like this some weeks later, to the scenes of the crime, as it were.'

'They do,' Punch said. It was three weeks since McNair had been outed as being in the wrong century. 'I appreciate you coming back to tie up the loose ends. Though I suspect the breakfasts in the Western had something to do with it.' Punch looked to the sea, now back below neck-level. 'Which boy?'

'Well – both. But I was referring to the Bosnian lad.'

'Uh-ha. Crime, trauma, is what they're supposed to be getting away from.'

'*Architects of post-truth?*' she marvelled.

'Certainly Bible John needs to up his game . . .'

'I'll now present the Crown Office and Procurator Fiscal with my completed paperwork and findings. I'll await news if the courts need me.'

'Oh, you'll be called. Prominent politician in the mix. This isn't going to be cleaned up quickly. Got half of CID staying in the Western.'

'I saw Blair made his tributes. One way to kill a political sex scandal.'

'And a wind farm.'

'Ghastly . . .' She looked to the sea. 'The ends some folk meet.'

'I've got media training directives up the gazoo. Cluny'll be hoping for the *Crimewatch* gig.'

Lydia Strathclyde released the passenger door. 'Always such a mix of emotions, no matter how complicated or high profile the case. Are you ever able to experience satisfaction, sergeant?'

'Not sure I think of it that way. A fire needs to be put out, I try to put it out.'

'No sense that you've solved a puzzle?' Lydia turned.

'Another problem usually morphs out of it. You just hope it's smaller.' Punch looked at the ferry, now taking in cars. Blah Blah Blah performing the circus act of untying various ropes from bollards. He couldn't fathom how somebody could see the ferry's insides, when you were just looking at it. To capture that on a page. Or maybe, he supposed, that was how he saw people.

'After a case, sergeant, I always think to myself, "I can use that information in the future." That drives me on. Then the work is feeding the work. In nature, the future informs the past.'

'Think on islands it's the other way around.'

'Making lemonade out of lemons, eh?' Lydia Strathclyde opened the door. Carved her bob with one hand. 'I used to think of islands as lonely places. Now I think cities are.'

Punch opened his door too, felt the wind on his skin. 'Aye, poor family in London. Kiddies lost a dad. Seemed quite a fellow, the civil servant. They'll be visiting, the family. Monteith's brief. She's softer than she appears.'

'And it seems the politician had sailed here before?'

'Flowers on the pontoon apparently.'

Lydia stepped out onto Craignure pier and closed the door behind her.

Punch exited from his side, put his hat on and opened the back door. He nodded to Blah as the man entered procedural overdrive. He took hold of the professor's bags. Closed the door and walked around the rear of the Ranger.

'Cluny will be accusing me of taking his jobs . . .' he attempted, making a small fuss of placing her bags next to her. 'Long way to come looking for a butler. Tulliallen will be all over it.'

'Thank you, sergeant.' She smiled efficiently. Eyes in there somewhere.

Punch wondered if this was the time to admit he was connected to Lockerbie, too? To explain she was standing on the exact spot he had waved Charlie off for that final time. But what was the point? It would be like trying to explain the music of limbs flying over a sandpit.

'For being so open to my methods,' she said. 'I mean.'

'I know what you meant.'

'I just feel very privileged to know exactly how something works.'

'The law?'

'Nature. When I go, sergeant, my ashes will be recycled and my molecules will be reused and reincarnated.'

'Into what?'

'A tree, a bluebell or a beetle. Still undecided. I prefer bacteria to some people.'

'There's an album title.'

'I've left a man over his failure to determine the correct species of mushroom.'

'Harsh. Though I'd leave a woman if she couldn't tell Jeff Beck from Jimmy Page.'

'Rod or Bob?'

'Eh?'

'For *your* reincarnation?'

'Keith Moon. Every time.'

She mocked the act of running away. Took hold of her bags, looked to him and then away. 'She seems a good woman. A keeper.'

Punch felt his face burning, just when he'd hoped the island was cooling down; reached for the roll-up behind his ear. 'Time to put your microscope away I'd reckon.'

'I deserved that.' She almost laughed. 'Be well.'

'I'll book you in for analysis of my front room,' he attempted. Not sure if it had been heard. He turned to leave and then stopped. Realising how it had sounded. He faced her again as she lifted her bags. 'I meant . . .'

'I know what you meant, sergeant. But you, erm, *wear it well*?'

'Neckringable. A little old-fashioned, but that's all right . . .'

Punch retreated, embarrassed, to the Ranger, before he went up in flames. He was under no illusions he was going to have to give himself a night behind the thick blue door for that. Jury was still out on the fan heater and bog roll. Though a bottle of Tobermory, headphones and a broom handle weren't up for debate.

He started the engine and performed a turn of the wheel. Drove slowly past the 'No Unauthorised Vehicles Beyond Here' sign. *So this is what it all amounts to? The ability to drive where a CalMac employee can? Real power.*

A tall, solid man waved him down.

Punch wound down his window.

'Blah,' he acknowledged. 'I know I'm not technically an employee but . . .'

'I'll turn a blind eye. For you, Ivor. Red tape coming at us all the time. Paint's still wet on one sign when they issue us another. You've had your hands full I hear. Hellish.'

'Uh-ha, Blah.'

'And the two yellow lines outside the Co to police too? Powers that be and all their blah blah blah . . .'

'At least they give me handcuffs.'

'Hi-Pockets *and* his lad. And two folk from away?'

'Uh-ha. The island never stops surprising us.' Punch nodded his hat to the mainland. 'Wish it all happened away.'

'Must be strange being buried when you're supposed to be doing the burying . . .'

'Me?'

'Billy the Box.'

'Oh, aye. Right enough. Okay, no rest for the . . .'

'Right, Ivor.'

Punch wound up his window and drove on down the pedestrian-only pier. One of the small luxuries of being the island's pair of handcuffs. At this moment, it was all he needed. Maybe an accompanying rasp and a stomp to complete the picture.

PLEASE MAKE SURE YOU CLAIM ALL YOUR BELONGINGS AS YOU LEAVE THE THEATRE

PUNCH ARRIVED BACK AT PEBBLEDASH HQ from dropping Lydia Strathclyde at Craignure. He turned into the gap between the station and the station house. Thankfully, Guinness was not on shift, though that didn't necessarily mean the PC's Ranger wouldn't still be parked to attention. The lad was the living embodiment of keenness as currency. He was thankful too that the forensic ecologist would by now be nearer the mainland.

Punch had arranged to meet at the rear of the police buildings by the lockup. She was standing in her customary black. *As Monday follows Tuesday.* Punch swung the Ranger around slowly. Killed the ignition. Opened the door and stepped out.

'Right.' He sniffed. 'You'd have been early, I imagine.'

'Always. Hello to you too.'

‘I’d have brought flowers, but . . .’ He felt air stick in his gullet. The association with flowers wasn’t helpful. He could tell Mary had clocked that too.

‘Ever the song and dance man. Even in primary.’

Punch lifted a brow as he walked towards the lockup. ‘Surprised you noticed.’

‘I noticed.’ She stood away from him. ‘The uniform. Really?’

Punch brushed his hands up and down his clothes. Realising he really had no other outdoor clothing. The uniform a kind of skin. Like Bob’s mouthorgan.

‘Semper Vigilo.’

She looked at him, askance.

‘What it says on my uniform shoulder. “Always vigilant.”’

‘Same in the playground. It’s fine.’ She motioned to his attire. ‘It’s who you are.’

Punch found the key on his ring and fitted it into the padlock on the lockup door. He swivelled the door open and immediately wished he had put the slaughter hooks away.

‘You spoke to MacLean about a service?’

He nodded.

‘Just us. Not sure your mum needs to go through it.’

‘Agreed.’

He walked into the space and bent to pick up, then bin, some bloodied rags. He pushed the table into the corner, by the meat fridge.

‘It’s not Harrods perfume counter I know . . .’ he said.

‘More a pop-up at the Salen Show.’

She stepped in behind him. He heard her heels stop. He turned. She was staring at an item covered by an off-white sheet.

‘No. That’s the drum kit,’ Punch said. He took a roll-up

from a pile already rolled on the table. Leaned into the flame. He sighed at the covered kit. Charlie's guitar boxed alongside it. 'Well,' he puffed, 'I suppose in fairness Ringo hasn't made it through Tulliallen.'

'Yet.'

'Aye. But why do we keep all these things … maybe Skerryvore has it right, after all?'

'Hayfield Hotel, no door no bell?' Mary slowly nodded.

Punch knew it was in recognition of the only other covered object.

'Look we don't …'

'Remove the cover,' she said.

Punch noticed a shard of light had landed on the ground right outside the door. Giving the impression they were separated from everything outside the lockup by a shift of tectonic plates.

He leaned to the bedsheet and pulled it away. It rippled like a sea. Revealing a child's car seat. Anchored. A beacon not of light, but darkness. To the past.

'Tigger …' She smiled, through sudden tears and a single sniff.

Punch had stuffed a few tissues in his pocket; poised there if needed. He turned and offered them to her, half expecting a child to be holding her hand. He'd hoped this acknowledgement of death could in turn reawaken life, their life, together.

'The toy,' she managed, taking the tissues. 'You kept it.'

'Well, I'd bought it a ferry ticket, so …' Punch pushed up a cheekbone.

Mary nodded. She walked to the car seat and carefully lifted the furry, striped animal.

'Where do you put it?' she asked.

'What?'

'All this?'

'This in here?'

'No. That's where you *store* it. But where do you put it? Carry it?'

Punch closed his eyes against smoke. *Is under the uniform an acceptable answer?*

'Huh.' Mary gestured with the tissues to the space they were in.

'What now?'

'You've finally established a Family Liaison Unit.'

'One name for it. Cluny would approve.'

'Just need a family now,' she said, softly.

'Sometimes, late at night, I sit on the best seat in the world and imagine he or she alongside me. Maybe with a crabbing line.'

'Where?'

'The bench overlooking the seafront at Ledaig. In front of the distillery. It's like sitting on water.'

'Better than feeling submerged in it.'

'Look,' he said, 'I thought we might . . . nah, maybe daft.'

'What?'

Punch dropped the roll-up from his mouth. Stood on it.

'Okay. This is either a good idea or a very bad one.'

They both walked out of the lockup. Punch pulled down the door and reset the padlock.

He opened the passenger door for her and walked around to the driver's side. All three of them climbed inside. Punch turned the ignition and drove out between the pebbledash.

They progressed down by her house and up though Creagan Park. Past the bottom of Raeric Road and down by the school. Children were playing in sandboxes outside the nursery. One was pointing to the sky. Punch looked and saw a bird swooping.

'Kingfishers are on the rise apparently,' he said, knowing it wasn't one.

He turned right at An Tobar and up Breadalbane Street.

'The kid's shoes hanging over the road outside Salen?' she said.

'Can't possibly reveal my sources.'

At the junction with Albert Street he swung them right and up past his old house. The whole time she sat holding the Tigger, cradled tight.

Punch pulled the Ranger over to the verge at the graveyard. *Once, all this, was all I needed.*

He opened his door and exhaled. Walked around, but Mary had already exited. They stepped up to the kissing gate. Punch could tell she was uncomfortable holding the furry toy, in clear daylight. In the Ranger the thing had all but required a seat-belt.

They passed through the creaking gate. Then stopped at the small gravestone beside it.

The Unknown Sailor.

They both took in the few words. A visitor, now part of the island. Punch looked at Mary and remembered jumping out on her from behind some of the bigger, Victorian-era graves, the ones with metal bars around them.

'I'm not sure,' he said. 'But this could all simply be about providing perspective.'

'Notes to an unborn child . . .' She pointed. 'The sky could read.'

He looked at her. 'Burns said, "We live our lives between the dead and the yet to be born."'

'Or the other way around.' She paused. 'Will you do it?'

Punch put his hand out and she placed the toy within it. He reached down and leaned the Tigger against the small grey stone.

He straightened up. He had used his right arm and needed to adjust his sleeve. He turned away to the sea, to Calve Island, eternally sleeping, or watching, or floating. For some reason it always chose to stay.

'I know why I came back here. From Inverness,' he said. 'There's more space for life.'

'None taken.'

'Uh-ha.'

'But why won't you live it then? Fill it?'

Punch let her question hang. White clouds clustered above; he looked in them for the chariots Dylan had sung of; knew the Ranger didn't quite cut it.

'Just because you can't go there, Ivor, doesn't mean I can't say how it makes me feel.'

He nodded. 'Guilty as charged. But grief is like fingerprints. Everyone's is different.'

The wind got up and he felt her hair brushing his face. He looked to the mainland, had to concede to the majesty of Ben Hiant. It made him feel very small. In a way it was reassuring to be evidence of scale prevailing. He took in the expanse of sea, that indicator of separation, also prevailing. He imagined the image of a dress or trousers out there waving back at him. Could have been persuaded there was an irregular light in the sky. But really, he felt speared by the flagstaff.

'We create a world where it means this much,' she said, looking to the grave and capturing her flyaway hair in her hand. 'And then it's taken away from us.'

Punch felt her shoulder nudge against his, a slight tremor coming from it. His body connecting with hers. He made it known he would accept her weight.

'Not all of it,' he said, as he looked to the sky, where he could swear he now saw a sleeping bear, or a baby curled in slumber, in the cloud formation.

ACKNOWLEDGEMENTS

Thank you to Ali McBride at Black & White Publishing for your faith in me and these characters, Emma Hargrave, Rachel Morrell, Harry Banham, Thomas Ross, Clem Flanagan, Tonje Hefte and all at Black & White for your combined work and support in bringing Punch and co to the wider world. Emma – thank you for your insightful editorial input once again, for your care of the characters and for always questioning and improving the text. To Rachel – thank you for your safe hands, guidance and positivity throughout the whole editorial and production process. Thanks to all at Bonnier Books UK, including Alice Dovey, Beth Whitelaw and Justine Taylor, alongside the art team for depicting the essence of the book in your wonderful cover image. It was just right.

To Pam, Sian, Reegan, and my mum – love and appreciation for your unwavering support. To Bonnie, for nose-nudging me when it's time to take a break (meaning '*walk*', where, yes, the ideas do flow). Thank you to my wider family all over the world – those with us and those departed but still 'around' – for your encouragement and inspiration; and to my uncle "Gus", Angus MacIntyre, well, just for being all that is you.

To my nephew, Ruari Macintyre, thanks for all your willingness, enthusiasm and efficiency on my various merch stands at gigs across both books and music over the years – here's to more!

Thank you: Gordon MacIean for your creative insight and friendship, my lifelong pal Marcus McEwan for allowing me to be inspired by your own gift for storytelling in both road trips and architecture; Anthea The Lovely for your kind gift of *The Lighthouse Stevensons* by Bella Bathurst; Ian Rankin, Val McDermid & Alexander McCall Smith for being inspiring storytellers as well as inspiring people; my cousin Didi Macintyre for our passionate discussions and always being in sync on plotlines; Duncan Swinbanks and all at Tackle & Books Tobermory; Rupert Davies-Cooke and the Original Writers Group for helping me find my voice; Chris Brookmyre for your kindness in taking the time to read the proof; Fiona Atherton at StonehillSalt PR; Jessica Hall at Radioactive Promotions; Ian Smith and all at Last Night From Glasgow; Thom & Rob at Sonic PR; Steve Taylor at Roam Artists; Soren Kristensen / SOLK Photography; Stephen Kelman for your writerly solidarity; Di Speirs for that line; John 'Tiger' MacArthur; and the gentleman and ultimate professional that is Billy 'The (*real*) Box' McClymont for allowing me to use his island-imposed nickname (inspiration for this character *only* in name!). I have written in other places about legendary childhood memories of bicycle jumps by Eenie Brown in Tobermory . . . but I want to make clear his safe and successful jumps have no connection with the fictional characters or events in this book. I would also like to acknowledge Veronique

Baxter at David Higham Associates for providing valued feedback on early versions of fictional road trips.

Elements within this text have been inspired, though wholly reimagined and fictionalised, by the BBC's *Desert Island Discs* episode featuring castaway Professor Patricia Wiltshire, as well as the opening lines of a wonderful *Guardian* article on Francis Bacon by the art critic Jonathan Jones. If there are any errors in the information gathered from any of the sources included above, then they are entirely of my own, and intended to serve the fiction.

And F . . . inally, I would like also to dedicate this work to the people of Mull, with my appreciation of the island's culture, landscape and folklore – and for allowing me an endless source of inspiration in both words and song.

– Colin MacIntyre, 2026

© Soren Kristensen/SOLK Photography.

Colin MacIntyre is a multi-award-winning songwriter, musician, producer, author for adults and children, playwright and educator, who has been publicly voted Scotland's Top Creative Talent at the Glenfiddich Sprit of Scotland Awards, as well #12 in the Greatest Scottish Artists of All Time public poll. Born into a family of storytellers, writers and musicians on the isle of Mull in the Hebrides – where his poet-bank manager grandfather, Angus Macintyre, was recognised as the island's 'Bard of Mull' – he has released ten acclaimed albums to date, most notably under the moniker Mull Historical Society, achieving three UK Top 20 albums and six Top 40 singles to date. His gold-selling debut album, *Loss*, topped many Album of the Year polls, and his single, "Watching Xanadu", made it into STV's Scotland's Greatest Album. His new MHS album, *In My Mind There's A Photograph*, is the second in a groundbreaking new-format series in collaboration with world-leading authors, which include Sir Ian Rankin, Nick Hornby, Val McDermid and Irvine Welsh. His debut novel, *The Letters of Ivor Punch*, won the 2015

Edinburgh International Book Festival First Book Award and the Guardian's Not The Booker Prize, and he adapted it for the stage as *The Origins of Ivor Punch*. He has toured worldwide, including with R.E.M., The Strokes and Elbow, has collaborated in song with a varied cast, such as Snow Patrol, Annie Lennox and Tony Benn, and has appeared on multiple festival and TV stages, including *Later with Jools Holland*. His memoir was *Hometown Tales: The Boy in the Bubble*, and his first book for children, with accompanying music, was *The Humdrum Drum*. He has written a multi-genre musical, *Culloden*, which is now in pre-production. Colin is also a music educator on several university programmes, and he has led the children's charity Mary's Meals in London. He once spent a year with the Scottish professional football club, Queen's Park FC, and, despite his absence of a working shield, he is a descendant of the Scottish Warrior Poet, Duncan Ban MacIntyre.

An Island Burning is the second in his 'Mull Mysteries' crime series, *When The Needle Drops* was the first.

You can find all things words & music for Colin at colinmacintyre.com & mullhistoricalsociety.com

Instagram: @colinmacintyremull & @mullhistorical
Facebook & X: @colinmacintyre @mullhistorical

Also By Colin MacIntyre

Novels

The Letters of Ivor Punch

The Mull Mysteries Series

When The Needle Drops

An Island Burning

Memoir

'The Boy In The Bubble' – Hometown Tales, Highlands & Hebrides

For children

The Humdrum Drum

For the stage

The Origins of Ivor Punch

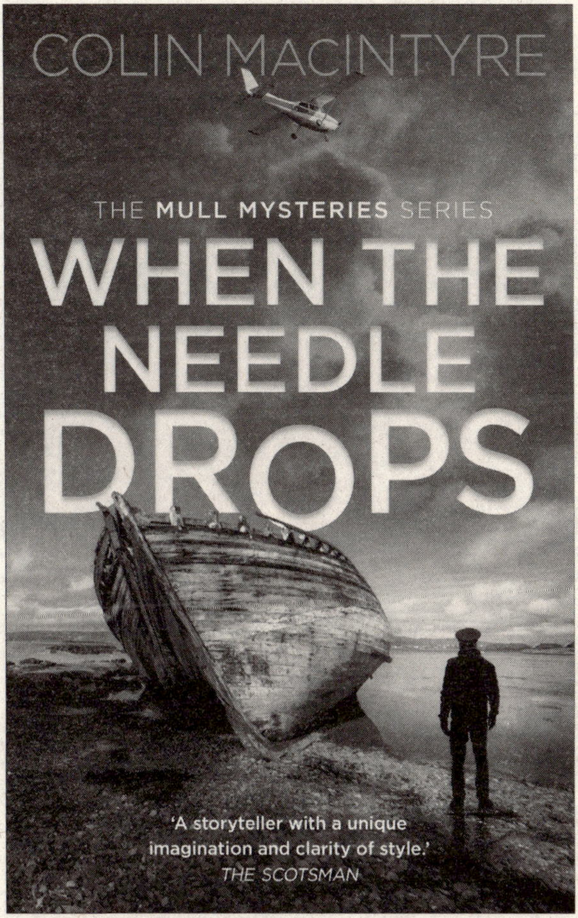

'A twisty mystery set on Mull, the island being a character in itself. Ivor Punch is a detective well worth spending time (and a dram) with'

IAN RANKIN

'A storyteller with a unique imagination and clarity of style'

THE SCOTSMAN